# SHRAPNEL.

## ISSUE #15     THE OFFICIAL BATTLETECH MAGAZINE

# SHR▲PNEL

## THE OFFICIAL BATTLETECH MAGAZINE

**Loren L. Coleman**, Publisher
**John Helfers**, Executive Editor
**Philip A. Lee**, Managing Editor
**David A. Kerber**, Layout and Graphic Design

Cover art by Germán Varona Galindo, a.k.a. Wallok
Interior art by Marie Baumgarten, Alan Blackwell, Jared Blando, Eldon
    Cowgur, Mark Hayden, Harri Kallio, David A. Kerber, Natán Meléndez,
    Benjamin Parker, Marco Pennacchietti, Tan Ho Sim

Published by Pulse Publishing, under licensing by Catalyst Game Labs
5003 Main St. #110 ▪ Tacoma, WA 98407

*Shrapnel: The Official BattleTech Magazine* is published four times a
year, in Spring, Summer, Fall, and Winter.

Available through your favorite online store (Amazon.com, BN.com, Kobo,
iBooks, GooglePlay, etc.).

ISBN: 978-1-63861-147-9

**COMMANDER'S CALL: FROM THE EDITOR'S DESK** ......... 5
Philip A. Lee

## SHORT STORIES

**A LESSON LEARNED**.................................... 8
Jason Schmetzer

**THE ALEXANDRIA JOB** ............................... 25
Giles Gammage

**SIGNING BONUS**..................................... 52
Jaymie Wagner

**NO DAWN ON THE HORIZON**.......................... 72
David G. Martin

**DUST TO DUST: A KELL HOUNDS STORY** ................ 94
Michael A. Stackpole

**TALES OF THE STRANGE BEDFELLOWS**.................110
James Hauser

**EL DORADO**......................................... 132
Chris Purnell

**WHERE I BELONG**.................................... 154
Tom Leveen

**SECOND TO NONE**....................................197
Russell Zimmerman

**INDOMITABLE** ...................................... 231
Robin Briseño

**BEHIND THE STICK**.................................. 249
Jason Hansa

**ACE DARWIN AND THE SECOND TRY FIASCO** ........... 314
James Bixby

**PICKING THE BONES**................................ 331
Alan Brundage

**SILENT PLANS**...................................... 354
Daniel Isberner

**SIX MONTHS ON THE FLOAT** ......................... 373
James Kirtley

**RAPTOR'S REQUIEM: CANTICLE** ...................... 397
Lance Scarinci

## SERIAL NOVEL

**LONE WOLF AND FOX, PART 3 OF 4**.................... 279
Bryan Young

## ARTICLES

**VOICES OF THE SPHERE:**
**SMALL BUT MIGHTY PROFITABLE** . . . . . . . . . . . . . . . . . . . . . 22
Stephen Toropov

**ELEVEN GOOD WAYS TO...RUIN YOUR MERCENARY COMPANY.** 68
Daniel Isberner

**WHERE THE PEN IS MIGHTIER THAN THE SWORD** . . . . . . . 104
Stephan A. Frabartolo

**SEA*LIST: ALMOTACEN ALMANAC.** . . . . . . . . . . . . . . . . . . . . . 129
Stephen Toropov

**WILL SCHEDULE IT FOR YOU:**
**COMBINED ARMS TECHS & ASTECHS** . . . . . . . . . . . . . . . 145
Ed Stephens

**MERCENARIES ENTERTAINMENT NETWORK DIGEST:**
**JUNE 3152.** . . . . . . . . . . . . . . . . . . . . . . . . . . . . . . . . . . . . . . .179
Ken' Horner

**GETTING PAID IN AN UNCERTAIN AGE.** . . . . . . . . . . . . . . . . . 245
Lorcan Nagle

**THE TRUTH ABOUT THE BOUNTY HUNTER?** . . . . . . . . . . . . 309
Lorcan Nagle

**THEY WALK ALONE: MERCENARY FREELANCERS** . . . . . . . . 327
Eric Salzman

## GAME FEATURES

**TECHNICAL READOUT: GLD-7R GLADIATOR** . . . . . . . . . . . . . 45
Wunji Lau

**UNIT DIGEST: OUTER REACHES DISCIPLES.** . . . . . . . . . . . . . 86
Eric Salzman

**UNIT DIGEST: LACADON VENGEANCE LEGION** . . . . . . . . . . 90
Eric Salzman

**CHAOS CAMPAIGN SCENARIO: RAINMAKER** . . . . . . . . . . . . 149
Eric Salzman

**TECHNICAL READOUT: THE UNTOLD MAULER** . . . . . . . . . . 183
Johannes Heidler

**UNIT DIGEST: BLAZING ACES.** . . . . . . . . . . . . . . . . . . . . . . . . . 224
Alex Fauth

**UNIT DIGEST: HALSTEN'S BRIGADE** . . . . . . . . . . . . . . . . . . . . 227
Zac Schwartz

**PLANET DIGEST: LE BLANC.** . . . . . . . . . . . . . . . . . . . . . . . . . . . 273
Eric Salzman

**UNIT DIGEST: 21ST CENTAURI PEREGRINE LANCERS** . . . . . 351
Stephen Toropov

**SUCCESSOR LORD: A CARD GAME FOR 3 TO 5 PLAYERS** . 369
Ken' Horner

**ALPHA STRIKE SCENARIO PACK: EMBERS OF THE PAST** . . 390
Ed Stephens

# COMMANDER'S CALL
## FROM THE EDITOR'S DESK

Salutations, MechWarriors! Remember back in issue #12, when we included a bunch of mercenary-related content to get people hyped for the *Mercenaries Box Set* Kickstarter campaign? And remember in #13, when I promised that, due to the stunning *$7.5 million success* of the crowdfunding campaign, #15 would be a double-sized all-mercenaries blowout issue? Well, you're now holding the fulfillment of that promise, and true to my word, it's literally the biggest *Shrapnel* issue ever, packed fuller than a *Union*-class DropShip on a trek across the entire Inner Sphere. It's got double the stories, double the game content, double the art—even more than #10, our last double-size issue! So I again want to take a moment and thank everyone who contributed to the campaign. This issue exists because of you!

Before I dive into the issue's contents, one thing that kept cropping up as I reviewed all of the stories and articles were little odd moments of kismet. For example, Giles Gammage's "The Alexandria Job" and returning BattleCorps veteran Chris Purnell's "El Dorado" both mention "Alexandria"; the planet and the Terran city, respectively. Jaymie Wagner's "Signing Bonus," a story set just after the First Succession War, mentions the planet Northwind (then a Capellan world), and then David G. Martin's "No Dawn on the Horizon," is set on Northwind itself during House Davion's infamous assault during the Second Succession War. It almost feels like these two authors coordinated so Wagner's story would foreshadow the events of Martin's. Other fun echoes include two separate mentions of the Bounty Hunter, one from an article written quite some time ago, long before we had planned to do this all-mercs issue; Mech-it-Lube shows up in two different places; the planet Freedom is referenced twice; and there's two completely unrelated instances of *Calliope*s, which are uncommon enough even I had to look them up to make sure I was thinking of the right 'Mech.

All of these odd little threads echoing between stories and game content throughout this issue further underscore how this giant, beloved universe with its many little tiny details can still find unexpected moments of interconnectedness and continuity, and serves as another reminder of how special and unique the *BattleTech* universe is. And speaking of special, don't forget: when the next issue drops, we'll be celebrating *BattleTech*'s 40th anniversary, so there's bound to be some fun goodies coming down the gravity well...

But back to the here and now. For fiction, every story in this issue features mercenaries of some variety or other. In addition to the aforementioned stories, we have tales from a bevy of veteran *BattleTech* authors. First, Jason Schmetzer's "A Lesson Learned" continues the story of the ilClan-era Gray Death Legion. Then we have not one but *two* Kell Hounds stories: "Dust to Dust," by none other than Michael A. Stackpole, and Russell Zimmerman's "Second to None," which is set in the St. Ives Compact shortly before the Clans arrived in the Inner Sphere. From James Hauser we have "Tales of the Strange Bedfellows," a fun piece about the origins of three disparate mercenary units who discover they might have something in common. Tom Leveen's "Where I Belong" follows a fallen arena gladiator desperate for a chance to pilot one of her merc unit's 'Mechs again. "Indomitable," Robin Briseño's first *Shrapnel* story, shows why being Dispossessed means more than just losing a 'Mech, and Jason Hansa's "Behind the Stick" follows a group of unconventional mercenaries desperate to find work on Galatea. In "Picking the Bones," Alan Brundage showcases former Republic troops fighting to stay one step ahead of the mercenaries doggedly hunting them and their mysterious cargo.

This issue also includes several follow-up stories. James Bixby continues the Ace Darwin saga from issues #6 and #8 with "Ace Darwin and the Second Try Fiasco." Daniel Isberner's "Silent Plans" comes right on the heels of "Tales from the Cracked Canopy: Silent Roar," also from #8, which takes the Silent Reapers to some dark places. (Keep an eye out for the forthcoming translation of Dan's Silent Reapers novel! This was originally published in Germany back in 2014, and we're excited to bring it across the pond in the relatively near future.) James Kirtley's "Six Months on the Float" chronicles the continuing travails of brand-new mercenary Leo Simonides from "Never Trust the Recruitment Posters" in issue #12, and Lance Scarinci's "Raptor's Requiem: Canticle" is a spiritual successor to "Yesterday's Enemy" from our very first issue, in which he brings the Crescent Hawks a step closer to the ilClan era. And last but certainly not least, the Fox Patrol's adventures on Alyina continue with the much-awaited Part 3 of Bryan Young's *Lone Wolf and Fox* serial novel.

For game content, it's more mercs all the way down. Kicking off the issue is "Voices of the Sphere: Small but Mighty Profitable," a look about the success of smaller merc units, and it includes the following Kickstarter-backer characters: Vincent Schons (for Vincent Schons), Reece Lennox (for Jonathan Bauleke), Operative "Nemo" (for Brandon Kosta), and Robert L. Mace (for Brandon Mace). The Unit Digests feature the Blazing Aces, the Outer Reaches Disciples, the Lacadon Vengeance Legion, Halsten's Brigade, and the Twenty-First Centauri Peregrine Lancers. This issue's Planet Digest: Le Blanc covers a merc-hiring world established after the Second Succession War. In the Technical Readouts, the GLD-7R *Gladiator* and the various *Mauler* iterations both have ties to mercenaries. Playable scenarios include "Rainmaker," a *Chaos Campaign* scenario involving Snord's Irregulars unearthing a dangerous Star League-era artifact, and "Embers of the Past," an *Alpha Strike* scenario pack where mercenaries assist the Silver Hawk Irregulars' invasion of the Wolf Empire.

Also, if you're looking to start your own mercenary unit or expect to tangle with one in a future battle, you can't go wrong with the advice from the articles in this issue. "Eleven Good Ways to...Ruin Your Mercenary Company" offers a wise list of *don't*s for any mercenary commander. "Will Schedule It for You" is a reminder to be kind to your techs and maintenance schedules, and "Where the Pen Is Mightier than the Sword" gives great insight for navigating mercenary contracts. "Getting Paid in an Uncertain Age" will help keep your pockets, accounts, and bellies full, the latest Sea*List bulletin for Almotacen will make sure you find the best local deals, and if you ever find yourself on your own, "They Walk Alone: Mercenary Freelancers" will remind you that even lone mercenaries have a viable place in the Inner Sphere. For those looking for some lighthearted downtime fun between employment contracts, look no further than the rules for "Successor Lord: A Card Game for 3 to 5 Players," the drama and hijinks from "Mercenaries Entertainment Network Digest: June 3152," and some rampant speculation on the true identity of our favorite masked mercenary in "The Truth about the Bounty Hunter?"

I also want to give special thanks to our regular interior artists, Jared Blando and Natán Meléndez. These two continue to blow us away with stellar work issue after issue, and for this double-size issue they both marched double-time to complete twice as many pieces as usual. And our Kell Hounds cover art, by Germán Varona Galindo (a.k.a. Wallok) is also spectacular, and really sets the tone for all the mercenary goodies found in this issue.

And don't forget: we're always looking to sign on some new mercenaries. If you've got what it takes to tell hard-hitting *BattleTech* stories, bring your reactor online, thumb off your weapon safeties, and fire your submissions our way. Remember: you miss all the shots you don't take!

**—Philip A. Lee, Managing Editor**

# A LESSON LEARNED

### JASON SCHMETZER

**HIGASHIIZU**
**GRAM**
**DRACONIS COMBINE**
**7 JUNE 3152**

The crowd reacted with a hungry growl as the man on the small dais in the front of the café raised a *wakizashi* over his head and shouted. Isobel Carlyle and her companion shared a look from where they sat in a row of single-table booths along the back wall, but said nothing.

The older man sitting next to Bel at the next table made a small sound, almost a sigh. Bel saw the small grimace of distaste before it disappeared. Her earbud translated the jingoist rhetoric from the speaker's native Japanese almost immediately, but it wasn't anything she hadn't heard or read since entering the Gram system.

"You do not approve?" Bel asked.

The other man glanced at her, his eyes flicking across both Bel and her companion, then looked to the stage. "My son."

"He is a talented speaker," Bel said.

"He is an idiot," the man corrected her.

Bel allowed herself a demure smile; it would have been rude to laugh. The café décor spoke to traditionalism; the colors were muted, grays and black and earth tones. Every table had a small dish of gojo berry jam. The crowd mostly looked middle-aged and soft. The garb they wore was semi-formal in cut, but inexpensive in material and craftsmanship. On Odessa, when Bel had been a younger woman, she'd have sat in a café like this with her brother and their minders and listened to people who looked like this drone on about the sad state of Lyran superiority.

"You do not agree with him?"

"He speaks of things he does not know," the father said. "As all children do."

"He speaks of war," Bel said.

The grimace flashed again, the barest micro-expression, but she saw it. White skin as the man's lips compressed across his mouth, lines of old pain borne across years around his eyes. Her grandfather had often shown the same face.

"He knows nothing of war. He is trained, yes. A fine graduate of Sun Zhang. But he has never fought. He has never stared death in the face. He has never been threatened, never made to know that his life could end in the very next instant. He has never had to accept all of that and continue." The old man looked at Bel. She saw his eyes flash across her face, taking in her head. "I see from your temples that you are a *gaijin* MechWarrior," he continued. "A Lyran, from the fashion. But you are young. Perhaps you do not yet understand what I mean?"

Bel smiled faintly. "I have seen death come for me," she said. "Felt its hand on my shoulder, seen it come for my comrades. And kept on. I know exactly what you mean. Some things can only be learned, never taught."

The old man regarded her, nodded, and went back to watching his son. Bel swallowed, forcing down the wash of emotion her simple words had brought to the surface. Images and sensations flashed through her mind, a mélange of cockpits and markets and explosions and BattleMechs bearing down on her. Her skin flushed cold. Goosebumps rose along her sides.

"As soon as he has finished?" Bel's large companion whispered.

She demurred.

"Your son," Bel asked the man beside her. "He is a man of honor?"

"As he understands it," the father replied. There was condemnation, not approval, in his voice.

"The lesson that can be only learned. You wish him to learn it?"

"He is my son," the man said simply. "Of course I do not." He paused to sip his tea, to look at his son. Bel saw a lifetime of fears and hopes flicker through the older man's eyes. "But if he is to succeed in the life he has chosen, he must."

He set the teacup down. It clinked, rattled as tremors from the man's fingers rocked it against the saucer. "My son," he repeated. Then he looked again at Bel, and past her. His voice changed. Hardened. "You wish to teach him?"

"I will have that sword," Bel replied with the same hardness. "But perhaps he can learn a lesson as well."

The man's lips compressed. He looked at the giant man next to Bel. "In my youth, I fought the Rasalhague Dominion. The warriors there were your size." His knuckles, wrapped around the teacup, whitened. "I have killed Ghost Bears before." His eyes, filled with emotion before, went dead and flat as a glacier.

Beside Bel, Curtain chuckled. "I too have killed Ghost Bears," he said quietly, for all his voice sounded like boulders clashing. "I have come here for my captain—" He inclined his head toward Bel. "—not your son."

"The sword," Bel repeated. "But perhaps a lesson?"

"A child must touch the kettle once, even though they have been told it is hot." The older man closed his eyes. "My son." When he opened them again, they were flat and cold. "I am Hikaru Tsukuda. If you kill my son, I will kill you, though I will die in the doing."

"I am Curtain. If I kill your son, I acknowledge the debt will be owed. Though I do not wish him dead."

Hikaru looked at Bel again. She nodded. He sat back in his chair, his back a little straighter. "I would not have him learn this lesson," he said. "He is my son. But he is chained to his choices."

Bel wanted to smile, to pat the old man on the shoulder, to say she understood. She had seen the same pain in her own father's face the day she shipped out for the Coventry Military Academy. But she said and did nothing. She knew it would have insulted him. No matter her intent, he would have considered it patronizing.

"Do it," she told Curtain.

The big man winked and stood up. He couldn't stand fully, because he was taller than the low ceiling, so he stepped out of the booth alcove. "Hiroyuki Tsukada!" Curtain's voice boomed across the room in a way young Tsukada's had not. "I will have that sword. You are not worthy of it."

Tsukada's voice, cut off mid-rant, was different. "What?"

"That is the sword of Isoru Koga," Curtain said. "MechWarrior of the Gray Death Legion and the Sword of Light, samurai of the Draconis Combine. He died on this world, killing a coward who bore your name. Undoubtedly some cousin." Curtain paused to let the susurrus of gossip that washed through the café dissipate. "I will have it. Give it to me."

Tsukada hefted the sword. "This is a sword of my family."

Beside Bel, Hikaru grunted almost imperceptibly.

"This is the sword of a warrior of the Combine," Tsukada continued, warming back to his subject. "This sword has the blood of the Dragon's enemies in its very steel."

"Then it is being tarnished by your touch," Curtain retorted. "Watch, everyone. It will shortly begin to rust. Cowards are poisonous to honor. Turn around, coward, and show these people the tattoo of the yellow bird on your lower back." In the crowd, someone snort-laughed. "I will have that sword, boy. Give it to me, and I will not embarrass you further. Show these people who you are. Hand it over."

"Who are you?" Tsukada asked.

"I am Curtain, lieutenant of the Gray Death Legion. MechWarrior. War Chief of the Condor Peoples. I have killed more MechWarriors than you have ever met, Hiroyuki Tsukada. I will have that sword. Give it to me, or I will pry it from your cold fingers."

He spread his massive arms wide. "I am justice for the soul of my departed comrade-in-arms. Even now, his shade watches and approves. I will have that sword."

"I will kill you for this dishonor," Tsukada ground out. Red colored his neck and face.

Bel bit her lip to keep from smiling. Predictability got you killed on the battlefield. There were many lessons young Tsukada needed to learn.

"There is no dishonor in the truth," Curtain replied. "Where shall we fight, coward?"

"Here," Tsukada snarled. "Now. There are dueling fields outside the city. My *Archer* will grind your bones to dust, *gaijin*."

Bel didn't need to see Curtain's face to hear the grin. "What a coincidence."

Bel stood, turned to Hikaru Tsukada, and bowed. "Tsukada-*sama*," she said. "My apologies for the language. It was necessary."

"He is my son," Hikaru said. "He wishes to be a warrior. There are things he must see to learn to be that." There was iron in his voice as he gripped the teacup. "He is my son," Hikaru said in the strangled voice of a father.

Bel joined the rush of people leaving the café.

"You are a witch," Curtain said, looking up at the BattleMech.

"I am nothing of the sort," Bel told him.

"How else would you know this Tsukada would pilot an *Archer*?"

"Luck," Bel said. When Curtain glanced down at her, she grinned an imp's grin. "I am a student of history. History repeats itself."

"A witch," Curtain repeated. "My *Regent* would have made this child's play."

"Your *Regent* wouldn't have been equal. Besides, there are parallels here. A century ago, Isoru Koga and Tsukada's ancestor dueled in *Archers* while the old Gray Death Legion was on-world during the Fourth Succession War. There is symmetry in using the same machines to recover his sword."

"Equality is for amateurs," Curtain said. He crossed his arms and leaned back, looking up the 8-meter distance to the 70-ton BattleMech's cockpit. "Where did this even come from?" The *Archer* was painted in the Legion's customary camouflage pattern, grays and greens, with the grinning skull of the Legion insignia painted on a thigh.

"Buthra's people dug it out of the junkyard on Garrison," Bel said. "Or the bones of it. His people have been putting it back together as they get the parts. It caught up with us as we left Pandora." Bel smiled faintly; Garrison felt so long ago.

After the mutiny that forged the Tamar Pact, Bel, her brother Ronan, and the core of what would become the new Gray Death Legion had escaped Arcturus for Garrison. There, they had built their first weapons out of scrap pulled from a kilometer-upon-kilometer sprawling salvage yard the Carlyle family held a stake in. Garrison had been a core Lyran military world for centuries. Buthra Azarri, the Legion's senior technician, had once told Bel it would be the work of ten lifetimes to dig all the treasure out of there. Even after the Legion formed and departed Garrison, small detachments and local hires continued to mine equipment for use or resale. With war again raging across the Inner Sphere, there was always someone willing to buy arms and armaments.

"Perhaps it was Koga's," Curtain teased.

"It isn't," Bel said, but her expression softened. "I like to think he would approve, though."

"I did not ask why, before we left," Curtain said, after a pregnant pause. "I was, and am, pleased to travel with you. To fight with and for you and the Legion. But this is beyond, I think, your annoying interest in history."

"We need symbols," Bel said, after a moment. "If the Legion is going to survive, to prosper, we need more than tradition and stories. People remember the old Legion, remember the stories. The Helm memory core. Defeating the Jade Falcons on Pandora. Fifteenth Hesperus. But tradition and history will only take us so far. We need real things we can feel, can touch. Symbols that connect us with that history."

"A sword will do that?" Curtain chuckled. "We could have bought any of those swords at the spaceport and said it was Koga's."

Bel frowned. "It wouldn't be the same."

"No, it would not," Curtain agreed, sobering.

"Koga was a great Legionnaire. He died here, on this world, after fighting in a 'Mech just like that one, over the matter of his reputation. That means something."

"It means he cared too much what meaningless people thought about him," Curtain inserted. "My honor does not come from other people."

"Your reputation does."

"Reputation is not honor."

"We have the whole jump series back to argue that," Bel said. "Koga had made a vow. He died carrying it out. That is a straightforward idea our new Legion must always be aware of. We make the same vow every time we sign a contract. That sword…" She paused. "That sword will be a reminder that we aren't the first people wearing the skull to make that deal. And we *dishonor*—" She grinned up at Curtain. "—their memory and sacrifice if we do any less."

Curtain grunted and looked back up at the *Archer*. After a moment he sighed. "A witch."

Bel rolled her eyes. "Just try not to kill him," she told the big man. "We don't need more vendettas chasing us across the stars." She slapped his elbow. "You don't need any more debts to owe."

Curtain chuckled.

In the *Archer*'s cockpit, Curtain finished the final pre-fight checklist and, satisfied the 'Mech was as ready as any of the machines held to Buthra Azarri's high standards, regarded the BattleMech of Hiroyuki Tsukada across the dueling field. It had the characteristic *Archer* blockiness, the wide stance and jutting torsos that hid the trademark long-range missile launchers. Tsukada had painted it flat black, with a Kuritan coiled-dragon insignia on the left chest, and a silver sword painted down the right arm. His battle computer told Curtain Tsukada's *Archer* was a -9K model, which meant the missile batteries had been replaced with four five-tube multi-missile launchers and its lasers with light particle projector cannons. Curtain chuckled. *Of course the child would choose that configuration.*

The theory of multi-missile launchers, which could fire standard long-range missiles or short-range missiles, was that the flexibility of extending firepower to any combat range gave the *Archer* more options to defeat an enemy. Curtain had studied MMLs, fought against them, even test-fired them during his time on Condor. As part of a lance or Star, Curtain would concede the -9K's designers were correct.

Fighting alone, here on the dueling field? Curtain chuckled again and toggled his weapons suite from standby to active.

Master Sergeant Azarri's technicians had rebuilt the *Archer* Curtain piloted to the standard Republic of the Sphere -7C model. It retained the iconic LRM-20s in the torso and the familiar medium-scale lasers in the arms and rear torso. Curtain approved of that loadout. He also approved that, like so much else of the Republic's blend of Inner Sphere and Clan, the weapons were all Clan-built, which meant tighter missile patterns and medium lasers almost as powerful as Inner Sphere large lasers.

Kuritan-built *Archer*s were meant to fight as part of a lance. Curtain's *Archer* was meant to *fight*. And it had one other asset he expected to use to his advantage. He smiled as the radio crackled to life from the range controller's office.

"Warriors," the bored male voice said, "do as honor demands. Combat will commence on the tone, in thirty seconds."

Curtain nodded almost imperceptibly in agreement. MechWarriors had fought duels almost since the first BattleMech walked off its assembly line so many centuries ago. In each of the cultures of the Inner Sphere, dueling remained, but it was influenced by that culture's relation to violence. In Curtain's Clan experience, a duel simply began. A duel in Federated Suns space might begin with an obligatory "Can your differences not be worked out by other means?"

Here on the Gram? "Do as honor demands."

In the seconds before the fight began, Curtain's mind flashed again with how he expected the minute or so after the tone to go. He had never piloted this *Archer* before, though he'd spent weeks in the simulator during the transit. Fighting this duel in his *Regent* would have been little more than muscle memory; he would have advanced his throttle and beaten Tsukada to the ground with the smashing maces of his ER PPCs. Curtain preferred his assault 'Mech. It was simpler: move toward the enemy, destroy the enemy. No noise, no confusion.

This duel would require different tactics. Not unfamiliar tactics. Just different.

A flat tone sounded. Tsukada's *Archer* stepped forward, covers flipping open to reveal the MML batteries in its chest. Curtain did nothing. Tsukada fired; his *Archer* disappeared beneath missile exhaust as twenty LRMs rippled out of the launchers and angled slightly up to reach Curtain's 'Mech.

Curtain slammed his throttle forward and angled the *Archer* left, twisting his torso right to keep Tsukada beneath his crosshairs. The 70-ton machine accelerated quickly into a run. Curtain felt for the *Archer*'s balance, settled his aim, and returned fire. His *Archer* shook as forty LRMs ripped out, twice what Tsukada had fired at him.

Tsukada's missiles exploded into the dirt behind the *Archer*'s heels. Curtain's 'Mech had been faster than Tsukada expected, which Curtain had counted on. The -7C was as fast as most medium BattleMechs. Curtain intended to use that advantage to the fullest.

Tsukada strode out the cloud of his own missile exhaust straight into the hailstorm of Curtain's missiles. Thanks to his skill and the support of the Artemis V fire control system adjusting the missiles' flight, more than three-quarters of Curtain's warheads exploded across Tsukada's 'Mech, staggering it. Armor plates, smoking and buckled, fell

to the ground at Tsukada's feet. *Archer*s carried heavy armor; Tsukada was still in the fight.

But Curtain knew he had already seized the initiative from the boy. The jingoistic samurai, confident of his social superiority, had already been blasted out of his own mental model for how this fight would go. Every step he took from here on was going to be in reaction to what Curtain did.

He had already lost. Curtain knew it, even if Tsukada did not.

The duel viewing area was a holotheater buried in a bunker. Bel approved.

She had been to worlds where dueling fields and proving grounds had outdoor bleacher-style seating where the interested could watch or wager on the outcome the BattleMech fights. Bel had been on too many battlefields to ever want to do that; the noise of combat was literally deafening, and while most of these worlds had thriving black market betting pools on how many stray shots would end up in the crowd, that sort of macabre natural selection had never appealed to her.

Instead, the Kuritans of Gram had hollowed out a massive underground bunker and buried a six-meter holotank in the front of it, as if it were a public holotheater. Bel sat near the center of the raised wall of seats, in a small area reserved for those personally connected to the combatants. She was, of course, the only person sitting in Curtain's section.

Across a small velvet rope, Hikaru Tsukada sat down. He glanced at her and nodded politely as he settled in. She inclined her head in return. Tsukada had taken the time to change clothes, to an out-of-date duty uniform of the Ryuken regiments. He wore no rank insignia, but their absence was clear: fabric, darker where the katakana had previously shielded the fabric from wear, stood proud on his high collar.

Around them, a small crowd, mainly people who'd followed them from the café, muttered, wagered, and made sounds of disgust or pleasure as the two BattleMechs moved. Bel ignored them, watching instead the holotank, where the two *Archer*s fought. She had little doubt of the outcome of the fight. Curtain was one of the best MechWarriors Bel had ever seen, but still...

She reached up and brushed an imaginary hand off her shoulder.

Curtain chuckled as the first short-range missiles appeared from Tsukada's multi-missile launchers, fired at their extreme effective range. The young samurai's *Archer* moved with jerky, uncoordinated movements, and Curtain knew it was not from damage. He'd shocked Tsukada nearly into fight-or-flight. The SRMs were evidence of that; Tsukada knew the short-legged missiles carried heavier warheads. He had to be banking on those same warheads blasting through Curtain's armor, the way his own heavier LRM barrages had done as they closed the range.

Bolstered by Curtain's own talent at gunnery and the supporting guide lasers of the Artemis V FCS, Curtain had replied two missiles to every one LRM Tsukada had fired at him as the two 'Mechs closed. Tsukada's *Archer*, already black-painted, was just *blasted* with missile impact craters, charred by smoke and flame. Sparks shot from a half-dozen places where the warheads had combined to dig deep. Tsukada had done his best to reply, but it wasn't enough.

Curtain's *Archer* bore a quarter of the missile impact craters across its armor, but several spots glowed with dissipating heat where Tsukada had gotten lucky shots placed with his light PPCs. Even then, though, Tsukada just couldn't seem to recognize and adapt to Curtain's *Archer* being fleeter of foot than his.

The wave of SRMs roared in, but most missed. Curtain rode out the few impacts, experienced eyes watching only peripherally for any new red—serious—damage indicators, but there were none. His LRMs *ker-chunked* into battery as fresh reloads fed into his launchers, but Curtain held his fire. The range had indeed closed. He changed target interlock circuits, bringing his lasers online.

He could have kept up with his missiles. Unlike Inner Sphere technology, which suffered in accuracy at short ranges, Clan-made LRMs were dangerous as soon as they left the launcher. Curtain could have kept blasting away until he was standing over the other *Archer*, crashing missiles down atop it like waves into a sandcastle on the beach, but he didn't need to. He could tell, from the way he moved and fired, that Tsukada had realized, probably for the first time, that death stalked the battlefield with him. He was probably feeling the uncertain, unconscious awareness that people died fighting battles like this. He would have known it, intellectually, but now the first creeping feelings of it being able to happen to *him* would be rising up.

What Curtain wanted young Tsukada to learn now was that death could come for him. That its form could be Curtain, war chief of the Condor Peoples, lieutenant in the Gray Death Legion. He wanted to take those first, unformed creepings of fear and give them form.

*His* form.

Tsukada needed to learn what it cost to be a MechWarrior, the lesson his father had quietly lamented he must be taught. Curtain had seen and heard the fear and resignation in the old man's voice. He had heard it a thousand times on Condor, from parents as children took their first steps to adulthood.

Curtain would teach him.

He dialed his crosshairs over the *Archer*'s left thigh, where repeated missile strikes had already weakened the armor, and let his targeting computer lock in the point of aim before he fired. Clan-built extended-range medium lasers hit with almost the strength of Inner Sphere large lasers. Combined, they hit almost as hard as his *Regent*'s ER PPCs.

Tsukada's *Archer* stumbled as Curtain cut its leg out from beneath it.

"He should have kept up with his missiles," someone in the crowd moaned. "He's gonna ruin my point spread!"

From the level of agreeable noises, Bel realized most of the crowd had bet against Tsukada. The elder Tsukada, next to her, snorted under his breath. When he glanced at her, she caught his eyes and raised her eyebrows in question.

"My idiot son," Tsukada murmured, just loud enough for the two of them to hear, "thinks these people ensorcelled with his words. They make the noises he wants to hear when he speaks, so he makes more of them." He glanced around the dark room. "If only he could hear this."

Bel opened her mouth, but the room erupted in noise. She looked to the holotank.

"My son," the elder Tsukada said, sounding half-strangled.

Tsukada's PPCs flashed blue-white actinics across Curtain's display. The holo image damped the glare, the shots had been close. Curtain ignored them. A miss was a miss, whether a micrometer or kilometer.

He brought the *Archer*'s nose around to point directly at Tsukada, whose BattleMech was barely a hundred meters away. The Kuritan samurai was backpedaling furiously, trying to keep the range open while still holding Curtain in his crosshairs, but it was a hopeless cause. Again, the young MechWarrior had miscalculated. His light PPCs had difficulty targeting beneath ninety meters, and Curtain's *Archer* was twice as fast forward as Tsukada's was backward.

Curtain passed ninety meters and kept going.

His ER medium lasers pinged as the capacitors recharged; he checked the targeting computer had held its point of aim and fired them. Both beams stabbed like scalpels at Tsukada's *Archer*'s thigh.

The armor there was gone.

The laser cut into and through the foamed ferro-titanium "bone."
Tsukada's 'Mech collapsed in a heap, its leg amputated mid-thigh.

Curtain slowed his speed as he approached the fallen 'Mech.
Tsukada, to his credit, was trying to turn the 'Mech over, to continue
to fire. Curtain put his own *Archer's* foot into the elbow of Tsukada's
machine and stepped down, crushing the limb. Tsukada's 'Mech flipped
over onto its back, cockpit canopy staring at the sky.

Curtain squatted his *Archer* down until he could press the emission
port of one of his lasers against the cockpit canopy.

"The sword," he sent.

Tsukada's *Archer* went quiescent as it was powered down. Curtain
stood his *Archer* up to clear the other MechWarrior's canopy. A moment
later, Tsukada emerged from the cockpit. He wore a black Kurita combat
suit, with a sweat-soaked white headband bearing the Kuritan dragon
in red stitching around his head. He carried Koga's sword.

The moment his feet touched the ground, he took off sprinting
toward one of the dueling ground APCs. Curtain upped his magnification
and caught a glimpse of young Tsukada's face when he twisted to look
over his shoulder.

He was terrified.

Curtain chuckled. "A debt that one owes me," he murmured. "For
the lesson."

Laughter filled the seating area as the duel ended. Bel ignored it. She
closed her eyes for a quick moment, breathing a silent thank-you to
gods old and dark that Curtain had survived, before opening them and
looking toward Hikaru Tsukada.

The old man sat still, back straight, clasping the knees of his
uniform. He watched the tank, which was replaying the collapse of
his son's *Archer* and then his son's flight to safety. Even in the dim
light, Bel could see the whiteness of his skin across his knuckles, the
not-quite imperceptible tremor in his forearms. While she watched he
swallowed, then stood and turned to face her.

"I thank you for the gift of my son's life," he said roughly. The bow
was not deep, but it was filled with emotion. "And for the lesson. Though
I might have wished he had learned one fewer."

Bel stood as well. "Better he learn this lesson now, while there is
time and opportunity to learn it fully." She returned his bow. "Tsukada-
*sama*. Your son has my property."

"I will see it is returned," the elder Tsukada said, gravel in his voice.

"I can be reached here," she said, handing over a small card. Tsukada took the card, bowed again over it, and departed.

Bel sat back down. She had no desire to queue up with the rest of them. She would wait.

Curtain stood to open the door to their hotel suite when the chime sounded. Bel remained where she was, engrossed in going over the mental inventory of her packing one more time. They were scheduled on a departing DropShip in the morning. Curtain had asked if they should defer, but Bel trusted the elder Tsukada.

"We have guests," Curtain rumbled, returning from the foyer with both Tsukadas. The senior still wore his Ryuken uniform, though he'd added a short sword to his belt. The younger trailed along behind, dressed in a duty uniform and carrying a short sword in a black cloth bag. Hikaru's face was impassive, but the younger man's face was flushed, his expression somehow set between haughty and confused.

"Tsukada-*sama*." Bel greeted the elder with a short bow. She merely nodded at his son.

"My son has something that belongs to you," the father said.

"You don't deserve—" the son began, but stopped at a hissed warning from his father. He held the sword out to Curtain, who'd come to stand behind Bel's right shoulder. "Here. Your traitor friend's sword."

Curtain made no move to take the sword. Tsukada's expression faltered, swinging fully into confusion for an instant, before the haughtiness returned.

"That is my captain's prize," Curtain said.

Tsukada looked at Bel and scowled. "You did not even fight."

"You had to be brought here by your father, like a small child who needs honor explained to him," Bel said. She reached out and took the sword from his hand before he stopped sputtering, then looked past him, toward his father. "My gratitude, Tsukada-*sama*. Truly. I wish you good fortune."

Tsukada the son barked a curse. "How dare you—" he started, but his father grabbed his shoulder and swung him around.

"How dare *you*!" he roared. "How dare you forget all that I have taught you! All that your mother sacrificed to get you into Sun Zhang. How dare you, defeated in honorable combat, flee the field rather than submit? Wait outside!"

The elder Tsukada's bow was deeper, once his son was gone. "Forgive my idiot son," he said to both Bel and Curtain. "He is clearly not meant to be a MechWarrior. I will speak with his colonel."

Tsukada looked past Bel, at Curtain, and bowed again. "I thank you," he said, looking at the floor, "for my son's life."

"I had no wish to take it," Curtain replied. "He may yet learn."

"I fear not," Tsukada said, straightening. "There are lessons sons need to learn."

He turned and walked to the door, but paused.

"There are also lessons fathers must learn about their sons," he said. And was gone.

# VOICES OF THE SPHERE: SMALL BUT MIGHTY PROFITABLE

## STEPHEN TOROPOV

Glamorous and heroic regiments steal the spotlight, but most mercenary units in the Inner Sphere are less than a battalion in size. Independent contractors, ambitious startups, specialists, and grizzled veterans scraping by—no two mercenary units are alike. We interviewed members of these scrappy smaller commands to see what life is like as one of the many small fish in the big pond.

—INN Report, 19 June 3152

### Vincent Schons, Freelancer, Son Hoa (Independent)

Corporate security work is good business for a sole proprietor. The smaller corps can't afford big merc outfits, and the bigger corps prefer to spread their jobs around to units their lawyers can still boss around. You do run the risk of getting hooked by some company store supply scheme when you're getting spare parts for your *King Crab* right off the assembly line, but that can be a blessing in disguise: manufacturers can grab BattleMechs from the assembly line, but it ain't like they've got a bank of iron wombs to crank out reliable personnel. You won't find a better retirement plan in this business than ending up as head of security for one StarCorps plant or another, after all.

### Zumac Morales, CO, Hardshell Guards, Tania Borealis (Free Worlds League)

Folks who say retainer work doesn't have enough action are idiots. Just because you aren't risking it all in an active war zone doesn't mean you're sitting around getting soft. Nobles and moguls who can afford to hire a lance of BattleMechs as a personal retinue don't do it because the MechWarriors look pretty. I'm getting paid good money to paint the bosses' crest on my 'Mech and use it for what it was designed to do: knocking skulls and scaring footsloggers. I couldn't care less about the politics; that's the mercenary dream right there.

### Reece Lennox, XO, Ortega's Outriders, Herotitus (Fronc Reaches)

To last in this business, you gotta have contingency plans for pissing off the wrong people. One of the perks of working small is getting lost in the crowd of wide-eyed startups. Say, purely hypothetically, you found your unit blacklisted for allegedly destroying the planetary governor's prized branth stables while you were putting the moves on her heir who was riding jumpseat for a training exercise. Well, a quick call to a good accountant and suddenly Jim's Reapers are in arrears and get dissolved, and your buddy Ortega can pick up all the equipment for a song while setting up his own bold new venture in private military enterprise. Then that totally new unit can take a security gig with a trader heading as far afield as you can find, and bang, you're back in business. Hypothetically, of course.

### Aina Baek, MechWarrior, Shady Ladies, Proserpina (Draconis Combine)

Outsiders consider smaller outfits as they do mayflies: short-lived, numerous, and below notice. Yet we have thrived for centuries, even through the harshest years, bound together by a legacy of excellence and a close-knit comradeship. The Dragon's periodic mistrust of ronin purged larger outfits from the market, but more nimble groups like us could be reclassified and continue operating— we have served the Pillar of Jade with renown since the times of my great-grandmother, and one day I hope my great-granddaughter will do the same.

### Adetokunbo Albrecht, Administrative Officer, The Metallicon, Markesan (Federated Suns)

Growing a merc unit is a process that feeds on momentum and luck in equal measure. The ups and downs are dizzying. We started as two lances in the Chaos March, rode out Stone's Peace as a reinforced company doing garrisons in the broken League. Gray Monday was good to us, we grew to a battalion by '39, then the old

*Overlord* we hired had a bad run in with a Cappie fighter wing. By the time we dug out of the debris, the techs could piece together enough spare parts to get nine 'Mechs running, and we were back down to two lances. We've doubled that since, but I wanna slap all them loudmouth greenhorns in the merc bars jabbering about how they'll command a regiment if you give them and their rusty *Chameleon* three years.

### Operative "Nemo" (rank withheld), Nine-Two Commando, Principia (Capellan Confederation)

Staying small isn't a failure to grow, it's about knowing our market niche. We've got a reputation as the best damn unit on the market for special operations. We don't need more troopers than we have for the jobs we do, and adding on some new team of tankers or prima donna 'Mech jockeys isn't going to earn us more pay than we'd spend on the new logistics and transport concerns. Staying at the size we are now, we can charge a premium because employers know we'll do the job right, and all our individual shares pay out better.

### Robert L. Mace, Avanti's Angels, Galatea (Isle of Skye)

The golden age of the freelancers is closing up, I think. When the hyperpulse generators went down and the Wall went up, any yahoo who welded an autocannon to a *MuckRaker* could make a living scaring bandits and splinter groups off to easier targets. Then bozos like Bannson gave way to real threats like Alaric and Malvina, and running solo became a death sentence. Nowadays it's join or die, and I know having a cause and comrades watching my back has agreed with me. Still, I do miss calling my own shots and taking my own jobs now and again.

### Tomici Parata, Employment Broker, Almotacen (The Hinterlands)

In all my years, I've never seen better opportunities for the little guys. Khans and House Lords all have their eyes on the big prizes, and whole swathes of space have fallen through the cracks. Folk stuck in one of those cracks still need protection, so the market for roving heroes to do that protecting is thriving. I don't mean to say it's all rosy, sometimes you're gonna have to get some blood on your knuckles to earn your keep. If you've got a BattleMech and the courage to use it, though, it won't take long to pay the bills around here.

# THE ALEXANDRIA JOB

## GILES GAMMAGE

**HEAVEN'S GATE**
**RYDE**
**LYRAN COMMONWEALTH**
**5 JULY 3020**

"No real names," said the patron. She pointed to them each in turn. "Chuck, Lemmy, Janis, and Patti. You can call me Lisa."

The back room of the "Gentleman Adventurers" club was dim and smoky, its space mostly taken up by a round table in the center. The four mercenaries lounged on black leather couches in hazy shadow around its perimeter.

"Chuck" had a stubby cigar jammed in one corner of his mouth. "I'm who?"

"Chuck," said "Lemmy." He wore sepia-toned aviators and a bomber jacket over a black tank top, an ouroboros tattoo of a snake biting its own tail on his neck. "Aw, don't complain. At least you get to be a verb, 'stead of a suicidal rodent."

"Lemmy, not lemming," corrected "Janis." She was a short, compact woman, yet her wild explosion of hair added ten centimeters. She nodded at "Lisa." "Pre-Exodus Terran entertainers. It's her thing."

"Patti" shrugged, instantly drawing everyone's attention. She was built like an *Atlas*, if an *Atlas* wore black leather, black eyeliner, and matching lipstick. "Who cares what the codenames are. You said you had a job."

The patron, "Lisa," took a paper tube from where it stood against a wall, placed it on one edge of the table, and with a flick of her wrist, unrolled it into a white-on-blue map.

"The job is a simple objective raid," she began.

"Simple?" echoed Lemmy. He lowered his sunglasses and gave her a long, steady look over the tops of the rims. "Lady, there's plenty of mercs who might hire other mercs to do a simple job, and no offense, but Snord's—sorry, *Lisa's*—Irregulars ain't one of them. Nothing you folks do is *ever* gonna be a 'simple' job."

Lisa shrugged. "Fine, not entirely simple then. It's no secret my unit has a reputation for—"

"Rampant looting?"

"—collecting memorabilia. That's caused some issues with our paymasters. Both our own employers and the opposition will be watching us. They will not be expecting *you*."

"So, you drop us in and we take all the heat?" Chuck asked. He dislodged his cigar and eyed it critically, as though it might answer his concerns. "Not sure I like the sound of this."

Lisa sighed. "Two million C-bills. Each."

"I say we hear her out." Chuck nodded emphatically and, with a toothy grin, returned the cigar to its nesting place.

"Thank you." Lisa spread her arms over the map. "Welcome to Alexandria. Currently occupied by the Draconis Combine. Once famous for some of the Star League's finest museums and art galleries."

"I thought your beef was with House Marik," said Janis.

"Very true, but my father..." Lisa began, then caught herself. "My CO believes there are profitable opportunities on the Combine border. We've identified the location of something valuable, but with all eyes on us, it would be...difficult for us to secure it ourselves. Which brings us to the job."

"I think I see where this is going," Janis nodded slowly. "What are we going to steal? Original recordings? Concert jackets? Signed guitars?"

Lisa tapped the map, where the scribble of a city nestled within a mountain valley. "Benedict Station. Home to some of humanity's most famous artworks: Camuccini's *The Death of Julius Caesar*, Sally Skinwalker's *Oleg and Mustafa*, and *Capellans Bearing Gifts* by Metropolix, among others. No? Well, they are fabulously valuable classics, all of them. My unit will be one of several that will land on Alexandria as part of a Lyran Commonwealth assault. While the Combine is busy with us, you will slip through their lines, retrieve the artworks, and return them to my unit's DropShip."

"Defenses?" Chuck asked.

"There's a garrison here, at Benedict Springs." Lisa traced the thread of a road from Benedict Station down to a city straddling a narrow river. "It's manned by the local militia with about a company of light armor. To avoid raising the alarm, you can bypass them entirely by jumping the gorge upriver."

"They'll still detect us though," Chuck objected.

"Our techs have restored some of the ECM capabilities of Patti's *Spector*."

"They got the original electronics in that thing to actually work?" Lemmy's eyebrows shot up as he looked from Lisa to Patti.

Patti shrugged. It was like watching a boulder hiccup. "What's it to you?"

"Just surprised is all," he said, raising his hands in mock surrender.

"If I may?" Lisa interrupted. "In any case, there's no garrison in the city itself. If you do encounter any patrols, Janis should be able to liaise with the locals. *Tanomu ne, Jani-chan*."

"*Ryokai*." Janis gave a thumbs-up. "*Makesete*."

"Okay, that doesn't sound too bad." Chuck grinned and leaned back against the wall with a contented puff.

"Huh, now let the other shoe drop," Lemmy said. "Why is a city that big deserted, and why's nobody ever fixed to grab this loot before? What's the catch?"

Lisa hesitated a moment. "Benedict Station might be a little...how should I put this? Irradiated."

"Come again?" Janis asked, blinking rapidly.

"The Benedict Station nuclear power plant was destroyed in 2819 during a Combine raid," Lisa explained. "Probably a mix-up with a name, as there was nothing of military value in the city, but there *was* an ammunition factory in Benedict *Springs*. The Combine mistook a nuclear power plant for the ammunition factory, blew up the control center, and the resulting core explosion spread several tons of cesium and strontium around, so the zone is still a little...warm."

"Great," muttered Chuck. "We're gonna die, aren't we?"

"Well, if you're not interested in two million C-bills..." Lisa shrugged.

"Hey now," Chuck protested. "Didn't say I was bailing. Dying rich is as good a way to go as any."

"Stay in your 'Mechs and you won't notice a thing," Lisa assured him. "Even if you get out, you should be fine as long as you don't lick the stonework."

"How'd a bunch of paintings survive a nuclear meltdown?" Lemmy wondered.

"Thought you'd never ask." Lisa reached for a corner of the map, and, with a magician's stage, flourish flipped it over. There was a cross-section diagram, like a map to an excavated pyramid, showing a building squatting above a long chimney that burrowed into the ground.

"At the beginning of the First Succession War, the paintings were moved from the gallery to a nearby underground vault, originally built during the Age of War." Lisa tapped a chamber at the bottom of the chimney. "It's about fifty meters down. There was a freight elevator, big enough for a BattleMech to ride down, but of course it will be inoperable.

Still, the shaft and vault itself should be intact under all the rubble. The sensors in Janis' *Ostscout* should allow you to find it easily."

Patti raised a bear-paw hand. "How are we going to get down there?"

"Lemmy's *Firestarter* will melt or blast away the elevator car, exposing the shaft below. Chuck's *Javelin* and Janis will then use their jump jets to maneuver down the shaft and reach the vault." Lisa traced a line down the chimney. "They will extract the content of the vault, rig up a sling, and use their jets to carry it back up to the surface. Lemmy and Patti will remain on guard above. You will then rendezvous back at our DropShip, and we all return to the Commonwealth for a well-earned reward."

Janis and Patti nodded, if grudgingly, while Lemmy seemed to think it over before shrugging to himself. "It's a lot of money," he admitted, then added softly: "For a merc."

All three turned expectantly to Chuck, who sat frowning down at the map.

"I don't know," he muttered. "There's a lot that can go wrong here."

"Always is," Janis agreed. She rolled up the map, slung it like a rifle over one shoulder, and sauntered to the door. The light beyond was bright, sheathing her in a silver glow. She paused and turned, and there was mischief in her smile. "You can always say 'No.' But I can think of two million reasons not to."

**BENEDICT SPRINGS**
**ALEXANDRIA**
**DRACONIS COMBINE**
**17 SEPTEMBER 3020**

*Tai-i* Mithras Li eased into the seat behind his desk and blew gently on his tea before taking a sip. He owed his unusual name to his parents' religion. They had been followers of Mithra, the ancient sun god, and as he basked in the sun, Li was half-tempted to believe in the god himself. Birds sang outside the window, the Jafar River shimmered and shushed to itself, distant ground cars murmured across the bridge.

*War has come to my home again, but you wouldn't know it here*, Li mused. *This was a beautiful planet, once. Before the Commonwealth and Combine ground it into dust between them.*

*Bah, let them grind each other.*

Under the desk, he kicked off his boots and wiggled his toes in relief. There were reports to read, paperwork to fill out, but they could wait. His eyelids grew heavy. Perhaps a short nap, why not, he had time. There was no hurry—

The door blasted open with a cannon roar.

Li's eyes flew open. His knee jerked up, smacking into the underside of his desk and sending a curling arabesque of hot tea flying into the air, where it hung for a moment before descending on him with scalding vengeance.

He yelped, leaped to his feet, stubbing a toe on one of the desk legs, transforming the yelp into a howl of pain. He hopped on one foot, simultaneously dabbing desperately at his uniform to dry the tea. "What the—"

An officer stood before his desk, looking at Li the way an astech might a faulty actuator. Li registered the frown, the frigid glare aimed at his socks, the green insignia at the other man's collar.

"*Sho-sa!*" Tam tried to straighten, still balanced on one foot, and saluted. He wobbled.

"*Tai-i* Li. I trust I am not interrupting anything? Your calisthenics, perhaps." *Sho-sa* Tomas Troth was a steel whip of a man, slim, his bearing stiff, elbows clenched to his sides, his hair brushed back and shellacked in place by a gleaming layer of gel.

"No, sir. Yes, sir, that's it, sir. Er, to what do I owe the honor, sir?"

"This sector has been quiet, hasn't it?"

"Yes, sir. Not a peep, sir."

*Sho-sa* Troth strode past Li to gaze out the window. He stood there for a long moment. "It is peaceful, isn't it?" he agreed, then whipped about fast enough to make Li jump. "That is all about to change. We have a report from a source placed with the Lyran mercenaries that the enemy is planning a raid on Benedict Station."

"Benedict Station?" Li laughed, then stopped when he saw Troth's expression. "You're serious? But there's nothing there, except five different ways to get cancer."

"Nevertheless. I want your men on alert, patrols out, watching the roads."

"Sir, my company isn't going to stop anything tougher than a light breeze."

"That's fine." Troth gave a piano-wire smile and cuffed Li on the shoulder. Both were meant to be reassuring, and both failed spectacularly. "Your job is to spot the enemy, not engage them. High command is sending a lance of BattleMechs for support."

## BENEDICT STATION
## ALEXANDRIA
## DRACONIS COMBINE
## 19 SEPTEMBER 3020

The BattleMechs lumbered through the wooded hillsides, the treetops swaying aside or snapping like twigs as the 'Mechs brushed past. Lemmy's *Firestarter* took the lead, a cartoon bulldog painted on one shoulder under the name "*Brutus*." Janis' *Ostscout* followed close behind, a rotund, vaguely egg-shaped 'Mech with a single laser jutting from its midsection, and a great length of canvas looped over one shoulder. It was followed by Patti's *Spector*, whose right arm ended in the menacing barrel of a Nightwind laser. Chuck's spindly *Javelin* brought up the rear, with twin short-range missile launchers embedded in its oddly out-thrust chest. It, too, shouldered a loop of canvas.

In his cockpit, Lemmy glanced at the display of the local area map and slowed to a stop. He called up a zoomed-in camera view of the hazy rooftops of a city.

"Coming up on Benedict Springs," Lemmy radioed. "Time to see if the Irregulars really got that bit of *lostech* on your ride to work, Patti."

"How come a bunch of vagrants like the Irregulars know how to work with *lostech*?" Chuck wondered.

"They used to be part of Wolf's Dragoons, haven't you heard?" Lemmy replied. "The Dragoons drop extinct Star League models as often as the Liaos lose star systems."

"Activating Guardian ECM," interrupted Patti.

The map immediately dissolved into static. Switching to thermal sensors produced a wobbling, oozing psychedelic spray of color that reminded him of an especially vile hangover. "Uh, Patti, I can't see a damn thing."

"Me neither," protested Chuck. "Every sensor just went haywire."

"Then it is working."

"Working?" Chuck yelped. "I thought the Guardian ECM only messed with the bad guys' signals?"

"The system in my 'Mech is four centuries old; it is a wonder the Irregulars could get it working at all. It is blocking the enemy's sensors, what more do you want?"

"Uh, to see where I'm going?"

"Try looking out the ferroglass." Patti clicked off.

Lemmy pursed his lips, then shook his head slightly, feeling the neurohelmet connectors batting against the back of his neck. He slid the throttle forward, cautiously, keeping his eyes on the forest floor ahead.

The gorge was wide but not impossibly so, composed of two sheer walls of multicolored rock, between thirty to forty meters high, above the white, frothing torrent of the Jafar River. The forest grew almost up to the edge, leaving just a small strip of bare rock on either side.

Lemmy pinged the far side to measure the distance, ignoring the rest of the display skittering across his HUD like an overexcited flamenco dancer listening to double-speed mariachi music. "I reckon it's about one seventy-five meters here," he sent. "Chuck and I should be able to make it, if only just. Janis, why don't you go first?"

"Why me?"

"Your walking egg has the biggest jets," Lemmy pointed out. "If you can't make it, not much point in the rest of us trying."

"Let Patti go first then."

"I should go last, to maximize our chances of evading detection," Patti said.

"Okay, then Lemmy or Chuck can go."

"There something wrong, Janis?" Lemmy asked.

Janis mumbled something in reply.

"Sorry, but I coulda sworn I heard you just say your 'Mech has a faulty gyro," Lemmy said sharply.

"Well excuse me for not having a factory-fresh ride like some freaking Wolf's Dragoons MechJock or a Star League museum piece like Patti here, so not everything's gonna be perfect. Okay?"

"Can you make the jump?"

"Of course I can make it!"

"Look, Janis, the sensors on your *Ostscout* are our only chance of finding the vault, and much as I would love to see your faulty death trap smear itself across the rock face, I would love even more to see two million C-bills, so lemme ask you again: Can you make the jump?"

"I told you, I can make it."

"Then after you." The *Firestarter* bent awkwardly at the waist and waved one handless arm toward the gorge.

Janis' *Ostscout* strode to the cliff, its feet toeing the edge, sending a small avalanche of loose stones down into the white-capped torrent below. She backed up two steps, paused, then hurled the 'Mech forward, igniting quad streams of superheated air on either side of its back, sending it lumbering into the air in a long, gently curving arc.

At first, all seemed well. Then at the zenith of its jump, the BattleMech wobbled. It tilted drunkenly to the left, then overcompensated and veered suddenly right, rapidly losing altitude, hurtling toward the sheet rock wall.

At the last moment, the *Ostscout* righted. The jump jets screamed, firing on full burn, angling the 'Mech forward, bringing up its feet so they only just clipped the far edge of the gorge. The *Ostscout* plunged head-first into the forest beyond, plowing a wide swathe of splintering destruction before coming to rest face-down on the forest floor with a thunderous crash.

"Janis?" Lemmy signaled. "You still with us?"

"Yeah, fine, fine," she replied after a moment. "Told you I could make it."

"That was some fancy flying." Lemmy sat back and sighed. "Let's try not to do that again, okay?"

*Tai-i* Li perched on top of the tank commander's seat, with the hatch thrown open, exposed to the air from the waist up. The inside of the Scorpion was stuffy and stank of unwashed privates. Li made a show of scanning the forests to either side of the road with his binoculars, but his vision was filled instead with a hundred ways to wreak his revenge on *Sho-sa* Troth, even now relaxing in what had once been Li's office.

"Sir?" Lance Corporal Faith Tam called from the musty depths below his feet. She sounded worried.

"Hm?" There was something at the edge of perception, a distant sound, like thunder, a slight tremor felt through his boots, or was it his imagination?

"Sir, there's something wrong with our sensors."

"You know what Quikscell quality is like, Tam. Be more of a surprise if anything in this deathtrap works the way it's supposed to."

"But sir, every sensor just went on the fritz at the same time. The enemy could walk right by us, and we'd never know."

"Oh no," Li said flatly.

"Sir?"

"Lance Corporal, the Commonwealth and Combine have mashed our home into mud over the last two centuries and the militia always, *always* gets caught in the middle. If we don't spot a single enemy for as long as I live, I will count it a blessing."

"Yes, sir."

"Anyway, the whole thing is probably a false a—aaaaah!"

A stand of trees to his left exploded in a rippling series of bangs, showering him in a rain of splinters and flying bark, obscuring the road in a sawdust haze. Through the smoke came a giant, impossibly tall, incredibly powerful. Unstoppable.

It stopped. One arm swung toward the tank and Li knew enough to recognize the murderous maw of a 'Mech scale flamer, a weapon that excelled in turning people like him into flaming lumps of coal that were not very much like him at all. He closed his eyes and whispered a heartfelt, if somewhat dishonest, prayer to Mithra detailing everything he would do if he escaped being roasted alive in the next five seconds.

He was interrupted by a voice in his ears. *"Sensha ichi-ichi, kochira wa eeto, eeh, ano...Pyrite Pirates no Chu-i Janis."*

Li risked opening his eyes a crack. A second, slightly battered BattleMech had appeared, and seemed to be placing a restraining hand on the arm of the other. A third and fourth 'Mech stood at the edge of the forest. He swallowed. Hard.

The voice sounded in his headphones again: *"Sensha ichi-ichi, kikoemasu ka?"*

Li hesitated, wet his lips with his tongue, then clicked his mic on. "Uh, sorry, I don't speak Japanese. Say again?"

The first 'Mech twisted to give the other what appeared to be a long look of disgust, then lowered its weapon arms.

"Lieutenant Janis, Pyrite Pirates. We, ah—that is—"

"You're our reinforcements?" Li asked quickly.

"Say again?"

"I heard we were getting BattleMech reinforcements. You must be it."

There was a long silence. "Yes, that's it. We are your reinforcements."

"Oh good. Lyrans are expected any day now." Li waved up the road toward Benedict Station. "City is that way, if you want to scout it out."

"Uh, copy that. Will do. Over and out."

The lead BattleMech regarded the Scorpion. Li gave it a cheerful wave and realized that was probably overdoing it. The 'Mech turned away and began to stride up the road in earth-shaking footfalls that made Li's teeth rattle and the Scorpion see-saw against its suspension. He kept waving until the last machine was dust and shadows.

"Uh, sir?"

"Yes, Lance Corporal Tam?"

"Sir, I don't think they were the reinforcements, sir."

"You don't."

"No, sir. Our reinforcements are supposed to be the Rasalhague Regulars sir, not some merc unit."

"What extraordinary insight, Lance Corporal Tam. Well, our orders were quite clear: Observe the enemy without engaging."

"Shouldn't we at least signal *Sho-sa* Troth? He'd probably change those orders if he knew the Lyrans were already here."

"Yes, yes he probably would," Li agreed. "Tell you what, Tam, can you do something for me?"

"Yes sir?"

"Shut up."

They strode through the verdigris ruins of Benedict Station. Vines besieged the crumbled walls, trees had invaded the streets, and everywhere masonry had surrendered to time and gravity, retreating back into nature. A few relics proclaimed the city's faded glory. The bottom half of a sign boldly announced the mercenaries could "*GET IT HERE!*" though it was unclear what "*IT*" was, unless it was weeds and rubble.

"Amazing," Chuck breathed.

"Amazingly garbage," Janis sniffed.

"Then your 'Mech fits right in," he countered.

The Geiger counter crackled in dry amusement.

Little of the Benedict Station Center for the Visual Arts remained standing above ground, save for a few wedges of concrete where the corners had once been, sort of a sketchy wireframe of the building's foundations.

"All right, time to earn your pay," Lemmy said to Janis. "Patti, if you could give the nice lady some bandwidth to work with?"

"Guardian ECM deactivated," Patti sent. "Work quickly, we are exposed. I will reactivate it once we have located the elevator shaft."

The screens in Lemmy's *Firestarter* snapped back to normalcy. He clicked through a few of the overlays and grunted in satisfaction. The Scorpion they had encountered was still there, at the limit of sensor range, but hadn't moved.

The *Ostscout* extended its arms straight out, palms down, and began to shuffle across the rubble like a zombie, twisting this way and that in a rhythmic pattern.

Lemmy chuckled. "You fixing to find it by witchcraft?"

"Sensors in the arms," Janis snapped. "Now hush. Some of us are working."

Lance Corporal Tam jerked up in her seat as sudden light stabbed from the sensor screens, bathing the interior of the tank in their glare. She blinked, squinted, tried rubbing her eyes to force them to adjust. She noted the position of the rest of the company, then the four red icons of unidentified signatures.

She studied them for a moment, chewed her lip and glanced up. *Tai-i* Li had not moved for a long while. *Indolent, cowardly ass is probably sleeping.*

She reached toward the comm station and slowly, carefully switched it on, wincing at the sudden sharp *click* of the button. Li did not move or react.

"Temple Base, Temple Base, this is Delilah One," she whispered hoarsely. "Contact, say again contact..."

The elevator shaft was blocked solid with debris; great slabs of concrete sprouting medusa tendrils of rebar, stone boulders, and two centuries of accumulated dirt. While Patti's *Spector* kept watch, the *Javelin* and *Ostscout* scooped away the rubble with titanic shovel hands and the *Firestarter*'s twin lasers blazed through metal spars and boulders too large to move.

The elevator car was wedged at an angle about a quarter of the way down the shaft, preventing the rubble from filling it completely, but also blocking access. It, too, was removed by the simple expedient of laser-bisecting it, allowing the two halves to tumble and fall to the bottom in a series of gradually fading bangs, ending in a final crashing crescendo.

"You're up," Lemmy said to Chuck.

Chuck's *Javelin* unslung the canvas from around its shoulder, threw them a jaunty salute, then fired a brief spurt from its jets to hang immobile in the air above the center of the shaft for an instant. "Tallyho!" he sent, and the 'Mech dropped straight down like a stone.

Lemmy winced and waited for an explosion and wasn't sure if he was relieved or disappointed when Chuck sent the all-clear from the bottom.

"I can see the vault, door looks intact," he said. "Give me a hand down here, Janis? I don't think firing a dozen SRMs in an enclosed area would be a good idea."

The *Ostscout* unslung the second canvas roll, paused at the lip of the hole, then fired its jets and descended far more slowly, hesitantly, and unevenly than the *Javelin* had.

There was a dust plume on the horizon, back down the road toward Benedict Springs. A black shadow at its center. Li raised his binoculars and adjusted the focus. He recognized the Baba Yaga hut silhouette of a *Cicada*, a Mech famous for its speed despite its ungainly box-on-chicken-legs appearance. The red "R" of the Rasalhague Regulars was stenciled on one blocky wing.

"Oh Ta-am?" he asked in a sing-song voice, lowered the binoculars, and looked down.

"Yes sir?" Her face radiated pure innocence.

"I don't suppose you know why there is a 40-ton death machine currently bearing down on us at top speed, do you, by any chance?"

There was a thoughtful pause. "Yes, sir."

"Thought you might." He raised the binoculars again and saw a trio of other BattleMechs behind the first: the high shoulders of a *Phoenix Hawk*, then a blocky-armed *Dervish*, and a *Clint* bringing up the rear. "Don't suppose you've also considered who is going to get blown to bits first when the big boys start shooting at each other, Lance Corporal Tam?"

The pause was somewhat longer this time. "No, sir."

The *Firestarter* and *Spector* stood on opposite sides of the elevator shaft. Over the external pickups, Lemmy could hear faint, metallic scrapes and rustling as Chuck and Janis dismounted from their BattleMechs and ransacked the vault below. Patti had reactivated the Guardian ECM so there was nothing to see on the sensors, and little else to do but stare at the view.

"What is the origin of the Irregulars' feud with Marik?" Patti was asking him.

"Oh, I dunno, probably stole something they shouldn't have," he told her. "Leave the grudges to the Houses, that's my motto. They're the only ones who can afford revenge. Never bet against the side with deeper pockets."

"Speaking of profit, what do you think they'll do with them?" she mused. "Sell them?"

"The art? Nah, that's the crazy thing, they'll just add it to their collection on Clinton."

"Seems a waste."

"Don't start on that, Patti. If you're looking for a big score, work for one of the Houses, or sell that ride of yours. Probably worth more'n a thousand paintings all on its ownsome."

"Then I'd be Dispossessed. Anyway, can't. It's been in the family for centuries."

"And now here it is."

"You're here, too."

"Don't I know it," Lemmy chuckled. "I know what I am. Takes all kinds of mercs to make a Succession War. At the top, you got your big brigades like the Twelfth Star Guards, your scrappy brawlers like

Hansen's Roughriders, your no-nonsense pros like the Centauri Lancers, then way, way down at the bottom, you got Snord's Irregulars. And a notch below them, you got the folks that do their dirty work. But you know what? They ain't so different from us. They're all in it for the money, no matter what they say. Wouldn't be mercs otherwise."

"You don't find this stealing...dishonest?"

"Nothing honest about taking money for killing folks, either. What's war all about anyway, other'n taking stuff that ain't yours from folks who can't stop you from taking it?"

"Strange opinions for a mercenary."

"Just honest is all. I'm in it for the payout, don't mind who's doing the paying."

Their conversation was interrupted by Chuck's *Javelin* popping out of the elevator shaft like a champagne cork from a bottle, bearing a canvas bandolier bulging with the outlines of crates and boxes.

"Everything good?" Lemmy asked.

"Never better," Chuck replied cheerfully. "Can't believe I was worried about this. Easiest money I've ever made. Come on up Janis, and let's get out of this irradiated rat hole."

"On my way," Janis acknowledged.

Lemmy listened to the familiar rumble of the *Ostscout*'s jump jets firing. The roar grew louder as the 'Mech slowly and carefully ascended, burdened by its stolen cargo, taking care not to damage it. Louder, still louder. Almost there. Home free.

He heard Janis shout something—panicked, rushed, indecipherable. The tone of the jump jets changed from rumble to shrill scream.

He heard Janis say, quite clearly and distinctly: "Shit."

He heard a detonation, then a caterwaul screech of metal on metal, then a titanic, echoing crash. A flash from the elevator shaft, a pulse of air, carrying a burst of dust and smoke.

And then: silence.

"Janis?" Lemmy walked to the edge of the shaft. "Janis—aw, hell."

Li clung miserably to the back of the tank's turret, goggles down, his shirt hiked up over his nose and mouth as the tank ate the dust kicked up by the four 'Mechs ahead. *Sho-sa* Troth had been in a jeep trailing behind the BattleMechs. He'd leaped down, strode across to Li's Scorpion, given the *Tai-i* the tiniest of disappointed head shakes, then waved Li out of the turret cupola with a whip-snap of his wrist.

"I'll take over."

The jamming was back, the sensors dead, but the enemy BattleMechs hadn't moved perceptibly the entire time they'd been on the scopes, so the entire force was converging on their last known location.

The cracked bones of the city reared up around them. Rustling avalanches of rubble shook loose as the BattleMechs thundered past. To his alarm, Li noted the tanks plunging into the city right behind them.

"You're not thinking of engaging them, are you?" Li shouted to Troth over the growl of the tank's engine.

Troth turned slowly, almost robotically, to give Li a steely glare. "I'm thinking of court-martialing you, Li."

"If you get into a shooting match, I'll be fried!"

Troth's garrote smile returned. "Wouldn't that be a shame."

The *Ostscout* lay on its back at the bottom of the elevator shaft. The left arm was missing, the left leg shredded and twisted below the knee, the cockpit half caved in, the ferroglass window shattered.

"What happened?" Chuck asked.

"Malfing gyro," Janis groaned. The 'Mech twitched slightly, scrabbled at the wall and tried to lever itself into a sitting position. The wall beneath its hands crumbled and it flopped back onto its back again. "Of all the—look, I'm stuck, left side jets are scrap and I can't get this thing to stand."

"Aw hell," Lemmy swore again. "Look, none of our 'Mechs are powerful enough to lift you out of there. Gonna have to leave it. Maybe see if the Irregulars will splurge on a search party after we get back."

"Well, don't leave me down here!" she yelped. "I don't want to come back glowing green with two heads."

"Of course not," agreed Lemmy. "We'd never dream of it. After all, you still got half the treasure down there."

"Nice."

"Alright, sit tight in there and I'll come down. You can hitch a ride with the loot on the way back up. Chuck, Patti, stay sharp. Let's not have any more unpleasant surprises."

Li crouched down, just peeking over the top of the turret. As he peered between the legs of the *Cicada* in front of them, he could just make out two BattleMechs with their backs toward him, standing by what looked like a square hole in the ground.

Two. Not four. Where were the other two?

"There's only two!" he shouted to Troth, still standing exposed in the turret cupola. The man did not turn, probably had not even heard him. Li reached forward to tug at the back of his uniform. "Only two!"

Troth jerked angrily away from Li's grasp. "What?"

Li opened his mouth to speak. Then he went blind.

A standard CDA-2A *Cicada* was equipped with two Magna medium lasers and a single small laser, a somewhat underwhelming arsenal for a medium BattleMech, and lacking a knockout punch. Which is precisely why the manufacturer, HartfordCo, had developed the -3C variant. In exchange for a lower top speed, this model mounted a Donal Particle Projection Cannon: A weapon that fired a searingly, blindingly bright nova of blue-white energy that turned even BattleMech armor to slag and cinders. A weapon very, very capable of delivering a knockout punch.

Patti never saw the bolt that struck Chuck's *Javelin* in the shoulder, shearing straight through the joint and sending the charred stump of the right arm pirouetting away. The canvas bandolier slung about the shoulder erupted into flames. The material snapped, spilling metal crates and boxes to the ground.

Patti pivoted her *Spector*. "Bandits!" she yelled. She brought up the Nightwind laser and fired a snap blast of cyan light at the *Cicada*, but missed, the bolt carving the air between its legs instead.

Lemmy's voice crackled from the bottom of the elevator shaft. "What?"

"Nooo—" Chuck cried as his machine staggered. He crouched the *Javelin* and tried to scoop up the artwork one-handed.

"*Move*, you idiot!" Patti yelled.

"What bandits?" Lemmy demanded. "What's happening?"

A score of long-range missiles came screaming down, loosed by the *Dervish*. A dozen explosions hopscotched across the back and head of the *Javelin*. The 'Mech went down on one knee, then pushed itself up just in time to take a double volley of fire from the *Clint* and *Phoenix Hawk* to the chest and face.

The *Javelin* rocked back on its heels, black smoke pouring out from a hole in the back of its head. It nodded once, as if to acknowledge its fate. Then tipped forward and fell with a crash, narrowly missing the elevator shaft.

"Chuck? Patti?"

"Sorry, Lemmy." Patti grabbed the remains of the canvas cloth and its contents with one hand as she fired blast after blast with her laser from the other. A PPC bolt arced just wide, while autocannon shells blew divots out of the armor over the right hip. Patti fired another shot, then turned and threw the *Spector* into a run, chased by a rain of missile fire.

Li fell back onto the engine deck of the Scorpion, great blobs of light dancing in his vision. He heard Troth shout "Fire!"

Then one of the enemy 'Mechs fired at the *Cicada*. And missed.

A line of murderous light scythed directly over the top of the Scorpion, close enough for the furnace heat to blister Li's exposed skin. *Sho-sa* Tomas Troth disappeared from the waist up, instantly annihilated, blown into a bloody cloud that splattered down about Li.

"Mithra..." he breathed. He looked down at his flash-burned hands, now doubly daubed in red. "Holy Mithra."

The *Spector* ran, then lurched forward as a PPC bolt struck its back, nearly sending it sprawling. Patti swore. She could outrun the rest of the Kurita lance and her ECM fouled their missile tracking, but the *Cicada* could keep pace, fire over iron sights, and had the range to hurt her even if it couldn't close the gap.

She angled for a gap between two ruined high-rise buildings, then veered so she was running straight toward one. A PPC bolt flashed by, thrown by her sudden change of course, and detonated against a wall in a storm of stone fragments.

As the wall reared up directly before her, Patti fired the jump jets, kicking the *Spector* almost vertically straight into the air, over the top of the building, then down on the other side, putting it directly between her and the *Cicada*.

Patti glanced at the 360-view strip above her cockpit canopy, saw the wall of concrete now between her and her pursuer, and grunted in satisfaction. *That ought to slow them down.*

A moment later, her smile disappeared as the building's wall exploded outward as the *Cicada* plunged straight through it.

"Orders?" someone was asking him. Li tried to wipe the blood from his goggles and succeeded only in creating a red-brown smear across his vision. He pushed them up onto his helmet. Lance Corporal Tam was looking at him expectantly. What was left of *Sho-sa* Troth lay in a heap beside the tank.

"Right, yes, orders." Li looked around. The BattleMechs had gone, leaving only the militia armor and a single 'Mech on the ground, next to what looked like a pile of industrial garbage. He pointed toward the downed *Javelin*. "Let's, ah, secure the wreckage. Might be salvageable."

As they drew closer, the "garbage" beside the Mech resolved into gray, white, and black steel containers, from which had spilled a collection of paintings, sculptures, masks, totems, and other objects onto the ground.

"Stop," he ordered, "STOP." Li slid down from the tank and walked hesitantly forward. He crouched by a frame and gingerly lifted it by one corner. He recognized it from a history textbook as one that had once been on display in Alexandria: *The Death of Julius Caesar*.

He was still staring at it when the *Firestarter* vaulted from the ground and landed a dozen meters before him. The impact sent him sprawling in the dust.

"*YOU!*" Li recognized the voice that boomed from the speakers. "*WANT TO BE A HERO?*"

"Absolutely not!" he squeaked up at it, still on his hands and knees.

"*GOOD,*" the 'Mech told him. It extended an arm, and a woman with a static halo of black hair slid down from the shoulder and hopped to the ground. *She looks irritated,* Li thought.

"*PAINTINGS ARE WORTH MILLIONS. DITTO THE 'MECHS. YOU CAN KEEP 'EM. UNLESS YOU'D RATHER FIGHT?*" The human-incinerating flamer was pointing at him again.

"Um, no?"

"*A MAN AFTER MY OWN HEART.*"

The 'Mech twisted in the direction the pursuers had gone, and broke into an earth-shattering run, leaving Li and the strange woman to stare after it, then at each other. She folded her arms defiantly.

"I'm, uh, Mithras Li." He extended his hand and noted her frown of befuddlement. "The name? It's, ah, a long story. Don't ask."

To his surprise, she just nodded and shook his hand. "Janis. Ditto."

Patti was out of the city and plunging through the trees. Green needle curtains and the pillars of pines flashed by on either side. She risked a quick hop, feathering the jets just enough to hurdle the next strand of trees. Blue light pulsed, impacted on the already-damaged right leg. Alarms hooted in her cockpit, announcing damage to the lower leg actuator.

The *Spector* landed awkwardly, wobbled, and she barely saved it from going over on its side. Patti swore. There was no chance of outrunning the *Cicada* now.

"Enough," she snarled. She found a break in the woods, a small clearing, and hobbled to a stop. She let the tattered canvas fall from the left arm, freeing up the two lasers mounted there. Her 'Mech was wounded and surrendered five tons to her opponent, but its PPC was chest-mounted and would be inaccurate in a close fight. "Let's do this."

The *Cicada* had stopped at the limit of PPC range, cautious, perhaps sensing a trap. With the ECM still active it would be blinded, wary of an ambush, and so it waited for the rest of its lance to catch up.

"Come on!" Patti yelled at it. She fired a blast through the trees. *"Come on!"*

A twin stream of fire rained down from the skies. In the space between the two 'Mechs, trees turned to blazing candles, then exploded into an inferno as flames leaped from branch to branch, trunk to trunk.

The *Firestarter* came down from out of the sun, a fiery angel, turning the forest into bonfire wherever it touched.

"Pick up your gear and run," Lemmy told Patti. "PPCs run hot, that *Cicada* won't risk running after us."

She scooped up the loot and ran.

The gorge yawned before them. Patti clutched the bag to the chest of her 'Mech, then jumped, as low as she dared, jets on, jets off, on, off, bobbing just above tree height, watching the jump meter drain down and down and down, and *now*. One last burst.

And she was across, Lemmy's *Firestarter* touching down on her right a moment later. The blackened, smoking *Cicada* emerged from the trees and skidded to a stop on the far edge. It fired a frustrated blast after them that succeeded only in singeing the treetops.

The *Dervish* came barreling through the woods behind it at top speed, ran straight to the edge without slowing, and fired its jets. Two-thirds of the way across, its jets stuttered, flickered and died. Forward momentum carried it for a moment, the arms flailed, the torso twisted from side to side, the arms sprayed desperate laser fire at the oncoming rock face. Then it plunged from view. A moment later, the earth shook in the thunder of an ammunition explosion and a black pillar of smoke shot into the sky.

The two 'Mechs ran for another hour before coming to a halt by unspoken agreement. They stood facing each other for a long while.

"Thank you," Patti said, almost grudgingly. "You saved me."

"Well, maybe," Lemmy agreed, then leveled the *Firestarter's* twinned lasers and flamers at her *Spector*. "But then again, maybe not."

"Betrayal?"

"Yup," he agreed again.

"That ambush was too perfectly timed... You tipped off the Dracs?"

"Right again."

"But you ran from them, same as us."

"Well spotted," Lemmy said cheerfully. "Luckily for me, the Irregulars and the Snakes aren't the only game in town."

"I could shoot." The barrel of the laser came up.

"You could, but that ride of yours is plenty beat up, so let's just act like adults, hey? Now, I ain't the mean type, so you can keep your great-grandaddy's 'Mech, but the artwork has to stay."

"And the two million C-bills?"

"A lot of money, no question there. For a merc. Peanuts for a House, though. I told you they're the only folks who can afford revenge. I'm afraid Miss Snord got herself outbid."

**LAKE MEEDE**
**ALEXANDRIA**
**DRACONIS COMBINE**
**1 DECEMBER 3020**

Rhonda "Lisa" Snord sat and stared at the holo delivered by the ComStar agent, her eyebrows knotted together, her jaw a steel trap. In the flickering blue light of the emitter hovered the long, bearded, and ascetic face of a man with a purple and black tattoo on his forehead. The man smiled.

"Janos Marik," she snarled softly.

*"I would invite you to the opening of my new art gallery, but I hear the Irregulars are short of travel funds these days,"* Janos smiled. *"Normally I'm not the kind to gloat, but I must say, that's music to my ears."*

## GLD-7R GLADIATOR

**Mass:** 55 tons
**Chassis:** MW240
**Power Plant:** DAV 220 Light
**Cruising Speed:** 43 kph, 54 kph with Triple-Strength Myomer
**Maximum Speed:** 54 kph, 75 kph with Triple-Strength Myomer
**Jump Jets:** Chilton 950 Improved Jump Jets
    **Jump Capacity:** 180 meters
**Armor:** StarSlab/3H Hardened with CASE II
**Armament:**
    1 Defiance Novashot Model 2 Plasma Rifle
    2 Diverse Optics Extended-Range Medium Lasers
    2 Diverse Optics Extended-Range Small Lasers
    1 TharHes 4 Pack
**Manufacturer:** StarCorps Industries
    **Primary Factory:** Son Hoa
**Communications System:** Telestar Model XB-82
**Targeting and Tracking System:** Starlight Seeker LX-4X

Following the success of the *Hermit Crab*, StarCorps on Son Hoa found itself in the curious position of being a profitable advanced BattleMech manufacturer on an independent Periphery world. The megacorporation's most far-flung branch was able to act without oversight from the Inner Sphere powers, had massive market share over a huge swath of space, and was a tempting target for every military force within ninety-plus light years. Brion's Legion, a mercenary unit under long-term contract for Son Hoa's defense, had relied heavily on its stockpiles of pre-Republic equipment for decades. Knowing that using a locally produced multirole machine would reduce service costs and logistics delays from off-world suppliers, StarCorps and the Legion agreed to collaborate on a solution. The facility's *Gladiator* line had been running since the Blakist war, producing a few -5R export units every year. With minimal capital expansion costs and only a few newly-sourced components, the -7R refit became both an economical and effective local defense unit as well as a distinctive addition to the Son Hoa branch's catalog for regional sales.

### Capabilities

The Jihad-era -5R is known for its durability, and the -7R pushes that feature even further. Sluggish on the ground, it relies on its enhanced jump capacity for mobility; its Triple-Strength Myomer is useful for maintaining speed on long marches, but difficult to keep active in combat due to the -7R's limited heat-control options. Nonetheless, the 'Mech's potent short-range punch and incredibly stout hide make it an excellent urban combatant and line-holder—and no small prize for pirates and thieves.

## Battle History

By the 3120s, Brion's Legion's contract with StarCorps had lasted so long that multiple generations of Legion offspring had been born, raised, and inducted into the unit. Many in these new generations saw themselves not as mercenaries but loyal defenders of their homeworld, working alongside StarCorps' corporate security forces, visiting Sea Fox merchant-warrior detachments and other local combat units to form an ad hoc but surprisingly effective planetary defense force.

In the late 3120s, Son Hoa came under attack from an unusually well-equipped pirate force calling themselves "The Final Gaze." After several successes on lightly defended border worlds, the Gaze were emboldened enough to strike Son Hoa with a pirate-point drop of unprecedented strength. As Gaze forces made a beeline from the plains toward the StarCorps depots in Hayestadt, the Legionnaires blocked the pirates' path with their *Gladiator*-7R's while support units from StarCorps CorpSec harassed the attackers with long-range fire, buying valuable time for the city to be evacuated. The Legion then withdrew, seemingly content to let the pirates loot the city now that the population was safe.

However, having sustained almost no internal damage, the Legionnaires quickly patched their armor and reloaded, then charged back into the dense urban battlefield. The pirates had anticipated an attack and set up a defensive line. The Legionnaires again used their *Gladiator*s as blockers, this time jumping them close to the defenders to occupy and channel them while fast strike units broke through toward the pirate transport assets. Taking losses and now facing a brawl in unfamiliar urban terrain, the pirates realized they had little to gain anymore and retreated to the wilds of former Circinian space. The widely publicized engagement marked the start of a downturn in pirate raids on Son Hoa that would last for decades.

## Variants

The increased presence of Sea Fox traders on Son Hoa has spawned two notable refits designed to fill specific product niches for both the Clan and StarCorps. The ClanTech-equipped -7R/SF seems lacking compared to the -7R, but this is intentional; its multiple ammo bins and eclectic weaponry make it well-suited to address a wide range of garrison contingencies (albeit in an unfocused, jack-of-all-trades fashion). The variant is commonly sold via Son Hoa's hiring hall to Periphery merc units that can't afford Omni technology or need a versatile anchor unit for urban deployments; the nearby Sea Fox offices offer payment plans of varying degrees of onerousness.

The unusual -9SF (known among Sea Fox pilots as the *Betta gladiator*, after a Terran fish species) mounts varied equipment to enable the machine to douse fires, weld seams, lift over 100 tons, and otherwise appear as a mundane spaceport IndustrialMech—an illusion quickly dispelled with one look at its right arm. When moving cargo, pilots can use a special diagnostic computer mode that runs the shoulder-mounted flamers in a repeating activation cycle, automatically keeping the 'Mech's enhanced myomers active and giving the -9SF the appearance of a steam-age automaton with a flame-spouting smokestack. Only produced by special request, the -9SF is almost always seen in Shoal Clusters (where it is considered a somewhat better prospect for glory in battle than most IndustrialMechs). Some merchants bring them on trade ships to increase cargo space by combining BattleMech and IndustrialMech capabilities in a single bay, but finding pilots can be difficult; few Trueborn warriors are willing to be perceived as glorified stevedores, leaving freeborn, *solahma*, or contract pilots as the go-to options for such expeditions.

## Notable 'Mechs and MechWarriors

**Commander Lionne Keller:** Lionnephryx Keller claims to be a descendant of Alex Keller, whose name is still famous on Son Hoa, but they have been unwilling or unable to produce any documentation, and positive genetic tests have been flagged due to suspected tampering. Lionne certainly has the same bravado and mystique as their putative forbear, but attitude alone has proven insufficient to persuade local authorities to grant access to the old Keller landhold on Son Hoa. Instead, Lionne rents modest quarters near the StarCorps complex, where they have steadily climbed the ladder (despite their near-total lack of academic credentials) as a lead test pilot and security coordinator.

**Star Commander Mullio:** A Trueborn warrior from a prestigious Bloodhouse, Mullio did not expect his service in the Sea Fox Watch to include acting as a glorified insurance adjuster. Even so, when tasked to investigate mercenary malfeasance on Sullivan in 3151, Mullio went without complaint. Realizing the potential need to bring large pieces of salvage back for evaluation, Mullio requisitioned *Gladiator* -9SF units for his team. When the Eleventh Ghost caught wind of Mullio's investigation, they attempted to ambush the Clan unit. Mullio and his Starmates held off the Draconis Combine Mustered Soldiery forces with accurate particle projector cannon fire while hauling away hundreds of tons of wreckage, which was eventually used to confirm that Scoleri's Sabres had betrayed their Federated Suns employers. Mullio's efforts earned him significant accolades, and the whole affair was instrumental in solidifying the Sea Foxes' reliability as mercenary contract brokers.

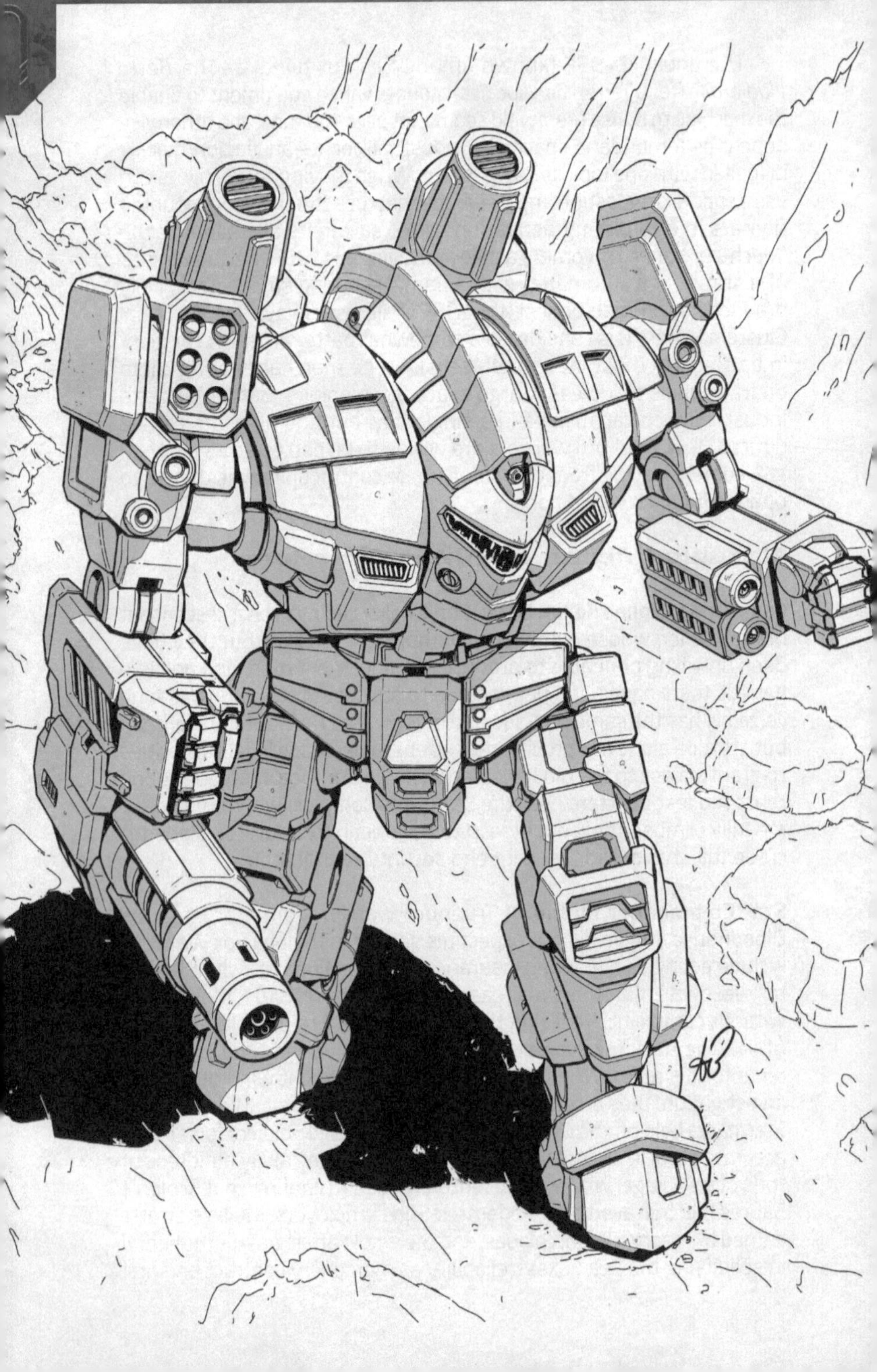

Type: **GLD-7R Gladiator**
Technology Base: Inner Sphere
Tonnage: 55
Role: Skirmisher
Battle Value: 1,890

| Equipment | | Mass |
|---|---|---|
| Internal Structure: | | 5.5 |
| Engine: | 220 Light | 7.5 |
| Walking MP: | 4 (5) | |
| Running MP: | 5 (7) | |
| Jumping MP: | 6 | |
| Heat Sinks: | 10 [20] | 0 |
| Gyro (XL): | | 1.5 |
| Cockpit: | | 3 |
| Armor Factor (Hardened): | 132 | 16.5 |

| | Internal Structure | Armor Value |
|---|---|---|
| Head | 3 | 9 |
| Center Torso | 18 | 19 |
| Center Torso (rear) | | 6 |
| R/L Torso | 13 | 15 |
| R/L Torso (rear) | | 6 |
| R/L Arm | 9 | 12 |
| R/L Leg | 13 | 16 |

| Weapons and Ammo | Location | Critical | Tonnage |
|---|---|---|---|
| Plasma Rifle | RA | 2 | 6 |
| Ammo (Plasma) 20 | RA | 2 | 2 |
| 2 ER Small Lasers | RT | 2 | 1 |
| SRM 4 | RT | 1 | 2 |
| Ammo (SRM) 25 | RT | 1 | 1 |
| CASE II | RT | 1 | 1 |
| 2 ER Medium Lasers | LA | 2 | 2 |
| Triple-Strength Myomer | RA/LA | 3/3 | 0 |
| Improved Jump Jet | RL | 2 | 1 |
| 2 Improved Jump Jets | RT | 4 | 2 |
| 2 Improved Jump Jets | LT | 4 | 2 |
| Improved Jump Jet | LL | 2 | 1 |

**Notes:** Features the following Design Quirk: Cowl.

Type: **GLD-7R/SF Gladiator**
Technology Base: Mixed Inner Sphere
Tonnage: 55
Role: Skirmisher
Battle Value: 1,748

| Equipment | | Mass |
|---|---|---|
| Internal Structure: | | 5.5 |
| Engine: | 220 Light | 7.5 |
|    Walking MP: | 4 (5) | |
|    Running MP: | 5 (7) | |
|    Jumping MP: | 6 | |
| Heat Sinks: | 10 [20] | 0 |
| Gyro (XL): | | 1.5 |
| Cockpit: | | 3 |
| Armor Factor (Hardened): | 128 | 16 |

| | Internal Structure | Armor Value |
|---|---|---|
| Head | 3 | 9 |
| Center Torso | 18 | 19 |
| Center Torso (rear) | | 6 |
| R/L Torso | 13 | 15 |
| R/L Torso (rear) | | 5 |
| R/L Arm | 9 | 12 |
| R/L Leg | 13 | 15 |

| Weapons and Ammo | Location | Critical | Tonnage |
|---|---|---|---|
| LB 5-X (C) | RA | 4 | 7 |
| CASE II (C) | LA | 1 | .5 |
| SRM 6 (C) | RT | 1 | 1.5 |
| Ammo (SRM) 30 (C) | RT | 2 | 2 |
| Ammo (LB 5-X) 40 (C) | RT | 2 | 2 |
| CASE II (C) | RT | 1 | .5 |
| 2 Imp. Hvy. Medium Lasers (C) | LA | 4 | 2 |
| Triple-Strength Myomer | RA/LA | 3/3 | 0 |
| Improved Jump Jet | RL | 2 | 1 |
| 2 Improved Jump Jets | RT | 4 | 2 |
| 2 Improved Jump Jets | LT | 4 | 2 |
| Improved Jump Jet | LL | 2 | 1 |

**Notes:** Features the following Design Quirk: Cowl.

Type: **GLD-9SF Gladiator**
Technology Base: Mixed Inner Sphere
Tonnage: 55
Role: Skirmisher
Battle Value: 2,119

| Equipment | | Mass |
|---|---|---|
| Internal Structure: | | 5.5 |
| Engine: | 220 Light | 7.5 |
| Walking MP: | 4 (5) | |
| Running MP: | 6 (8) | |
| Jumping MP: | 4 | |
| Heat Sinks: | 10 [20] | 0 |
| Gyro (XL): | | 1.5 |
| Cockpit: | | 3 |
| Armor Factor: | 176 | 11 |

| | Internal Structure | Armor Value |
|---|---|---|
| Head | 3 | 9 |
| Center Torso | 18 | 26 |
| Center Torso (rear) | | 9 |
| R/L Torso | 13 | 19 |
| R/L Torso (rear) | | 6 |
| R/L Arm | 9 | 17 |
| R/L Leg | 13 | 24 |

| Weapons and Ammo | Location | Critical | Tonnage |
|---|---|---|---|
| ER PPC (C) | RA | 2 | 6 |
| PPC Capacitor (C) | RA | 1 | 1 |
| Targeting Computer (C) | RA | 2 | 2 |
| 2 Flamers (C) | RT | 2 | 1 |
| SRM 4 (C) | RT | 1 | 1 |
| Ammo (SRM) 50 (C) | RT | 2 | 2 |
| CASE II (C) | RT | 1 | .5 |
| Lift Hoist | RT | 3 | 3 |
| Lift Hoist | LT | 3 | 3 |
| Small Pulse Laser (C) | LA | 1 | 1 |
| Fluid Gun | LA | 2 | 2 |
| Ammo (Fluid Gun) 40 | LA | 2 | 2 |
| Triple-Strength Myomer | RA/LA | 3/3 | 0 |
| 2 Jump Jets | RL | 2 | 1 |
| 2 Jump Jets | LL | 2 | 1 |

**Notes:** Features the following Design Quirk: Cowl.

# SIGNING BONUS

### JAYMIE WAGNER

**HANGDORF PROVING GROUNDS**
**10 KILOMETERS OUTSIDE GALATEA CITY**
**GALATEA**
**LYRAN COMMONWEALTH**
**5 MARCH 2822**

Mark Hazzard heard the *ping* as his *Ostsol*'s targeting computer registered a new contact, and took a moment to breathe before he swung the 'Mech around to face a simulated target being projected by the equipment at the Hangdorf proving grounds.

His sensors told him a Galleon tank had somehow popped up from the ground, but a quick look through the cockpit window revealed an I-beam with a few sheets of rusted armor plate crudely welded on to provide him with something to shoot.

He wished that he could pay for a one-on-one range session with remotely operated tanks or another MechWarrior, but right now he had to watch every credit until they had a new contract. Mark had over a hundred mouths to feed, so an hour of shooting fake tanks would have to do to help him stay sane.

After twelve years of piloting for the Free Worlds League Military and another three of mercenary work, he barely needed to think about lining up a shot on the move at the 'Galleon' with his lasers.

*One second...two seconds...three seconds...*

The reticle flashed gold as his sensors matched the finer focusing of the lenses with the crude input of his joystick, and his thumb smacked down on the stud for his medium lasers to send two lances of solid light into the "side" of the tank, followed by one of the Tronel heavy lasers set into the 'Mech's breast.

Slagged armor dripped from the plates onto the much-abused ground, and a chunk of I-beam joined the puddle of cooling metal as his computer reported the target had taken minor armor damage to its turret from one of the lasers, but the two that hit the flank had blasted road wheels and made the theoretical Galleon throw a track. That kind of damage would have easily taken a real tank out of the fight, while the equally theoretical return fire his computer reported had barely managed to score the armor on his left leg.

It wasn't much like a real battle, but as he took a breath of air that was just enough above room temperature to tell him *Hustler's* heat sinks needed to work a bit to disperse the waste heat his shots had generated, the world made sense for a few seconds.

See target, zap target, fight on. Easy.

Nothing like the constant uncertainty he would face when he cracked the hatch and let reality back in.

Then his radio crackled with the static that had plagued the machine's comm systems since his mother had inherited the *Ostsol* from his late uncle during the Star League Civil War, and an amused alto voice came over the line.

"About done out there, boss?"

Mark rolled his eyes even as he turned toward the general direction of the proving grounds' exit. "I suppose I am, even if we're apparently giving up on proper comms today."

"I will be professional when we have a new contract for me to be professional with," Iris informed him dryly.

"I suppose that's fair enough," he admitted as *Hustler's* strides ate up ground. "Any particular reason you're checking in?"

"Well, first, you are my adorable husband, and I would like to have dinner with you."

"Aww. Thanks, love."

"You're welcome! Also, second, because I'm your XO and we've got a contract to look at, ASAP."

"You couldn't have led with that!?" Far too many contracts for smaller units were time sensitive. You never knew who else was being considered, or how long the offer was going to be on the table.

He could hear the barely suppressed laughter in Iris's voice, static or no static. "I could have, but this way I got to ask you out!"

Mark grinned and shook his head as much as his neurohelmet would allow. Five years and change, and the honeymoon went on. "Roger that. Hazard Six is returning to base."

Even at a leisurely 35 kph, per the Proving Ground's rules for BattleMechs moving from the firing range to the 'Mech bays, it didn't take long for Mark to reach the set of berths they had rented for the unit while they recovered and refit.

A few of the techs heard his approach and shifted from maintenance work to guiding him to one of the open repair bays. The rest of the tech crews kept working on the repairs they'd begun while on the way to Galatea, a laundry list that never seemed to end.

Mark settled *Hustler* into position, ran through the shutdown checklist, and set to disconnecting his cooling vest and life-support feeds. The heavy neurohelmet was the last to come off with a soft grunt. Stupid thing felt like it was twice as heavy as the model he'd used with the First Fusiliers of Oriente, but the Duchy's quartermasters had split every hair possible when he'd submitted his discharge papers. Even though he'd started his career in the battles to defend Oriente after Thaddeus Marik had hung them out to dry, Duke Carter Allison had apparently instructed the logistics office to make it as difficult as possible for anyone planning to muster out while the Fusiliers of Oriente were rebuilding their strength after their final campaign against the Capellan Confederation.

*Hustler* might have been his family's 'Mech, but the neurohelmet and the cooling suit he'd been issued were both considered property of House Allison, and the best replacements he could find on Galatea hadn't been much to write home about.

Mark half suspected the only reason he'd gotten *Hustler* away from the hungry quartermasters at all was because the BattleMech's deed had been kept in his personal effects storage, and not on file in a drawer somewhere the Ducal bureaucracy could have decided to 'misplace' it.

The cooler air of the 'Mech bay raised goosebumps on his skin as he headed to the cherry picker that had come to meet him at the cockpit hatch, and he wasn't surprised to see Carole, their chief tech, operating the lift basket.

"Have fun blasting a few dummies, Major?"

Mark felt like he'd been punched, his good mood deflating. "Well, I was until you called me major."

Carole shrugged, then held out a clean shop rag with one hand while retracting the lift with the other. "Still your rank on paper."

"Yeah. On paper."

On paper, they'd still been at three-quarters strength when they'd finished their last contract. As long as you didn't count the many who were still nursing their wounds, their wrecked machines, and their badly dented morale.

Their real available assets when they'd reached Galatea had been a lot closer to company strength, at best. That hadn't helped much with getting employers to give them a look, either. Not many planetary governments or interstellar corporations wanted to pay full rates for a unit that could barely muster a third of its strength.

He took the offered towel and used a few seconds of scrubbing his damp hair and face to give himself a chance to get his equilibrium back.

Back when Iris, Carole, and a couple companies' worth of MechWarriors and tank crews had decided to make a go of it with him as mercs rather than potentially get shoved into the meatgrinder of the Capellan front again, he'd really been a major, or close enough for government work.

They'd even managed a sweet first contract for their newly formed Hazard Duty battalion, picking up a garrison assignment from the Lyrans to sit on Cruz Alta in case any of the old Rim Worlds remnants still eking out a life as pirates decided to try to hit the food reserves or outgoing water shipments that supplied most of the other border worlds nearby.

It had been nice and quiet for the first two years, giving them a chance to drill and polish their formations, developing their own tactics and organization rather than aping what they'd learned in the Fusiliers. They'd just started to consider an offer to extend their contract for another three-year hitch when the war found them again, but not from the pirates they'd been anticipating.

The Second Marik Militia had decided to stage a raid in force on Cruz Alta, skipping over the spaceport and grounding on the planet's southern continent, Abundance. Mark had ordered their recon units to get into position once they'd confirmed the raiding *Overlords'* orbital track, and soon had reports of Marik Militia 'Mechs and tanks sweeping through parts of the Turley and Mykonos districts, clearly looking for something.

After some discussion with the Altan government, they'd sent an HPG message out to the Alarion Province HQ to call for aid, then tried to set up a series of hit-and-run raids to harass the Marik forces and buy time.

It *should* have been a tough but manageable fight, especially with Mark and the locals having better knowledge of the terrain, but the Second Militia had thoroughly scouted out the plains and forests of Abundance and anticipated several of their attacks. What should have been quick, mobile engagements often turned into pitched slugfests, with Mark's command lance taking heavy fire as they executed a withdrawal or lent their weight to attempts to break through the Militia lines.

Worse, the Second Militia had been brutal in their counterattacks, grouping fire and blasting 'Mechs, tanks, and the local defense infantry with equal fervor. By the time elements of the Forty-Fifth Lyran Guards made planetfall, Hazard Duty had taken 60 percent equipment losses and buried almost a third of their personnel.

The damage and salvage clauses in their contract had helped the unit make good on at least some of the machines, but people were a lot harder to replace when you were standing on the edge of the Periphery, so they'd decided to pass on the Lyran offer and travel to Galatea to see what might be scared up now that the Great Succession War seemed to be coming to an end.

"Hey," Carole's voice broke into his woolgathering. "Major? Boss? Mark? Pick up the phone!"

Mark shook himself out of his funk just as the cherry picker's basket touched the ground with a rattle. "Sorry. Got lost in my own head for a second."

"I noticed," the veteran tech observed. "So. I heard we got a new contract offer."

"Apparently, yeah." He straightened up and took another look around the repair bays. "How do we look as far as machines go?"

"Getting there," Carole answered as she opened the gate and waited for him to step down. "Most of our tracks and hovers we could repair or recover are ready for duty, and Bravo Company's looking good."

That meant their recon and cavalry assets were back up to speed, but Mark also knew what kind of shape their heavier equipment had been in.

"Okay, and Alpha Company...?"

Carole's sour expression said it all. "I think I can get Mitch's *Black Knight* working again, mostly. I managed to find a replacement arm with a bit of haggling, but the comm system and active probe are both shot, and it'll take time to get replacements—if I can get them at all. Of the remaining 'Mechs, your machine and the XO's *Orion* are good to go, but Bayfield's *Champion* isn't worth saving at this point, and the rest are all missing important pieces. I can put a couple more back together, but it would help if we had bodies to put in the seats."

Mark winced. Bayfield used to say their dad had chosen not to leave with Kerensky, and had gone home to the Free Worlds with their former Star League Defense Force 'Mech instead. They hadn't really had qualms about leaving the Fusiliers to become a merc, but they had maintained the egg-like 'Mech with a quiet pride—and the fatal Gauss slug Bayfield had taken in one of their last engagements had really been meant for him.

"How much is left of the *Champion*? Can we get any use out of it?"

Carole shook her head. "Nobody on this side of Terra makes parts for the Lubalin's dual ammo feed, and the engine shielding took so much spall damage when the ammo blew that it looks like Swiss cheese. Even if I got a new Vlar and patched it up, we'd either need to put a lower quality gun in the torso or make it into an overweight *Cicada*."

He grimaced at the idea, and Carole's expression shifted into one of sympathy. "Sorry. I know you were hoping to get it back up and running, but nobody's got spares worth a damn for Hegemony-built 'Mechs at this point."

Mark let out a grunt, then tried to get himself back to thinking practically. "I know you probably looked into parting it out, so you might as well tell me what you can do."

The chief tech's eyes had a pleased light in them that always made him think she'd gone a bit feral. If there was one thing Carole Sunthakaram loved more than working on 'Mechs, it was scrounging and haggling.

"Got a tech over with the Arcadian Cuirassiers who's pretty desperate for some StarSlab ferro-plating, and some guys calling themselves the Black Lances said they'd pay for the chassis and remaining weapons. Not enough to get us a full replacement, but I might be able to scrounge for some other parts to help the heavies up or grab something like a *Centurion* or a *Treb*."

Mark considered, then nodded. "Okay. First priority is trying to get our heavier stuff on its feet—we're supposed to be a line formation, not just a recon unit. If you can't find what you need...we could use some extra fire support. A *Trebuchet* would work—and so would some missile tracks."

"Right. I'll see what I can dig up, and keep you posted. If that new contract sounds like we might need something in particular, let me know."

"I haven't said we're taking it yet."

Carole raised an eyebrow. "Sure. You're just coming by every couple days to go zap things for an hour or two because you're trying to keep in shape."

Mark rolled his eyes, but acknowledged the hit as he left Carole to her work and went to the locker room for a shower. He still had to make dinner—and look over a contract.

By the time he'd showered, changed, and gotten back to the temporary housing complex where the unit had rented most of an apartment block, Mark was thinking more and more about what that contract offer might look like, and what Hazard Duty might need to meet it.

Carole was right about spares not being available for what had been state-of-the-art Hegemony or SLDF tech, but rugged beasts like his *Ostsol* were going strong, and armored vehicles and VTOLs were easy enough to obtain on Galatea, as long as your credit was good.

Pilots and crews might be more of an issue. It seemed like five new mercenary outfits put out their shingle in the hiring halls every day, and the battles for recruiting veteran MechWarriors were getting fierce—especially if they could bring their own 'Mech with them.

The losses they'd taken meant that they could try fishing out of the pool of candidates who had either lost the family 'Mech or been using someone else's equipment in their previous service, but even a lot of those were long on enthusiasm and short on experience thanks to the bloody battles of the last few decades.

On the whole, they tried to avoid completely green candidates, but if their employer wanted them at full strength the minute their DropShips touched down at their posting, he might need to talk with Iris about bending that rule.

Mark stepped off the elevator, walked the five meters or so toward their apartment, and Iris opened the door with a grin, her eyes filled with excitement.

"I never understand how you can time that so well," he greeted her as he let himself be wrapped into a quick but heartfelt kiss.

"I'm a professional," Iris noted as they disengaged. "Also, Carole let me know you were on the way."

"You have pretty much everything covered," Mark replied on his way to the kitchen. "Why am I the one in charge again?"

"You cook better than I do, and Carole isn't nearly as good in bed."

Mark let the remark hang in the air for a few seconds before letting out the laugh he'd been struggling to hold back.

"Oh, god," he pleaded once their laughter died down. "Please don't ever, *ever* repeat that. Especially not on an open channel."

Iris grinned as she settled down at the table with her noteputer. "I do know how to keep a *few* secrets. Besides, letting it be known we have a contract on the table got us some more applicants while you were out."

"Sneaky woman."

"Sure am. Now, what's for dinner?"

Mark looked in the fridge, considering what they had available. "We still have half a loaf of bread and some ground chicken. Kota sandwiches and some of those little frozen spanakopitas?"

"Works for me, boss."

Half an hour later, the kitchen had a pleasant aroma of toasted bread and curried meat as Iris pulled out a data stick that still had the Mercenary Review Board security seal wrapped around it. "Ready to take a look?"

Mark swallowed a bite, then nodded. "Let's have it, Mrs. XO."

It only took a moment for her to pull the security tab, slot the stick, and throw the document up on the 'puter's holographic projector, the MRB and ComStar logos rotating in the air for a few seconds before it began to read out.

**TO:** *Major Mark Hazzard, Hazard Duty.*
**FROM:** *Adept Aodhan MacCnag, MRB Liason*

*Major,*
*As your designated liaison from the Mercenary Review Board, it is my pleasure and duty to provide you with the following contract offer from the Capellan Confederation Armed Forces Mercenary Liaison Office (Tikonov).*
*Thank you for entrusting the MRB to act as your bonding agent. I will be in my office at Galaport if you have any questions or concerns about the contract you would like me to direct to the client.*
*The Peace of Blake be with you.*

"Huh. They're really pushing that crap, aren't they?"

Mark grunted. "I suppose so. I'm more concerned about how the others would feel about taking a job from the Capellans than I am about someone deciding the HPG repairman should be a saint."

Iris paused the display, her green eyes turning thoughtful as she met his gaze. "Let's start asking that question here, then. Mark—if the money's good and the terms are reasonable, would you feel comfortable in the Confederation?"

He looked down at the table as he thought through her question, drumming his fingers against the table as he turned it over in his head a few times.

"We saw some nasty stuff from the partisans on Lukla and Sappho," Mark finally admitted as he looked back to his wife, "but those were people fighting tooth and nail for their homes. If someone had invaded Kiyev while we were on planet, I would have fought just as hard and as dirty."

Iris nodded, waiting until he finished to ask her next question. "How about taking orders from the CCAF?"

That got another grunt. "Well, I don't think we're too likely to end up reporting to someone who has a grudge from back in '16 or '17. Even then, we aren't fighting for Oriente or the Free Worlds. We're there to be professionals and get paid."

"That's about what I was thinking. So, let's take a look." Iris grinned as she opened the next file. "Besides, it'll be easier to sell the others on it if we know what the paycheck will look like."

**GALATEA CITY
GALATEA
LYRAN COMMONWEALTH
8 MARCH 2822**

Three days and seven interviews after the Capellan offer had come in, Mark sipped his coffee and looked over the lance and company commanders who were occupying just about every horizontal surface in his living room, with Carole holding up the back corner of the wall.

They were the surviving core of the unit's founders. Trusted friends and basically family at this point. He knew they all wanted to see Hazard Duty get a new job—but they also would speak their minds about any problems they saw.

He glanced over to where Iris stood by their bookshelves, and smiled at her not entirely subtle thumbs up before he turned back to give his people—his *officers*—his full attention.

"Okay, everyone. You can probably guess what I brought you in to talk about, so let's get to it: Our MRB rep sent us a contract offer with an interesting signing bonus. I believe it's a good move for us, but I want your input before I shake hands on it."

Several of them straightened up, or leaned a bit forward with curiosity as the noteputer on the coffee table sprang to life.

"You're looking at Nopah," he continued as the slowly rotating world with three primary continents pulled out to a map of its star system. "Specifically, Nopah VII, but I don't think anyone actually calls it that except on their tax forms."

Mitch raised a hand, and Mark nodded for her to go ahead with the question.

"Where the hell is Nopah?"

The joke broke up some of the lingering nerves in the room, and Mark let the chuckles die down before he nodded to Iris to zoom the map out further.

"I'm so glad you asked, Mitch. Nopah's in Capellan space, about four jumps from the Suns' border, and three-ish from the Combine border, depending on the route." He took another sip of his coffee before nodding to Iris to take over, the display shifting back to the orbital view of the planet.

"It's not right on the border," Iris continued, "but it's just close enough to everyone that if things go hot again, it *could* be a target."

"Not that there's a lot to hit," Mark observed. They'd practiced the pitch for six hours, and, so far, it was going as smooth as glass. "There are some nice forests for logging, but something like seventy percent of their economy is agriculture or aquaculture, and processing or packing facilities to export luxury goods and exotic timber out to the rest of the

Tikonov Commonality. They're a lightly developed agricultural world, a lot like Cruz Alta was, but not a priority target by any stretch of the imagination."

He wasn't shocked to see a few people grimace at that, but only one spoke out loud—a veteran of Cruz who had lost most of his platoon over the course of the fighting.

"Cruz Alta wasn't supposed to be, either."

Mark glanced over at his XO, and she gave him a little nod before turning her attention back to the room. "I hear you, Ben. But there are a few reasons we think this will be different, and a few things we can do about it." Iris tapped on her noteputer's keyboard, and the star map reappeared, with Nopah highlighted in gold.

"So—here's Nopah again."

She tapped a few more keys, and three worlds closer to the Confederation's border lit up in gold.

"Tigress, Ruchbah, and Basalt are one jump away, and according to the gazetteer research we could do, currently have front-line CCAF troops stationed on planet in addition to the local garrison."

Another tap, and two words lit up in red—one a bit to the east of the gold cluster, and the other to the north.

"Tikonov is two jumps away, so we know an HPG message there could get us support within a few weeks at the worst. Maybe faster if they have an L-F JumpShip charged up and ready."

Mark let the room ponder that a moment before he took over again.

"The other red dot is Northwind—and they're just barely outside the 30-light year radius. That means if someone tries a deep raid, we have no less than five systems with multiple standing regiments available to come and back us up—or save our asses."

He could see the gears turning in their eyes, and his heart beat just a little faster. They were getting it.

"More importantly, just like the XO said—*we* learned from what happened on Cruz Alta. If Hazard Duty takes this job, we'll have two and a half months of transport time. We're going to use that time to plot out the planetary landmasses and study every nook and cranny on the map—and after we settle into our primary garrison outside of the planetary capital..."

"Cocula," Iris broke in.

"Cocula, we are going to start running recon operations over every centimeter of soil, shifting between all three continents until we know them like the back of our hand—and the rest of the unit will be drilling and running training exercises, rotating between garrison duty and in the field every couple of months."

Mark put his coffee cup down so he could open his hand up to the assembled officers. "Within six months of landing, you and your people are going to know how to set up, screw with, and hammer the *shit* out of anyone who tries to come calling until they surrender or flee."

There was a moment where no one reacted, then someone uttered 'Hell yeah' under their breath, and Mitch started to clap.

"That was good," Iris noted with a grin as the applause and enthusiasm spread. "Inspiring! Ten out of ten, honeybun."

Mark ducked his head to conceal the goofy grin that spread across his face, but he knew he was too pale to hide the blush on his cheeks as he tried to school his expression. "Okay, okay, everybody settle down! Seriously! We aren't done here yet!"

It took a minute for the room to quiet down, and it was Carole who spoke up next. "What have you got, Major? Is this the *interesting* signing bonus you mentioned?"

Mark grinned over at his XO. "Care to share the good news?"

Iris tapped the keys, and the contract terms appeared in the air, scrolling through the initial boilerplate and payment details until the relevant section was highlighted in bright green:

### 10: SIGNING BONUS

*In exchange for acceptance of the Contract, the Confederation Ministry of The Military (hereby referred to as the 'Employer') will provide, by the Grace of Her Celestial Wisdom, a package of no more or less than four (4) BattleMechs in battlefield-ready operating condition, with each BattleMech weighing no less than 45 tons and no more than 55 tons, and a fair market value of no less than 4,000,000 and no more than 5,500,000 C-bills per unit.*

*The BattleMechs will each be provided with sufficient spare parts and operating consumables for no less than two (2) years and proper storage and repair facilities on-site at the primary garrison facilities for your exclusive use. This clause also will provide an exemption to the normal purchase/sales tax due to the planetary and Commonality governments for said 'Mechs and equipment.*

*__Note:__ If the Company (Hazard Duty LLC) should voluntarily resign or be determined to be in violation of contract by the Employer or the Mercenary Review Board within the first two years of their employment, the Company is liable for all taxes and fees associated with the acquisition and use of the vehicles and equipment defined in this clause, plus 50% of the value of the provided BattleMechs in the first year, or 25% in the second year.*

Carole was practically drooling as she read through the details. "So...four free 'Mechs as long as we do our jobs?"

Iris nodded. "Plus spares, ammo, and anything else we need for the first couple years of the contract."

Trey, one of their recon lance commanders, eyed the contract language skeptically. "The Caps got their asses kicked by half the Sphere in the Great Succession War. What do they even have to give away?"

"Nanking factory's still standing," Carole observed. "Pretty sure they still have tooling for *Shadow Hawk*s there. It's possible they might have refurbished *Hunchback*s or *Centurion*s, and you can't spit on a battlefield without a 50/50 chance of hitting a *P-Hawk*."

Mark nodded. "That's about the same conclusion the XO and I came to when we first went over the details. No matter what they give us, we should be able to make something viable out of it."

Trey gave a soft "Huh" before he looked back up to meet Mark's eyes. "So, who gets the new 'Mechs?"

"We'll figure it out when we get there," he promised. "I don't want to count these chickens until they hatch."

Iris tapped the keys one more time and the presentation disappeared, leaving the two of them standing together in front of the room.

"Now, with all that said...are we in, or are we out?"

**OVERLORD-CLASS DROPSHIP *THE MAGNIFICENT WANDA***
**NOPAH**
**CAPELLAN CONFEDERATION**
**24 JUNE 2822**

"Okay, people—just like we planned it."

Mark flexed his hands around his joysticks, watching the altimeter on his HUD slowly tick down.

As former military DropShips went, the *Wanda* had mostly lived up to her name; after almost three months of rattling around in a tin can, he and the rest of Hazard Pay were ready to get off and see some sky.

Listening to his unit comms in one ear and a feed from the DropShip's bridge in the other, he did his best to keep a calm and focused attitude and not give in to his excitement.

"One thousand meters...nine hundred...eight hundred...seven hundred...six hundred... ATC beacon is locked... Five hundred... four hundred... Landing pad designated... Two hundred... Landing struts locked and barberpoled... One hundred... fifty...twenty-five... Touchdown!"

The rattle and roar of the *Overlord*'s engines and retros cut out, and the *Ostsol* rocked slightly in its 'Mech cradle as the massive ship settled, shock absorbers hissing and sighing as they took on the weight.

"Okay, Major," the *Wanda*'s captain announced, "We are locked in. Doors open in five."

"Thank you, Captain. We appreciate the smooth ride. Hazard-Six out."

A flick of a switch, and he was on the unit comms for good. "Hazard, this is Hazard-Six. Doors opening in five. Arrow Company, Roadrunner Company, Hammer Company, deploy and form up once you are clear. Alpha Company, on me."

As if on cue, a buzzer sounded and yellow warning lights began to flash as the massive bay doors that ringed the bottom third of the ship undogged and began to open, the faintly red-tinged light of Nopah's sun shining over their freshly painted vehicles and 'Mechs.

The vehicle companies rolled and hovered down the ramps, the bright red armor contrasted with strips of yellow and black, and Mark gave the last of their heavy tanks a chance to clear the ramp before he sent *Hustler* forward, leading the command lance onto the spaceport tarmac.

Ten minutes after the DropShip's landing, Hazard Duty was in parade formation, each company in neatly ordered rows facing a small reviewing stand where the planetary director and assorted VIPs had watched them disembark and assemble.

The *Ostsol*'s external mics picked up enthusiastic clapping and cheers as they were officially welcomed to Nopah, and Mark thumbed the external arm controls so he could bring the 'Mech's arm up in a proper salute, the other 'Mechs capable of the action mimicking him a moment later.

Another wave of applause followed, and Mark let it fade before he opened his external speakers.

"Director, Hazard Duty stands ready to take up our post to protect the people of Nopah."

He let the salute drop, the other 'Mechs following again in a slow wave while a woman in a deep green suit with subtle ivory trim walked to a small podium, her voice amplified to carry across the tarmac.

"Major Hazard, on behalf of the people of Nopah, we welcome you. We are glad to see such professionalism and skill from our new protectors, and we look forward to many years of peace and protection beneath your shield."

This show had been just as planned and rehearsed as the pitch of the contract to their unit, but Mark still felt a swell of pride at the sincerity in the Director's voice.

"Thank you, Madame Director. It's good to be home."

Once they'd dispensed with the pomp and circumstance, they traveled around the city to the garrison base that would serve as their new home for the next few years. Mark was as excited as anyone to get a look at their new lance, but he waited for every other 'Mech and vehicle to get parked in their new berths before he finally followed the techs on traffic duty to *Hustler*'s new bay.

He shut down the 'Mech, unhooked himself, and ran through everything to ensure the *Ostsol* would be ready to go if needed before he exited the hatch and headed over to the same cherry picker Carole had been using back on Galatea.

"Major."

"Chief!" Mark grinned as he accepted the shop rag, even if he didn't really need to towel off after such simple parade duty. "Did you enjoy the show?"

Carole nodded, but there was an odd hesitation. "I did. Now, about those new 'Mechs..."

"Yeah," he nodded. "Can't wait to see what they have for us."

Carole's expression wasn't the excitement or satisfaction he would have expected.

"You...had better take a look for yourself."

"Two *Blackjack*s, a *Chameleon*, and a *Scorpion*?! What the hell are we supposed to do with those?"

Iris gave him a look that said she understood his frustration, but she was ready to move on now. "They're practically brand new. Less than a hundred operational hours on each of them—that's something, at least."

"Sure," Mark agreed as he went to their new liquor cabinet and pulled out a tumbler and a bottle of bourbon. "But that's because nobody wanted to set foot in them—except the *Chameleon*, I suppose."

A training 'Mech wasn't so bad—especially since they'd all seen them pressed into service for combat, and the *Chameleon* had enough firepower to make an opponent pay for dismissing it as nothing but an academy cadet's ride.

The *Blackjack*s were a different story. Those had carried a bad rep for as long as Mark could remember. He still heard the story about a brand new one going into an engagement against Taurian infantry and

getting blasted apart because the armor had fallen off. Not to mention, the narrow feet always looked one stiff breeze away from losing traction and sending the whole 'Mech to the ground in a heap.

Then there was the 'bucking bronco' ride that was the *Scorpion*, and the tendency for pilots to need anti-nausea meds before and after routine patrols, let alone a combat sortie.

"We were expecting to turn those into an extra lance for Bravo, or a seed for a Charlie company if we had a good run here. But these are *deathtraps*, Iris! Trey already sent me a message saying he'll quit if we try to assign him the *Scorpion*!"

Iris hummed. "Yeah, I know, but I don't think that'll be a problem."

Mark finished pouring a finger into the glass, then slowly capped the bottle. "You...know something I don't."

Iris grinned. "I usually do."

"...Okay. Lay it on me."

Iris turned her noteputer around so he could see what was pulled up on the screen. "The governor would like to know if we'd be willing to use our 'additional assets' to provide training for potential MechWarriors in their Home Guard."

Mark sipped his bourbon, and let it burn on his tongue for a moment before he swallowed. "Right...okay. So, we do some cadre work with them in exchange for...?"

"An extra million C-bills every year to defer operating costs."

Mark blinked. "That's...pretty damn good."

Iris grinned. "And if we put trainees in them, we don't have to worry about anyone trying to quit."

Mark set the tumbler down on their new coffee table. "You really *do* have everything under control."

"That's why you married me, isn't it?"

"I mean, I can think of a *few* other reasons. So, XO—may I get you a drink?"

Iris's eyes sparkled as she stood up to put her arms around his neck. "Sure...in about eight months."

Mark's eyes went wide as he hugged her close. "Eight months...!"

"I was late, so I went to check with the nurse on the *Wanda*...and after we got my *Orion* into the bay, I snuck out to go see a doctor, and he confirmed it. I'm somewhere between six and seven weeks pregnant."

A thought crossed Mark's mind, and he started to grin. "Well. Here I was upset about our signing bonus, and it turns out we got something even better than I was hoping for."

# 11 GOOD WAYS TO...
# RUIN YOUR MERCENARY
# COMPANY

## DANIEL ISBERNER

*Gladiator Gazette*, November Edition 3151

Hello and welcome to our newest installment of "11 Good Ways to..." This quarter we're covering mercenary companies—giving you a chance to profit from good advice and some humorous experiences other mercenary companies have had.

### 1: Accept obscure currencies

The collapse of the HPG network, and later ComStar, had severe consequences. Not only did the Inner Sphere lose its reliable network of interstellar communication, but the loss of the C-bill as a universal currency that allowed mercenaries to switch employers made life very difficult.

While House currencies are not ideal, it is strongly advised to not follow in the footsteps of Caram's Marauders and accept planetary scrip from some backwater planet. While they came to Galatea flush with coin, no one had ever heard of the Reisling Mark before. What they thought was a smart plan—and absolutely no one understood what made them think that—turned out to be the cause of their demise. There are, of course, exceptions to this. But unless you have someone around who can make sure the Lushann francs you are offered are real, stay away from them—or you'll get further trying to barter for supplies with toilet paper.

## 2: If it sounds too easy, go for it

There are far more mercenary contracts out there than actual mercenary companies. Some of those contracts have been out for years or even decades. The most famous contract was open for over a century—despite a massive payment offer for a seemingly easy job.

In 3026, Tchamba offered a contract to investigate a supposed Star League research installation on their moon. Get in, grab everything you can find, get out, get rich. No one taking the contract for 121 years should have been the first clue, but the Michel Brothers seemed clueless. They took the contract, went in...and detonated a hydrogen bomb in the facility, which everyone who had done their research knew was there. Why did they think the contract had stayed open for so long?

## 3: Ignore orders

One should not have to say this to any military unit, but it remains one of the most prevalent reasons mercenary companies fail. While they might not die in a horrific explosion, ruining your reputation will destroy you anyway.

In 3122, the Badess Boyz (that is not a typo) took a contract on Ljugarn to defend it against pirate raids. When the pirates attacked, the planetary garrison ordered the mercenaries to fall back and wait. Badess Boyz did not listen; seeing this as a slight against their reputation, they attacked in the middle of a nature preserve that was not only host to a century-long experiment, but also the main tourist attraction of the planet. While they handily defeated the pirates, the damage to the preserve and experiment caused by the fighting was catastrophic. Not following orders had destroyed the main source of their extra-planetary income.

## 4: Overembellish your forces

You might think this goes without saying. Sadly, it does not. It has become a trend in recent years for mercenary companies, especially new ones, to state force sizes they don't really have. The most famous example was the Hard Hitters in 3001—who somehow managed to get a hold of a JumpShip and four *Overlord*s, while their actual 'Mech force was one lance and a few infantry soldiers. I am sparing you the gory details, but the pirates who killed them were very happy with their new transport capabilities.

## 5: Spend your forces

You remember number three? There are exceptions!

When your employer throws you at targets you cannot defeat and who are outside of your contract parameters, you cut your losses and go! Many mercenary companies die because they think they must do the impossible to maintain their reputation.

The dead don't need a reputation.

### 6: Fail at basic math

If you take on a contract, run the numbers. What will it cost to get to your assigned base of operations? What will it cost to maintain your equipment over the course of the contract? What will an engagement cost you? What unforeseen circumstances might befall you (yes, you should expect the unforeseen)?

Count up all of that—then double it. Then see if the sum your would-be employer is offering is more than that. After all that, negotiate for more.

There are companies that offer "contract viability proofing." If you are new, you should take them up on their offer. Otherwise, you might end up indebted to your employer.

### 7: Be a lot of individuals

Starting fresh is always hard. More so if you are alone or small and feel like you require more soldiers in your unit to take on a good contract.

Of course, you can hire MechWarriors left and right to get this big job over there, but before you do, you should train. Become a cohesive unit before you take on any real job. There are many examples of this going wrong, but one of the most striking ones is Peter's Tigers.

In 3100, they took on a contract to take out a sizable pirate company. Founded only a month before they took on the assignment, they hired two dozen MechWarriors and their equipment in the week before they went off on the DropShips their employer offered. While also ignoring number six, they landed on the pirate moon three months later and were overrun.

Half of the MechWarriors did not comprehend the orders they got or thought they were smarter. Others were unfamiliar with their lancemates and ran straight into their allies' line of fire. You can grab the trivid recordings from the departing DropShips pretty much everywhere. They became the number-one slapstick hit in 3101, and the revenue allowed for the hiring of a real mercenary unit.

### 8: Scouting is for losers

Okay, this one is easy: recon, recon, recon.

Don't follow the example of Bryan's Castles and walk into a full battalion of enemy units with your one medium lance. Just...don't.

## 9: Blindly trust your employer

This might sound strange, but it is always worth checking into who you are tying your unit to. While reputation is important to a mercenary company, it is also important for employers. If your employer has a reputation to not follow through on their obligations, what makes you think *you* should trust them?

## 10: Don't load up on ammunition

Many mercenary companies try to use as many energy weapons as possible to not run into this situation, but there are things you cannot achieve with lasers, and often you have no choice regarding the type of weapons your 'Mechs pack. Because of this, having a good supply of ammunition is important.

There are few things that will turn the tide of battle faster than the click of your ammunition feed running dry.

## 10a: Only for you!

Don't just supply your command 'Mech. This will not just be a problem in battle, but Max's Mustered might become Stephen's Mustered after your MechWarriors mourn their dead one time too many and hang you.

## 11: Take a contract from the crazy House Lord of the season

This might be the most important point of them all. While most of the Great Houses are more or less trustworthy, there is always at least one Great House run by a loon. Romano Liao, Caleb Davion, Takashi Kurita... Opening a history book will show you many crazed heads of state.

While you cannot always foresee them going crazy mid-contract, no one should have taken a contract in the Draconis Combine after their "Death to Mercenaries" edict. Still, many did, thinking they could somehow be the exception... And while the Draconis Combine is currently okay with mercenaries, who is to say this won't change tomorrow?

# NO DAWN ON THE HORIZON

### DAVID G. MARTIN

**THE CASTLE
CROMARTY CITY
NORTHWIND
CAPELLAN CONFEDERATION
5 NOVEMBER 2841**

"Someone better tell me who the hell those inbound DropShips belong to!" Colonel Brandon Gibson slammed his fist on the meeting-room table. The question was not rhetorical. He expected answers, and quickly, from someone in this room. His glowering gaze scanned the members of his command staff.

Most of the junior officers in the room tried their best to evade the steely glare from his cool blue eyes. With a stature of just over 180 centimeters, Brandon's small bushel of ruddy red hair and tight beard only recently began showing the first signs of graying. Colonel Gibson stood at the head of the command table, openly fuming as he waited out the silence, every bit the picture the rest of the Inner Sphere held in their minds when they thought of a Northwind Highlanders MechWarrior.

"They're Federated Suns, sir," Lieutenant Daran Rossling finally spoke up.

"Of course they are, Lieutenant," Brandon snapped, "but which regiments?"

"As best we can tell, it's the Davion Assault Guards, the Thirty-Third Avalon Hussars, and two other regiments we've yet to identify," Captain Jaina Kerr said.

"So at least four regiments?" Brandon asked.

"So far, yes," Kerr said.

"Blast it all!" Brandon said, slamming his hand on the table again. "We can't repel that kind of attack. Is there any hope the Chancellor will send us support? Perhaps other Highlanders regiments? Who is closest?"

Brandon Gibson, the newly installed colonel of the Third Kearny Highlanders, had just begun rebuilding the regiment since returning to Northwind after hard campaigns along the Capellan Confederation's border with the Suns. The recruitment and procurement was on track to have them fully operational by midway through next year, and the Armed Forces of the Federated Suns must have somehow realized Stuart's Highlanders, the other regiment currently on-planet, was not at full strength. As of that moment, the Third was capable of fielding two understrength battalions, but just barely. And that was after pressing into service all the training 'Mechs and vehicles at the academy.

"There has been no response from CCAF command yet, sir," Lieutenant Rossling said.

"How long before they are here?" Brandon asked.

"A little over fifty-six hours until they reach Glasgow orbit," Kerr said. "Once they have the moon secured, it will be a scant day before they can make landings on Northwind."

"I need to confer with Colonel Armstrong," Brandon said, dismissing his staff with a wave of his hand.

"Do you *really* think those bastards will stop with just the Castle and Cromarty City?" Brandon asked.

"Ah...weel...no," Colonel Bart Armstrong finally admitted. "I dinnae ken they will, Gibson. Your plan is a good one, and the right one. But I have tae take my regiment tae defend the city as best we can."

Brandon nodded. "I know, Colonel. It has to be done. Keeping a strategic hold of both the Castle and Cromarty City itself for as long as possible is the only hope any of us have. I am just sorry the Third is no position to help."

"We'll try tae hold 'em as best we can, Colonel," Colonel Armstrong said from the other side of the vidscreen. "The best ye can do is try tae get the civilians out and an' safe afore they break through tae ye."

Brandon nodded, but had nothing else to add to Armstrong's assessment of the situation. He turned and looked out his office window toward the tree-lined horizon of the distant Cairngorm Mountains. A storm hovered above the range, mirroring Brandon's outlook on the future for Northwind and its people.

"We'll be grateful for any time you can give us, Colonel Armstrong," Brandon finally said, turning back to face the vidscreen. The two colonels offered each other a parting salute, both knowing this would be the last time they spoke.

As the screen went dark, Brandon turned back to face the window, staring out at the mountains for several moments. Those mountains represented Northwind's last and only hope of holding out until help might arrive, but he knew in his heart that help would not come. The other Highlanders regiments were on the brink of exhaustion from the war, and CapCon commanders would not let them or any other forces off the front lines to help defend this place. Brandon reached out to open a desk drawer, his gaze tearing away from the distant mountains to look at the contents. He took out the bottle of scotch and the small glass next to it and sat them on the desk.

Brandon Gibson sat down at his desk and took a deep breath. Throughout the centuries, as the Northwind Highlanders regiments served as mercenaries all over the Inner Sphere, a Highlanders regimental commander had always sat at this desk. The pride of sitting in this seat was almost as coveted as the position of leading one of the regiments, a rare honor Brandon never dreamed he would achieve, until he had done it. He would likely be the last Highlanders commander to sit here for a very long time. But he would do everything in his power to ensure the seat was covered in as much FedRat blood as possible before a Davion commander dishonored it with their sassenach arse.

Brandon poured himself a glass of scotch and held it up, his eyes meeting the gaze of a portrait on the wall. He nodded and downed the glass in a single gulp and smiled wryly back at the visage of Colonel Tobias Stuart, the ancient Highlanders commander who first called this room his office.

"That'll have to do, I'm afraid," Brandon said before rising from his seat and walking out of the silent office.


**SOUTHERN SPUR CANYONS**
**CAIRNGORM MOUNTAINS**
**NORTHWIND**
**CAPELLAN CONFEDERATION**
**11 NOVEMBER 2841**

Colonel Brandon Gibson walked out of his command tent and surveyed the Highlanders' encampment. Though, at this point, "encampment" constituted a liberal definition of the word. The soldiers looked like they had been through hell and back, and Brandon knew how true that was. The arm patches on the surviving MechWarriors he could see showed a mix of what was left of both the Stuart's Highlanders regiment and his own Third Kearny.

All gathered, the survivors numbered less than a battalion, perhaps two overstrength companies, if he was honest. The attackers had been ruthless in their landings and their subsequent taking of Cromarty City and the Castle. The last message Brandon was able to get to the ComStar techs simply said, "Northwind lost." He knew the other regimental commanders would have received it by now, but nothing could be done to save the Highlanders on Northwind now. The AFFS had no interest in taking prisoners, not even among the civilian populace. Those bastards weren't allowing anyone to surrender until FedRat troops had complete control of the planet.

Brandon hoped there had been at least some time to get some of the populace away from the cities, out into the more rural areas where the AFFS troops might leave them mostly alone once they saw the civilians were no threat, but that hope was fleeting at best. Northwind was burning, and help was nowhere on the horizon.

"Colonel!" Captain Kerr ran up to Brandon as he continued walking along the few tents that had been hastily set up between the forest trees. He waited a moment for Kerr to catch her breath. She was an excellent officer who, under different circumstances, Brandon would have bet on to go far in her career with the Highlanders.

"Yes, Captain," Brandon eventually said after she had caught her breath.

"Scouts report they're coming, sir," Kerr replied. "It's time."

Brandon didn't reply right away. He looked into the eyes of the men and women around him, the ones who had just heard Kerr's report. Most looked scared. All of them looked angry. One woman bearing the patch of the Third Kearny on her shoulder looked like she was about to devolve into a feral rage now that she was face-to-face with her inescapable doom.

Brandon turned to face Kerr and nodded. "Very well, Captain. This place is as good as any to make our final stand."

He looked around at the peaks of the mountain canyons surrounding them. They had been backed into a corner, and there had been nothing they could do about it. Backed into the fight of their lives.

"Just like the Royal Black Watch," Brandon said, more to himself than to anyone standing around him.

"Sir?" Kerr asked.

"You remember the story, right, Captain? After the traitor Amaris killed the last Lord Cameron and all of his family, the Black Watch fought on to the bitter end, eventually causing so much damage to the enemy that only nuclear weapons could finally take them out."

"Aye, sir. Every Northwind native knows the tale, sir."

"But we are not the Black Watch," Brandon said, again more to himself than anyone in particular.

"Aye," Kerr replied, folding her arms and setting her jaw to match Brandon's defiant tone.

The other soldiers around Brandon and Kerr dispersed to report to their 'Mechs for their final ride as Northwind Highlanders. The two officers stood in silence, watching the only Highlanders soldiers left on Northwind prepare for their death battle. Nobody had any heroic delusions that their stand would be as grand or storied as the Black Watch's, but Brandon harbored a silent hope and a prayer in his heart that they would nonetheless be remembered for what was about to happen.

"Contact!" The callout came from down the line, a Stuart's Highlanders *Phoenix Hawk* on recon, according to Brandon's screen.

"Stick to the plan," Brandon responded.

The plan was simple but delicate. One domino falling in the wrong direction would doom them all, and with little hope to begin with, Brandon had only decided on this plan because it had the best chance of grinding down the most AFFS forces before the Highlanders' eventual demise.

The canyons in this part of the Cairngorm range were narrow enough that BattleMechs traversing them had to advance in single file. That alone would help with the numbers game, especially since the Highlanders knew the breakouts in the canyons where lance-sized units could concentrate fire on choke points. It wasn't much, but it was something to hold on to.

The Davion Assault Guards' aerospace assets had yet to arrive, so if the Highlanders could cause enough damage to the ground forces before then, it was possible to draw out the fight enough to discourage the FedRats from pursuing the survivors. But the canyons were a dead end at the far side. The Davions had to turn back, or there would be no other way out.

In the cockpit of his *Thunderbolt*, Brandon Gibson heard the final stand begin. Laser fire streaked into the sky from both ends of the canyon network, and flights of missiles arced high above the trees before diving back down under the forest canopy. Captain Kerr's *Shadow*

*Hawk* stalked a little ahead and to the right, waiting for the time when their two 'Mechs would join the fight.

"The Davions have entered the canyons," Kerr reported.

That was the signal.

"Okay Highlanders," Brandon said over the regimental comm channel, "time to make 'em pay! For Northwind!"

The calls came back over the channel, echoing Brandon's battle cry. There was little point in strict comms discipline at this point, and Brandon heard the open comm channels as they were flooded with transmissions of bagpipes blaring as the few Highlanders remaining on Northwind marched toward the enemy.

Brandon did not have to wait long to get into the action. The Davion Assault Guards were not stopping for much, relying on their armor and the weight of their assault to push the Highlanders back. Brandon's first engagement was with a *Rifleman* that had drifted just a little too far from their lancemates. Catching the pilot out, Kerr and Brandon fell on the errant Davion BattleMech like wild Picts from the Alba of old, mauling the *Rifleman* beyond recognition in just a couple of minutes and disappearing back into the woods before the rest of its lance could properly support it.

"Colonel." The call came from Major Patrick McGraw, the ranking surviving officer of Stuart's Highlanders, who oversaw the northern flank.

"Major," Brandon answered.

"Sir, they're pushing hard here," McGraw said. "They have us backed up to the secondary canyon position already, and they aren't letting up. Their armor is so tough, and it's like they are taking this fight personally."

"Hold out as long as you can, Major," Brandon ordered.

"Aye, sir, but there's something else," McGraw said. "A dust storm is blowing in, Colonel, from the west. It's coming in right behind them, and I don't think they know it yet. We'll have one doozy of a wind tunnel situation in these canyons in about thirty minutes."

"Copy that, Major," Brandon responded. "If we can hold out until then, it might mitigate those aerospace assets of theirs. Try to break out when the storm hits if you can manage it and get as many of your people as possible to the B4 series of canyons. Hopefully the Third can meet you there in the confusion."

"Roger," McGraw said. "McGraw out."

The dust storm hit with a sudden fury Brandon imagined as a mystical extension of Northwind's own spirit, protesting the Davions' presence

on the planet. As the dust surged in between the BattleMechs of both sides, screens flickered as dust pelted and clogged sensor arrays.

Brandon's *Thunderbolt* swayed as the winds whipped through the canyon. He turned on his external microphones to listen for sounds in the storm, and was greeted by a moaning cacophony of high-pitched whistles as the wind tumbled between the Highlanders BattleMechs near him.

*Northwind herself protests this atrocity.*

Some lighter 'Mechs might have had trouble staying upright if the pilot was caught sufficiently unaware, but the Davion units on the other side of the fight were unfortunately all too heavy for such good luck. The only reason Brandon kept a fixed position on Kerr's 'Mech was because he had her unique transponder displayed on a secondary screen. As the visibility decreased, shots started to go wide, lasers and missiles hitting rocks and canyon walls nowhere near their intended targets. Pilots on both sides started to chase ghosts, and Brandon needed to get his remaining troops in line first to have a hope of gaining advantage in the chaos.

Before the dust storm hit, the remaining forces from the Third consisted of Brandon and Kerr, and about eight or nine other BattleMechs. The initial fighting had ground down both sides, but the Davions were still clearly on the better end of the stick. Taking advantage of the moments of chaos, Brandon had pulled his forces back to the B3 canyon area, effectively creating a battlefield that gave the Highlanders only one direction to shoot in. Time was short, but if they could manage to re-form quickly enough and join McGraw's forces, the Third might be able to push back for the first time since entering the canyons. But there were no BattleMechs from Major McGraw's unit in sight when Brandon's forces reached the rendezvous.

"Major McGraw," Brandon called over the comm. He received only static in response. Not completely surprisingly, the dust storm was unseasonably heavy, and had allowed the Highlanders to withdraw from the Davion forces without much reprisal. It would take a moment for the heavier Davions to catch up. Brandon had held out hope they would be able to meet up and make a concentrated stand here, but McGraw's absence meant only bad things.

"—ibson...cau...et to you..." it was obviously McGraw's voice attempting to pierce the blowing sand and dust between the two units, but Brandon could not make out what the major was attempting to convey.

"Sir! They're here!" Lieutenant Jill Speakman's voice reached out to bring Brandon's attention back to the direction of the advancing Davion forces. Speakman's *Guillotine* was already firing by the time Brandon's *Thunderbolt* reached the vantage point on a small rise.

There was no time to wait for McGraw now. They would have to retreat farther into the canyons, removing any possibility that the two units would be able to link up.

*Damn these Davions, and their mothers, too!*

"Fall back!" Brandon ordered. "Into the canyons, now! Speakman, you're with me on rear guard until the rest get in."

"Roger—" Speakman confirmed.

The next second, a PPC bolt impacted the *Guillotine's* cockpit, smashing what was left of the armor and internal structure and exploding into a brilliant flash of light right in front of Brandon's cockpit. Just like that, Speakman was gone, too.

Brandon blinked several times, frozen by Speakman's abrupt demise. His *Thunderbolt* began rocking with hits from lasers and light autocannon fire. The Davions were in a firing position on his location. He had to move. Speakman's BattleMech hadn't finished falling to the ground before Brandon snapped out of it. Soldiers had died in front of him before, but, this time, each one hurt with more impact.

Brandon's *Thunderbolt* fired back at the two lances of Davion Assault Guards on the short hill below him. He held a brief advantage, yes, but his one 'Mech would do nothing against two assault lances.

"Colonel!" Kerr's voice broke into the sounds of weapons fire and impacts as Brandon's *Thunderbolt* lost tons of armor standing on the ridge. Her voice was enough to get Brandon to move. He wasn't trying to die on that ridge, but something inside told him it was either on the ridge or in the canyons. He did not know specifically why, but Speakman's death had broken all hope Brandon held of any of them surviving the day.

Brandon moved his BattleMech off the ridge and into the opening to the canyons. It was not long before the Davion 'Mechs followed, and the final siege of the canyons began.

At first, the dust storm made everything better for the Highlanders and worse for the Davions. Combined with the canyon choke points Brandon and the Third took full advantage of, for a time it looked as if the Highlanders might manage to make a dent.

But the Davions just kept coming.

In a turn just past the choke point they had just fallen back from, Brandon found himself facing two Davion BattleMechs as he covered the latest retreat. A battered *Hunchback* that refused to die and a relatively fresh *Griffin* had managed to gain entry to this stretch of canyon and were working as a very effective team to corral Brandon's larger *Thunderbolt*.

In a move Brandon saw coming, telegraphed by the *Griffin* pilot, the lighter BattleMech engaged its jump jets and soared over Brandon's 'Mech, landing somewhere behind him. The ruse might have worked against a less experienced pilot, but Brandon knew turning his back to the *Hunchback* would spell certain doom. While this *Hunchback* appeared to have run out of ammunition for its massive autocannon, Brandon would not take the chance that the pilot was, perhaps, clever enough to have conserved one final last shot for just such an opening.

Instead, Brandon pushed forward, away from his own troops and toward the *Hunchback*, who suddenly began maneuvering from side to side, as if the pilot did not know how to respond to his maneuver. The *Thunderbolt* shook under the impact of laser fire from the *Griffin*, but he ignored it for now. Nothing he could do about it anyway. The *Hunchback* had to die first.

Brandon kept a wary eye on the opening to the west, but, so far, no more Davion BattleMechs had moved through the position to make their presence known. He wasn't about to ask why, and pressed the advantage while he still had one.

Having long since run out of missiles, Brandon let loose with his BattleMech's battery of lasers. Heat flowed into the cockpit as the *Hunchback* bore the salvo with little grace, the 'Mech wobbling on its feet over the uneven ground.

*Yeah, not so fun when you're the one being bullied, is it?*

The *Thunderbolt* shuddered as something heavier than lasers hit it from behind, a massive hit and loss of armor registering on the 'Mech's left leg. The *Griffin* had drawn a bead with its PPC, and Brandon's timeline for dealing with the *Hunchback* had just gotten much shorter.

Brandon throttled up and surged his *Thunderbolt* toward the rattled *Hunchback*. He didn't have much room in the canyon, but he had enough to get up to enough speed for a short charge. It was not his first choice, but the heat level of his BattleMech could use a short break. Physical combat in BattleMechs was a good outlet for rage anyway, and in that moment, Brandon Gibson was nothing if not rageful.

His *Thunderbolt* took another hit from the *Griffin*, but Brandon did not care. This *Hunchback* had to die now. It tried to avoid the charging heavy BattleMech, but the *Hunchback* had nowhere to go that Brandon could not easily follow. Attempting to back up and hoping to score a lucky hit, the *Hunchback* fired its lasers. When Brandon got into what would have been the range of the smaller 'Mech's autocannon, the massive gun bore remained quiet.

Until it did not.

Erupting in a massive wave of explosive light and sound, the *Hunchback* expended the last of its ammo at the quickly approaching Highlanders 'Mech. The shot was good, too, impacting on the *Thunderbolt*'s torso, shredding the remaining armor. Brandon ignored the screens telling him his BattleMech's torso armor had been breached on the left and middle sections and raised its left arm as he closed in for the kill.

Brandon's 'Mech collided with the *Hunchback* in a crash of wrenching and bending metal and myomer. Surprisingly, the *Hunchback* took much more damage to critical areas than the *Thunderbolt*, and a few seconds later, Brandon shook his head to clear his vision and was rewarded with the sight of the *Hunchback* lying on its back, a huge rock sticking up out of what used to be the cockpit.

Brandon took a deep breath, turned his *Thunderbolt* around, and raised his large laser toward the *Griffin*, which was partially hiding behind a tree on the other side of the small canyon alcove.

"Your turn," he said over an open channel.

"They're breaking thr—" Kerr's shout was drowned out by the sound of her BattleMech exploding next to Brandon's badly damaged *Thunderbolt*. He winced, expecting the worst as a small miracle spared his own 'Mech from further damage. Only a hit to an ammo bin would cause an explosion like that, and Brandon grimaced, nodding in respect as he heard his friend's death both over the comms and through his cockpit.

"Pour on the fire!" Brandon yelled out to anyone who was still listening and capable of following the order.

The downed Davion Assault Guards BattleMechs in front of them were testament to the Highlanders' determination to hold the canyons against the onslaught, but this was a numbers game they would not win. After several hours of fighting with no word from McGraw or any elements of Stuart's Highlanders, Brandon had given up hope that any kind of help might be on the way.

Brandon fired his overheated large laser at an approaching *Goliath*. The beam was absorbed by the walking tank's leg armor as if he had merely spit at the giant quad BattleMech. For every *Atlas* or *Orion* the Highlanders managed to down in the narrow choke points, another heavy or assault class 'Mech was ready and willing to take its place. Brandon didn't know what demons drove the Davions, but they advanced with little regard for their own lives. Perhaps it was the knowledge that the Highlanders could not possibly win that drove them, or maybe a lust for battle simply gripped their hearts.

Whatever the case, Brandon had never seen any force advance with the madness he witnessed from the Davions.

"Sir! The storm!" someone called over the comms.

Brandon looked at his weather overlay screen. The storm was breaking up. Not good. That meant aerospace assets would soon be able to fly above the canyons and bomb the remaining Highlanders into oblivion. They were out of time. The Davions would not be retreating today. It was clear with how many of them had already been ground into the canyon floors that no price was considered too heavy for the goal of annihilating the remaining Highlanders.

*This is how it ends for us. Not unlike the Black Watch after all, just minus the nukes.*

"Fall back again," Brandon said into the comms.

"There's only five of us left, sir!"

"Then you shouldn't trip over each other as you follow my orders!" Brandon snapped back, much more harshly than he would have liked to speak to a scared soldier who was about to die, but now was a terrible time for his orders to be questioned even in the slightest.

It did not matter if following the order would ultimately get them nowhere. Brandon knew the exercise was meaningless. There was no cover, and there were not enough of them left for it to matter anyway. But his blood would not let him simply give up. Never in all the lifetimes of the Highlanders could he abide by giving up. It just was not in the DNA of a member of Clan Gibson to do so.

The remaining Highlanders withdrew one last time, moving back into the narrowest stretch of canyon yet, barely a crevice in the rocks, if Brandon was being honest. Only four of them remained now. Brandon had passed the downed form of Lieutenant Lawrence Evans' *Enforcer*, the last officer other than himself, on his way through the final chokepoint.

"This is it, sir," Lieutenant Maisie McNamara, the pilot of a *Hermes II* said. "Nowhere else to retreat to."

The young pilot sounded scared, and Brandon had no words to comfort him. He was scared, too. But not for himself. Brandon was scared for the people of Northwind, for the regiments scattered out across the stars, and for his planet itself, for which tomorrow's dawn would usher in a terrible and tragic chapter of its story. But he would not live to see any of that. Others, those in the future who bore the Highlanders insignia on their uniforms, would have to fight that evil. Right here, in this canyon, was the darkness that came for him. But that would not break him.

"Hold here," Brandon said. "Form a line, and fire at anything that moves. If you fall, well done, Highlander. If you can get back up, all the better. And if you can make just one more of them fall with you, then I can ask no more. Godspeed, all of you."

After his speech, Brandon turned on his external speakers and opened his comm unit for general broadcast. He selected one of his favorite pieces of bagpipe music, a patriotic song that, according to the records, had been played by the original Highlanders who settled Northwind after leaving Terra and establishing their new, free home.

The bagpipes blared, his every deep breath of the few he had yet to take swelling his pride for his homeland and people, and Brandon steadied his heart for the end.

They waited. But the Davion Guards did not come. The canyon grew quiet as the storm blew out, and after some minutes, there was only sky above them and canyon around them.

Brandon lowered his head. He knew what was coming. The Davions finally had their fill of spending their soldiers on killing off the last of the Highlanders. The rain was probably already on the way.

"Farewell, my darling Northwind," Colonel Brandon Gibson said over the open channel, looking to the now clear and vibrant sky above him, and witnessed the sky grow dark again with the bombs that would end his story.

### FIRST KEARNY HIGHLANDERS COMMAND CENTER
### KYRKBACKEN
### CAPELLAN CONFEDERATION
### 30 NOVEMBER 2841

Colonel Timm McDougal's hands shook as he read the report. Northwind had been taken. The AFFS had annihilated the two Highlanders regiments on the planet, killed to the last soldier. But that was not enough for the AFFS bastards. From what reports had made it off Northwind, the invaders had turned on the people next, pillaging, burning, and doing all manner of other unspeakable things to the citizens of Northwind.

"You've read these?" McDougal looked across the desk at his aide-de-camp, Lieutenant Rebekah Faal.

Faal shook her head, "No, sir. I wanted you to be the first with the news, so you can decide how best to proceed."

"Well, it's obvious to me," McDougal responds. "We're going to Northwind."

"What about the other commanders?" Faal asked.

"What about them?" McDougal grumbled

"Will they be as willing to go against CCAF orders and leave our posts? Not to mention, none of the regiments are in combat-ready shape, least of all the Second, which reports indicate is at less than twenty percent strength."

McDougal grumbled again. Faal was right. The remaining Highlanders regiments had been used as the front-line spear tips in the latest campaigns against the AFFS, and their strength was nowhere near what would be needed to retake Northwind. The Highlander in McDougal wanted to get on a JumpShip right now and head off into the void to save his homeland, but the commander in him said that would be folly. It would be months, more likely years, before the Highlander regiments were built back to sufficient strength to even consider retaking Northwind from the Federated Suns. Years of oppression the people would have to endure.

McDougal thought about his friend, Colonel Gibson, and the last message the commander of the Third Kearny had gotten off the planet.

*Northwind Lost.*

The Highlanders had spent their entire existence as mercenaries, protecting the interests of other planets, other peoples, other leaders who valued their service about as much as a kitchen cook values the sponge that cleans their dirty pots. And when it came down to the most important thing, the jewel in the hearts of every Highlander scattered among the stars, they had failed. Northwind was now further away than ever, and McDougal knew in his heart he would not live long enough to set foot on her again. This present war would see to that, even though it showed signs of dying down, the fighting would never truly be over.

And the Highlanders would have to bear the burden of failure for the duration.

"Well," McDougal finally said, "I guess I better prepare a statement for the troops. Have this information disseminated to the other regimental commanders, along with an invitation to join us here to discuss the future of the Highlander regiments."

"Do you think anything about the present situation will change?" Faal asked.

"I don't know," McDougal answered, "but nothing will ever change if we sit here and do nothing. And no Scotsman ever tolerates doing nothing for long."

# UNIT DIGEST:
# OUTER REACHES DISCIPLES

### ERIC SALZMAN

**Nickname:** Ryan's Rebels (never publicly used)
**Affiliation:** Mercenary
**CO:** General Yu-Seng Wong
**Average Experience:** Veteran/Fanatical
**Force Composition:** Two mechanized infantry regiments, one bomber wing, one artillery battalion, one JumpShip squadron
**Unit Abilities:** Off-Map Movement (see *Campaign Operations* [*CO*] p. 85) and False Flag (see *CO* p. 84)
**Parade Scheme:** Gold with red trim
**Operational Period:** 2223–2688

## UNIT HISTORY

The Fourth Alliance Grand Survey of 2235 counted 619 colonized worlds surrounding Terra—five times more than in 2168. Terran attempts to maintain direct rule over its rapidly expanding territory led to growing excesses by the Expansionist Party government, which imposed steep taxes, set unrealistic production quotas, appointed inflexible and capricious governors-general to bind the colonists to Terran-made laws.

The Ryan Cartel, which operated vast fleets of ice ships to carry water to arid and otherwise uninhabitable client worlds, had driven much of the rapid expansion. Though the Cartel served the Expansionist Party's territorial ambitions, its founder, Rudolph Ryan, secretly colluded with the opposition Liberal Party to smuggle dissidents and technical specialists out to the colonies, making them more self-sufficient and capable of resisting Alliance authority. Ryan's murder in 2185 only accelerated this process as his son, David, took over both the Cartel and the smuggling operations.

Though the Expansionist Party controlled the Alliance Global Militia (AGM), Colonial Marines, and the Alliance Global Navy (AGN), Liberal Party leaders maintained their own covert military assets. Only known to a few top leaders, the Party had long supported the New World Disciples, a terrorist organization responsible for the assassination of dozens of Expansionist heads of state and Alliance Parliament members. After the AGM destroyed the Disciples' Himalayan base and forced their leader, Elias Liao, to flee off-world (with help from the Ryan Cartel), the Liberals sheltered the remnants of the Disciples, more determined than ever to resist Expansionist domination.

In the 2220s, David Ryan formed a new paramilitary organization around the remnants of the Disciples, training and equipping this group to perform cadre duty for independence-minded colonial governments. Cartel iceships smuggled personnel and weapons to client colonies. Under Rudolph, the Cartel had been in the practice of helping anti-Expansionist groups settle uncharted worlds by equipping colony JumpShips, then reporting the ships "lost to misjump." David escalated this practice, "losing" six JumpShips crewed by the Disciples and packed

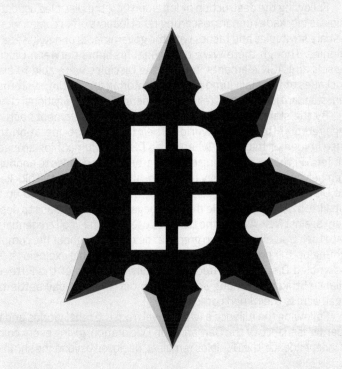

with military-grade gear diverted from Alliance Global Militia depots by highly placed Liberal Party sympathizers.

When the world of Freedom declared independence in 2235, elements of the Disciples were already present, and they immediately offered their services to help train and organize the planetary militia. Thanks to the Ryan Cartel's extensive JumpShip network, the Disciples learned four other worlds also planned to secede. General Wong sent emissaries, offering the Disciples' services as mercenary auxiliaries. Sevren, Morningside, and Ryde accepted, but Summit's government, wary of the Disciples' terrorist history, refused. Thus, Summit was defenseless when General Seth Van Doren's Twenty-Third Alliance Striker regiment occupied the world and reportedly massacred ten thousand civilians.

On Freedom, Disciples advisors helped fortify Jefferson City and took part in the sortie that overran the Fourth ParaCavalry's siege lines and captured their artillery. Records indicate they significantly increased Alliance losses before perishing when the city was overrun. At Ryde, the Disciples used the ORDS *Free State* to mine the system's jump points, destroying Alliance troop transports. (The AGN's inexperience in waging a spaceborne military campaign left them vulnerable as Ryan Cartel captains directed the Disciples to the AGN's standard arrival coordinates.)

Following the destruction of Jefferson City, the Disciples used their ships as blockade runners, escorting rebel leaders off occupied worlds to share strategies and tactics with the governments of newly seceded colonies. Though there were occasional firefights between Disciple vessels and AGN elements in orbit, the Disciples were able to avoid blockades at the main jump points by entering and exiting systems at non-standard jump points, relying on superior Cartel navigational charts.

By the start of 2237, the Disciples had small elements actively engaged on fifteen rebel worlds. Their largest joint operation took place in June of that year, when three Disciples JumpShips arrived in the Terra Firma system, using Liberal Party-supplied codes to announce themselves as the troop levy from Liao. Allowed through the blockade, the Disciples grounded their troops at the AGM staging area on the outskirts of Austerlitz. While the AGM began drawing up plans to deploy them against New Avalon, the Disciples used their falsified credentials to place their trademark "fusion grenade" devices throughout the complex, lighting up the pre-dawn darkness with catastrophic explosions. The assembled Disciples fell upon the surviving troops of the Fifteenth Alliance Striker Regiment, wiping them out in a two-day battle that raged across the ruined complex.

Following the Alliance's withdrawal from the rebel worlds and the Liberals' issuance of the Demarcation Declaration, giving every colony its independence, the Disciples remained deployed beyond the shrunken

Alliance borders. With their experience, mobility, and reputation from the rebellion, their services were in great demand with newly formed planetary governments in need of security. Maintaining their relationship with the Ryan Cartel, they hired out to approved clients and provided escorts for trading ships. As shields-for-hire against the rising tide of banditry in the now lawless Inner Sphere, the Disciples established themselves as one of the very first interstellar mercenaries. They opposed the Terran Hegemony's Campaigns of Persuasion, fighting for the Dieron Federation, Tikonov Grand Union, and Chisholm Protectorate. They protected Ryan Cartel interests through the Age of War, but disbanded in 2688 when the Cartel declared bankruptcy.

Centuries later, their colors and insignia would be adapted and flown as the banner of Redjack Ryan, an illegitimate member of House Ryan, perverting the Disciples' legacy of anti-pirate operations by making the unit's hidden nickname, Ryan's Rebels, synonymous with depraved banditry of the worst sort.

## COMPOSITION

The Rebels typically deployed in units no larger than company size, providing security for rebel leaders and training militias on the use of smuggled weaponry and irregular tactics to take advantage of the Colonial Marines' weak points. During the uprising, the Rebels could deploy two regiments of infantry in vehicles suited to wilderness travel, an artillery battalion, a wing of Torrent-class bombers, and a six-ship squadron of up-gunned *Aquilla*-class transport JumpShips, each carrying six heavy shuttles and two *Saturn* Patrol Ships.

# UNIT DIGEST:
# LACADON VENGEANCE LEGION

## ERIC SALZMAN

**Nickname:** The World Wreckers
**Affiliation:** Mercenary
**CO:** Major Crispulo Aguinaldo
**Average Experience:** Regular/Fanatical
**Force Composition:** 1 Medium BattleMech battalion, 1 heavy armor battalion, 1 jump infantry battalion with VTOL transport, one mobile artillery battalion
**Unit Abilities:** Enemy Specialization—Federated Suns (see *Alpha Strike: Commander's Edition* [*AS: CE*] pp. 103–104 or *Campaign Operations* [*CO*] p. 84)
**Parade Scheme:** Black, with a bloody red tear painted below BattleMech cockpits and on vehicle forward hulls.
**Operational Period:** 2828–2862

## UNIT HISTORY

Lacadon was settled by Filipino colonists in 2649, using massive atmospheric processors and water filtration units from the Terran Hegemony world of Brownsville to tame its atmosphere. The terraformed world soon proved its value to the Capellan Confederation, with a booming economy, a mining industry exporting vast quantities of germanium and other valuable ores, and exotic foods for nearby worlds. To safeguard this bountiful world without exceeding strict Star League limits on front-line military assets, the Capellan Confederation Armed Forces stood up an overstrength Home Guard regiment, known to its populace as the "Lacadon Legion."

On 3 May 2809, in response to the Confederation's peace proposal, the Thirteenth Syrtis Fusiliers and Seventeenth Avalon Hussars made combat landings on Lacadon. Their orders from the First Prince were to cause as much damage as possible, pulling Capellan resources away from the main thrust around Chesterton. The undisciplined Fusiliers relished the opportunity to retaliate against the Confederation for "pirate" attacks during the Third Hidden War, devastating the capital city of Miagao. Though the Lacadon Legion was able to turn the Fusiliers aside at Bangsamoro and Iloilo, the rampaging Davion forces broke through their lines and inflicted heavy damage on the main atmospheric processing stations at Manhayang before withdrawing off-world.

When post-war reconstruction efforts began in 2821, Capellan assessors determined that the damage to the terraforming systems was irreparable, given the nuclear destruction in 2811 of the Brownsville production centers. They estimated Lacadon's environment would revert to an uninhabitable state by 2830. The Davion offensive had inflicted similar blows to several other, more heavily populated Capellan systems. With its merchant marine shattered by Davion commerce raiders, the Confederation lacked the lift capacity to evacuate every world. Despite the urgent need, Lacadon was deemed too low on the priority list for immediate assistance.

Unwilling to accept their world's fate, the Lacadon Home Guard transformed into a mercenary unit, freeing itself of Home Guard deployment restrictions. The newly renamed "Lacadon Vengeance Legion" signed its initial contract with the Lacadon planetary diem and launched a retaliatory raid against the Federated Suns system of Caria in 2828. Not only was Caria the baseworld for the hated Thirteenth Syrtis Fusiliers, but it also had Brownsville-model atmospheric processors. While the Legion's BattleMech battalion struck the Fusiliers' dependents at their laager in Ionia, its heavy tanks and artillery kept the bulk of the Fusiliers bottled up at Fort Andanus and in the capital of Lycia. Though the Legion openly broadcast its desire for revenge against the Fusiliers, their attacks were primarily distractions, enabling their infantry to escort Lacadonian engineering crews to the Carian atmospheric processors at Caunos and Bargylia, where they stripped the units of transportable components and scuttled the husks that remained.

The Legion struck again in 2829, this time targeting the Seventeenth Avalon Hussars on Turko. Forewarned by the government on nearby Caria of the Legion's intent to strip Turko's reprocessors, the Hussars dug in around their terraforming stations at Alabalik, handily repulsing the Legion's initial probes. Unable to breach the Davion defenses, the Legion brought forward its artillery battalion and unleashed a sustained barrage that obliterated the complex. They fought back the Hussars' attempt to overrun and silence the artillery, then withdrew in good order, leaving yet another dying Davion world in their wake.

Penetrating deeper behind Davion lines, the Legion hit Aggstein in 2830, crushing its Planetary Guards and stripping its terraforming equipment down to the wiring. A delegation from the capital pleaded with them not to seize their vital infrastructure. In response, Major Aguinaldo transmitted a copy of Chancellor Ilsa Liao's 2808 peace proposal, suggesting they take their complaints up with Prince Paul.

With the components from Aggstein and Caria raids, Intelligentsia teams were able to effect stopgap repairs and get Lacadon's reprocessors working again. They warned, however, that the damaged machinery would require a steady supply of parts to keep functioning. Accordingly, the Legion continued to execute raids throughout the Capellan March, targeting worlds for *lostech* components.

The constant raids took a toll, cutting the Legion's strength by two thirds as of 2860. When House Davion launched Operation Winter Garden that year, the Legion returned home. Even after Chancellor Dainmar Liao offered an armistice in mid-2861, the Davion offensive continued, hitting Lacadon in early January 2862. The Legion made a brutal last stand against the Blue Star Irregulars' 1894th Light Horse regiment at Manhayang, dying to the last soldier for the world they'd fought to save.

Only days after their sacrifice, word came that the Chancellor had agreed to cede Lacadon to the Federated Suns as part of his armistice agreement. The Federated Suns used Lacadon as a military staging point and listening post to monitor the border, doing little for the world or its citizens. As the reprocessors began to fail once more, House Davion abandoned the world, dooming hundreds of millions of inhabitants.

## COMPOSITION

The Lacadon Vengeance Legion is built along the lines of a standard CCAF Home Guard regiment of the Star League era. Better equipped than those of the late Succession Wars era, it was led by Major Aguinaldo's medium BattleMech battalion, which served as a hammer to the anvil of the Manticores, Bulldogs, Demons, and Von Luckners in the armored battalion. A battalion of jump infantry with integrated Ripper VTOLs served as the unit's scouting force and also as spotters for the Marksmans and Thors of its mobile artillery battalion. They followed CCAF doctrine of the era, pinning opposing maneuver elements in place, then bringing massed artillery to bear against enemy concentrations.

# DUST TO DUST:
# A KELL HOUNDS STORY

## MICHAEL A. STACKPOLE

**KELL HOUND HEADQUARTERS
ARC-ROYAL
DISTRICT OF DONEGAL
LYRAN COMMONWEALTH
9 MARCH 3028**

*"Come be a mercenary,"* she said. Dell Thompson slowly exhaled. *"It'll be fun,"* she said.

Dell sat in the reception room in a battered metal chair painted white to match the antechamber's white walls and the panels of the drop ceiling. The glass and stainless-steel table in the middle of the room had a couple of tablets featuring magazines that hadn't been updated in the calendar year. Because this was the District of Donegal, half were in Irish, and because it was the Lyran Commonwealth, most of the rest were in German. She'd found two she could actually read. The one in English detailed plans for fantasy fighting 'Mech leagues based on results from Solaris, and the other was something called *Sushi Today*. The wonderful pictures made her both hungry and a tiny bit homesick.

*For a home I've long forgotten.*

The door to the inner chamber opened and there he was, shaking hands with another returnee—returning him to the rest of the unit. *They're both smiling. That's a good sign, right?* She nodded. *It's got to be a good sign.*

Colonel Morgan Kell's smile shrank as he glanced in her direction. "Delyth Thompson, yes?"

Dell nodded again, then got to her feet, snapped a salute and said sharply, "Yes, sir."

The man nodded back, his dark brown eyes betraying nothing as he returned the salute. He stepped aside and waved her into the office. "Sorry to have kept you waiting. I've looked forward to meeting you."

"Yes? Sir? Thank you, sir." Dell fought to keep a tremor out of her voice and scored herself an utter fail on that subject. *What did Boris say about me?*

Holding herself as erect as she could, Dell marched past him into the interior office and slowed about halfway to the chair askew there in front of the desk. The man's office had simple appointments, the desk and the chairs in keeping with those in the reception area. A computer terminal took up a third of the desk toward the window side, and a small holoprojection plate sat on a table in the far corner, but otherwise the place felt spare, almost sterile. *Not what I expected from a man in his position, not at all.*

The only sign of personalization consisted of a small digital picture frame sharing the table with the holoprojector, and an honest-to-God, leatherbound book on the desk corner opposite the terminal. The gold embossing on the spine proclaimed it to be a bible. The frame played through a series of static shots of Morgan—a much younger Morgan—smiling, posed with friends during happy times.

"Please be seated." Morgan gave her a nod as he came around the desk. "You prefer to be called 'Dell,' yes?"

"Yes, sir." She sat, positioning herself forward so she'd not slump.

Morgan assumed his place behind his desk. "At ease, Dell. The purpose of this interview is just to get to know you. And to thank you."

"You've got nothing to thank me for, sir."

"You're here, and that's grounds enough." He glanced at the terminal's screen, tapped a key, then returned his gaze to her. "People who were with us fifteen years ago—like Meredith Devlin, who brought you and Boris Vereker in—they put a lot of faith in me. I asked them to go away and wait until I summoned them back. I asked them to find people like you, who they could bring here when it became necessary to reconstitute the Kell Hounds regiment. That as many came back as have, well...humbling." He fell silent for a moment. "They did everything I asked of them and then some.

"But you, you're atypical. No formal military training, no Academy, no enlistment or service record. You own your own 'Mech, you've been fighting on Solaris and you're enough of a leader that both Mr. Vereker and Ren Jensen, your tech, elected to follow you here." He folded his hands together on the desktop. "Why would you leave Solaris—notwithstanding the excitement you've had over the last six months—to come join a unit that is going to see a ton of serious action?"

Dell glanced down at her hands. "There was no way I couldn't come, sir."

"Yes, I understand Meredith can be quite persuasive..."

"No, no, it's not that." Dell half-smiled. "I mean, yes, with a sharp stare and snapped word she could convince a bullet it didn't want to go ripping through someone. But..." Dell felt her throat closing up. "Man, this is weird."

Morgan Kell sat back, brushing fingers over his beard. "What's weird?"

"On Solaris, Meredith played the Unknown Mercenary type of fighter. Didn't say anything about her past and was kinda tight-lipped in general. But sharp, real sharp. Didn't miss a thing; and got a bunch of us out of some very serious trouble. So, when she approached me and Boris about joining up, I found out for the first time that she'd been with the Hounds. You know, it's one of those things. You hear about legendary units—Wolf's Dragoons, the Northwind Highlanders, everybody—and you think maybe, someday, I might be good enough to be considered. And when you get the offer, you think for a moment, 'Are you sure you mean *me*?' I—I looked around the room to make sure there wasn't someone else she was asking."

He spread his hands. "But you *are* here, now."

"Yeah, but maybe I was never supposed to be." Dell shrugged. "And maybe it was fated."

The man's dark eyes narrowed. "I have the impression, Dell, that I'm missing a detail or three that could help me understand."

She took in a deep breath and slowly exhaled. "I'm sorry, sir, it's just I didn't expect some of the things coming up. That file there, in your computer, it's got me originating on Mara or Addicks, right? Somewhere in the Draconis March. Big blank spot before I start piloting 'Mechs in games on Solaris?"

"Pretty much." Morgan met her gaze openly. "What is it I should know?"

Dell exhaled audibly. "This isn't the first time we've met, Colonel."

The man's head came up. "I don't seem to recall..."

"You couldn't." Dell leaned forward, elbows on her knees, and stared down at the floor. "At least I hope you don't, because those aren't days I want to remember."

The thing Dell remembered most about that time was that the winds howled and sand hissed through the air. It was the sand season, had always been. Wasn't a day she didn't remember coming through the

dust lock into the house, standing there between two doors, shaking off her clothes, stamping her feet to drive the dirt out of wrinkles. She always wore clothes too big—hand-me-downs from her cousin Olive—and always in layers to make it tougher for the sand to get to the skin. Dell would pull off her shirt and had learned young how to snap it like a whip and watch a beige cloud get sucked up into the vacuum sand-eater humming overhead.

When she emerged as clean as she could be, her mother would douse her in lotion. Dell hated it. The stuff smelled like some rotten plant from a faraway world and would just make the sand stick to her skin. But her grandmother would insist, warning her no man would want a woman who had skin rough as sandpaper. That didn't make sense to Dell at her youngest, but as she grew older, she understood. The wrinkles on her grandmother's face looked like they'd been carved by the cyclones, and Dell had never seen any man give her grandmother so much as a second glance.

Life on Mallory's World hadn't been pretty or exciting, no glamor at all. Both her parents worked in the factories, turning fungal fibers harvested from the otherwise infertile wastelands into personal sanitation products. They created the 'adult protection products' in a variety of sizes and colors, guaranteed to suit the fashion sense and lifestyle of the most chic and dynamic people in society.

Or their children who'd not yet been toilet trained.

Even as a child, Dell had known creating diapers wasn't the sort of higher purpose philosophers encouraged people to pursue. But she'd never been hungry, never wondered where she was going to be sleeping that night. Her parents loved her. Her grandmother, too, despite all the weird stuff she spouted as rules to live by. It wasn't a great life, but it wasn't a bad one, either.

And then the Second Sword of Light had to spoil it.

Back then, Dell couldn't figure out why the Draconis Combine would send troops to conquer Mallory's World. Once upon a time, the world had been a fertile breadbasket, but previous battles to possess it for exactly that reason had destroyed the ecosystem on three of the continents. Now, instead of producing the stuff that would go into the body, the world supplied the means to catch what came out. For reasons she had never been able to fathom—even as an adult—House Kurita wanted the world.

More specifically, they wanted the factory district, and landed on it hard.

The dust storm had lightened up that day. Dell and her grandmother, along with other folks in their little village, climbed to the top of a dune and watched as ovoid DropShips disgorged a phalanx of giant war machines. The Second Sword of Light's bright red paint scheme shone brilliantly against the grey-brown of the sand and the slate-grey of the factory's concrete walls. Vivid red-light beams shot out and things exploded on the ground. Dell recalled watching autocannon fire rip through aircars in the parking lot, relieved that her parents always took the train.

The reality of what was happening didn't hit her, largely because of the range from which she watched. The 'Mechs appeared the same size as they did in holodramas, so it seemed all make-believe to her. Even the blaring of air-raid sirens meant nothing, since all the dramas had that, too. She even expected to hear theme music play and for tall 'Mechs in blue and white and red—the Fourth Davion Guards—to swoop in and rescue the factory.

And, as an adult, she realized she had picked those colors only because she was sure the man on the coins, First Prince Ian Davion, would be coming to their rescue. And, again, it took becoming an adult for her to understand that wars don't conveniently package themselves to fit in between ads for fast food and aircar lube.

So, the occupation began. No more than two weeks—that, she'd discovered reading about Mallory's World in Jay Mitchell's history—but to her it had been forever. Her mom had returned home. Her father remained at the factory, ostensibly to work loading or unloading whatever the Dracs wanted from the place. That's what her mom said. But Dell knew the truth. She wasn't so young she didn't understand what a hostage was.

A Combine 'Mech company sought billets in their village, taking only the best for themselves and complaining everyone in the place was filthy and barely human. Dell's grandmother would have poisoned every one of them had the Dracs not taken Mr. Driscoll out and shot him in the street because, apparently, he didn't know how to make tea properly. Two soldiers stayed in Dell's house, parking their 'Mechs in the yard to stand sentinel.

The skinny one, Dell had a hard time remembering.

She always carried a knife on the off chance she ever met the fat one again.

Time didn't move at all. They stopped living, and just spent their time fearing. A couple of afternoons—clear days, the miraculous sort of days the villagers all used to celebrate—the Drac soldiers started drinking. They didn't have any trouble drinking the wine from the New Helen vineyards from the next continent to the west, but they complained it wasn't *sake* or wasn't as good as the wine from a half-dozen other worlds.

Their complaints heaped one upon the other, with each soldier getting angrier than the one before. They demanded more wine, and folks brought it to the heart of the village, sacrifices to supplicate an angry priesthood who could command the giant metal gods could destroy the village at a whim.

But more wine wasn't good enough. They wanted entertainment, and the fat one from her house pointed her out. "That one," he'd called. "She should sing for us. Sing, little one."

Dell remembered standing there half-hidden in the shadows of the growing dusk, shivering despite the summer heat.

The man rose swiftly from his chair and stamped a foot. "Sing, damn you, or I will march my BattleMech through your wretched little mushroom."

The other Dracs laughed, and Dell's cheeks burned. Because of the cyclones and the scouring winds, all the village buildings had heavy roofs capping them. Columns supported and anchored the roofs, making the village appear as if grown out of the fungus the people harvested and used in the factory. Dell had always thought of the village as magical because of it, and because that's what she gleaned from the faery stories her mother used to tell her at bedtime.

The fat one ruined that.

Even as a child, a child who had perhaps watched too many holodramas, Dell knew she should sing some bold song, some patriotic song, a song that would sink into the man's gut and twist his insides into a knot. She was pretty sure that had she been able to call such a song to mind, she would have blared it out loudly, and would have made her mother proud.

But if she'd known such a song, it wouldn't come to her. Not that night.

So, terrified that the man would smash her house, she began singing, singing the only song she could remember. It had to do with a very small spider and a waterspout and rain—which they never had much of—and the sun that came and dried up all the rain. She repeated the verse over and over again. With each repetition the other soldiers laughed harder and harder, but the fat one, his face just reddened.

She looked into his eyes and saw death. She didn't know that's what it was. She just saw a hollow in him. The laughter rasped against his soul, scouring away the thin veneer of humanity inside him. Whatever had stayed his hand up to this point, it had gone.

He took one step toward her, then the radios they all wore crackled with sharp, fast words. Her Japanese hadn't been good enough to catch what was said. She knew now that the combination of military jargon, call signs, and slang might as well have been its own language. But the words had a greater effect than the laughter, and focused the fat man. He snapped orders and the party dissolved. Soldiers ran to their 'Mechs and as the last of the wine glugged out of an overturned bottle, the Combine 'Mechs headed north toward the factory.

Dell had wondered why the fat man hadn't kicked her house as a last bit of pettiness. Or why he hadn't stomped her into jelly as he strode past. It took many years for her to understand that as furious as he had been with her, as shamed as he felt in that moment, what he'd been told over the radio—and what else he learned as he plugged into his *Panther*—had presented him with an existential threat. A threat which made a little girl irrelevant.

Dell almost felt cheated. *How dare he forget me, dismiss me!* Her anger built, and she let it, because anger beat the hell out of being terrified.

She marched off in the wake of the Combine 'Mechs. She climbed into and out of the crumbling craters they'd stomped in the sand. She struggled her way up the dune where she'd watched them before. The Combine 'Mechs, these livid red soldiers rushing toward the factory, she felt as if they were running from her. That made her happy.

And what happened next made her even happier.

From the west came a scarlet storm. These 'Mechs also favored a red paint scheme, but added black for their arms and legs. Helicopters similarly decorated streaked through the sky, brilliantly backlit against the golden sunset. Missiles streaked down, stringing a garland of bright explosions across the landscape. Beams flashed—sporadic from the Combine side and plentiful from the new 'Mechs. Some J. Edgars sailed in, raising dust clouds that helped obscure their compatriots, their medium lasers stabbing coherent light into the 'Mechs that had so recently fled her village.

Fled from her.

Return fire ripped into one of the hovercraft, snapping it in half. The rear dug its way into the ground while the front half tumbled across the sand. As if emboldened by that one tiny victory, a lance of light 'Mechs surged forward from the Combine lines. Her heart rose into her throat. It could have been the fat man and if he won, he would return to punish her for her transgression.

But then another 'Mech appeared. She'd not known what it was then, but just its fluid motions as it strode forward marked it as special. Blocky and tall, it mocked the smaller 'Mechs. Then the launch pods on its shoulders snapped open and fire blossomed. Missiles, a seemingly endless stream of missiles, arced through the sky. They looked to her like a mythical rainbow made of fire and smoke. She stood there, her mouth open, as they rose and gracefully turned toward the ground.

And smothered the Combine 'Mechs with explosions. Dozens of bright lights strobed through the cloud of dust and smoke and armor bits, some of them so thoroughly blasted she could hold a dozen armor fragments in the palm of her hand. She had. She had collected many of them.

The attackers, whom she learned very soon were the Kell Hounds, boiled into the valley housing the factory and the village. She didn't know the word at the time, but *relentless* fit her memories perfectly. The Combine troops gave ground almost immediately. They headed farther north, a few of them blasting the factory with missiles out of spite. The blue lightning of particle projection cannons replied as if the thunderclouds of desert dust had joined the battle. The sizzling beams melted armor and picked apart 'Mechs. Those that escaped, village wisdom soon had it, had only traveled faster because they were traveling a limb or two light.

As night fell, the battle moved farther north. Flashes of light, red spears and blue lightning, lit the darkness. Seconds later came the reports of the blasts. The intervals between them grew, and by the time explosions had become distant sparks, her mother came and got her, leading her home for a dusting, lotioning, and a night's sleep.

The next day, she woke with the sun and went out. The battle had moved away, so far away she could see nothing, nor could she hear anything. The only sign it had happened were the broken war machines and other detritus. She searched for the fat man's *Panther*, hoping she'd find it, then telling herself every single explosion she'd seen had hit it and that the biggest piece she'd find would be smaller than a nail clipping.

She started searching for those bits, but found her father instead. Exhausted, masked with dried blood from a cut over his eye, but otherwise okay, he smiled when he saw her. She'd dropped her armor shards and run to him, then happily led him home. Her father told everyone that she'd saved him, his brave little girl who had come out looking for her father.

She didn't contradict him.

And later, the Dracs killed him before she could ever tell him the truth.

Dell glanced at the window for a moment, then back at Morgan Kell. "So maybe we really didn't meet, sir, but that's not how I'm going to remember it. I was just a little girl in a village so small it didn't even have a name. And you, in your *Archer*, you saved every one of us. So, when Meredith asked if I'd join the Kell Hounds, yes was the only answer I had."

"I see." Morgan nodded slowly. "I've heard many a MechWarrior tell a similar story of losing loved ones to an enemy and deciding to join the military to exact revenge. But you, you chose to go to Solaris and become an entertainer."

"Why?"

"Yes."

"Vengeance, sir, is stupid. Even when they killed my father—I was all of thirteen when it happened—I realized I could kill the guy who did it, but what then? Someone else would take his place. And another one and another one. And then someone who loved the guy I killed, they'd come after me or someone I loved. Where does it end?"

Morgan rose from his chair and looked out the window. "You know I've re-formed the regiment to go after Yorinaga Kurita, the man who killed my brother."

"Yeah, but from what you said, it's not *because* he killed your brother." Dell studied his silhouetted profile. "You're going after him so he won't kill anyone else's brother."

Morgan turned toward her. "He also commanded the troops who killed your father."

"I know." She stood. "You and your brother created the Kell Hounds to be a unit so good no one would want to face them. You wanted them to be so powerful others would decline to go to war against them. Given the nature of man, that's the only way we'll ever stop wars. So, your invitation gives me a chance to be part of that. I'm glad my skills give me the opportunity to further your dream."

"Welcome to the Kell Hounds, Dell Thompson." The man extended his hand in her direction. "Let's see what we can do to end war forever."

With a broad smile, Dell took it. "Yes, sir."

# WHERE THE PEN
# IS MIGHTIER THAN THE SWORD

### STEPHAN A. FRABARTOLO

## CONGRATULATIONS!

You are now registered as a mercenary with the Mercenary Review Board (MRB)!

From now on, you are protected by the universally accepted auspices and regulations of ComStar's MRB. This includes, but is not limited to, legitimate combatant and POW status privileges and, in case of mercenary/employer disputes, fair contract arbitration through the MRB.

## MERCENARY STARTUP BRIEF: CONTRACTS (REV. NOV 3048)

ComStar is strictly neutral. Thus, neither ComStar as a whole nor the MRB specifically are party to a mercenary contract; rather, the contract is entered between the employer and you, the mercenary. The MRB is merely a facilitator and impartial arbitrator. It is important to remember that the MRB has no part in negotiating or drawing up contracts. Contracts will always be recorded and processed as submitted by the parties, barring violation of MRB tenets.

And the contract must be honored. A bad contract, even a single poorly worded clause, can cut short your career, turn a battlefield victory into a crushing financial defeat, and stop your forces cold just as effectively as an enemy assault battalion hot dropping on your position. In this sense, the pen is indeed mightier than the sword! You are therefore strongly advised to seek expert legal counsel when drawing up a mercenary contract.

That said, as a rough guideline (that in no way should be construed as legal advice), here is an overview of some of the more frequent issues encountered with mercenary contracts:

## Mission Contracts

There are fundamentally two types of mercenary contracts. The first is objective- or mission-oriented, and it calls for a specific goal to be achieved, like an escort mission or destruction of a particular target. Mission success and payment can be measured directly against the mission objective. These are often relatively simple contracts. At their core, they only need to specify the parties (mercenary and employer), the objective, and payment.

But none of these aspects is as simple as it sounds.

### Identity of the Parties

A mercenary contract will invariably stipulate who the parties are, and their identity will be vetted by the MRB. This is important because any contract is binding only between its direct parties.

And yet, it can happen that mercenaries are unaware of who they are really working for. Employers sometimes use shell companies to hide their identity, if only to distance themselves from the operation in question. This is not illegal per se. But in very rare cases, bad actors outright pretend to be who they are not, in violation of the MRB's registry tenets.

A more common problem is that both parties typically are legal entities and, as such, may undergo sudden and substantial change in size, composition, power, and relative value (or solvency) yet technically remain the same legal entity for the purposes of the contract. For this reason, employers often stipulate a minimum size, composition, or skillset for units on long-term contracts, and reserve the right to reduce pay for the time these conditions are not met. Similarly, mercenaries are well advised to avail themselves of ComStar banking and the escrow, credit, and insurance options offered in conjunction with MRB-sponsored contracts, to mitigate the risk of an employer turning out to be unwilling or unable to pay for services rendered.

### Mission Objective

If a mercenary contract is entered with a specific objective, that objective must be described in sufficient detail to determine if and when it has been achieved. The wording can make all the difference here, and this is indeed at the core of many of the conflicts that end up in MRB arbitration.

The stated mission objective and whether or not it was achieved is often contentious because it usually determines the payment and is also highly relevant for the mercenary's MRB rating.

This goes both ways. A mercenary is not obliged to participate in actions that are not directly part of their specified mission or otherwise go beyond the contract. For example, if the contract is only about defending a specific facility, then it does not extend to objectives outside of that mission statement, such as counterattacks or defending the employer's assets elsewhere. Conversely, a mercenary unit contracted to destroy a specific facility may find their employer is not liable for combat damage sustained while fighting the target's defenders if the contract does not mention it.

## Payment

Payment models are legion. While high-profile mercenary units are often paid in C-bills, this is the exception rather than the rule. It is far more common for mercenaries to be paid in House bills, bonds, titles, hardware, salvage rights, services rendered, or any combination thereof. For garrison and defense contracts in particular, employers like to offer payment in the form of shares in the objective to be defended.

The parties are free to agree on whatever payment they choose, and payment clauses consequently range from simply calling for payment of a certain reward after the mission objective was achieved (and implicitly, no payment unless and until then), to elaborate rulesets covering different base salaries, combat bonuses, reimbursements, et cetera for different components of a mercenary unit, sometimes down to rates for individual BattleMechs or man-hours for techs. While mission contracts tend to link payment to mission goals, long-term service contracts usually opt for a salary model with bonus payments based on circumstances.

Thanks to ComStar's escrow system, mercenaries can be sure they get paid as long as they can prove they fulfilled their mission and honored their obligations.

## Long-Term Contracts

The other main type of contract is for service time instead of a specific objective. Examples include retainer, garrison, or cadre duty. Essentially, the mercenary is tied to their employer for a prescribed period of time, with no specific mission beyond a loose definition of the services to be rendered. Such contracts are significantly more complex, with correspondingly more pitfalls. For example, if the base payment sans bonuses is insufficient to pay for a unit's upkeep, an employer could put financial pressure on the unit by simply refusing them a chance to earn bonus payments.

Additional relevant concerns that should be addressed in any long-term contract (which are sometimes relevant for mission contracts) include:

## Status of Forces Agreement

This establishes the legal framework for a mercenary's presence in their employer's space, namely what laws and jurisdiction they operate under. Most legal status issues are already covered through the MRB, but interaction and integration with the employer's regular military forces—and here, particularly ranks and command rights—need to be considered.

## Dependents

Family-based mercenary outfits or large units often have a significant supply train and dependents that are not part of the combat forces proper. The contract needs to be clear on what part(s) of the whole unit is under the employer's orders, what parts the unit is allowed to bring along as dependents, and the status of such dependents—legal status, freedom of movement, and housing being the most important aspects.

## Supply

One noteworthy aspect is how a unit's upkeep, supply, and maintenance demands are met. Larger units, especially those fielding BattleMechs, often lack the tech staff and equipment to properly maintain their vehicles. Even during downtime, there is a steady demand for services, spare parts, and consumables. Frequently, these supplies and services are provided through the employer's military. In fact, this will usually be the only viable venue. To recoup the money paid to their mercenaries, many employers require some or all the maintenance and supply to be purchased through the employer's military. This, too, is often a contentious issue when mercenaries overspend or otherwise find that their regular maintenance and supply expenditures exceed their regular payment, driving them ever deeper into debt.

## Other Considerations

There is a plethora of ancillary subjects a mercenary contract might cover, some of which may be obligations outlasting the contract proper such as non-disclosure agreements. Two that stand out are as follows:

**Liaison Officers:** On long-term contracts or for larger mercenary units, employers regularly place a liaison officer with the mercenaries. The exact extent of the liaison officer's powers and duties is highly dependent on the nature of the contract, and can range from a mere contact person to a representative of the employer with full command rights.

**Transportation:** Transportation clauses clarify if or to what extent the employer is responsible for safe travel for the mercenaries, or, if they have their own spacecraft, to what extent these are part of the contracted assets and at the employer's disposal (or part of the unit's dependents). Since the vast majority of mercenaries have no transport assets of their own, a typical arrangement for mission-oriented contracts is that the employer is responsible for safe insertion and extraction. A garrison contract might merely include reimbursement for reasonable travel costs aboard regular cargo vessels.

Mind that without a transportation clause, travel and insertion are entirely the responsibility of the mercenary.

**Bludgeon:** Thanks for nothing ComStar! What's this blathering about identities? If the money is good, what does it matter where it comes from?

**Arrowhead:** Reilly's Armored Cavalry is perhaps the best example for what can happen if you are hired through shell companies. Not many survived that suicide mission. And remember when pirates posed as the Jandex Corporation back in '45-46 and lured several small units into ambushes with fake plum contracts to steal their 'Mechs?

**LoneStar:** As far as ComStar was concerned, it was Jandex whose name had been sullied and who had to pick up the pieces afterward. They never mentioned the vetting process. It's never the MRB's fault when something goes awry. But they can't spell out "company store" either in this worthless joke of a document.

**Bullseye:** The same vetting process that failed to blacklist a merc unit that worked for the Oberon pirates and Helmar Valasek. Yeah. Totally neutral and infallible.

**Arrowhead:** Piracy is an action, not an affiliation. The Oberon Confederation and Santander's World are both established political entities. In this fashion they are no different from a Great House. It is not illegal to work for them unless you commit criminal acts in the process.

**LoneStar:** Oberon hires out their forces like mercs, but they aren't registered with MRB and the MRB still tolerates it.

**Arrowhead:** The MRB acknowledges there are quasi-mercenaries such as the armies of small states or noble estates. Or even the corporate security forces and militias in the Combine that exist but aren't allowed to properly register due to that "Death to Mercenaries" issue. The MRB also tolerates units with high fluctuation that amount to mercenary cartels, like the Lone Wolves or the WhipIts. What's your problem?

**LoneStar:** The MRB panders to the Houses and mercs will always draw the short straw in their so-called arbitration.

**Arrowhead:** Funny. The Rasalhagians said the opposite after most of their mercs successfully bowed out of fighting in the Ronin Wars. I think you're complaining about bad contracts, not bad arbitration. Get a competent hiring agent.

**Ceredwyn:** Worth noting that many of the more egregious stories that go around merc campfires never actually saw MRB arbitration, either because neither side called for arbitration or because they were outside the MRB to begin with. Hard to know what really happened when you only heard one side of the story, and not even firsthand...

# TALES OF THE
# STRANGE BEDFELLOWS

### JAMES HAUSER

**BRUNSWICK SPACEPORT**
**SACKVILLE**
**DUCHY OF TAMARIND-ABBEY**
**FREE WORLDS LEAGUE**
**7 AUGUST 3149**

A cloud of dust cut among spherical and ovoid metal mountains on a wide gray plain. The leading point of the cloud dodged between the silent, parked DropShips. It weaved around large ground transports and utility trucks, and slowed as it approached the ramp of a green Clan *Overlord-C*-class DropShip with a jade-colored katana as the only decoration on its hull. The hover jeep that spawned the cloud stopped at the ship's bay entry ramp, where it was met by a pair of armored Elementals. After a brief conversation, its occupant drove the jeep up the ramp and into the ship.

Captain Giovanna Rudolpho-Majors, commanding officer of the mercenary company Demeter's Avengers, parked next to a 'Mech cubicle and stepped out of the vehicle. She took a moment to sweep her long red hair away from her feline cheekbones, glancing around the immense 'Mech bay as she did so.

As she was escorted to the elevator by an unarmored Elemental, Giovanna noted how several of the 'Mech bays had no signs of recent occupation. At the end of the row, in a darkened bay, sat a partially disassembled *Turkina* assault 'Mech lashed to the bay moorings, as if it had not been unpacked since the DropShip had landed.

Minutes later, she entered a spartan conference room occupied by a pair of warriors wearing generic Jade Falcon overalls, minus the Clan emblems. They rose. Both were obviously older warriors, and the warrior to step forward had a wide, strong face and light brown hair graying at the temples.

"Welcome to the *Ichabod Thastus*, Captain Rudolpho-Majors. I believe this is your first time aboard this ship."

"It is, Star Captain Vormand." She shook his hand and turned to the other warrior, a woman of olive complexion, with gray-streaked black hair tied back. "Star Commander Illyana—Good to see you again."

Vormand gestured to a seat, and Giovanna scanned the room to learn what these warriors considered to be spartan. Her understanding of Clan customs told her to get to business.

"Forgive my short notice, but I needed to see you about a contract issue," she said. "Our contract is expiring soon, and Minister Gomez is being stingy with the conditions. He's been telling us we are asking for significantly more from him than you or Manitou's Boys. I am here to find out if he's just playing us off each other. If you do not find it offensive to your honor, I thought we might compare our contracts."

"This would be welcome. I was not bred for commerce, and I believe I have not negotiated well, especially considering how poorly our compensation is covering our needs. Were we bidding for combat, I would be in very comfortable territory. But we are not, and I have no training for the mercenary life."

Captain Rudolpho-Majors nodded, but spoke very carefully. "We were surprised when we were told we would be sharing garrison duties with a group of Jade Falcon mercenaries. We are very curious about that."

Star Captain Vormand frowned and gazed off, as if into a faraway distance. "I assure you, we did not disgrace ourselves. We did not begin our new lives with the expectation of ending up this way."

He paused, apparently debating whether he should remain guarded or trust this unknown commander with their story.

"It all started about thirteen years ago..."

**OUTSIDE HAMMARR**
**SUDETEN**
**JADE FALCON OCCUPATION ZONE**
**4 APRIL 3136**

Star Captain Vormand scanned the chaotic landscape through the viewport of his *Summoner* OmniMech with dismay. Clouds of smoke rose from dozens of places where Jade Falcon warriors had turned their weapons on each other. Malvina Hazen's DropShips had landed and disgorged troops to reinforce the Falcon warriors sympathetic to her cause. He had mobilized his unit to defend Khan Jana Pryde against Malvina's Hazen challenge for control of the Clan. Somewhere up in the blackness of space, the two warriors had fought on the hull of the flagship *Emerald Talon*, and the Khan was dead.

So was the soul of the Jade Falcons.

Malvina Hazen would reshape the Clan in ways few ever had, and the direction she would take disgusted Vormand to his core. He knew the Watch would take note of who Khan Pryde's loyalists were. Word had gone out that there would be a major announcement in the Falcon's Perch in the center of Hammarr.

His command was busy collecting survivors and equipment in the foothills. It had been some of the most painful fighting he had ever seen. These were fellow Jade Falcons. He hated them for how their warped outlook would shame the Clan, but lamented how killing them would weaken the clan. The worst of it was not knowing who to shoot at. The Khan had gathered much of the *touman* on Sudeten to destroy Malvina's force, and he was surrounded by strangers. Some were honorable, others were Malvina's abominations. It was difficult to tell who each warrior was, and he was sure his forces had killed both.

"Star Captain, we have incoming aerospace forces that are not transmitting an IFF. It looks like a swarm of...*neg*...not fighters. Three large contacts, probably DropShips, but flying in very tight formation."

The Star Captain could see a bright yellow light in the sky. It wasn't the color of engine exhaust, but instead the yellow of atmospheric friction. White flaming chunks were splitting off from this second sun which seemed to be breaking up.

"Where is that headed?" Vormand blurted out as the snow of the landscape turned yellow. There was a bright flash, his 'Mech shook violently, and he fought to keep it upright. As his 'Mech just barely calmed, it was smacked again by a shockwave. Regaining control of his senses, he gazed at a massive expanse of smoke and flame that mushroomed into the sky where Hammarr had been. Chunks of debris pinged and hammered his 'Mech.

Communication channels were flooded with confusion. Vormand switched to his unit channels and ordered his warriors to check in. Satisfied with their answers, he dialed up the emergency channels to find them a cacophony of scared, confused, and pleading voices. A picture began to emerge of the *Emerald Talon* diving under power into the atmosphere. Reports had come in that the *Talon* was in ruins and in a decaying orbit, but he knew it couldn't have found Hammarr randomly; it had been aimed.

And it answered only to Malvina Hazen. She had already begun her purge, and apparently was not concerned that the Clan capital was collateral damage.

"This is Squawk actual. Does anyone have eyes on the spaceport?" Star Colonel Buhallin broadcast over the Cluster-wide channel.

"This is Squawk Three Rico," one of the recon Stars replied. "The spaceport seems to be within the zone of destruction, but I can have my Star there in ten minutes. What am I looking for?"

"Functioning DropShips."

"Sir, the DropPort was a little crowded, so several transports were grounded eighteen klicks southeast of us. We will have better luck there."

The Star Colonel ordered his loyalists to rendezvous at the site. The mass of smoke that concealed Hammarr was growing and spreading like a giant, ravenous amoeba. Fires sprouted all around him where bits of Hammarr had landed and set trees alight. His unit formed up and marched for the DropShips in good order. Other 'Mechs were paralleling them, but they did not seem like pursuing Malvina loyalists. Vormand noted how quiet the channels were.

Within the hour, they arrived at the airfield. He found several DropShips there, and directed the survivors to the nearest *Overlord*-class DropShip, the *Ichabod Thastus*. A few Elementals were standing at the base of the entry ramp in discussion with a crewman. Vormand changed channels to hear the conversation.

"Squawk actual, the chief technician wishes to speak to you," one of the Elementals said.

"Put him through using your mic."

The chief technician crossed his arms and looked up at the Star Colonel's *Turkina*. "I'm sorry, sir, but I cannot let you board, on orders of the Chingis Khan."

"Malvina is not here. I am," retorted Reynard Buhallin.

"Nevertheless, she is the Khan of all of us now, and she has ordered that no one leave."

Buhallin ordered his Elementals to move away from the ramp, then marched up to the ramp and stepped on the chief technician. "Does anyone else have any objections?"

The only response was the distant sound of BattleMech footfalls.

"My fellow Jade Falcons, our Clan is now led by an abomination who not only kills conquered worlds, but our own enclaves. She has destroyed all of Hammarr to eliminate those who oppose her, and will use equally destructive means to eliminate all opposition within the Clan. Many of us will be purged instead of dying for the good of the Clan or the Founder's dreams for humanity. Should you survive that, you will become her butchers, and your codex and Bloodheritage will be forever tainted by association with that malignancy. I am leaving

Sudeten to chart another path to fulfill Kerensky's vision. All those who wish to go with me should board this ship now."

At first, no one moved, but soon BattleMechs, armored vehicles, and armored infantry boarded the DropShip. A fair number stood beyond the DropShips, unwilling to leave their Clan.

Vormand looked around one last time at the world of his birth, feeling sick at the notion of how badly it had been wounded, and the thought he would never see it again.

### *OVERLORD*-CLASS DROPSHIP *ICHABOD THASTUS*
### BRUNSWICK SPACEPORT
### SACKVILLE
### DUCHY OF TAMARIND-ABBEY
### FREE WORLDS LEAGUE
### 7 AUGUST 3149

"Star Colonel Reynard Buhallin took the survivors to known Jade Falcon enclaves in the Republic. There we hoped to form a Clan-in-exile, but each time we were overrun either by Senatorial Alliance or House troops. In our last battle there, Star Colonel Buhallin was killed, and I assumed command. We considered joining another Clan, but even if we were not rejected outright and passed on Trials of Position, we would be relegated to *solahma* units to await a slow, pointless death. The Clan Protectorate passed on us, but are willing to trade. And we are unwilling to swear a *rede* of allegiance to any House lord.

"This left us few options. With no income or lower castes to meet our needs, continuing as we were would have left us all dead of starvation. All that was left was the mercenary life. The warriors that were still with us had survival instincts too strong to simply end their lives, so we fought in the only way we could. We became the Jade Swords."

Giovanna nodded. "It was a gradual progression then?"

"*Aff.* We were no longer officially a part of an outside hierarchy when we were defending the enclaves, so we got used to independence. And we continued to do what we needed to survive.

"What about you?" Vormand asked after sipping his coffee. "How did you and your fellow warriors become mercenaries?"

Giovanna considered the question for a moment. "Well, it started after my time in the militia was up. My grandfather and I were exploring an uninhabited area back home on Wildwood—in the Magistracy of Canopus. We came across part of a BattleMech sticking out of a hill.

After we dug it out, we found five others, and assumed they were Blakist raiders who ditched their rides when they missed their DropShips off world. This was about nine years ago..."

**APPROACHING DOLPHIN ISLAND**
**WILDWOOD**
**MAGISTRACY OF CANOPUS**
**10 JUNE 3140**

*The world is made of blue*, Giovanna Rudolpho-Majors reflected as her hover jeep glided across a causeway that seemed to stretch into infinity. Below and beside her, a shimmering turquoise expanse of water continued to the horizon, where it met the sapphire blue of the sky. Off to her right, the great blueness was broken by a wave of cumulonimbus clouds rising off the glades on the mainland. In places, sheets of rain cut through the air to the ground. Ahead, a green fuzziness rose along the length of the horizon, announcing she was nearing Dolphin Island. Soon, the causeway ended, and she drove among thick forests of both Terran and native trees. After a few kilometers, she spotted a sign with the word "*Whatever*" carved into it and turned off. Soon she was maneuvering in a parking lot full of rental cars and a tour bus.

She stepped out of her jeep into the Whatever Commune, founded by Connor Henry in 3053. Connor was part of the massive wave of immigrants that swelled the planetary population during the thirty-first century. He came to Wildwood to flee from the oppression of his day job and immediately found his way to a busy sidewalk and began preaching about his deeply held conviction that loafing was a sacrament. Before long, he had a holoshow that was transmitted in one form or another across the planetary communications networks and thousands of followers. In time, one of his disciples suggested they migrate to an island not far off the coast in the tropics. Sensing an opportunity for increased tourism, the local government provided a small stipend, prefabricated housing, and planted fruit trees to help keep them from starving. Content in the knowledge that his commune was secure, Connor began writing his Great Book, but procrastinated too much and died before he could finish the first chapter.

Giovanna walked down a dirt path between the trailers and watched tourists taking pictures of the various residents, who dozed in lawn chairs in the colony's signature bathrobe, shorts, T-shirt, and sandals. Raised voices caught her attention, and she recognized one of them as belonging to her grandfather. Quickening her pace, she found her long-haired, bearded grandfather in a grove of trees surrounded by a throng of bathrobe-clad locals, all sitting or lying on the ground.

"That's a crock and you know it!" he argued. "With all due respect for Wise Connor, sometimes you do have to get up and do a few things for yourself. The proverbial roof won't fix itself."

"You push the sacrament too far, Michael. You're asking your brothers and sisters for help. How are we to enjoy the Peace of Connor if we must labor for you? The early Travails of Hunger taught us it is proper and necessary to pick fruit and prepare our food *if need be*, but what you are doing puts us firmly on the slippery slope to labor," replied a member of the circle. "Isn't that right, Brother Finnorn?"

With a pause, Brother Finnorn replied, "I'm not making your arguments for you. I labor for no one. That is what the Unenlightened are for. Which reminds me: I need to get my robes cleaned."

"All right, fine," her grandfather spoke somewhat sarcastically. "I won't ask anyone for help anymore. Can I go now?"

"We would speak more on this," replied the inquisitor, "but I don't feel like it. Just remember, do not disturb your brothers and sisters with requests for labor, or we will be forced to cast you out."

Grandpa Michael stepped over a reclining member of the council and responded "Whatever" with a hint of sarcasm. The circle raised their hands and all chanted *"Whatever"* reverently. He spotted Giovanna and greeted her as she walked alongside him.

"Problems, Grandpa?"

"Damned fanatics! I'm surprised most of them haven't died of exposure. I'm glad you came to visit your poor old grandpa. I need you to help me with some maintenance on the sly."

"I can do that, but Mom asked me to speak to you about something. She wasn't completely forthcoming, but she said you had something important to tell me."

"Tell you about what?"

"Well, my time in the military reserves is up, but I was thinking of enlisting in the regular MAF as a MechWarrior. I qualified on a *Locust* during my service and took courses in tactics. When I told Mom, she expressed concerns that buying a decent rank would put me heavily in debt and I would just end up as Capellan cannon fodder. She also said you could offer an alternative."

"Did she now?" He glanced around. "Let's talk about this in my office."

As he led her into his humble abode, she once more marveled at how neat his shelves were in contrast to the piles of clothes and other personal items strewn on the floor. He stepped over to the table and cleared junk off the surface and the chairs, then gestured for her to sit.

"I apologize for the mess, but around here you need to keep up appearances," he said and took a breath. "Kiddo, we have a bit of a family secret; a scandal even."

"You mean besides my grandfather being a member of a laziness cult."

"Yeah, besides that. It was my father's secret. He was born on Thorin around the time the Clans invaded the Inner Sphere. During the fighting that turned that region into the Chaos March, he was orphaned and taken in by the Word of Blake."

Giovanna's eyes went wide. "Did he—"

Grandpa Michael held his hand up. "Yeah, he eventually joined the Word of Blake Militia and was part of a raiding party from the Sixteenth Division that landed on Wildwood during the Jihad. His unit had no stomach for what they were being asked to do, so the six of them faked being destroyed by the defenders, and the other Blakists left.

"They decided to do their best to blend in. Three tried to get home, but were run over by a hover bus on the way to the spaceport. The other three got jobs and started new lives, like my father. One killed himself and left behind no family. The other one got a job in investment banking."

"So, what does this have to do with why Mom sent me?"

"It has to do with what they left behind. They buried six 'Mechs, and I know where they are. It's a three-hour drive northwest of here. With that many machines just waiting to be dug up, you have some choices. You can grab your favorite and join a merc unit, or you can grab all six and start your own. Did you make any friends in your unit?"

She nodded.

"MechWarriors, techs?"

"Yes."

"Good. We'll say I found 'em while hiking in the mountains. Just the same, they'll need to know we can't talk about their origins to anyone outside the unit. The last thing you need is a Regulan hit squad determined to slag your 'Mechs. Start making your calls."

The winds blew off Paria Plateau, gently sprinkling the cliff face with sand. They blew over the group standing at the base of the cliffs and down into the wide, flat, light-orange valley below them. At the bottom, a deep, wavy ravine cut the valley in two.

Grandpa Michael, his eyes hidden by dark glasses, stood almost heroically as his bathrobe flapped in the wind. He shouted words of encouragement and direction as the others shoveled sand off the 'Mech buried inside the cliff face.

Based on what they'd already uncovered, Giovanna assumed they were excavating an *Archer* heavy 'Mech, and dug where the cockpit hatch was likely to be. After a few hours, they had burrowed down to it and popped the hatch open. The familiar smell of human sweat, made just a bit more acrid from decades of baking in the sands, greeted her.

She climbed inside, sat down in the command chair, and powered up the computer. She and one of the techs spent a few hours cracking the system's security protocols, after which she removed the neural patterns of the previous owner so she could install her own. Once the computer accepted her as the new master of the 'Mech, she powered it up. The *Archer* groaned as its arms and legs pushed its sandy shroud away and freed itself from the cliff. She triggered the sensors and found five other metal contacts embedded in the cliff face. Using her 'Mech's hands, she cleared off enough sand from the other hibernating 'Mechs for the three other MechWarriors and two techs to scramble up and wake their machines.

By evening, they had unearthed a *Rifleman*, *Dragon Fire*, *Trebuchet*, *Locust*, and a *Mercury*. They pitched their tents around a campfire near the feet of their 'Mechs.

"It looks like they just laid them up against the cliff and pushed sand over the edge to bury them," noted one of the warriors, Clytemnestra Holt. Her blond hair was tied back in a rough ponytail with a lock of hair hanging down behind each of her cheeks. The fire light glinted off the tiny, double-headed battle ax dangling from her necklace as they sat around the fire and ate. The battle ax signified she was an adherent of the ancient Minoan goddess Pipituna. She harbored a deep-seated aversion to the Capellans, fearing their political system would spread to the Magistracy. "That *Dragon Fire* was used exclusively by the Blakists, and is bound to attract unwanted attention."

"I know," Giovanna replied. "We're going to have to disassemble it and sell the parts individually. The nice thing about it is that that engine is a 300 XL. The weapons are up to modern standards, so they'll fetch a good price too."

"What about the *Mercury*?" asked Rupert Mehta, one of their two techs, as he stroked his dark goatee. "It was also used by the Word of Blake, and we could get money for its parts too."

"It's been around since the Star League, and everyone has used them at some point. It may get a suspicious glance or two, but will pass muster," Giovanna replied. "We'll have to remove the C$^3$i computers from all of them. They wouldn't pass muster, but I don't want to throw them away either. We may need them in an emergency someday."

"We could take the money from the *Dragon Fire* and buy commissions." MechWarrior Arlene Dubois brushed a lock of brown hair from her round face as several rock squirrels howled at each other in the distance.

Grandpa Michael chimed in. "That still leaves the problem of you being used as Capellan cannon fodder. Unless you want to end up fighting the Republic or even the Clans, you need to become mercenaries. You'll also need to find a place to sell those parts. If memory serves, there are military equipment dealers on Krimari."

"Before all of that, I know a place where we can stash the 'Mechs and disassemble the *Dragon Fire*. We'll also sandblast what's left of the paint on 'em," Giovanna suggested.

"Yes." Grandpa Michael nodded. "You'll also need a name for your merry band of mercenaries."

They all sat in silence for a few minutes, while the rock squirrels howled at each other.

"What about Demeter's Avengers?" Arlene Dubois finally suggested.

Clytemnestra chimed in: "A goddess name. I like it."

It stuck.

### OVERLORD-CLASS DROPSHIP *ICHABOD THASTUS*
### BRUNSWICK SPACEPORT
### SACKVILLE
### DUCHY OF TAMARIND-ABBEY
### FREE WORLDS LEAGUE
### 7 AUGUST 3149

"So, we traveled to Luxen, also in the Magistracy, and sold the parts. We picked up a pair of Arrow IV Trailers and sent messages to some of the independent worlds in the Free Worlds League. That led to a pair of garrison jobs punctuated by the occasional raid from pirates or League mini-states. We adopted a half-dozen orphaned MechWarriors and tankers, with their machines bringing us up to a mixed 'Mech company."

"I'm pretty good with finances, so we've been able to keep our heads above water. But we could command much better pay if we were a larger unit. I imagine your DropShip must boost your pay significantly." She gestured around the room.

"*Neg*, not significantly. Minister Garcia said it did not contribute to our performance clauses unless we used it to intercept incoming fighters and DropShips. And he complained this ship took up space at the DropPort."

Giovanna snorted. "He's full of it, that cheap bastard. He complained that our *lack* of a DropShip meant he had to provide a base with repair facilities and barracks. Your DropShip also means you can deploy to the enemy's landing zone faster and reduce the amount of damage raiders and pirates do to his precious planet."

Vormand pulled out his data pad and made some notes. "I will bring up this point with the minister in three months."

Giovanna pointed to his data pad. "Could you show me your contract? Maybe I can help you out with that. It's a shame we can't negotiate our contracts at the same time... Wait..." She grinned. "Maybe we can."

## ROSARIO MUNICIPAL DROPPORT
## SACKVILLE
## DUCHY OF TAMARIND-ABBEY
## FREE WORLDS LEAGUE
## 7 AUGUST 3149

Captain Miles Nguyen eyed the hover jeep sitting next to his unit's *Triumph*-class DropShip, the *Fancy*. The commanders from the other two mercenary units had come for a visit. Knowing the others were coming, he'd had his unit, Manitou's Boys, practice their marksmanship.

His hands shook a little as they grasped his *Marauder*'s controls. He felt like a fraud. He wasn't a warrior and despite all the drills, he knew his unit would be in trouble when facing a determined opponent. Everyone was depending on him, and when the time for action came, he feared he would let them fatally down.

Giovanna and Vormand sat in the front seat of her hover jeep parked in the shade of the *Folly* and watched the MechWarriors of Manitou's Boys practice shooting.

Giovanna's arms were crossed over the steering wheel. "They still shoot like techs."

"It has not been that long since our last joint training session. Perhaps a month." Vormand winced as the unit's *Marauder* wobbled while it turned and fired its PPCs at the practice target.

Giovanna nodded at the approaching 'Mechs. "Do you think they scheduled this demonstration to show off their improved gunnery skills?"

"If they did, they failed."

"At least their armor crews can shoot straight. And they have a DropShip."

A male voice came over her comm. "This is Captain Nguyen. I apologize for my tardiness, but practice makes perfect. Please pull up into the DropShip's bay."

"We'll follow after your 'Mechs get on board. We wouldn't want to get underfoot," she said, and cut the transmission.

"That is most wise," Vormand said as they shared a grin.

Inside, the scene was much busier than it had been on the *Ichabod Thastus*. It had the feel of a small town at lunchtime. As the 'Mechs maneuvered in their bays, their techs moved in to secure them. Notably, there were no signs of uniforms anywhere. People of all ages moved around the brightly lit, white-painted chamber, carrying or pushing loads. A small group of children seemed to be racing each other. A small pack of red and orange ferret-like mammals swarmed into everything, apparently hunting for food.

A crewman ushered the two newcomers into a conference room with assurances that their commanding officer would be with them shortly. Minutes later, Captain Miles Nguyen stepped through the door, his hair still wet from a quick shower.

"Sorry to keep you waiting. I had to change and shower to not offend you with cockpit stench." Hands were shaken and the three sat down.

As an icebreaker, Giovanna began. "I've been meaning to ask, what does Manitou refer to?"

"It's a town on Andiron where we all grew up." Miles shook his head. "It was a place where hope went to die. I grew up on stories of the golden ages of Andiron and the Circinus Federation, when someone could prosper based on their intelligence and hard work. We were told stories of the ranchers who spent their days shepherding their cattle across the wide plains and the vast farms that stretched to the horizon.

"All that ended near the beginning of the Jihad, when the Blakists came to Circinus. At first, they were a blessing with the technology they brought. Eventually, they brought a Regulan task force that annihilated Circinus and the Blakists. Then the Regulans had their way with the rest of the Federation. After the Regulans departed, pirates and other cast-offs moved in and had their way with what was left of the Federation. We were born in this age of regret, where technology began to fail and the pirates preyed on everyone, even each other. The herds diminished by the year as exporting off world became difficult and expensive, and the pirates stole livestock to suit their needs. Say what you will about the McIntyres, but they were pirates who appreciated the value of law and order, at least in the right sense. But the pirates who came after didn't see the value in civil order. The uprisings they inspired also demonstrated they were too well armed.

"Manitou made a name for itself as a place where some of that beloved *lostech* could become working tech once more. Wheeled vehicles drawn by draft animals left our town under their own power. As time went on, it got harder to restore those vehicles, because deliveries of replacement parts from off world were fewer and farther between. But our prosperity soon became a curse when a group of pirates noticed us and seized the town. A few years went by before a bigger and badder group of pirates took Manitou from the first group of armed miscreants with the predictable civilian casualties and collateral damage. Twice more, the town 'upgraded' to a new set of pirates until we decided to do something about the final group of half-drunken sadists.

"In spite of the pirates' best efforts, most of us had access to weapons and knew how to use them. Previous attempts at throwing off the pirates had failed because rifles weren't very effective against 'Mechs and tanks, and even when they were, another pirate band would simply help themselves to the newly opened territory.

"We'd had enough of that, so I made a plan."

**MANITOU**
**ANDIRON**
**CIRCINUS WASTES (FORMER CIRCINUS FEDERATION)**
**20 OCTOBER 3144**

Miles Nguyen looked around as he walked through town. In minutes, it was due to begin. The walk was a final check that everyone was ready to go. As he went, he locked eyes with each of the operational leaders. All of them nodded; all were ready.

Dozens of people stood about cheerily talking, putting a car back together, passing fast food through a window to a customer, laughing, cursing a work animal, and handing out more alcohol to their pirate overlords. If the pirates had been looking more closely, they might have noticed the townsfolk weren't normally this cheery. Today, they were too cheery—and that should have been cause for alarm.

Ahead, the pirate's *Triumph*-class DropShip, the *Fancy*, squatted in the middle of the plain like a bird sitting on a massive nest. A few armored vehicles formed a ring around the massive ship, but most were inside. A gradual epidemic of breakdowns tied to bad lubricants had the townspeople hard at work on the vehicles inside the ship. A lance of 'Mechs were also arrayed outside, facing the town. On Miles' suggestion, each of those 'Mechs had just gotten a computer check. It had been years since the planet had gotten a software update for their 'Mech's systems, but they would be getting one in less than two minutes.

Jack Tsimopolous sat in the cockpit of his aging *Marauder*, pondering who was the greater enemy: the other pirate bands, or his own. He believed Thinby Mather was bound to make his move soon, so he made sure that either Zanna or Siddiq were standing guard in their 'Mechs when he wasn't in his. Zanna's *Shadow Hawk* could hold its own against Mather's *Griffin*, but he worried that Siddiq's *Locust* wouldn't be able to buy enough time. The loyalty of the armor crews was the big wildcard factor. Jack had had Nguyen install kill switches on the machines of pilots he didn't trust.

He looked out the viewport at the armored units surrounding the landing field. Several of them had the kill switches, so he felt secure. He gazed over at the town. There was a lot more activity than normal, and they didn't seem to be doing their normal slinking around for some strange reason.

Out of the corner of his eye, he saw all the screens on his control panels turn blue. A message appeared on the screen.

AN IMPORTANT UPDATE IS IN PROGRESS. THIS CAN TAKE A FEW MINUTES...

A dialog box appeared: 1% COMPLETE. DO NOT TURN OFF THIS SYSTEM.

Jack frowned. System updates always left him feeling vulnerable, not that he'd seen many of those in recent years. He glanced back at the town and noticed people running around. Some were handing things to others. Rifles? They huddled, then turned toward the landing field and began running. Others ran through town in small packs and muffled cracking sounds bounced through his canopy.

He grabbed the stick and flipped the switches to charge the weapons, but nothing happened.

2% COMPLETE. DO NOT TURN OFF THIS SYSTEM, the computer chided him.

"Stop it!" he howled as armed townspeople closed on his defense line. "STOP IT STOP IT STOP IT!" he roared. It ignored him, and he banged on the screen with both fists. He frantically poked the screens everywhere with his index finger, then flicked every switch he had. He kicked the foot pedals with all his strength, and they squeaked back at him.

The 'Mech didn't move.

He glanced up and watched the rioters climb onto his tanks. *Why haven't the tanks fired?*

He dug his personal communicator out from under his seat and screamed, "What the hell is going on out there?" on the emergency channel. Voices responded and were cut off by sharp cracks. One tanker said he couldn't get anything to work. He heard part of a boom and then nothing from the tanker. He looked up to see smoke rising out of the hatch of a Hunter light tank. He watched in horror as figures on top of the Demolisher assault tank popped open the hatch, dropped something inside, and scampered away from the opening. Smoke gushed out, and the figures jumped into the opening with their rifles.

4% COMPLETE. DO NOT TURN OFF THIS SYSTEM.

"STOP IT!" He pounded on the controls again and winced at the pain coursing through his hands. Then he heard it. Something was clanking on his 'Mech. It sounded like someone was climbing. He reached under his seat for his sidearm. The sounds were now at the hatch. He leaned over farther, and his cooling tubes yanked at him. His fingertips brushed something that could be the gun. He recognized it as the holster, and it was empty.

Then the hatch opened. A figure outside calmly said, "Is this what you are looking for?" Then they leveled it at Jack and took careful aim.

As Miles ran toward the ship, he watched a body drop unceremoniously out of the *Marauder* and flop on the ground. He huffed and puffed as a hover vehicle bristling with armed townsfolk drove up beside him and someone yelled, "Get in!"

He jumped in and accepted an offered rifle. "What do you hear from our people in the *Fancy*?"

"We have most of the ship, including the hostages." Vena Lambrecht gestured to the ship.

"Good. Who controls *Fancy*'s guns?"

"We cut power to the fore and port guns, so they don't control that. We have to stay out of their other arcs."

The vehicle pulled onto the ship's ramp and drove up into the cargo bay. A thin, smoky haze hung over the otherwise brightly lit, white-painted chamber. In the distance, one of the lights flickered over a vehicle cubicle. Closer to Miles, splattered blood stained the white walls just over a dead body. He couldn't tell if it was a pirate or one of the townspeople.

"How much of the ship do we control?" he called out.

"We have everything but the bridge, Miles," answered Lyssa Spagnoli as she walked around the corner. "We killed seven of them, including sentries. We have three dead and two wounded. The engines are offline, so the *Fancy* isn't going anywhere."

"Good." He patted her on the shoulder, strode to an intercom station, and picked up the receiver. "Bridge, this is Cargo Bay Two."

After a pause, "Cargo Bay Two, go ahead."

"We have control of the ship."

"Which 'we'? Who are you?"

"Miles Nguyen."

"Miles? The chief tech? Are *you* responsible for this?"

"Yes," he responded matter-of-factly.

"The boss will kill you as soon as—"

"He rises from the dead? His body is at the foot of his 'Mech. The vehicles and 'Mechs on the tarmac are under our control. Most of the pirates in town were liquored up and easily killed. This just leaves you, Captain Narayan. It's time for you to surrender."

"Surrender? Do I look stupid to you? You'll kill us just like you did the others."

"No, Captain, we need you and the bridge crew. Most of us are planning to leave this hellhole. It's no place for decent folks anymore, and we don't know how to fly this ship. You do, and you haven't done any of us harm."

"How do I know I can trust you?"

"You don't. But the one thing you can trust in is starvation and dehydration. You have no food and water on the bridge, and the average person will die after three days without water. We simply have to wait you out. Oh, and did I mention all the looted cash is sitting in town, so even if you could reestablish communications between the engines and the bridge, you wouldn't have any money to pay for the JumpShip?"

Captain Narayan pondered his situation for half a minute. "Let's meet in the conference room."


**TRIUMPH-CLASS DROPSHIP FANCY**
**ROSARIO MUNICIPAL DROPPORT**
**SACKVILLE**
**DUCHY OF TAMARIND-ABBEY**
**FREE WORLDS LEAGUE**
**7 AUGUST 3149**


"After we wiped out Tsimopoulos' thugs, we found ourselves with the equipment of a small military." Miles shrugged. "We knew the other pirate groups would try to move in on us again as soon as they learned of our situation, and the consensus among the townsfolk was there was no future for anyone on Andiron. We grabbed the pirates' loot and negotiated a partnership with the crew of this ship. We loaded up most of the town and departed for the Free Worlds League. With all the military equipment aboard, we thought we could make a great life for ourselves as mercenaries."

"Wait." Giovanna frowned. "Most of the town is on this ship?"

"It wasn't a big town." Miles shrugged. "All of the spare vehicle bays have been converted into apartments or machine shops. Anyone who isn't working as a warrior is working in the shops. We do piecework for local manufacturers and repair equipment for anyone with the cash. When the warriors aren't busy, they help out with the tech work."

Miles paused as he noticed Vormand wincing.

"Everyone talks about how glamorous and exciting the mercenary life is, but no one talks about how hard it is to stay solvent. That's why we've got everyone working our small cottage industry on the side."

Giovanna saw her chance. "And of course, it doesn't help when your employer is playing you against the other units on the planet."

Miles frowned. "Playing us against each other?"

"In the terms of our contracts. When we ask for better terms for pay, expenses, salvage rights, et cetera, the minister says the other units are willing to work for less and if we're not happy with them, we can leave, and he'll just hire another mercenary company. If we were a battalion in size, then we could command better agreements. A better contract would mean better financial stability, and if a battle went badly and we lost a company's worth of units, our losses would be painful, but survivable."

"This is why we have come," interjected Vormand. "If our three commands were to merge, we would be stronger as a group."

"But...you're a Clanner." Miles shifted as his brows knit. "Warriors are supposed to go it alone."

"*Aff*, within a Clan, we are. Right now, we are anything but a Clan."

Miles quietly tapped his finger on the table as he mulled it over. "My people will not take kindly to getting ordered around by strangers."

"Vormand and I talked about it on the way over. The unit would be run more or less democratically for major decisions. Every warrior and tech would have a vote. But there would be a strict chain of command in combat situations. For the mid-level decisions, the three of us would form a council."

"Did you discuss the chain of command on the way as well?" Skepticism crept into Miles' voice.

"We did. Vormand seems like the obvious choice to be our overall unit commander because of his extensive combat experience in the Jade Falcon worlds and the Republic. If anyone's going to keep us alive in a tough fight, it's him."

"What about the one-on-one fighting style of the Clans? That could put us at a disadvantage."

Vormand nodded. "*Zellbrigen* died with most of our unit in the Republic. Those of us who survive learned pragmatism, though there are some lines we will not cross."

Miles nodded and turned to Giovanna. "What about you, Captain? Where would you fall in all of this?"

"Depending on which of the two of us has the most combat experience, the executive officer slot would go to them. I've seen combat in five raids and survived. I also have formal military training courtesy of the Canopian government. I mean no disrespect when I ask about your experience."

Miles paused. "You have more than I do."

"Do you have any objections to me being the second-in-command?"

"I will not contest it, assuming my people agree to the merger."

**DEFENSE MINISTRY HEADQUARTERS**
**TIGHFIELD**
**SACKVILLE**
**DUCHY OF TAMARIND-ABBEY**
**FREE WORLDS LEAGUE**
**23 AUGUST 3149**

As they exited the Defense Ministry, the senior officers of three just-dissolved mercenary units stared up at their command 'Mechs. Each 'Mech had an identical paint scheme: red at the top, fading to orange in middle and tan at the bottom. They also sported an insignia of a Greek goddess resting a jade green sword on her shoulder.

"Those colors are really growing on me." Giovanna gestured at the 'Mechs. "What was the inspiration?"

"Querlaks," Miles replied. "They are native to Andiron, and we keep them as pets aboard the *Fancy*. We let them roam free because they eat all the pests. They also are good watch animals."

"Well, I am glad we all agreed so effortlessly on a unit paint scheme, insignia and name," Vormand said. "Especially the name. I could have seen that debate going on for days."

"What's not to love?" Giovanna responded cheerfully. "It's not a name that screams 'We're overcompensating' like 'Death Stalkers.' It's not a dull name that sounds like some bureaucrat had to name a bunch of units in a hurry and just gave us a number and unit type like 'Seventy-First Hussars.' It's poetic, and has a hint of mystery:

"The Strange Bedfellows."

# SEA*LIST ADS:
# THE ALMOTACEN ALMANAC

### STEPHEN TOROPOV

[Weekly bulletin from the Governing Board of the Almotacen Hiring Hall. Distributed via local network and hardcopy on Almotacen, the Hinterlands, 3 June 3152.]

## EMPLOYMENT OPPORTUNITIES

**Bouncers Wanted**

Looking for a bit of work between contracts? Security personnel needed for a venture to reclaim premises in the Wastes for a new saloon. Payment options include kroner , stock in the venture, or free drinks at the bar, the proportion of each negotiable. References from current or previous employer required, contact Chaz Turcol at the Third Street Boarding House.

**Golden Opportunity for Reputable MechWarriors**

Veteran freelancer seeks reliable lancemates for lucrative off-world contract. All arrangements are strictly above board. Transportation and equipment maintenance is to be provided by the client, climate on target world is balmy. Ideal candidates will own their own BattleMechs, display initiative, and be willing to follow orders without second-guessing, moralizing, or undermining unit discipline. Serious inquiries can be made at The Malacca Lounge after 11:00 p.m. Ask the barkeep for Georgette.

## PUBLIC NOTICE

The Twenty-First Centauri Peregrine Lancers, on authority of the Governing Board of the Almotacen Hiring Hall, hereby proclaim that the following individuals, corporations, and units have been found in flagrant and unwarranted breach of an honestly agreed and fairly-drafted contract:

- Fortuna Pannichello
- Gloria Pannichello
- Ford's Falcon-Killers
- Condorcet Commercial Enterprises, Incorporated
- Ernesto Calvin Condorcet, agent of the above organization
- Steven P. Frohnhoefer
- The Undead Battalion and all personnel confirmed to be in their employ

The above listed individuals and organizations are therefore to be considered *BANDITS*. They may not avail themselves of *ANY* services offered by the Almotacen Hiring Hall. Those engaged in contracts under the authority of the Almotacen Hiring Hall shall *NOT* enter into agreements or arrangements with them. Armed forces party to a contract brokered at the Almotacen Hiring Hall who encounter them on the field of battle are entitled to *FULL* salvage rights for any equipment retrieved after dispatching them. Honest business is the lifeblood of the Hiring Hall, and those that deal in bad faith should know there are consequences for dishonesty.

## LOCAL INTEREST

### Fostering Trade and Fine Cuisine

Buy your provisions in comfort at the DropPort District Agricultural Association weekly market! Browse selections including the finest off-world delicacies and bulk rates on prepackaged shelf-stable rations in comfort in our fully indoor facility away from the dusty Almotacen weather! Monthly memberships are only five Fox Credits; merchant's booth rentals, only fifty Fox Credits. Dues help pay for the market's many amenities, including complimentary produce scales, air filtration and conditioning, and security personnel. The DPDAA, bringing the bounty of the stars to your mess hall!

### Grudge Match

Tonight at the Training Fields, Grueber's Gorgons will face off against the Eighty-Third Medellin Minutemen in a lance-on-lance grudge match! These two units have been one-upping each other's simulator course scores for weeks and will finally come to blows! The battle will be joined at 2040 hours, books close ten minutes prior. Get your bets in and watch the action at one of six fine participating Pit Lake recreational establishments!

## Community Cooperative Supports You!

Support Almotacen's development and get the freshest possible foodstuffs by joining the Tramtown Native Farmer's Crop Share Association. Our open-air market is healthful and welcoming, and we specialize in supplying locally grown ingredients to the growing food service industry. Admission to weekly Market Days is free, guests may not bring firearms and DropPort District Agricultural Association (DPDAA) members will not be admitted. Interested in joining the Crop Share Association as a food supply specialist volunteer security officer? Speak to one of our friendly agronomists at the Future Farmers of Almotacen table by the entrance.

## LIMITED ENGAGEMENT!

Hear the most raucous ~ *SALURIAN HYPERSCREAM*~ ensemble in Coreward space also known as the Howler Monkeys mercenary company as they blow the doors off the *RANSACKED RANCH BAR AND GRILL* with pure sound! Recently arrived from a stint in the Barrens, the musical mercenary maestros are playing every night until a new contract sends the company out into the stars once more! You \*\***KNOW**\*\* they're gonna be snapped up soon, so this is an opportunity true \*\***HOWLERHEADS**\*\* can't afford to miss!

## PERSONAL MESSAGES

### To Hazel

I'm willing to forgive the unfortunate coolant incident if you'll forget the Ovan Slyack infestation. Let's get the band back together, never been a better time—and I've got a lead on where Banquo hid the haul from Esteros. If you're willing to talk, meet me on the south shore of Pit Lake at dawn in three days. I'll be off-world the day after. —Hans

### Missed Connections

**You:** the gorgeous redhead who pulled up to the 11:00 p.m. shadow puppetry show at the Malthus Mansion in your Swiftwind. **Me:** the Sea Fox merchant who called your bluff at the drax table after the show. If you are willing to try the whims of fortune again, meet me at the same table next Friday night—I have access to a shipment of fine plumberry wine that goes down best with a bold companion.

# EL DORADO

### CHRIS PURNELL

**KENNEDY BEACH**
**OBERON VI**
**OBERON CONFEDERATION**
**19 JANUARY 3020**

[**Interview IE-2930-A-Oberon:** Subject is Heinrich Sladik, a 43-year-old MechWarrior of Lyran citizenship. Membership in McCall's Legion confirmed via the Mercenary Review Board. Subject was previously employed by Richard's Panzer Brigade and Carson's Renegades. Interview was conducted at the Lying Bastard, a seaside tavern located at 5312 Beachside Lane in Kennedy Beach on Oberon VI. Subject was remunerated with a bottle of Grimm's Grim Spiced Rum. Subsequent expenditures for alcohol and *tapas* did not exceed fifty C-bills, and so were not itemized.]

"They actually care what happened to Captain McCall? Hahaha, fine, I'll tell you what happened out there but first, you better get me a bottle of grog to whet my whistle.

I'd joined up with Ernesto McCall back on Galatea after a bit of a disagreement with Big Daddy Whitman. I'd spent my savings, and was desperate to find a new command before the old ball and chain caught up to me. Captain McCall had a good reputation for paying his MechWarriors on time and getting choicy contracts. He was a baron, or at least he claimed to be, old Rim Worlds nobility out on Apollo. Maybe that's why he was able to dodge the company store scams in the FedSuns before he came back to recruit.

It was just the twelve of us, a full company of 'Mechs. But a full company in working order. He was smart to invest in having enough techs on hand. Big Daddy had cut some corners there, and it was showing by the time I left. He had a DropShip too, a *Union*-class in the best shape I'd ever seen that he called the *Rowe*. I expect that's what got his foot in the door with you people. Or maybe he'd already been involved with your lot, and that's why he had a DropShip in good repair. I dunno, he was a real charming fella and usually real open, but, looking back, he kept a lot of real details close to the chest.

My first deployment with the Legion was late 3015, just a garrison and training job on Toland. Real boring stuff, trying to get the local militia to shape up and sending the odd pirate raid packing. I can't say I was happy there, but at least there were some bars and local girls to keep things a bit fun now and then.

Captain McCall broke the news to us of the Interstellar Expeditions contract at the Christmas mess party. He thought all the booze and music and food would put us in a jolly mood, eh? I suppose it worked, since we got up and boarded the *Rowe* after the hangovers wore off. We were up and lifted off by the new year, 3017. We were to provide muscle for survey teams operating out in the coreward Periphery. And there were the usual rumors about a lost Star League cache circulating around.

You heard of El Dorado? I don't mean the FedSuns world, it's an idea they named that planet for. Back on old Terra, it was a city of gold, glimmering just out of reach for explorers. Every mercenary hobbling about the Periphery has this notion that, just maybe, there's some *lostech* cache they can find out there. A Castle Brian, a loaded-up Star League DropShip, or a bunch of Kerensky's old depots still filled with ancient 'Mechs. I'd have sure liked to replace my *Commando* with one of them fancy Star League models with a computer that could shoot for you and a toilet that would wipe your ass.

The difference between all those legends and hopes and dreams is that we found our El Dorado. That's what happened to McCall's Legion and why we disappeared, and God *damn* McCall for taking us out there!

It didn't start out all that bad. We'd spent six months outside Lyran space and covered a half-dozen system surveys with not a sign of anything or anyone. Just airless rocks and comets and dust in four of 'em. Only noteworthy thing we'd seen was one habitable planet with a half-built city on the shores of a continental lake. Dwight, that is Dwight Sanderson, our IE liaison, found out it was a colonization effort that'd been abandoned after the settlement company went bankrupt. They'd gotten around to stocking the lake with salmon, though, so at least we had some fine dinners.

Can't deny we were getting the itch when we first entered the Thebes system. That's what the locals call it. I don't remember the IE designation, and we were picking up broadcasts from the zenith point, so we started using the name among ourselves pretty quick.

First briefing was on the *Rowe* about a day after we jumped in. Captain McCall was in fine spirits. Dwight looked a little less happy, like the captain had talked him around on something, but not all the way.

We found out what that something was when he had the holoprojector display the second planet in the system. That's when he pulled up an old data slate he claimed was a family heirloom showing the same planet. Continents were all the same, it was labeled Thebes. Didn't have the system designation or jump coordinates though. He said he'd been looking for this planet the whole time, and that his family had held an estate on it back during the Rim World Republic days.

Dwight brought up some of the broadcasts we were picking up from the planet. Radio and analog TV signals confirmed the people there were still thinking of themselves as Rim Worlders. He said the overall tech level was pre-spaceflight, but with reference to some preserved technology dating at least from the early Star League.

The short of it was they were going to contact the planetary council and have the captain press his claim to the world. In the meantime, we were going to paint our 'Mechs flat black and add on some shark insignias. Yeah, everyone was guessing we'd just been enrolled in the Rim Worlds Army.

Can't say I cared too much. The Amaris Coup was centuries ago, and from what McCall was saying, his family had stashed a giant hoard of strategic metals on this world before it went down. It wasn't the SLDF cache we were all dreaming of, but he promised us enough germanium to make us all millionaires. Maybe we did have C-bills in our eyes clouding our judgment, I s'pose.

We landed the *Rowe* outside the capital city, after McCall and Dwight had spent some time negotiating with the locals. They called the city Alexandria. Went with some weird classical white marble motif and an open-air plaza where they handled official meetings and such. Couldn't have been more than fifty thousand inhabitants, maybe a million people on the planet all told. They were still driving around in fusion-powered cars though, even if they looked like they'd come out of some historical documentary from the Age of War.

So, you're wondering why we didn't just take what we wanted? I mean, first of all, we were mercenaries, not pirates. Second, you know all that rot about how a company of BattleMechs can conquer a world? Yeah sure, if a Great House has a couple regiments of infantry following up on them. It was just the twelve of us and our 'Mechs and the *Rowe*, out there in the middle of nowhere. And if the captain's words were true, we'd need to stick around a while to load everything up. I didn't care to spend all my time inside my *Commando*, worried some local would stab me to death if I stepped out.

Hell, we wanted to enjoy the place after all that time cooped up. And they threw us a great party after we presented ourselves. Lots of *raki* and fresh fruit and real meat and vegetables, and that night they hosted us at a temple-looking building that was actually a dance club. Marty, that's Martin Singh, God rest his soul, brought out his Regulan techno-fusion record collection and the locals all loved it. We all had a great time.

McCall and Dwight spent that time talking with the planetary council. Headed by an old biddy named Theodora. From what I heard, she seemed relieved we weren't pirates and was charmed by McCall. Well, not the only person ever charmed by him. He spun them a tale about how he was going to use his troops and resources to drive the Commonwealth off Apollo and restore the Republic. They ate that bullshit up. Seems they'd been hoping for a savior ever since they'd been cut off by the war. Usually, it's planets pining for the Star League instead, but it's common enough out in the Periphery.

Now, we weren't stupid. Marty, he was one lance commander, I commanded one, and Ginny Westlake commanded the other, and we all insisted we go see this estate of the baron as soon as possible. The captain obliged, we borrowed a nice car and took it about an hour's drive out of Alexandria. I was surprised to see the estate was still intact and cared for by the planetary government. And, sure enough, there was a warehouse on the grounds full of valuables. Not just germanium, but also gold and silver, gemstones, and the like. There was also a navigation core in the library of the estate which had just been sitting there, unopened, for a couple hundred years.

McCall used his heirloom dataslate to open up the core and it pulled up a bunch of coordinates of systems around Thebes. Other planets suitable for settlement, where Amaris hid depots and caches of weapons for some kind of guerrilla fight. No telling if any of them were intact or not, but we started getting even greedier. If that devil Stefan had stashed away some of his Star League 'Mechs or technology, we could have gotten away as billionaires, not just millionaires.

We should have just taken the money and left.

It all started to go tits-up soon after. The first bit of bad business came a week later. The captain had started living out of the estate and we were summoned over from the *Rowe* one evening on an emergency. He sent a bunch of cars to pick us up, all hush-hush like. He had us assemble in a conference room, just the Legion staff, none of his techs or DropShip crew. That's when he dropped the bombshell that Dwight was dead.

I don't know what happened and I never did find out for sure. Captain McCall said he'd had a heart attack that morning and passed away before medical staff from the city could arrive. I dunno, Sanderson was a bit high-strung, but seemed like he was in pretty good shape to me. I'm not saying the Cap'n killed him, now. I don't know. But he was real anxious that our IE JumpShip not get the news. He said he was afraid they might jump out of the system and head back to Lyran space and leave us stranded.

Now, the survey team from IE had already started work in Alexandria, so I don't know how he thought he could keep it from them for long. He somehow managed to fob off the captain of that JumpShip for a solid two weeks anyway. But the survey team packed up and left back to their own civvie *Mule* afterward and, as soon as they docked, they left the system. We weren't happy about that to say the least, though McCall told us they were just going to survey one of the RWR caches from the data core. I didn't really believe him then, given how that whole thing with Dwight's death played out, but if we were stuck, we were stuck, and wasn't anything anyone could do about it.

After being marooned, we had to get a lot more involved with the planetary council. They'd already agreed that McCall was the noble liege of the world by right of inheritance. Now, what they'd set up to run the planet was an elected council of thirteen members, who elected a head from among their own number. Theodora had been president of the council, and she was the one really working with McCall, but they weren't unanimous welcoming us in. A small group were kind of standoffish or even hostile, despite swearing loyalty to the captain as their lord.

One of 'em, a councilman named Stefan, named after that pig Amaris himself, was probing us with questions all the time. Shoulda killed that bastard earlier, but the captain said he wanted to be 'clement,' like the Caesars of old, he said. That got old Jules gunned down in the Vatican for all the pardons he gave, but he was the boss, so what he said went. We toed the line and kept our mouths shut when the locals like him asked us for details about the Inner Sphere. But he found ways to get some people to talk, the clever little rat. But that only became a problem later.

The problem then was the captain getting a little too big for his britches. He was letting the "liege this," "my lord" that go to his head. He didn't make us call him Your Highness, but he started putting on the airs of a monarch instead of a mercenary commander. He even held a big coronation at the Forum in Alexandria, where we had to line up and parade in our 'Mechs for the crowd. Theodora even crowned him with some golden leaves like some philosopher in the ancient history vids Ginny liked watching.

And the speech he gave sure was something. He claimed he was going to become the Consul of a new Republic once he secured the rest of his inheritance. That the oppressed peoples of the Lyran Periphery remembered their roots in the Rim Worlds and were ready for someone to come liberate them. That the Star League was dead and would stay dead, so it was time for the Rim Worlds to rise again. They really ate that bullshit up. Seemed like the whole damn city was crammed into the Forum or watching from the streets outside and the applause was loud as thunder, even inside my 'Mech.

Me and Ginny called him out once we got back to his estate. He said he was just playing to the crowd. That he didn't mean it, but he had to keep the local rubes on side until the JumpShip returned. He clasped me by the arm and said he was just trying to buy a little time. That in a few months we'd be in the VIP boxes at Solaris enjoying the high life.

But then he had us give a briefing to the Council about his plans. Real fantasy stuff there. He'd highlighted the Rim World caches and told them once he could secure enough ships, he could outfit a whole division of 'Mechs. He'd recruit a brand-new Republican Guard from Thebes and some other systems nearby, liberate Apollo, and spark uprisings in the surrounding systems. He talked about hiring Wolf's Dragoons and signing an alliance with House Kurita and House Marik to keep the Lyrans off our backs as we rebuilt the Rim Worlds. Hell, he halfway convinced me he was serious and even had a chance, not that I liked the talk of treason against the Archon.

Of course, they didn't know who the hell the Dragoons were, and I expect that was well enough, 'cause I doubt they'd have responded well to the name of the Black Widow, ha ha ha ha!

But everyone on the Council seemed satisfied, even that dog Stefan, so they turned the militia over to us to train up.

"Consul" McCall even formed a *leibgarde* from a bunch of the locals who swore direct allegiance to him. Which, fair enough, a 'Mech company makes for bad bodyguards no matter how it works at the Court on Tharkad. But I felt like he was getting a bit too out of touch with the company with all the scraping and bowing he had going on around him. And while training the locals kept us and them busy, it turned out that was a terrible idea all around. We could only show them just enough to get themselves killed on a battlefield while making them organized enough to act as a single unit elsewhere.

No prizes for seeing what was coming there.

There was a bit of a lull following the coronation, though. Things seemed almost nice for a bit. The captain was playing king, and we were looking to our own interests. Marty got himself a sweetheart among the locals and a side-gig of sorts as a deejay at the local club. Ginny kept herself busy taking over day-to-day running of the company. And as for me, I took up fishing most afternoons. Caught myself a whopper of a bass one evening as a personal best. My lance had fish-fries down on the lakeside just about every weekend with plenty of booze and a roaring bonfire. Life was pretty good, is what I was saying.

We still hadn't heard anything about the JumpShip, though, and it was making the spacers anxious. The crew of the *Rowe* was discouraged from going into town or having too much to do with the locals even after McCall crowned himself. I suppose he thought that would keep the Council reliant on him if they ever wanted out of orbit, but after a while, the techs and crewmen started sneaking out into Alexandria. That's when one of 'em turned out a lot less discreet than Marty was with his gal, and it came to bite us all in the ass. And it all came crashing down on top of us right after we'd had a band of pirates beat the shit out of us.

That was the fifth of January, right after we'd celebrated the new year. The locals treated that like their biggest holiday, and we'd gone along, so I was coming off a week-long bender. Had just drank a bottle of beer in my quarters for a bit of the hair of the dog to get my headache under control when I got the call to get my ass over to the *Rowe*, along with my MechWarriors. That took an hour or so to round everyone up, and I can't say it was a pleasant experience.

Once we got there, we were rushed into the briefing room. Captain McCall had got there ahead of us. I already knew it was serious business 'cause he'd left all the routine up to Ginny as his second-in-command. We got some brief greetings before he turned on the holotank and let us know a JumpShip had entered the system, and it wasn't IE. Given the state of things, we expected that meant pirates because who the hell else would be out here, the damned Star League Defense Force and mad old General Kerensky?

They didn't bother hailing us or sending any demands, so we got busy getting the defenses ready. We gave the locals a rough and ready course where they could put a satchel charge into a 'Mech to really ruin its day. Didn't have high hopes for that, but they did far more than I ever expected. But not against those damned pirates.

So, I was in command of the recon lance of the Legion. I had myself in my *Commando*, Julien Chen in his *Vindicator*, Amy Bonet in her *Firestarter*, and Maksim Fedorov in his *Jenner*. I ran a pretty tight ship as lance sergeant, though I'd have to admit we'd been out of the cockpit too much after arriving on Thebes. Marty led the strike lance with his *Rifleman*, and Ginny was effectively commanding the heavy lance from her *Orion*. They would have been down a 'Mech because "Consul" McCall rarely took the field, but that day he was out in his *Zeus*, so we were at full strength.

We thought we were fortunate when the pirates descended well up north of Alexandria, at least until the captain realized they were headed straight for his estate. So, we hauled ass up to meet 'em, with his precious *leibgarde* dug in around the warehouses to protect the goods. We were about an hour from contact when we got our first look at what we were up against, and for a moment, I thought we'd wipe the floor with them.

I never did find out whose band they were with, I'll say upfront. There was a company of 'Mechs, backed up with some armor and at least a couple battalions of infantry. They were painted olive green with no insignia. Near as anyone ever figured out, they must have taken our JumpShip and learned about what we were doing, so they were screwing with us by taking the SLDF colors. But they were pirates, and we were mercenaries. Didn't leave any question who'd win in our minds.

By the time I made contact with their lead, one whole lance of the enemy had dragged itself off across the two other lances. *What a real shitshow,* I thought, *they couldn't even keep their elements together.* But what I didn't count on, what none of us could have imagined, is they had an entire fragging *company* of Gray Notons!

I'm not exaggerating. I'd pulled my lance up in a solid position covered by wooded hills running north-south parallel to the main road running to the capital. I stepped my *Commando* out to get a better look at what we were facing from nearly a klick out and barely had any time to take it in before I started taking laser fire. I called them out as fools, but they didn't close the range that far before the first alarms started going off as I lost armor. Chen tried to engage at range with his PPC as I stumbled back, but he was on the losing end of the exchange, and we were outnumbered six to four, so we fell back. I had Amy torch the woods to provide us some smoke to get back to meet up with the rest of the company.

Yeah, maybe you're thinking I was a coward? Well let me tell you something. Ain't nothing that any captain or colonel or First Lord can pay you to make up for being Dispossessed. My family thought naming a 'Mech was foolishness, but that *Commando* had been in our line for a hundred years and the meal ticket for my father's father onward. If you haven't piloted a 'Mech for years, experienced all the feedback possible from a neurohelmet, felt the rush as you gambled your life against the heat capacity of—oh, never mind. But that emptiness lasts and there's nothing that can fill it, no matter how you try.

So, we fell back. Let the pirates run into the main force. Felt sure Ginny and the captain would send them off with our heavy metal.

But as we pulled out of the woods, we saw a couple of *Stingray*s zooming overhead before breaking into a slash into the middle of the company. Marty's *Rifleman* was the only real anti-air we had, so he tried engaging them, which just drew their full attention. I saw the PPC beam lance right through his torso and set off all his ammo. He still had most of it left, so his 'Mech was blown sky-high before his lance even engaged those pirate 'Mechs coming after us. Can't say that left

us feeling too confident and it was even worse when I realized I hadn't seen him punch out before the blast.

There's not really a whole lot more to it. Captain McCall moved all of us up into the woods to try a short-range melee, where we thought they'd be disorganized. They were, but it didn't really matter. They were just better than us. I dunno where a whole goddamned stable of Solaris stars came out from to wreck our day, but that's what happened.

Captain McCall, I'll give him this, was the last one of us out of that furball. He stood at the edge and fought the pirate lord. His *Zeus* against the pirate *Thug*, well, plus some buddies of the pirate. He lost and punched out. I lost Maksim covering me as I ran back under fire to pick him up in my *Commando*'s one hand, and when I finally pulled out, half my armor display was in the red.

They were between us and the McCall estate, so we just ran west until we finally broke contact for good. The pirates didn't bother chasing us. They knew what they were about and sacked the estate good. Killed the whole *leibgarde*, too. They fought to the bitter end for the Rim Worlds. I wish they'd just fled.

We spent about two weeks waiting out while those pirates completely wrecked the estate. I'd never seen such thorough destruction before. Less of a sack than a controlled demolition. They packed up everything of value, set off their charges, and drove off back to their DropShips. All that money, the navigation core, just about everything we'd come here for was lost except some germanium we'd already loaded aboard the *Rowe*. Captain McCall was real quiet the whole time, but there wasn't anything we could do but watch our dreams die.

After they finally left, we stopped by the estate site to see what we could salvage, but there was nothing. It'd been picked clean. At least they bothered to deal with the corpses, we wouldn't have had the manpower for a mass grave. We were eight MechWarriors with six operational 'Mechs, counting my *Commando* that had more holes than armor left. And we had to slink back into Alexandria. We weren't exactly expecting a warm welcome there either.

We saw "Consul" McCall return on the reentry into his capital. He'd been in touch with Theodora and set up a Council meeting at the Forum where he'd try to win the city back over. I thought he was out of his mind, maybe the loss of his *Zeus* had pushed him over the edge. At that point, with Marty dead and Ginny out of commission, I was effectively leading what was left of the company. I went behind his back a bit, made sure Amy and Julien were ready to intervene in their 'Mechs if things went bad.

The meeting didn't go bad, it started bad and got worse. The forum was packed with locals, and they booed McCall as he entered with us.

Seemed they weren't too keen on seeing us again after we'd gotten the best and brightest of the locals killed off at the estate.

Theodora was up there at the speaking platform, forming a solid phalanx with the rest of the Council, impassive as could be. But that rat bastard Stefan was just beaming with puffed up pride and I knew he had some kind of trick on hand. We saw what as soon as McCall stepped up to the podium to try to address everyone and was halted by the sergeant-at-arms.

Stefan took the floor first and called out for a squad of militia to bring up their guest. They had a bosun from the *Rowe* in tow, in chains. Stupid bastard had been with one of Stefan's honeypots when the pirates landed. Pretty obvious he'd been beaten and tortured, but they brought him up to the podium anyway and had him claim McCall was a liar and a fraud. That he wasn't even really Ernesto McCall.

To hear the bosun tell it, the *Rowe* had been purchased and outfitted in the FedSuns in 3009 as the *Freebooter* by one Ernesto Chavez. That being Captain McCall at the time. He had some corporate shares on New Syrtis that provided him income that let him buy out the title of a dead family line on Apollo. That had come with all the assets of the Barony of McCall, including the dataslate and all the information about Thebes. He'd just changed his last name to his barony and started masquerading as a direct descendant of the last true Baron of McCall.

Now, our captain could be an enigma, but I know a Lyran accent when I hear it and he spoke German like some overeducated Tharkad aristo. I'm not sure of the truth, mind, but it was pretty obvious Stefan had gotten his confession out by torturing the poor sap. Captain McCall raised the same objection, shouting loud enough to be heard over all the swoons from our audience. Called Stefan the liar and a jealous such and such who just wanted to seize power himself and betray the Rim Worlds and so on.

That was when Theodora stepped up and asked the captain a simple question. What, she said, was the meaning behind the central device of the McCall coat of arms?

McCall confidently answered that the oak tree was a symbol of strength and resilience with deep roots that kept it from being toppled, even by the strongest winds. Seemed like a good answer to me, but it was wrong.

It was the acorn in the coat of arms that was the real central device. A proof of the seed of Amaris that would regenerate and be reborn in due time. McCall was either a fraud or his family had forgotten their real origins in the mists of time. Either way, she said, they owed him no loyalty.

I could see where this was going, so I dialed in Amy and Julien to get in ASAP.

The crowd was going nuts and starting to toss garbage at us, and the militia squad on the stage was moving to arrest us. I had a foldout needler though and shot first while trying to push Captain McCall and the rest of our group out. That started a panic, and it was sheer chaos once the militia started shooting again. I thought they'd missed and some of their shots went into the crowd and caused a stampede. We would have been blocked out, but fortunately Amy arrived and no one felt like taking on a *Firestarter* while we ran out under it.

The militia was still shooting at us though, so Amy covered our withdrawal. Well, if you've smelled burning human flesh once, you've smelled it enough. I think that's all I need to say about that.

We were almost free and clear when some asshole on the seats nailed the captain with a beer bottle. They made 'em strong there, strong enough the bottle didn't even shatter. He went limp right away and I had to drag him out to the escape car. Julien was out there on overwatch, and no one wanted to tangle with a 'Mech, so we could load him up and zoom away on a rendezvous with the *Rowe*.

The captain never woke up; he went into a coma and died three days later, leaving me more or less in charge of what was left of the company.

The council of Thebes declared us bandits, and maybe we were at that point. We had to eat, and they weren't going to feed us willingly. The militia couldn't come close to taking us head-on, so we could take requisitions where and when we wanted. But I got sloppy about four months in. Militia pulled off a decent ambush when we moved into the suburbs of Alexandria. One of them put a satchel charge right where I'd showed them to, in the knee actuator of my *Commando*. And that's how I joined the ranks of the Dispossessed.

We got lucky a couple months later when a new band of pirates landed. These guys were uh—completely unaffiliated with my current employers in Oberon, but very reasonable. They were disappointed the estate was so thoroughly looted, but we had a haul of germanium in our hold, and they had a JumpShip collar open. All we had to do was stand aside as they sacked Alexandria. And they did that, boy did they ever. The damned Forum was rubble by the time we—they finished.

We happened across Stefan fleeing the city, and I'll just say we gave him what he deserved.

Our new acquaintances kept their word. We gave them the germanium, they let us get off that cursed planet. The crew of the *Rowe* elected to sign up with the pirates, but they were kind enough to let us get off at Oberon VI first. From there we all went our separate ways, and I don't really know where the rest of the survivors are now. Probably for the best.

There's a lot that happened I still don't know what to make of it. But I'll never forgive Captain McCall for not taking the germanium and just heading right back to the Inner Sphere when we still had the chance. I'm sure Dwight and your IE people could have been convinced too. But he just let that Consul business go to his head. He wound up dead, and I'm a washed-up instructor out here on Oberon.

Getting a bit morose now, ain't I? It's the rum and the sunset. But I reckon we're at the end of the story, and I've got places to be."

[**Interview Postscript:** McCall's Legion was hired December 3016 to provide security for the Sanderson Expedition to former Rim World Republic space. IE registered JumpShip *Trailhead* was provided for transportation. The expedition disappeared, and was presumed lost with all hands in a mis-jump in 3018. This account by a MechWarrior previously part of McCall's Legion provides an alternative possibility that bears further investigation.]

# WILL SCHEDULE IT FOR YOU: COMBINED ARMS TECHS & ASTECHS

### ED STEPHENS

## TECH/ASTECH COMPENSATION REVIEW: DECEMBER 3151

**To:** Commander James Northey, Battleaxe Co.
**From:** Executive Officer Gil Dawson

Commander, please find below the requested report of my findings on Kandersteg, based on your orders to "Ask around, talk to the lads, ladies, and others in all the repair bays, make sure we're taking care of our techs." I have arranged the report into bullets of salient points for your ease of consumption.

### Hazard Pay Continues to be Indispensable
A recurring theme I heard was "I can earn in a year what would take me ten to earn back home." Every world today needs skilled techs to rebuild and maintain equipment, so aside from getting away from home, why would anyone join a mercenary company to do the same job but elsewhere? I recommend we continue to offer baseline pay as just enough for basic expenses, with generous hourly hazard-pay rates for any work done in an active conflict zone. Note: I emphasize the word "generous": if we retain techs who have a great deal of experience on *our* equipment, we have a competitive advantage.

### Recurring Equipment Training for Users Could Pay Dividends
I talked to several commiserating infantry techs. It seems the X791 Tactical Infantry Helmet (more commonly referred to as the

"Steiner Clam") loses its anti-personnel laser reflective coating when used to cook a can of Uncle Bill's Magic Beans over a fire. The techs also had on the wall a list of infantry gear that should *NOT* be used as a hammer, which included rifle butts, rifle muzzles, rifle receivers, rifle sights—actually, any rifle parts—magres goggles, canteens, satcom radios, mortar tubes, and of all things, dog tags. It seems possible we could save costs in equipment replacement if our infantry were trained in proper usage and maintenance of their equipment. The techs also recommended I look into wax drawing sticks for the infantry battalion; however, I was unable to ascertain their intended combat purpose.

### Loyalty Is Not Necessarily Expensive

One of the less colorful groups of technicians I spoke with had recently terminated their employment with a mercenary company due to, of all things, a disagreement on pronunciation. They were a group of techs specializing in Wing-in-Ground-Effect vehicles.

They argued, at length, despite my lack of disagreement, that since "G" stands for "Ground," it must be pronounced with a hard "G." Thus the acronym must be pronounced *WHY-Geeh*. You will find their names and perscomm IDs at the end of this report; they have agreed to an interview, but only if we use correct pronunciation. It seems they are more than willing to hire on for reasonable rates (despite WiGE techs not being easy to come by), provided we pay them with the simple respect they ask.

### Total Benefits Package: Support and Counselling

I believe it would be prudent to ensure our staff has access to the appropriate level of mental health counseling and support. My encounter with the crew and techs for a competitor's Pike (the plasma cannon variant) was something I will never forget. They sat in a circle around a bar table, staring with dead eyes, as they took bets on who could hold their hand over a pocket soldering torch the longest. As far as I'm concerned, they all won: the smell was unforgettable. I imagine witnessing firsthand the horrors that can be unleashed on an infantry platoon with the weapons you maintain, which can tend to cause issues.

### Reduction in ChemTest Stringencies

Before explaining this point, I feel it bears repeating that you ordered me to mingle with the local crews.

I spent an evening with the lead techs of the Kandersteg Militia DI Multipurpose VTOL wing. (Of note, militias on Kandersteg appear to be procuring the DI en masse to transport squads of Hantu armored infantry for shock deployment, a concept I thought you might find familiar).

The last thing I remember was the lead tech, Mario, opening his third case of 4 C's cider. When I was finally awoken several hours after reveille by the militia MPs, I found the DI techs had already been at work for many hours, none the worse for wear. They seemed to find my discomfort amusing.

We may consider a performance-based ChemTest compliance program, as opposed to one strictly based on numbers. The militia DI VTOLs were in nothing but tip-top condition.

### Wars Have Been Fought for Less

One of the local legends making the rounds in the hiring halls here is of a nearby engagement between two mercenary companies—fighting over a crew of techs and astechs who specialize specifically in the Saxon APC. Legend has it this crew is able to fabricate hover inducer coils better than the originals, shortening lift and drop times to hasten redeployment in the field. Apparently, Primal Company attempted an assault on the encampment of the Mongrel Machine with the intent of capturing this crew for their own employ.

Now, as our dependents are fully aware (given that every year or two they're captured and held hostage by some faction or another), our noncombatants are a weakness in our company. We should review our list of crews and make note of any potential targets of opportunity for our competitors.

### Final Thoughts

I hope you find these observations helpful, Commander, and I commend you for your concern for these most vital members of our company. One final thing I observed was this: nearly every vehicle shop I entered had—on the wall, placed as one would place a shrine of devotion—an old and tattered notice proclaiming, *"If you do not schedule time for maintenance, your equipment will schedule it for you."*

# CHAOS CAMPAIGN SCENARIO: RAINMAKER

## ERIC SALZMAN

*It is as was prophesied! The heavens shall open in all their glory and bring life! The sands shall bloom and prosper!*

—Leicester Benedikt, Council of Water

*Yeah, about those malfin' "prophecies"...leave me out of 'em!*

—Colonel Joshua Snord, Snord's Irregulars

At the height of the Star League, the Department of Mega-Engineering (DoME) achieved renown for its almost unfathomable feats of terraforming.

In 2754, DoME set its sights on the Rim Worlds Republic planet of Butte Hold. The thinly populated, lawless desert world was deemed a suitable testbed for a new terraforming program, with no oversight from the planetary government and an expendable local population. With SLDF forces providing security against bandit raids, DoME began construction in the depths of the Throline Desert.

The Periphery Uprising and subsequent Star League Civil War forced the cancellation of DoME's efforts. Decades of catastrophic warfare destroyed project records, and a massive sandstorm buried the equipment, leaving no traces. Local legends told of a vast treasure buried beneath the sands, and half-remembered promises made by DoME engineers were passed down as prophecy.

In 3149, Interstellar Expeditions dispatched an archaeological team to Butte Hold, seeking the DoME installation. Given the region's reputation for banditry, IE contracted mercenaries as security for the dig. In 3151, Snord's Irregulars were on duty at the Throline excavation when the archaeologists made a breakthrough, uncovering the command module. As they worked to restore power and run diagnostics on the centuries-dormant device, long-range sensors detected an inbound Hell's Horses force.

Colonel Joshua Snord took part of his forces to intercept the Clan raiders, hoping to buy time for the archaeologists to evacuate the dig site. What he didn't count on was the team accidentally activating the *lostech* terraforming machinery in their haste to depart.

## TOUCHPOINT: STATIC SHOCK

This scenario can be played as a stand-alone game or incorporated into a longer campaign using the *Chaos Campaign* rules (available as a free download from https://store.catalystgamelabs.com/products/battletech-chaos-campaign-succession-wars).

For flexibility of play, this track contains rules for *Total Warfare* (*TW*) and Tactical Operations: Advanced Rules (*TO:AR*), with *Alpha Strike: Commander's Edition* (*AS* or *AS:CE*) rules noted in parenthesis, allowing the battle to be played with either rule set.

## SITUATION

**THROLINE DESERT**
**BUTTE HOLD**
**NEW OBERON CONFEDERATION**
**18 JANUARY 3151**

Pursuing Oberon Confederation raiders that had eluded capture in the Republic of the Barrens, the Sixteenth Hellraiser Trinary followed a false lead that brought them to Butte Hold's Throline Desert. Finding only an Interstellar Expeditions archaeology team and their mercenary security forces, Star Captain Borjigin took umbrage at the mercenary commander's mockery and ordered his Trinary to engage and destroy the Inner Sphere sellswords, intending to win a quick battle against inferior foes, then claim the archaeologists and their discovery as *isorla* for the Hell's Horses. When the ancient *lostech* device activated, Borjigin's Trinary found itself in a fight for its life against both the mercenaries and the very ground beneath their feet.

## GAME SETUP

*Recommended Terrain:* Barren Lands #1 (Clan Invasion Box), Barren Lands #2 (Clan Invasion Box).

Lay out the mapsheets with their narrow edges touching. The Attacker (Clan Hell's Horses) selects one narrow edge as their Home Edge, and the Defender (Snord's Irregulars) designates the other narrow edge as their Home Edge. The Attacker enters from their Home Edge at the start of Turn 1. The Defender may begin deployed anywhere within five hexes of their Home Edge.

### Attacker

*Recommended Forces*: Sixteenth Hellraiser Trinary (Eleventh Mechanized Cavalry Cluster), Clan Hell's Horses.

The Attacker consists of 100 percent of the Defender's strength, with one OmniMech Star, one Vehicle Star, and one Battle Armor Star. If desired, players may roll on the Hell's Horses RAT in *Tamar Rising*, pp. 122–124. Star Captain Borjigin pilots a *Doom Courser*.

### Defender

*Recommended Forces*: Snord's Irregulars.

The Defender consists of four BattleMech lances comprising 100 percent of the Attacker's strength. Joshua Snord pilots an HGN-732b *Highlander*, and his XO, Elizabeth Sneede, pilots her RFL-3N (*Sneede II*) *Rifleman* FrankenMech. For the rest, players may roll on the Mercenary RAT in *Tamar Rising*, p. 118.

## WARCHEST
**Track Cost**: 1,000

## OPTIONAL BONUSES

**+500 Ride the Storm (Defender Only):** The activation of the *lostech* device has brought a sudden and unexpected storm to the Throline Desert. Heavy Rainfall (see *TO: AR*, p. 57 or *AS: CE*, p. 58) conditions apply.

**+500 Bring the Thunder (Attacker Only):** The Defender has access to two Sniper artillery pieces located at the dig site, five mapsheets away (see *TO: AR*, pp. 147–154 or *AS: CE*, p. 47).

## OBJECTIVES

**Bring Me His Head:** Disable/Destroy the Enemy Commander (Borjigin/Joshua). **[750]**

**Run The Gauntlet (Attacker Only):** Each Attacker unit exiting the Defender's Home Edge Before Turn 10. **[100]**

**Fighting Retreat (Defender Only):** Each Defender unit exiting the Defender's Home Edge on or after Turn 10. **[100]**

## SPECIAL RULES

### The Great Machine Awakens!

At the start of each turn, the Defending player rolls 1D6. This represents the number of hazards that will activate following the Movement phase that turn. Once movement is complete, repeat the following steps a number of times equal to the number rolled at the start of the turn.

If using hexless terrain, do the following: Each player rolls 2D6, re-rolling ties. The player with the higher number measures that many inches from their Home Edge, and the player with the lower number measures that many inches from a side edge of their choice. The hazard appears where the two measurements intersect, affecting a 2" radius around the intersection.

If using Hex Maps, do the following:

1) The Defender and Attacker each roll 3D6. Whichever has the higher total will place the hazard marker on the map where their Home Edge is located. Re-roll ties.

2) Subtract 2 from the lowest total; this will represent the first two numbers in the hexagon coordinate selected.

Example: Rolling a 2, 3, and 1 would total 06. Subtracting 2 identifies column 04 as the target hex.

3) Subtract 2 from the highest total; this will represent the last two numbers in the hexagon coordinate selected.

Example: Rolling a 4, 6, and 5 would total 15. Subtracting 2 identifies row 13 as the target hex. Combined with the above, the hazard will appear in Hex 0413.

4) If there is already a hazard at that location, it deactivates. Remove the marker.

5) If there is no hazard at that location, roll 1D6 and consult the following table:

1: Pit—A Depth 3 (*AS*: 3") pit opens abruptly. Any unit in the affected area suffers a Level 3 Fall (see *TW* pp. 68–69). (*AS*: Apply 1 damage from the fall. To move out of the location, the unit will need to ascend a 3" incline.)

2: Pylon—A Level 3 (*AS*: 3") pylon rises out of the desert floor, with a CF of 120 (*AS*: CF 12). Any unit in the affected area must make a Piloting Skill Roll at a +2 TN penalty or suffer a Level 1 Fall (see *TW*, pp. 68–69), being displaced randomly (roll 1D6) to an adjacent hex. (*AS*: Automatically apply 1 damage.) Units successfully making the roll will remain standing atop the pylon.

3: Hot Spot—Intense heat radiates from the ground, adding 10 Heat (*AS*: 1 Heat Level) to any unit in the affected area.

4: Explosion—A system fault causes an explosion. BattleMechs suffer 2D6 damage (*AS*: 1 point of damage) to their legs in five-point clusters; vehicles suffer the same amount of damage to their Rear.

5: Bolt From the Blue—Stormclouds gather over the battlefield, and a massive lightning strike envelops the affected area, dealing 10 points of damage (*AS*: 1 point of damage) to all units there (see *TO: AR,* p. 57 if you want to randomize the damage using the Lightning Bolt Table).

6: Smoke—A plume of Heavy Smoke (see *TO: AR*, pp. 45–46 or *AS: CE*, p. 167) erupts from underground vents.

### You Must Evade Additional Pylons

At the end of the Weapon Attack phase, if any elevated pylons are within fifteen hexes (*AS*: 30") of other elevated pylons, great electrical arcs crackle between them, dealing 10 points of damage (*AS*: 1 point of damage) to the front arc of any units in hexes (*AS*: or in a 2"-wide band) between the two pylons. Once made, the connection remains active until a pylon is destroyed, and any units entering the affected area will immediately take 10 damage (*AS*: 1 point of damage) to their front arc. Jumping over the affected area avoids the hazard.

## AFTERMATH

The Irregulars intercepted the attacking Horses, who had come fruitlessly seeking Oberon Confederation bandits and were happy to take out their frustrations on the mercenaries. Neither side expected the desert around them to suddenly come alive with partially functional, long-dormant *lostech*. Leading his forces in a fighting retreat through the increasingly hostile battlefield, Snord was able to hold the Horses back until the region became lethally impassable, enabling the Irregulars to fall back to the relatively quiet dig site and evacuate with the Interstellar Operations team, leaving the surviving Horses to fight their way free and return to their own vessel.

The *lostech* terraforming device ionized the atmosphere over a large section of the Throline Desert and generated a colossal low-pressure system that drew in moisture from the surrounding seas, unleashing a hurricane-strength storm and causing unprecedented flooding of the desert wastes, drowning the dig site under a small new inland sea. The storms eventually subsided, enabling the Council of Water to evaluate whether the region's weather patterns have been permanently affected.

# WHERE I BELONG

## TOM LEVEEN

**CRATER TOWN
GALATEA VI
FEDERATED COMMONWEALTH
6 JUNE 3047**

The woman lounging in the cockpit of the *Enforcer* could have been mistaken for a man, which suited her fine. Each line on her weathered face told a story, blending effortlessly with scars, such that one could not be distinguished from the other. Only yesterday she'd re-shaved her gray-blond hair into her standard flattop, a style she'd kept since her warring days.

Her eyes were closed behind yellow glasses she wore whenever she was awake; glare was a big issue for her these last few years. Black buds tucked into her ears played a mix of ancient classical music. Tonight: Dvořák. Her feet, clad in oil-resistant boots, tapped out rhythms on the 'Mech's front console, her desert camouflage pants crinkling softly with each motion.

The cockpit canopy was open and she could hear her boss, Devin, shouting up at her. She ignored him. She was on break, dammit.

"Hey, grandma! Milly!"

Milly, keeping her eyes closed and a half smile on her face, lifted both middle fingers and conducted an invisible symphony with them down toward Devin's voice. She wasn't a technical magician like that old, bald asshole John-Michael Glass, but Milly knew Devin liked her best. Nobody here in the former Sheepdog Mercenary stable had more years in and around BattleMechs than Milly. No one alive, anyway.

Devin's head appeared over the edge of the cockpit. He wasn't smiling. "Milly, I just need a thumbs up on this 'Mech's nav system, is it done or not?"

Milly scowled and yanked the buds from her ears. Sitting up in the command couch, she rasped, "The panel's on, isn't it? My tools are put away, aren't they? Get a life, boss."

Devin was ten years her junior and it showed in his brown eyes. He could be a hard-ass when the situation called for it, mostly with the younger techs in the Sheepdog bay. With thirty years of warfare and another three on Solaris under her belt, Milly didn't frighten easily. She gave Devin full marks for his tech skill with BattleMechs, but the kid hadn't seen real shit. Just the game battles played in the town's namesake crater arena.

"You've been up here for thirty minutes," Devin said, theatrically scanning the console for any sign the *Enforcer* wasn't ready to roll.

"Then I've been on break for thirty minutes. Go ahead, test it."

"I'll have Joel take a look. Come on down, you got another job."

"Ah, shit, Devin."

"You're always griping about working in a bay, so I'm giving you what you always wanted, Milly."

He scaled down the ladder as Milly turned off her music and followed. "You're giving me this *Enforcer*? How generous!"

Devin stepped aside as Milly hiked down, landing with a soft groan. Her lower back wasn't what it used to be, and her left knee felt more like a stone mortar and pestle, grinding away whatever cartilage remained.

"How about a truck?" Devin said, walking her toward the enormous 'Mech bay doors, which were rolled up to admit the fading light of sunset. Milly worked graveyard, a holdover from her Solaris fights.

Milly rooted around in her pockets for her cigarettes and matches. She lit one and blew smoke only a little bit away from Devin's face. "What are you talking about?"

Devin gestured toward the four enormous, six-wheeled flatbed trucks fifty meters away, being driven out of the motor pool. "Salvage from our last win—"

"Ha! *That* was a few bouts ago."

"—and the stable's just found a buyer, and we need the money."

Milly squinted at the assembly of four vehicles. "You want me to drive one of those damn things across the desert to Galaport? Huh-uh, no thanks, Dev. Find some other idiot with time on her hands."

Devin kicked invisible stones with the toe of his boot. "It's, uh, kind of an order, Milly."

"A *what*?"

"Maybe you haven't noticed, but the Sheepdog stable is in a rough patch. We need this sale to keep afloat till we can get another pilot and BattleMech up."

"Maybe they should put someone in the arena who has some experience." Milly blew a perfect smoke ring in emphasis.

"You mean MechWarriors without a debilitating addiction?"

Milly spat on the concrete. That was a low blow, and she could see on his face that Devin knew it.

Not that he was wrong.

Devin gripped a handful of her jacket sleeve, pulled her in close, and lowered his voice. "This shipment needs to go out tonight. We got no warriors right now, Milly."

Milly spoke through clenched yellow teeth. "You got *me*, Devin. I can do it. Gimme that 'Mech, I'll win the next five bouts."

"We don't know if Benny's gonna walk again after that last fight. Micha's having trouble with her left eye, and Carlito's neck is gonna take months to heal up. All our 'Mechs are too shot up to be of any use for weeks except for that *Enforcer*. Yes, you are my vet, and that's why the stable boss wants you to take the trucks. They need someone with experience to lead the convoy in case the Guild decides to take a shot."

"The Guild won't attack anyone on the open road." The local bandits and their light 'Mechs caused plenty of trouble, she knew, but no one had ever reported an assault on the main road.

"They haven't *yet*, that doesn't mean they won't. This sale's too important. Come on, Milly. Just do this for me, huh? Drive the lead truck. The buyer's only on-world for the next two days, we got to run this convoy tonight to get there on time."

Despite herself, Milly glanced back at the *Enforcer*. Its broad black canopy screen seemed to gaze back at her, beckoning. "If I'm in a truck, who's riding shotgun?"

"Joel."

"*Joel*? He's twelve years old!"

"He's nineteen, and needs the experience before we can put him in the crater."

"Devin, at least put me in the *cockpit*, for God's sake. Let Joel drive the damn truck."

Her boss pressed his lips together and shook his head firmly.

Milly mirrored Devin's grip on her sleeve by grabbing his. With her free hand, she lifted the shades to the top of her head so he could see her eyes clearly. "It's been three months since I had a...an incident. Come on, Devin. Let me just go for the ride, please?"

She hated the tone in her voice and could tell Devin did too. It didn't befit her. Or, hadn't, until relatively recently. Until Solaris. A lot of things had changed after Solaris.

She didn't have to tell Devin what she was thinking: *If I can't pilot a BattleMech for a goddamn milk run, what the hell good am I?*

"You're driving the truck," Devin said softly. "I'm sorry, Milly, that's how it's gotta be. The stable would kick me out if I let you anywhere near a cockpit. Me *and* you, both. You'll be in charge of the convoy. Then you and the others take a day off when you get there, if you want."

He leaned closer, whispering, "Prove you can handle being in a place like Galaport without losing your shit, and I'll put in a good word, all right? I know the owners want you in the arena, but they have to know who they're getting. Are they getting the ace pilot from Solaris, or an elderly junkie vet who couldn't shoot straight unless it's into her own arms?"

Milly shoved him away, puffing furiously on her cigarette.

Devin scowled. "Hey! I'm the best friend you got, grandma. No one else here gives a shit who you used to be. That time's over. Right now, you're a washed up em-dub with a drug habit and a hundred tons of debt. So, take the convoy and prove them wrong, and I'll do everything I can to get you in the crater. Or stay here and solder more wires for the rest of your life."

"What if I don't come back from Galaport?"

Devin shrugged sarcastically. "Then I guess I have my answer." He began walking back into the bay. "But I hope you will. It's your call, Milly." Then he was gone, shouting orders at a couple techs screwing off instead of working.

Milly blew out smoke and stomped on the butt, grinding it into the concrete. She pulled her yellow shades down and glared west. Sunsets were nothing spectacular on Galatea, not the parts she'd been to, anyway. Pollux during her last stint before heading to Solaris; now *that* world had sunsets. Part of the reason, she knew, was the dust kicked up by combat and the smoke curling up from war wreckage. It turned the most banal of sunsets into glowing fire.

Across the broad expanse of concrete, the cargo trucks were being lined up. She saw the Sheepdog stable's youngest MechWarrior, Joel— still more of a trainee, in Milly's mind—hustling about with boxes of parts small enough to carry by hand. Joel must've been 195 centimeters, a slim, gangly kid who could barely fit in a cockpit. He wore his dirty blond hair long, and his face gave the impression that someone had just yanked hard on his usual ponytail.

Milly whistled and shouted, "Joel!"

The young man froze, wide-eyed, then saw who was calling. Quickly, he put the box on the bed of one of the trucks and raced over to her. "Hey-hey, Milly!"

"You're driving the *Enforcer*?"

"Yeah, yeah, that's what Devin told me."

"Splendid. Go check the nav computer before we head out."

Joel glanced into the bay as if to study the 'Mech. "Are—are you coming with us? Devin said—"

"Yep. I'm driving the lead truck." She almost added, *because I'm obviously too old and useless to do anything else.*

"Great, great!" Joel beamed as he smiled brightly.

He, at least, knew who she was. Who'd she'd been. He worshipped her, and she knew it. It depressed her to admit, even only to herself, how much she needed the admiration. She'd always excelled at life-and-death combat, but the roar of the Solaris crowd—only heard in the clubs and parties after a victory, but still—was the greatest intoxicant in the world.

*Well,* Milly thought bitterly, *second greatest, anyway. Right, grandma?*

"Yeah, I'm pretty great," she said. "So go on, git. We ride out in thirty."

Joel's smile somehow grew bigger as he tipped her a nod and ran into the bay toward the *Enforcer.*

"And slow down," Milly muttered. Damn kid ran everywhere.

Pausing to rub her knee, Milly then limped toward the vehicles.

Half an hour after sundown, Milly kicked back against the lead truck, one boot flat against the fuel tank as she smoked and eyed her motley team.

This was half of what remained of the once-venerated Sheepdog Mercenaries. She'd joined them after their fortunes turned sour and they'd become this stable of Galatea arena gamers. *After all,* she mused with a sneer, *only a unit whose fortunes had turned sour would ever want me, considering the shape I'd been in at the time.*

Joel occupied the *Enforcer,* walking it to the front of the line of vehicles. In the truck behind Milly's, a know-it-all tech named Rand stood on a step stool, hovering over the truck's engine while his teenage daughter, Airin, climbed gracelessly into the passenger seat. Rand was teaching her everything he knew about engines, whether combustion or fusion. Milly had a sense Airin harbored a crush on Joel—they were near the same age *and* height—but didn't know the girl quite well enough to give her a hard time about it. Milly tried to avoid Rand whenever possible; the guy was insufferable. Based on the size of the cargo boxes and tarps on his truck, Rand was hauling the biggest and most expensive salvage.

Next came a talented tech named Glass, starting up his truck. Glass was a short, bald man who looked like he'd recently sucked a lemon, but who could crosswire a BattleMech with the finesse of a neurosurgeon. Behind him, an assistant tech with the unfortunate moniker of Shaggy revved his engine. Milly had seen Shaggy with his shirt off in the 'Mech bay, and the nickname suited him even before taking into account his thick, curly beard.

"Ready, ready?" Joel called from the *Enforcer*'s PA system.

Milly clenched the cigarette between her teeth. "Shounds good," she said around the butt as she hauled herself into the cab. A joint in her lower back popped, and she suppressed a grimace at the pain.

*Maybe you really are too old for this, grandma.*

Coughing out smoke, Milly pulled the door shut and started the truck. Through the open window, she waved her hand and sent the big vehicle rumbling over the concrete toward the stable compound's gate.

"Comm check, comm check," Joel said into the set in Milly's ear. "Are we green?"

"Green, copy," Milly said. "Truck Two?"

"Truck Two, copy," Rand said. "But listen, Mill, I got a theory... Why don't we just cut through the hills?"

"Negative, we're taking the dry lake as usual. Truck Three, green?"

"Truck Three, copy," Glass snapped.

"Truck Four?"

"Truck Four, copy," Shaggy replied in his deep and geographically ambiguous brogue. "Tallyho, aye, mum?"

"Copy," Milly said, and goosed the truck a little quicker toward the gate, which lumbered open at their approach.

"Mill, just hear me out," Rand went on as Joel took the lead and walked the *Enforcer* through the open gate. "If we take the hills, we'll save a full day's travel. I need to see my wife. And I do mean *need.*" He gave a lecherous cackle.

"Copy that, and still a negative," Milly said. "Another day won't make a difference. We're taking the dry lake."

"But my boys!" Rand argued. "It's been months since I seen them. Come on!"

"Rand, shut up." Milly sighed. She guessed he'd tried to ask some higher-up at the stable to take the shortcut and been roundly rejected.

The convoy rolled out of the compound.

One inescapable feature dominated the local area: a massive crater dating back several millennia. Its steep sides and deep basin formed a natural and perfect arena for BattleMech competitions of the sort found on Solaris, but without the glitz or odds of survival. Stables, also like those on Solaris, had formed around the perimeter of the crater, some popping up and disappearing with notable regularity, while a few had withstood the test of time and had their eyes set on breaking into Solaris tournaments or being noticed by houses in need of mercenaries.

Rent was free for abandoned compounds like the one the former Sheepdog Mercenaries now occupied. If another stable wasn't using the buildings, they were open for the taking. The real money in Crater Town came from betting and salvage. To the victor stable of any bout went the spoils.

The Sheepdog Mercs were a middling stable when Milly landed the tech job. Her reputation hadn't preceded her quite this far when she arrived on-world two years ago. Since then, the stable had slowly climbed the ranks of these outback BattleMech matches, right up until their ace, a middle-aged ex-merc named Dixon, got himself killed. Since then, Sheepdog's fortunes had sunk abysmally. Milly was well-aware the rest of the community—MechWarriors, techs, bettors, bookies—were about to write off the stable as a lost cause.

She didn't want that to happen. Too many people knew who she was now and what she'd become, and weren't about to hire her, not when there were other options. Sheepdog, who didn't realize her history until after she'd already established herself as a decent tech, was her saving grace at the moment.

*Just put me in the arena*, Milly thought once again as the convoy rolled along through the featureless desert. *I'll turn this whole damn stable around.*

She'd grown up with the First Sirian Lancers, learning about 'Mechs the way other kids learned about blocks and dolls. Decades of good service with a respected unit ultimately led her to the game world of Solaris. There she found notoriety as one badass 'Mech jock, who knew—most importantly—how to put on a show. Any em-dub with a lick of experience could enter an arena and slug it out. It took showmanship to give viewers a thrill.

When viewers were thrilled, money flowed.

Millicent "Milly" Olson had been one of the best until the fame caught up with her, as it did so many rising stars on the game world. Fans threw themselves at her, mobsters courted her, the rich and powerful brought her to their parties. At first, she drank, because that's what people did on Solaris; the planet was one big damn party. Then came pills, to ease the aches and stress that came with being a successful MechWarrior. When those weren't enough, on the urging of her new "friends," as she thought of them at the time, Milly moved on to mainlining opiates into her blood.

No combat adrenaline, no amount of money, no sex in the world had ever made her feel like the drugs did. Within months, her game lagged, then fell apart completely. Her winnings evaporated, and her "friends" suddenly didn't call her. Mobster heavies wanted to know when the money she was borrowing was getting paid back.

*And that's how fast it happens*, Milly thought as she stared at the endless expanse of cracked earth illuminated by her headlights. *Snap.*

*That fast. Now here you are, driving a truck across the desert. Good job, MechWarrior.*

"Joel, you keep an eye on those scanners," she barked into her radio to redirect her dismal thoughts. "It's gonna be a long night."

"Copy, copy," Joel said. "You don't, uh...you don't think—"

"No, I don't. The Guild's a bunch of cowardly assholes, they're not gonna pounce across a flat open plain like this where we could see them coming. Don't worry, kid, but keep an eye out all the same."

Rand's voice broke in. "Milly?"

"I don't want to hear it, Rando."

"Don't call me that. Listen, I'm just saying, if we cut through the hills—"

"Did you not just hear me tell Joel the Guild won't jump us while we're crossing dry lake? The hills are too perfect for an ambush. Let it *go*."

Rand didn't respond.

The Guild were marauders, or fancied themselves as such. Penny-ante thieves, dime-store hoods...not the biggest kids on the block by any stretch. But even petty gangsters could fire a gun that could hit you in the face, and the Guild had BattleMechs. Trucks, 'Mechs, and human bodies didn't take well to lasers, no matter how shitty the pilot firing them. Easier just to follow the worn tracks across the scorched, cracked earth of this long-evaporated lake bed into Galaport.

Milly lit another smoke. The radio stayed silent, so she jabbed the earbuds in and tuned to Mozart's *Requiem*. It suited the landscape: dark, dry, endless.

She missed the lights and sounds on Solaris. Walking any of the big strips at night was like being inside a trideo pinball game, writ large. Milly ached to return. Even after all the years of real-life combat, the celebrity attached to Solaris still beckoned. She could admit that much, now, looking back. And was that so wrong? An orphan girl who'd spilled plenty of blood in her lifetime and had it spilled in return... Was it so terrible to yearn for a little notoriety?

The drugs had derailed everything, and Milly didn't argue that. The last binge she'd admitted to Devin had only come after almost a year clean and sober. She would not do it again.

Watching Joel pilot the *Enforcer* across the cracked lake bed, Milly didn't even try to tamp down an electric jolt of jealousy. He had his whole life ahead, and was making good use of it so far. She'd give anything just to be where he was right now, eased back in the couch, watching the dust and darkness drift by. As a tech, she had full access to the BattleMech's controls... Maybe when they stopped for a break, she could convince him to trade, just for a while? Their little secret?

Milly spent an hour mentally developing this gambit when the lights behind her, reflecting in the rearview mirrors, suddenly veered off to Milly's right.

"The hell!" she barked.

It was as if an assault 'Mech had kicked Rand's truck and sent it spinning. Then she realized: no, it was not an attack.

It was Rand.

Even without proper scanners or being able to see in the dark, Milly knew instantly why he'd suddenly jerked his truck that direction: one klick that way, a dry riverbed wound through a mix of steep and shallow hills, and led damn near to the doorstep of Galaport.

The sonofabitch was breaking protocol for his wife and other two kids.

Admirable. And irretrievably stupid.

Milly snatched her radio. "Rand, don't you do it!"

The receiver crackled back. "Come on, Milly, you know I'm right, let's just get this over with."

"Rand, goddammit!"

Rand actually laughed. Milly couldn't even tell if he was forcing it or not. "Just fall in behind me and let's drop these loads so we can have two whole days at the port."

The rest of the convoy had stopped by then, kicking up salty white dust that mimicked laser shots as it floated in the beams of the headlights.

Milly was momentarily pleased to hear Shaggy pop on to the radio. "You're jackin' us up, Rand! Less go, get back in line, aye?"

"Uh-oh!" Rand joked, asshole that he was. "Look at me, I'm almost to the riverbed. Somebody better come protect me from the big bad Guild, oooh!"

"I'm gonna stab you in the throat," Milly said.

Joel broke in. "Milly, Milly? What do we do? We can't just let her—I, I mean *him*—"

"Shut up, Joel." So, he did have a thing with Airin. Milly hadn't lost *all* her instincts, anyway.

"Aye, let him go," Shaggy said. "Let him get killed, we'll make do with our own cargo."

Milly pressed her radio button. "Rand? Your daughter is in that truck. You want to be an asshole, fine, don't risk her life for this."

"*You have no one,*" Rand said, his voice suddenly quite low over the radio. "I haven't seen the rest of my family in months. *Months.* I'm flooring it down this riverbed and I'll be at the port by dawn. You do what you want. Rand out."

"Rand. Rand!"

Silence.

"Well, that's just ducky," Glass said.

"Let 'im go," Shaggy said.

"Milly?" Joel said. "I—I can't just...you know?"

Milly flipped off her yellow shades and rubbed her eyes. *Dammit all!* She should listen to Shaggy, let the asshole go on his way. But then, if something happened to the cargo, the stable would be screwed. And she wasn't any more likely than Joel to let Airin get into danger.

Even as she thought this, Joel nudged the *Enforcer* a few steps to the right. "Milly? Please, we should...you know?"

*And if something does go south*, Milly thought, tightening her grip on the wheel, *they're gonna need you, Millicent.*

*You?* another, more cynical voice broke into her mind. *The elderly junkie vet?*

"I'm sorry, Milly," Joel said over the radio, and pushed the *Enforcer* ahead toward Rand's disappearing red taillights. "I—I have to."

"Copy that," Milly said to herself.

She pressed the gas pedal and twisted the wheel right.

*Damn that Rand.* She held the mic close to her mouth. "Whatever happens next is on you, Rando."

His only response, as she and the others drove quickly to catch up to him, was an arm out the window and a finger raised.

"Yeah, keep it up and I'll bite it off," Milly grumbled.

The convoy rolled on.

Milly had no idea what sort of rock formed the bulbs and swells of the hills their route curled through. Basalt, maybe. In the light cast by the trucks, the hills were purple-brown. The dome-shaped growths reminded her of pimples growing up from the skin of the ground, ranging in height from about a meter to twice as tall as the *Enforcer*.

Their path, carved by a long-extinct river now as bone-dry as the lake they'd been crossing, made Milly's heart beat a little quicker. The riverbed made serpentine twists and turns. Around any given corner, the Guild could be lurking, waiting in ambush.

She hoped Rand was anxious about this legitimately dangerous idea now that they were in the thick of the hills. The flat path was only wide enough for two trucks to roll side-by-side, and then only at times. Milly had given the order to stick to single file. Joel had taken the lead again to use the *Enforcer*'s scanners.

Even without being in the command couch herself, Milly knew those scanners were next-door to useless in this terrain. There could be a hundred Guild 'Mechs hiding out behind the tall hills, cold and quiet, and the *Enforcer* would never detect them until it was far too late.

*Which is why*, Milly thought, over and over and over, *we shouldn't be in this place to begin with, Rand, you assault-class asshole.*

No one talked. It was late, and Milly felt sleepiness dragging fishhooks at the corners of her eyes. But no stopping now. They'd have taken a short break after clearing the dry lake, probably around dawn, before continuing toward Galaport along a more established route. Now, with this shortcut, it was best to truck along until the bright lights of the port were readily visible.

When her radio hissed, Milly blinked to hydrate her eyes. She hadn't been sleeping, but definitely droning.

"Uh, Milly?" Joel's voice seemed high.

"What is it?"

"Maybe—maybe nothing, but I thought I saw a heat sig?"

He said it like a question. Milly wriggled her tired ass in the seat and rubbed her knee. "Did you or did you not, Joel?"

"It was small, maybe an animal?"

Milly scanned left to right and back again. Galatea was known for active wildlife, but the majority of it resided underground. They hadn't passed anything even remotely resembling water since leaving Crater Town, which sat atop an underground oasis.

An animal? Wandering around in the dry dirt? Maybe.

But unlikely.

Milly glanced at the speedometer. "Joel, I'm clocking only forty kph right now, can you speed it up without falling over?"

"Uh...maybe," the boy said. "I-I mean, I can try."

"Try. Everyone? We're picking it up, let's shoot for sixty."

"Sounds good to me," Rand broke in.

"You don't say another word, Rando," Milly said. "Like, ever."

Rand took the time to press his own radio button just so she'd hear him laugh into it. Milly began plotting just how badly she was going to beat his ass when they got to Galaport.

Despite his relative inexperience, Joel did well navigating the twisting riverbed. He got the *Enforcer* moving at a good clip. Not quite full speed, Milly could see, but considering the sharpness of the turns and the narrowness of the path, the kid was doing well.

*Hell*, she thought. *Some of these hills are high enough he'd just bounce right off them and keep going.*

She permitted herself a rare, grim chuckle at the thought just as Joel's voice screamed through her speaker. *"Contact!"*

Milly slammed on her brakes just as she made a left turn, following the *Enforcer*. Even before the cargo vehicle came to a halt, the jarring

bright red glare of laser fire erupted against the BattleMech, casting Joel's machine into silhouette.

In a span of time hardly measurable, Milly somehow managed to think: *And so it begins. This is where we die. Thanks, Rando.*

Joel's *Enforcer* stumbled backward. For a heart-clenching moment, Milly thought the 50-tonner was going to land right on top of the cab, crushing her flat. But the young pilot kept the 'Mech upright and fired his autocannon back at the ambusher.

The truck speakers erupted with voices as the rapid, dull grunts from the *Enforcer*'s AC fire rattled Milly's bones. She scrambled for the radio.

"Stay in the trucks, *stay by the trucks*, that's what they want, they won't risk blowin' 'em up!" Milly ordered and cussed poetically.

Joel pushed forward, laying down more fire against his attacker as Milly crashed out of the cab of her truck. It was practically wedged between two medium-height hills—a perfect choke point. She didn't want to risk Joel's BattleMech toppling on her.

As 'Mech gunfire whined loudly above her, Milly instinctively raced back toward Rand's truck. "Roll back, you sonofabitch, roll back!" she screamed, waving her arms the direction they'd come. No more than few hundred meters away, just a few minutes ago, they'd driven through an open area, enough room for the trucks to turn around.

Rand stuck his head out the open window of the cab and had the audacity to shout, "What's happening?"

She could have shot him herself.

Milly took a deep breath to bellow over the sounds of the 'Mech combat occurring just a few meters behind her, when she caught sight of movement to her right. She skidded to a stop.

Terror sent a slurry of ice through her limbs as a metallic hand crept over the top of an eight-meter-tall hill like a silver spider. Harmless sparks from Joel's battle acted like momentary flares, illuminating the distinctly human-faced *Wyvern* BattleMech slowly peering around the hill.

And aiming its right arm at Rand's truck.

Though the 'Mech had no myomer in its face, the *Wyvern*'s villainous leer seemed like a grin to Milly.

Instinctively, she spun and leaped away from the vehicle as twin small lasers sniped from the *Wyvern*'s arm.

Milly hit the ground, her joints bursting from the impact. As quick as she landed, the old vet was on her knees, spinning to see what damage the enemy 'Mech had caused.

Millicent Olson had killed. She'd seen death. She'd buried friends and obliterated foes. But the image, sound, and smell assaulting her now was unlike anything she'd experienced.

Rand fell out of the truck's cab atop its twisted, melted scrap of a door, which had given way from its hinges like a rotten tooth. He was still alive as he rose to his feet, reaching for his face. On the left side of his skull, most of the tissue and hair was just *gone*, revealing glistening bone. From the hole where his mouth used to be came a sound like a clogged drain giving way beneath punishing acid. The smoky odor of burned flesh and hair reached Milly's nostrils, gagging her even as Rand fell once more.

He no longer moved.

*"Daddy!"*

Airin's shriek from the other side of the truck pierced Milly's ears over the horrific sounds of battle. Milly, fighting against the pain and stiffness in her own body, leaped for her and wrap-tackled the girl to the ground before Airin even cleared the hood of the truck.

"Don't look!" she hissed into the girl's ear. *"Don't look!"*

Over the ruckus of combat, Milly heard Shaggy shouting curses. From her vantage on the ground, looking beneath Rand's truck, Milly could see his boots as they raced toward Rand's motionless corpse. "Aw, Christ!" he bellowed.

Milly watched Shaggy drop to a kneeling position. A high-pitched mechanical shriek pinched her eardrums, followed by a crashing explosion.

"Stay here!" Milly barked at Airin and pulled herself off the stunned teenager.

She whirled to the front end of the truck to take stock and saw the *Wyvern* was stumbling backward. Smoke rose from its right shoulder.

Milly looked to Shaggy as the gruff tech got to his feet and dropped a single-shot SRM-2 launcher. He looked wildly around for a moment before their eyes met. "I keep one in the back just in case!" he shouted.

The night lit once more with fire. Milly and Shaggy raised their arms against the glare.

It was the *Wyvern*, launching into the sky on jump jets that scorched its torso and legs. Milly anticipated a new attack, but the 'Mech flew away from them, alighting momentarily on a taller peak. The jets fired again, taking the *Wyvern* farther away.

"Retreating," Milly breathed, and thought, *Thank God.* Either the pilot was a straight-up coward, or the 'Mech had damage she hadn't seen, and the MechWarrior couldn't risk even the relatively weak blow from an SRM-2.

She spun toward her own truck. The BattleMech engaged with Joel's *Enforcer*—she saw now it was an old *Blackjack*—also lifted into the air and flew away from the scene. Milly watched the pair of 'Mechs jump away, making sure they weren't just angling for another attack.

Once it was clear they were hightailing, Milly got to her feet and pointed at Rand's remains. She shouted at Shaggy, "Cover him!"

Shaggy draped his coat across the still-smoking corpse as Milly limped back to Airin. The girl had pushed her back against the passenger-side front tire, arms wrapped around her knees, eyes wide.

Milly took a knee, which crackled painfully. "Grab my wrists. Grab 'em. Squeeze."

Airin obeyed, clearly on autopilot.

"Good. Now tell me your name."

"Airin. Airin. Airin..."

"Good. Okay." Milly ran her palms over the girl's entire body, occasionally checking her fingers for blood. Nothing. "Okay. You stay right here, you hear me? That's an order."

"My dad—"

"He's gone. You stay right here."

*Joel*, Milly thought as she hiked to her feet again. *Goddammit, where's Joel...*

Milly passed Shaggy, who was wiping his mouth and staring at Rand's limp legs. "Glass," she called to the hairy man. "Check him."

Shaggy ran back to Glass's truck as Milly turned the bend in the riverbed past her own vehicle. She sucked in a breath as she took in the *Enforcer*, lit by her truck's headlights.

The BattleMech had lost armor in its torso. Great chunks were missing, but Milly saw no internal structure showing.

That wasn't what scared her.

The *Enforcer* had taken what looked like a point-blank blow to the head. Instinct told Milly it came from the *Blackjack*'s autocannon, not a laser blast. A narrow hole was cut into the side of the 'Mech's head, near the neck, opaque and fatal.

"Joel? *Joel!*"

Slowly, a bloody hand appeared out from the darkness of the cockpit, waved once—and fell limp.

Glass and Shaggy were physically unhurt and worked together to extricate Joel from the cockpit of the *Enforcer*. Once the boy was safely down, Glass scampered back up with his tool kit and squeezed his plump body in through the hole.

Joel shrieked, then clamped his mouth shut as Shaggy laid him out on the dirt beside Milly's truck. Joel's left thumb was missing and bled freely into the dust. His face was black from smoke, but unblemished. Shaggy liberated the standard-issue med kit from Milly's cab while Milly checked Joel the way she'd checked Airin. When her hands crossed his ribcage on the left side, she felt something like loose cereal under her gently probing fingers.

Joel shrieked again.

"Right," Milly said, and touched his cheek. "You did good, Joel. You're a mess, but you're alive. Sit tight."

Jaw clenched like a vice, Joel nodded, once.

Shaggy bandaged the boy's hand, following that with a small dose of painkiller. Milly salivated at the sight of the hypo and walked quickly to Airin's side.

She instructed Airin to sit with Joel, which the girl did—and followed orders not to glance at the covered body of her father. Under Milly's direction, Shaggy picked the dead man up and took him to the bed of his truck, where they secured him under a tarp.

This grim business done, Shaggy and Milly walked back to the feet of the *Enforcer* to await Glass's diagnosis.

"We shood turn aroon, Milly," Shaggy said, crossing his arms and scanning the hills. "Forget all aboot this mess."

"Then what? The stable needs the money. We don't get it, it folds, and we all fold with it. You got another gig lined up, Shaggy? Want to put in a good word for the rest of us?"

"Huh!" Shaggy grunted. "Soom of us have better words than others!"

She might have kicked his shin in other circumstances. Milly said nothing, smoking three cigarettes until Glass gingerly pulled himself from the *Enforcer* and climbed down.

"Cockpit's jammed shut," the bald tech reported. "The head's pretty well stripped of armor. No way it'll eject, either. It's got power and weapons, but the AC's on empty. Left torso and arm lost a bunch of weight, but they're holding."

Milly nodded, mostly to mask the pain in her knee and back. She hadn't been hit by a single thing, but her body roared at her.

She badly wanted a hit. One of those painkiller hypos was looking mighty fine.

Instead, she just nodded again.

"What's yoor plan, then, mum? We go back now, at least we're alive, Milly. All we've got oot here is a jacked-up 'Mech, and we're down a MechWarrior and a driver."

Milly spit into the dirt. She'd already made up her mind.

"We've been sitting too long already. The Guild'll come back, and with friends. We need to make best speed to the port. I'll drive the 'Mech."

Glass coughed. "Milly? It'll walk, and it'll turn, and the lasers will shoot. But that head is gone. It takes so much as a BB shot and this 'Mech is out. May as well drag it behind a truck and sell it for scrap. The kid did good, but it wasn't cheap."

Milly gazed up the length of the BattleMech. "If it moves and shoots, it'll do."

"No, you're not hearing me. You'll have practically no protection in the 'pit.'"

She eyeballed him. "If it moves. And shoots. It will do."

"Milly!"

"Just get in your trucks. Let's go." Milly jabbed both men with her fingers until they shuffled toward the vehicles.

Milly moved to stand over the two teens. Airin looked up. Tears reflected across her cheeks in the glare of the headlights.

"Airin?" Milly said, in a gentle voice she hadn't known she possessed. "Can you drive my truck?"

"My dad..." Airin said, and Joel squinted a pained, questioning glance up at his boss.

"I know, sweetie, I know. But we are in a big boiling pot of liquid shit right now and I need to know if you can bear up for just a little while longer."

"Where is he? I want to—"

"You cannot see him right now. You can't. Shaggy took care of him; we'll treat him properly. I need to know if you can drive that truck, though. Your dad taught you everything he knows, and the best way to honor him is to prove it, right here and now. I want you to get home to your mom and your little brothers, got it?"

Airin hesitated before hurriedly wiping her face and snuffling up snot. She stood and lifted her chin.

"Atta girl," Milly said. "You got this. Go on."

She slapped Airin on the arm, and the girl went, casting a look back at Joel on the ground.

Joel was breathing though pursed lips. Milly rubbed her knee.

"How about you, cowboy? Think you can move?"

"If...I don't...breathe," Joel gasped, wincing and laying his bandaged left palm on his ribs.

"Breathing's overrated, right?" Milly nudged his foot with her boot. "I'm gonna stand right here, you show me if you can get up or not. Otherwise, I leave you here to rot."

Joel stared. "Is that...a joke?"

Milly grinned. "Mmm, like, seventy-eight percent, yeah. Come on. Show me."

"Okay. Just...let me think."

He stretched out his right arm experimentally; lifted himself a couple centimeters, and fell back with a tight groan. Joel followed that with several other slow gestures, trying to find the least painful way to get to his feet. None worked.

"Well," he breathed, "I-I guess...it's this, then."

He raised his right foot, knee at a right angle, and stretched his right arm over his head.

"Aw, shit," Milly said, intuiting his maneuver, and wincing on his behalf.

Using his leg and arm for momentum, Joel flung himself into a sitting position with a scream that echoed through the hills. Then, as if moving faster than he dared to think about it, he got a foot planted and unfolded himself to a standing position.

"Easy..." Joel whimpered. A single tear dribbled from one eye.

"I'm field-promoting you to general," Milly said, getting an arm under him. "Let's get you buckled in. We're gonna get to Galaport, and I want you to marry that girl."

Somehow, briefly, Joel smiled.

It wasn't easy to slither into the *Enforcer*'s cockpit through the jagged hole in its head, but Milly managed with only minor scrapes. Sharp spears of jagged metal stabbed at her with every move to get inside. Her back and knee seemed to flash red under her clothes.

Yet as she wormed into the command couch, the pain somehow seemed to lessen. It was as if the seat had been specially molded for her body. Despite the need for urgency, Milly gave herself a moment to let her hands drift across the various controls and interfaces of the cockpit.

*Home*, she thought. *It feels like home.*

Accidentally smearing a bit of Joel's blood on the MRE panel shook her back to reality.

She donned the neurohelmet and used her tech credentials to run through the 'Mech's start-up sequence, bypassing the safety protocols she felt she could get away with. The fact that a breeze blew through the hole in the *Enforcer*'s head made that choice easy. Glass was right. She was damn near naked in here. One or two rounds from a 'Mech machine gun would end this little jaunt in a hurry.

Start-up complete, Milly gave the big war machine a little juice. The *Enforcer* took a confident step forward.

"Atta boy," she whispered, then said, "Comm check."

She'd reorganized the convoy, putting Shaggy in the lead, then Glass, then Joel and Airin. Shaggy'd proven himself useful in a jam; she wanted him closer to her. Everyone checked in, even Airin, with a proper response, impressing Milly. Joel's voice was strained, but he answered.

"Off we go," Milly said, and started at an easy pace that she gradually increased as she guided the BattleMech around the hills. "If you can't keep up, say something."

It had been years since she'd driven a 'Mech into combat, but the machine responded to her as easily as the cargo truck. It took only a few minutes before she was able to top Joel's earlier speed.

"Okay, Millicent," she said aloud as the *Enforcer* cruised along. She took a sharp turn, lasers ready. "You can do this. Just a few more hours to Galaport, and all's well."

The convoy rolled on.

Her scanners stayed clean and clear as Milly led the trucks further into the hills. She checked in every fifteen to twenty minutes, and her drivers reported back each time.

An hour passed.

Then two.

"Maybe you've done it after all, mum," Shaggy said at the top of hour three. It sounded as though he was eating something.

"Oh, good, jinx the whole thing," Milly retorted, but secretly grinned. A small but bright ray of hope had begun to develop in her belly, despite her attempts to chase it away. There was no dismissing Rand's math, anyway; another hour from here, and they'd be clear of the hills, with the bright lights of Galaport in the distance. It'd be another hour after that before they actually reached the place, but at least they'd be in the open again along the way.

Safe.

Milly turned the *Enforcer* left around a hill.

Then broke the war machine right, raising the 'Mech's arms.

Her heart beat once...twice...and seemed to still.

Four BattleMechs stood before her in a rough semicircle about fifty meters away. She instantly recognized the *Wyvern* and *Blackjack* that'd ambushed them, but now they were joined by a *Centurion* and *Vulcan*.

Two hundred or more tons of war against her medium 'Mech with a hole in its head.

The moment she made the turn, her *Enforcer*'s heat map flared to life, clearly showing the four machines. Once again, the hills had acted on their behalf. This was their turf.

Everything Milly thought next took less than a moment to pass through her mind.

*This isn't Rand's fault anymore, Millicent. This is yours.*

*You could have turned back, saved their lives, even if the stable collapsed. But you wanted this fight. Didn't you?*

*Let's be honest, grandma. You wanted to bring these trucks to the port so the Sheepdogs would have to let you fight.*

*Well, congratulations, junkie.*

*You got your fight.*

Her heart began to beat again, fueled by adrenaline...and realization borne from experience.

In the space of one additional second, Milly's entire adult lifetime of combat spit out a readout in her brain as if the *Enforcer*'s screens were embedded in her vision:

*Their armor is almost perfect except for that* Blackjack.

*They don't like to fight.*

*They probably suck at it.*

*Joel's never been in combat and still scared that* 'Jack *away.*

*If they were good enough or brave enough to be mercs, they'd be in a unit.*

*If they were good enough or brave enough to compete, they'd be gaming on Galatea, never mind Solaris.*

*The* Wyvern *jetted after one blow from an SRM-2.*

*These are Dead Mercs. Bandits who can't even get contracts anymore.*

*So, while they've got the numbers and the firepower—*

"They're shit warriors," she said.

Maybe, despite their apparent overwhelming advantage, Milly still had a shot.

Maybe.

Milly calmly tapped her commlink. "Shaggy. I'm gonna make a hole. You drive these trucks through it and don't stop for anything."

"Milly," Shaggy broke in, his voice an octave higher. "Christ, mum, maybe we should—"

She shut off the link.

Drew in a shuddering breath.

And opened fire.

One of the Guild pilots spoke through a loudspeaker just as the *Enforcer* let loose with its large laser: "Stop where you are and get out of the *holy shit*!"

Everything in Milly's past—all the scuffles, brawls, and outright slugfests she'd endured and won coursed through her body at the speed of light. Everything she needed to know about her own 'Mech's current weakness, everything about her opponent's strengths. All of it.

*Offense.*

*Fewer casualties when you advance than when you retreat.*

The Guild had selected a spot in the hills that might have made for a decent arena. There was room enough to maneuver, but not enough to run. The four of them stood, lined up, facing her, blocking the open area's only other exit. Two tall hills like lamp posts stood on either side of the path where the dry riverbed continued on its way.

She just had to make room for the trucks.

Milly charged forward, firing the large laser at the *Centurion* that mostly blocked the path to the exit. The *Centurion* backed up past the two guardian hills, raising its right arm in response to the *Enforcer*'s laser melting a chunk of armor off its left side. Milly twisted her 'Mech's shoulder to dodge what was sure to be a withering assault of autocannon.

The shot never came.

Milly grinned savagely. *The* Centurion *AC strikes out again.* It was a well-known flaw in the design.

She sent another large laser blast into the 'Mech, and followed up with a small laser shot as she closed with the *Centurion*. Both shots landed center mass, and again the *Centurion* backpedaled.

A short heat warning rang in her ear. Already the *Enforcer* needed to cool. She had a burst or two left before risking overheating.

*Damn,* Milly thought. *Better watch that heat gauge, grandma.*

The other three MechWarriors may have been stunned by her courageous attack, but now they joined the fight. The *Vulcan* on her right let loose a barrage of machine-gun fire. A stream of flame spat from its opposite limb, engulfing the *Enforcer*, making Milly wince against the heat. The hole in her 'Mech's head, at least, faced the other direction, or she'd have been roasted alive. Even amidst the battle, Milly's warrior mind reported the *Vulcan* had not fired its own autocannon.

*Ammo's hard to get for a bunch of thugs, eh?*

Armor flaked off the *Enforcer*'s right arm and shoulder. Milly had little use for that appendage at the moment, and the *Vulcan* had stupidly remained in one place, so she took the opportunity this presented.

Like a barroom brawler, Milly swung her 'Mech's heavy right arm in a backfist. The blow caught the *Vulcan*'s protruding head on the chin, sending the lighter 'Mech skipping backward into a tall hill.

Cheering herself on, Milly turned left—and saw eternity in the black barrel of the *Wyvern*'s large laser.

*Shit!*

She lowered the *Enforcer* into a crouch and ran full speed at the *Centurion*, who now took aim with its AC again even as its red lasers punctured the night and careened toward her.

The *Enforcer* took the lasers into its left and right shoulders. Liquified metal drooled from its skeleton, pooling on the dry riverbed—

And this time, the *Centurion*'s autocannon worked.

High-velocity slugs slammed into Milly's BattleMech, shredding armor from the torso... and head. Alarms cried out. Sparks showered across her as something pinched her hard in the left flank.

Shrieking through her clenched teeth, Milly raced ahead and sent a right hook toward her attacker. Behind her, plinking at the *Enforcer*'s softer rear armor, the *Wyvern* and *Blackjack* offered fire support to their comrade.

Milly's physical assault caught the bulkier 'Mech in the chest. The blow tore plates from the *Centurion* and sent the enemy 'Mech stumbling backward, then spinning away to the left.

The path was clear.

*"Shaggy, GO!"* Milly shouted into her comm and fired her jump jets. *Time to give them a showstopper.*

The *Enforcer* jetted upward as Shaggy led the trucks in a full-tilt drag race for the opening between the hills. Milly slammed her 'Mech to the left, hovering for a moment over the *Centurion*—

*The audience'll love this*, Milly thought.

—and brought her machine crashing down atop it.

The sound of splintering metal, the odor of ejected coolant, and the sensation of her spine being twisted by godlike hands all coalesced into a sensory overload for pilot and machine alike.

Then she was falling helplessly toward the hills. Milly worked her controls in blind fury, operating on utter instinct. Luck played a hand— she managed to keep the *Enforcer* somewhat on its feet only by virtue of pinwheeling backward into a tall hill. The BattleMech reclined there like a too-cool teen leaning against an arcade wall.

And that suited her fine.

*"WOO!"* Milly cried as the *Enforcer* came to rest for a moment. She could hear very little and she distantly felt twenty-eight different kinds of pain in her body, but *goddamn*, it felt good to be where she belonged.

*Focus!* her instinct ordered. *This ain't over.*

Gasping, Milly righted the *Enforcer* and took a broad step, creating an arch with the 'Mech's tall legs just as the first truck, Shaggy's, roared beneath them.

In the arena-shaped area, the *Wyvern* took flight, firing its entire complement of lasers at Milly. Shots landed on the *Enforcer*'s torso and legs, but didn't punch through—not yet, but whatever armor remained was tissue-thin.

Milly took careful aim and released two measured blasts from her own large laser as the *Wyvern* tried to alight on a hilltop. The *Enforcer*'s heat warning blared again. Milly grinned savagely as a cool breeze eddied through the hole in her BattleMech's head.

*Cheap-ass air conditioning!* she thought—or perhaps screamed.

The second shot from her large laser caught the slender *Wyvern*'s right arm. Armor blew off.

The *Wyvern* fired its three lasers again, and all three struck the *Enforcer* just as the *Blackjack* and *Vulcan* leaned into the gap, as if peering together from either side of a doorway, firing their own weapons.

The *Enforcer* rocked as the salvo of laser fire penetrated its armor. More alarms flared red in the cockpit.

Milly brought the 'Mech's right arm up and lengthwise across its body, then balanced its left-arm large laser atop it. Knowing she was risking a shutdown, Milly sent one laser straight down the middle as the last of the trucks rumbled between her feet.

The red light missed both the *Blackjack* and *Vulcan* entirely...but they got the message. Both 'Mechs yanked back, concealing themselves behind the hills.

Growling, Milly glanced at her sensors. The convoy was off and running behind her, charging full speed to get out of this death trap.

*Perfect. Now give 'em the grand finale, then meet up for drinks...*

Despite the 'Mech's critical heat level, Milly prepared to lay down fire at the *Wyvern* just as the enemy 'Mech was taking careful aim back at her. The *Wyvern*'s shots went wide, punching holes in the rocky hills on either side of the *Enforcer* as Milly marched her BattleMech toward the arena space.

Her large lasers smashed into the slender opponent, and, as she'd hoped, that was enough for the pilot. The *Wyvern* didn't even return fire as the jump jets on its torso and legs went off, lifting the 'Mech up and away from the fight.

Milly reached the break in the hills where the other two opponents were waiting. She stepped in between them and lifted both arms up, pointed at their heads. Her AC was out of ammo, but they didn't know that. Sometimes, she knew, a little bit of audacity was all that was needed to win. Based on her sensors and the epic heat searing her body, if she used the lasers, the *Enforcer* would unequivocally shut down. And that would be that.

The two MechWarriors didn't hesitate as Milly trained her weapons on their cockpits. Both lifted into the air and followed their *Wyvern* compatriot away from the site of the battle, leaving the ruined *Centurion* behind. Milly pointed her large laser, ready to fire at them if they changed course. They did not, fortunately—not only was the *Enforcer* too hot to risk the shots, she was in far too much pain to properly target them anyway.

But she knew it would've looked good to the audience.

The audience...?

Milly blinked, and realized she was close to swooning. *No audience, grandma. That fight was for real. Now for hell's sake, fall in behind those trucks and...*

Milly looked down at her abdomen. Clearly, shock dulled the worst of the pain she knew she must be in. And she figured there was quite a bit of it at the moment, based on what she saw.

"Okay," she said lightly, barely daring to breathe. "All right."

Delicately, she sent a radio signal to the convoy.

Shaggy answered it. "Aye! Still in the land of the living, Milly?"

"Still here," she said softly. "Everyone good?"

"All clear," Shaggy reported. "But I want oot of these hills."

"Copy. Keep moving. I'm right behind you. Don't stop. Head straight for the port."

"Copy that, Milly. We're goin' to the buyer's bay, it's on the outskirts. Big red buildin', can't miss it."

"Right. See you there."

She clicked off and tested the *Enforcer*. Despite the flashing red over most of its schematic, it was still mobile and responsive.

Milly carefully turned the BattleMech around and headed for the riverbed.

Milly lost all sense of time, tracking it only as a matter of degrees of lost body heat. The *Enforcer* cooled as she walked it, and her core temperature seemed to fall with it. By the time she could see Galaport in the distance, beckoning with its white, orange, green, and red lights, the sun was just beginning to peer over the horizon. She was glad to see it, though it did not warm her.

She found the buyer's bay easily enough, just as Shaggy had described. Milly walked her 'Mech into the bay, stopped the *Enforcer* in an empty tech berth, and powered down. Then, she merely sat, staring blankly at the consoles.

Smiling.

"Milly, Milly?" Joel called from somewhere below, his voice pinched. "You okay?"

*How much pain he must be in*, Milly thought. *But he still wants to know how you are. Nice boy.*

But she had no answer.

A moment later, she heard someone climbing up to the cockpit. Was it Devin? Was she back at the Sheepdog bay? No, Solaris, maybe. No...

"Aye! Milly! You did it, mum. Come on oot."

Milly could not reply. After a moment, Shaggy's shaggy face appeared.

"Milly. Time to start our vacation. What do you want to... Oh, glorious Jesus."

He turned away, screaming into the bay, "Glass! *Glass*! Get a medic! Put 'em in a cherry picker! Now!"

Milly patted the tech's hairy forearm as he gazed in horror at the gore in the cockpit. Her voice was a damp whisper. "How's Joel?"

"Don't talk, Milly, he's fine, he'll be all right. We're gonna get you outta here."

"It's okay," she said. "It's okay. I'm where I belong."

"Milly," Shaggy said, licking his lips. "You've been *run through*, mum. You—You're *pinned* in here."

"Yeah. Pretty stuck."

"Someone's comin', don't worry. *Medic!*"

"Shaggy. Can you. Get me. A smoke...?"

"Sure, sure, Milly, anythin'. Where d'you keep 'em? Aye?"

Milly didn't hear the question. She heard nothing anymore.

But she was where she belonged.

# MERCENARIES ENTERTAINMENT NETWORK DIGEST: JUNE 3152

### KEN' HORNER

The life of a mercenary, with constant travel often in foreign realms, can make staying up on the latest holovid shows difficult. The Mercenary Entertainment Network will keep you up to date on the latest happenings of your favorite programs and, hopefully, introduce you to new ones as well.

### *THE STEINHEARTS*

A docudrama based on the Steiner Family, this holovid has stood the test of time and is once again on top of the ratings and award lists.

### The Latest

The Tharkad court is thrown into chaos as Alyssa Davidion arrives from the Federated Stars, bringing up old wounds from a previous generation. Despite her visit, the ambassador from the Free Planets Collective is unfazed and boldly blames Rudinger Steinheart for the increase in pirate attacks along his nation's periphery border. All the while, Princess Alexandria is dodging would-be suitors thrown at her by nearly every family member. During an insurrection, Octavia Kelso-Steinheart narrowly avoids capture by the Clan Watch due to Clan infighting, but must choose between continuing to lead her resistance alone or accepting assistance from reawakened legend Donovan Rocker, with such assistance sure to come with conditions.

### HANSE IN CHARGE

Using the nostalgia and legend surrounding Hanse Davion, this show features near-identical look-alike Uwe Stuart as Hanse Davion reimagined as an action hero set in the 3020s. Rather than providing leadership from the top, whenever evil strikes, typically from Maximillian Liao, Hanse is very hands-on at jumping into the situation and fixing it himself, usually celebrating at the end with a big meal at Triple-F.

### The Latest

The students at the New Avalon Institute of Science are missing class at an alarming rate. Hanse investigates, only to find out someone is pumping sleeping gas into the dormitory! Not only that, but his team discovers the waitlist for NAIS has been inundated by Capellan citizens. Can Hanse find the mysterious gasser before the professors dismiss the innocent students and NAIS educates the next generation of Capellan scientists?

### SAAD YOUSUF: BOUNTY HUNTER

A fictional show that recreates the exploits of modern bounty hunters, Saad Yousuf leads his team as they track down wanted criminals, from rogue mercs to pirates to even individuals from one realm wanted in another. Saad's bright orange *Verfolger* leads his 'Mech lance that works in conjunction with the jump infantry squad commanded by his on-and-off love interest, Srettha Manet.

### The Latest

The team lands on Batavia to capture Baron Gleeson, who has taken advantage of the chaos of the Federated Suns invasion to carve out his own fiefdom. Gleeson's on-planet rival helps them at first, but double-crosses the team after an exhaustive battle to corner and capture Gleeson. Will they let Gleeson go in exchange for his help to get off-planet, or will they be forced to fight yet another battle against the odds?

### A RED-HOT LIFE

This docudrama recreates the rise, fall, and resurrection of the most notorious band of the thirty-first century, Theras and Her Red Deltas. Presented as an eight-part limited series, actors recreate the successes and failures of the band, often over-dramatizing (but not by much) the real-life spectacle.

### The Latest

Despite Gunthar Carbonetti leaving to pursue a solo career after a huge argument with Theras, the band is still trying to finish their latest album with the record company breathing down their necks. Rudolph

X'dova attempts to handle songwriting as well as both rhythm and lead guitar until they find a replacement for Carbonetti, but Theras' excessive partying is pushing Rudolph to the limit. Also, the beautiful and talented synth player Kira Rystal isn't helping the situation by demanding more solos.

### MECHBALL

The Lyran world of Noisiel has offered various sporting events performed in BattleMechs since the middle of the thirty-first century. Only lasting twelve days, the games have grown in popularity, and this year, an extended season of Canadian style football played in BattleMechs, MechBall, is being trialed. The show not only follows the six teams' exploits on the field but, behind the scenes, also looks at the preparation they do and their private lives as they balance their sport and their families.

### The Latest

After a concussion to starting quarterback Trina McMasters, the Golden Hawks have stunned the top two teams behind newcomer Gaston Ng. With McMasters clear of the concussion protocol, which way will the Golden Hawks go? Over on the Battle Otters, Paula Vallejo has quickly adapted to a *Banshee* after her *Charger*'s leg was crippled in the last match, and is terrorizing the offensive backfield. The biggest news in the league may be the collapse of the Crimson Vipers as Conner Olson and Yoro Diop broke up, destroying team chemistry more brutally than any opposing team could.

### THE REACHES

This reality show follows various MechWarriors on Solaris as they try to climb from obscurity to stardom. While there is plenty of drama from the arenas and repair bays, the conflicts between the cast add yet another level of conflict to the program. Despite being labeled as "un-reality," the show is popular across the Inner Sphere.

### The Latest

Daxton seems one win away from the Unlimited class, but his particle projector cannon capacitor is burned out, and he only has a few days to get a replacement before his next match. Jianne has been accepted into the Black Pegasus stables, but is about to be ambushed by Gretchen, who has been cheating on her with Jamison, the hottest pilot in Black Pegasus. Joining the cast is Lydia Coyote, a fresh arrival from Clan Space in her *Kingfisher*.

### DAOSHEN LIAO: JUNIOR HIGH CHANCELLOR

This Republic comedy finds Daoshen Liao as the head of Sian Junior High. Only he is aware of who he is, and everyone else laughs off his claims of being the Chancellor of the Capellan Confederation. The signature line is his cry "But I'm the Celestial Wisdom!" and the reply, from any actor on the show, "For this school, yes, sir!"

### The Latest

Sian Junior High has been assigned a new janitor. He insists on helping the teachers out, seeming to be better at their jobs than they are. When alone, the older man calls Daoshen by name and says he is Maximillian Liao, but any time Daoshen tells another person, the janitor laughs it off as a joke. Meanwhile, Daoshen needs to learn to make dumplings for the staff party, and has no luck at all in the kitchen.

# TECHNICAL READOUT: THE UNTOLD MAULER

## JOHANNES HEIDLER

When the Clans invaded, the *Mauler* was the newest, baddest assault 'Mech House Kurita could field, so new its details were still secret. Or so initial ComStar readouts told readers at the time. Other media begged to differ.

*Mauler*s were already so common in the Draconis Combine Mustered Soldiery that Theodore Kurita used them as the poster child of a joint marketing campaign with the newly founded Mercenary Review and Bonding Commission, to announce the end of the "Death to Mercenaries" doctrine. Furthermore, even the Federated Commonwealth fielded some *Mauler*s on the Clan front, and featured them in propaganda holovids. Far from the enigma ComStar believed it to be, the whole Inner Sphere was talking about the *Mauler* by the time the dust settled on Tukayyid.

Wolfnet later detailed the 3030s Kuritan origins, but the Davion-Steiner forces had another specific reason to target *Mauler*s for capture even ahead of ComStar-supplied Star League 'Mechs in the War of 3039. In the prior decade, they had clashed with it once before—on the other side of their border. For it was House Liao that first created a *Mauler* prototype and used it in field trials. Shock and paranoia over the Concord of Kapteyn's joint military project were a powerful motivator to the Department of Military Intelligence's MI2, which quickly gained thorough knowledge of the assault 'Mech. In the 3040s, the Armed Forces of the Federated Commonwealth judiciously deployed its few captured *Mauler*s in quiet assignments on the Lyran Periphery border, where they could be operated despite a dearth of replacement parts. So, the *Mauler* faced the Clans in all invasion corridors, establishing its hard-earned, enduring fame.

## Capabilities

Most *Mauler* arsenals focus on a bank of light autocannons, backed up by shoulder-mounted missiles and arms housing secondary energy weapons. The result is a flexible support unit rather than a traditional assault 'Mech. Doctrinally, the *Mauler* always suited the Federated Commonwealth more than its originators.

## Battle History

All handcrafted Capellan *Mauler* prototypes were deployed with the Fourth McCarron's Armored Cavalry in their "Long March" until the debacle on Beten Kaitos. During the push into the cauldron west of the planetary capital Nantucket, the prototypes were well equipped to engage the retreating New Avalon Institute of Science Training Cadre. Against the Cadre's light 'Mechs, the *Mauler*s lived up to their name with accurate, long-range barrages. However, this became a drop in the bucket when the hidden First Davion Guards poured over the ridge. In the ensuing melee, the lumbering 'Mechs became easy targets. Two of the prototypes fell alongside Lady Hamilton, and became MI2's most precious salvage.

After becoming readily available to the Federated Commonwealth in the 3060s, *Mauler*s commonly served on both sides during the Civil War. On Eaton, some survivors of Fifth Lyran Regulars were trying to regroup after the unit's destruction on Freedom in February 3066. Unfortunately, the planetary governor was fully aligned with the Free Skye Movement, and had hired small mercenary bands to attack the Loyalists' supply routes at Barlow's Gap in the St. Andes Mountains. After two such attacks, the Regulars prepared an ambush of their own in a side gulley with a fire lance led by a *Mauler*. When the mercenaries tried their trick again, its sudden appearance was enough to scatter the medium 'Mechs. Pursued by long-ranged autocannon fire whenever they reared their heads above the ridges beyond the Gap, they called off any further attacks. The mere presence of a *Mauler* had pacified the staging area. Alas, the misfortune of the Fifth continued, as their failed counterattack on the well-protected gubernatorial mansion led to the unit's final demise.

## Variants

Two early minor *Mauler* variants existed. When the initial production of MAL-1R outstripped that of the new Victory Nickel Alloy ER models, some—designated MAL-1Y—used the same Tronel large lasers as the *Daboku*. Captured *Daboku*s, deployed in Federated Commonwealth with the MAL-1X-AFFC designation, swapped the LRMs for quad SRM 4s. Their fewer but more pronounced missile ports are an easy identifier of the variant in early Clan Invasion footage.

## Notable 'Mechs and MechWarriors

**Captain Zachary Miles "Hawk" Hawkins:** The executive officer of the ad hoc First Somerset Strikers was a key figure in the *Mauler*'s early fame, as he piloted one during their early exploits. While Hawk lost the assault 'Mech during the brief reconquest of Somerset in November 3050 (and actually piloted a *Wolfhound* in the strike on Barcelona in 3052), his *Mauler*'s legacy lives on. With its early prominence in the Strikers, the holo series based on their exploits inaccurately featured *Mauler*s as ubiquitous opponents to the Clans. *First Somerset Strikers* became the most popular series since *Immortal Warrior*, and truly cemented the fame of the *Mauler*.

**Champion Michael Romney:** Michael Romney shot to fame not only for winning the 3048 Solaris Grand Championship, but also for doing so in one of the Liao prototype *Mauler*s. While the exotic 'Mech's provenance is unconfirmed, Starlight Stables' Davion alignment and NAIS' proven activities on-planet point to one of the spoils of Beten Kaitos. Romney used his fame to secure a place as the stable's chief instructor, where he mentored Bassem Dichari to reach the semi-finals in three consecutive years, using the same *Mauler*.

Type: **Mauler MAL-1X-AFFC**
Technology Base: Inner Sphere
Tonnage: 90
Role: Juggernaut
Battle Value: 1,286

| Equipment | | Mass |
|---|---|---|
| Internal Structure: | | 9 |
| Engine: | 270 | 14.5 |
| Walking MP: | 3 | |
| Running MP: | 5 | |
| Jumping MP: | 0 | |
| Heat Sinks: | 14 | 4 |
| Gyro: | | 3 |
| Cockpit: | | 3 |
| Armor Factor: | 152 | 9.5 |

| | Internal Structure | Armor Value |
|---|---|---|
| Head | 3 | 9 |
| Center Torso | 29 | 23 |
| Center Torso (rear) | | 8 |
| R/L Torso | 19 | 15 |
| R/L Torso (rear) | | 5 |
| R/L Arm | 15 | 16 |
| R/L Leg | 19 | 20 |

| Weapons and Ammo | Location | Critical | Tonnage |
|---|---|---|---|
| Large Laser | RA | 2 | 5 |
| 2 SRM 4 | RT | 2 | 4 |
| Ammo (SRM) 25 | RT | 1 | 1 |
| 2 AC/2 | RT | 2 | 12 |
| Ammo (AC) 45 | RT | 1 | 1 |
| CASE | RT | 1 | .5 |
| 2 SRM 4 | LT | 2 | 4 |
| Ammo (SRM) 25 | LT | 1 | 1 |
| 2 AC/2 | LT | 2 | 12 |
| Ammo (AC) 45 | LT | 1 | 1 |
| CASE | LT | 1 | .5 |
| Large Laser | LA | 2 | 5 |

**Type: Mauler MAL-1Y**
Technology Base: Inner Sphere
Tonnage: 90
Role: Sniper
Battle Value: 1,460

| Equipment | | Mass |
|---|---|---|
| Internal Structure: | | 9 |
| Engine: | 270 XL | 7.5 |
| Walking MP: | 3 | |
| Running MP: | 5 | |
| Jumping MP: | 0 | |
| Heat Sinks: | 11 [22] | 1 |
| Gyro: | | 3 |
| Cockpit: | | 3 |
| Armor Factor (Ferro): | 206 | 11.5 |

| | Internal Structure | Armor Value |
|---|---|---|
| Head | 3 | 9 |
| Center Torso | 29 | 27 |
| Center Torso (rear) | | 10 |
| R/L Torso | 19 | 26 |
| R/L Torso (rear) | | 10 |
| R/L Arm | 15 | 22 |
| R/L Leg | 19 | 22 |

| Weapons and Ammo | Location | Critical | Tonnage |
|---|---|---|---|
| Large Laser | RA | 2 | 5 |
| LRM 15 | RT | 3 | 7 |
| Ammo (LRM) 16 | RT | 2 | 2 |
| 2 AC/2 | RT | 2 | 12 |
| Ammo (AC) 45 | RT | 1 | 1 |
| CASE | RT | 1 | .5 |
| LRM 15 | LT | 3 | 7 |
| Ammo (LRM) 16 | LT | 2 | 2 |
| 2 AC/2 | LT | 2 | 12 |
| Ammo (AC) 45 | LT | 1 | 1 |
| CASE | LT | 1 | .5 |
| Large Laser | LA | 2 | 5 |

# MAL-1PT5 MAULER

**Mass:** 90 tons
**Chassis:** Earthwerks Class 100PT
**Power Plant:** GM 270
**Cruising Speed:** 32 kph
**Maximum Speed:** 54 kph
**Jump Jets:** None
    **Jump Capacity:** None
**Armor:** Kallon Royalstar
**Armament:**
    2 CeresArms Medium Lasers
    2 Delta Dart LRM 15 Racks
    4 SarLon Autocannon/2
**Manufacturer:** Earthwerks Incorporated
**Primary Factory:** Tikonov
**Communications System:** CommuTech Multi-Channel 10
**Targeting and Tracking System:** BlazeFire Sightlock

When House Liao requested proposals for a more powerful BattleMech than the *Vindicator*, then the backbone of its military, part of Earthwerks' bid was an assault 'Mech named the "*Mauler*." The new creation aimed for combat effectiveness at ranges where targets could not respond. Anemic arm-mounted lasers offered only token protection, with their huge baffles intended not as battering rams, but to accommodate future upgrades. However, Earthwerks' other entry, the *Cataphract*, was more effective at conventional ranges, much cheaper, and easier on logistics, literally reusing parts from other BattleMechs. Deemed the worse alternative, the *Mauler* never saw production beyond a half dozen custom prototypes.

In the field tests during McCarron's March, the *Mauler*s were so effective at supporting an engagement from the sidelines that their pilots affectionately called it the "*Linesman*"—though come March 3023, this moniker would seem like a curse to Liao's Strategios. Earthwerks traded the *Mauler* plans to Luthien Armor Works, where they were filed as Project *Nainokami* and then proposed as a basic platform during the better-known post-Helm Project *Daboku*. Stuck between two members of the Concord of Kapteyn, the Federated Commonwealth consistently preserved the *Mauler*'s proper name, decades before receiving the 'Mech through legitimate channels.

## Sub-Variant

Earthwerks' final prototype sported large lasers, using a smaller engine to save mass. Before the availability of *Iostech*, the MAL-1PT6 was a dead end, with glacial speed and completely overtaxed heat sinks, but it created the template most *Mauler*s have followed since.

Type: **Mauler MAL-1PT5**
Technology Base: Inner Sphere (Introductory)
Tonnage: 90
Role: Sniper
Battle Value: 1,400

| Equipment | | Mass |
|---|---|---|
| Internal Structure: | | 9 |
| Engine: | 270 | 14.5 |
| Walking MP: | 3 | |
| Running MP: | 5 | |
| Jumping MP: | 0 | |
| Heat Sinks: | 12 | 2 |
| Gyro: | | 3 |
| Cockpit: | | 3 |
| Armor Factor: | 200 | 12.5 |

| | Internal Structure | Armor Value |
|---|---|---|
| Head | 3 | 9 |
| Center Torso | 29 | 30 |
| Center Torso (rear) | | 9 |
| R/L Torso | 19 | 28 |
| R/L Torso (rear) | | 6 |
| R/L Arm | 15 | 20 |
| R/L Leg | 19 | 22 |

| Weapons and Ammo | Location | Critical | Tonnage |
|---|---|---|---|
| Medium Laser | RA | 1 | 1 |
| LRM 15 | RT | 3 | 7 |
| Ammo (LRM) 16 | RT | 2 | 2 |
| 2 AC/2 | RT | 2 | 12 |
| Ammo (AC) 45 | RT | 1 | 1 |
| LRM 15 | LT | 3 | 7 |
| Ammo (LRM) 16 | LT | 2 | 2 |
| 2 AC/2 | LT | 2 | 12 |
| Ammo (AC) 45 | LT | 1 | 1 |
| Medium Laser | LA | 1 | 1 |

**Notes:** Features the following Design Quirk: Stabilized Weapon (Autocannons).

Type: **Mauler MAL-1PT6**
Technology Base: Inner Sphere (Introductory)
Tonnage: 90
Role: Sniper
Battle Value: 1,270

| Equipment | | Mass |
|---|---|---|
| Internal Structure: | | 9 |
| Engine: | 180 | 7 |
|    Walking MP: | 2 | |
|    Running MP: | 3 | |
|    Jumping MP: | 0 | |
| Heat Sinks: | 12 | 2 |
| Gyro: | | 2 |
| Cockpit: | | 3 |
| Armor Factor: | 200 | 12.5 |

| | Internal Structure | Armor Value |
|---|---|---|
| Head | 3 | 9 |
| Center Torso | 29 | 30 |
| Center Torso (rear) | | 9 |
| R/L Torso | 19 | 28 |
| R/L Torso (rear) | | 6 |
| R/L Arm | 15 | 20 |
| R/L Leg | 19 | 22 |

| Weapons and Ammo | Location | Critical | Tonnage |
|---|---|---|---|
| Large Laser | RA | 2 | 5 |
| LRM 15 | RT | 3 | 7 |
| Ammo (LRM) 16 | RT | 2 | 2 |
| 2 AC/2 | RT | 2 | 12 |
| Ammo (AC) 45 | RT | 1 | 1 |
| Small Laser | H | 1 | .5 |
| LRM 15 | LT | 3 | 7 |
| Ammo (LRM) 16 | LT | 2 | 2 |
| 2 AC/2 | LT | 2 | 12 |
| Ammo (AC) 45 | LT | 1 | 1 |
| Large Laser | LA | 2 | 5 |

**Notes:** Features the following Design Quirk: Stabilized Weapon (Autocannons).

# MAL-2R MAULER

**Mass:** 90 tons
**Chassis:** Alshain Class 101
**Power Plant:** GM 270
**Cruising Speed:** 32 kph
**Maximum Speed:** 54 kph
**Jump Jets:** None
**Jump Capacity:** None
**Armor:** New Samarkand Royal Ferro-Fibrous with CASE
**Armament:**
> 4 Bright-Bloom Extended-Range Medium Lasers
> 2 Federated 10-Shot LRM-10 Launchers
> 4 Mydron Model D-rf Light Autocannons

**Manufacturer:** General Dynamics (Refit)
**Primary Factory:** Ozawa
**Communications System:** Sipher Security Plus mk.II
**Targeting and Tracking System:** Matabushi SuperSentinel

The years following the Truce of Tukayyid saw an unprecedented era of close cooperation between the Federated Commonwealth and the Draconis Combine. Having contributed greatly to the *Mauler's* fame, the AFFC received many more through trade agreements.

House Davion has a lasting fascination with autocannons, and invested heavily in advancing their technology in the 3050s. Next to the *JagerMech*, the *Mauler* was predestined as a testbed for the resulting weapons. In a partnership with Luthien Armor Works, General Dynamics of Ozawa opened a refit facility with a new variant, the MAL-2R. It centered around cutting-edge light Ultra autocannons, while remaining simple and sturdy. General Dynamics seemed to draw as much from the original plans as from the imported, modern LAW chassis it performed its magic on, creating a combination that focused squarely on the new guns.

## Sub-Variant

Autocannon development continued, and by the early 3060s, rotary autocannons were available. The MAL-2D gained mass for the increasingly massive cannons by downgrading the shoulder box launchers to medium-range missiles—also readily available through LAW. As both the lasers and missiles were now all but vestigial, the MAL-2D became a developmental cul-de-sac. Though doubtlessly effective, it had poor mission endurance and did not offer tangible improvements in firepower.

The political situation changed dramatically soon after, putting an end to further Davion development of the *Mauler*.

Type: **Mauler MAL-2R**
Technology Base: Inner Sphere
Tonnage: 90
Role: Juggernaut
Battle Value: 1,586

| Equipment | | Mass |
|---|---|---|
| Internal Structure: | | 9 |
| Engine: | 270 | 14.5 |
| Walking MP: | 3 | |
| Running MP: | 5 | |
| Jumping MP: | 0 | |
| Heat Sinks: | 12 [24] | 2 |
| Gyro: | | 3 |
| Cockpit: | | 3 |
| Armor Factor (Ferro): | 206 | 11.5 |

| | Internal Structure | Armor Value |
|---|---|---|
| Head | 3 | 9 |
| Center Torso | 29 | 27 |
| Center Torso (rear) | | 10 |
| R/L Torso | 19 | 26 |
| R/L Torso (rear) | | 10 |
| R/L Arm | 15 | 22 |
| R/L Leg | 19 | 22 |

| Weapons and Ammo | Location | Critical | Tonnage |
|---|---|---|---|
| 2 ER Medium Lasers | RA | 2 | 2 |
| LRM 10 | RT | 2 | 5 |
| Ammo (LRM) 12 | RT | 1 | 1 |
| 2 Ultra AC/2 | RT | 6 | 14 |
| Ammo (Ultra) 45 | RT | 1 | 1 |
| CASE | RT | 1 | .5 |
| LRM 10 | LT | 2 | 5 |
| Ammo (LRM) 12 | LT | 1 | 1 |
| 2 Ultra AC/2 | LT | 6 | 14 |
| Ammo (Ultra) 45 | LT | 1 | 1 |
| CASE | LT | 1 | .5 |
| 2 ER Medium Lasers | LA | 2 | 2 |

**Notes:** Features the following Design Quirk: Stabilized Weapon (Autocannons).

Type: **Mauler MAL-2D**
Technology Base: Inner Sphere
Tonnage: 90
Role: Juggernaut
Battle Value: 1,745

| Equipment | | Mass |
|---|---|---|
| Internal Structure: | | 9 |
| Engine: | 270 | 14.5 |
| Walking MP: | 3 | |
| Running MP: | 5 | |
| Jumping MP: | 0 | |
| Heat Sinks: | 12 [24] | 2 |
| Gyro: | | 3 |
| Cockpit: | | 3 |
| Armor Factor (Ferro): | 206 | 11.5 |

| | Internal Structure | Armor Value |
|---|---|---|
| Head | 3 | 9 |
| Center Torso | 29 | 27 |
| Center Torso (rear) | | 10 |
| R/L Torso | 19 | 26 |
| R/L Torso (rear) | | 10 |
| R/L Arm | 15 | 22 |
| R/L Leg | 19 | 22 |

| Weapons and Ammo | Location | Critical | Tonnage |
|---|---|---|---|
| 2 ER Medium Lasers | RA | 2 | 2 |
| MRM 10 | RT | 2 | 3 |
| 2 Rotary AC/2 | RT | 6 | 16 |
| Ammo (RAC) 90 | RT | 2 | 2 |
| CASE | RT | 1 | .5 |
| MRM 10 | LT | 2 | 3 |
| Ammo (MRM) 24 | LT | 1 | 1 |
| 2 Rotary AC/2 | LT | 6 | 16 |
| Ammo (RAC) 45 | LT | 1 | 1 |
| CASE | LT | 1 | .5 |
| 2 ER Medium Lasers | LA | 2 | 2 |

**Notes:** Features the following Design Quirk: Stabilized Weapon (Autocannons).

# MAL-1KX MAULER

**Mass:** 90 tons
**Chassis:** New Samarkand Class 201 Endo Steel
**Power Plant:** Hermes 270 XL
**Cruising Speed:** 32 kph
**Maximum Speed:** 54 kph
**Jump Jets:** None
**Jump Capacity:** None
**Armor:** Wakazashi Standard Plate
**Armament:**
> 2 Lord's Light 5 Snub-Nose Particle Projection Cannons
> 2 Shigunga Long Range Missile 15-Racks
> 4 SarLon MiniCannon Light Autocannon/5

**Manufacturer:** Luthien Armor Works
**Primary Factory:** New Samarkand
**Communications System:** Sipher Security Plus mk.II
**Targeting and Tracking System:** Matabushi SuperSentinel

The final mystery of the *Mauler* was its lack of variants since the Jihad. LAW's developmental experimentation in the late 3060s sought to perfect a new weapons suite focused on medium ranges while improving the armor to suit an assault 'Mech. It did not fare well.

As in a prior attempt to update the BattleMech—3062's MAL-3R—the *Mauler*'s volatile CASE had to be discarded to accommodate new autocannon solutions, thereby undermining the quest for increased resilience. Additionally, the particle projector cannon overburdened the lower arm actuators. Increased armor mass required the use of a bulky endo-steel structure, reducing internal space, and allowing a small cockpit, cramping the MechWarrior, too. This aggregation of compromises prevented any investment in retooling the main production line. Only few examples of the MAL-1KX were finished, most being used as platforms for the development of the experimental *Banzai* melee assault 'Mech. After finding solutions for the actuators, if not the CASE, the weapons suite was instead mounted on the old MAL-1R chassis for production purposes, resulting in the widespread MAL-1K. With that, LAW cut its losses and stopped further development post-Jihad. Until the *Mauler* was refurbished with Clan weaponry following the Nova Cat Rebellion, Kurita's iconic BattleMech would become long in the tooth.

## Sub-Variant

Professor Wheeler of the Sun Zhang Academy suggested a last concept prior to the end of *Mauler* development. An updated weapon package centering around Thunderbolt missiles and variable-speed pulse lasers seemed promising, but was unfortunately implemented on the -1KX chassis, inheriting its flaws.

Type: **Mauler MAL-1KX**
Technology Base: Inner Sphere
Tonnage: 90
Role: Juggernaut
Battle Value: 1,678

| Equipment | | Mass |
|---|---|---|
| Internal Structure: | Endo Steel | 4.5 |
| Engine: | 270 XL | 7.5 |
| Walking MP: | 3 | |
| Running MP: | 5 | |
| Jumping MP: | 0 | |
| Heat Sinks: | 12 [24] | 2 |
| Gyro: | | 3 |
| Cockpit (Small): | | 2 |
| Armor Factor: | 272 | 17 |

| | Internal Structure | Armor Value |
|---|---|---|
| Head | 3 | 9 |
| Center Torso | 29 | 43 |
| Center Torso (rear) | | 14 |
| R/L Torso | 19 | 28 |
| R/L Torso (rear) | | 9 |
| R/L Arm | 15 | 29 |
| R/L Leg | 19 | 37 |

| Weapons and Ammo | Location | Critical | Tonnage |
|---|---|---|---|
| Snub-Nose PPC | RA | 2 | 6 |
| Ammo (LAC) 40 | RA | 2 | 2 |
| LRM 15 | RT | 3 | 7 |
| Ammo (LRM) 16 | RT | 2 | 2 |
| 2 Light AC/5 | RT | 4 | 10 |
| LRM 15 | LT | 3 | 7 |
| Ammo (LRM) 16 | LT | 2 | 2 |
| 2 Light AC/5 | LT | 4 | 10 |
| Ammo (LAC) 40 | LA | 2 | 2 |
| Snub-Nose PPC | LA | 2 | 6 |

**Notes:** Features the following Design Quirk: Stabilized Weapon (Autocannons).

Type: **Mauler MAL-3K**
Technology Base: Inner Sphere
Tonnage: 90
Role: Missile Boat
Battle Value: 1,622

| Equipment | | Mass |
|---|---|---|
| Internal Structure: | Endo Steel | 4.5 |
| Engine: | 270 XL | 7.5 |
| Walking MP: | 3 | |
| Running MP: | 5 | |
| Jumping MP: | 0 | |
| Heat Sinks: | 12 [24] | 2 |
| Gyro (Compact): | | 4.5 |
| Cockpit (Small): | | 2 |
| Armor Factor: | 279 | 17.5 |

| | Internal Structure | Armor Value |
|---|---|---|
| Head | 3 | 9 |
| Center Torso | 29 | 44 |
| Center Torso (rear) | | 14 |
| R/L Torso | 19 | 28 |
| R/L Torso (rear) | | 10 |
| R/L Arm | 15 | 30 |
| R/L Leg | 19 | 38 |

| Weapons and Ammo | Location | Critical | Tonnage |
|---|---|---|---|
| Large VSP Laser | RA | 4 | 9 |
| LRM 15 | RT | 3 | 7 |
| Ammo (LRM) 16 | RT | 2 | 2 |
| 2 Thunderbolt 5 | RT | 2 | 6 |
| Ammo (Thunderbolt) 24 | RT | 2 | 2 |
| LRM 15 | LT | 3 | 7 |
| Ammo (LRM) 16 | LT | 2 | 2 |
| 2 Thunderbolt 5 | LT | 2 | 6 |
| Ammo (Thunderbolt) 24 | LT | 2 | 2 |
| Large VSP Laser | LA | 4 | 9 |

# SECOND TO NONE

### RUSSELL ZIMMERMAN

**KELL HOUNDS HQ**
**WUHAN CITY**
**AMBERGRIST**
**ST. IVES COMPACT**
**6 FEBRUARY 3048**

There's something about lectures that makes them kind of blur together into one never-ending, indeterminable stretch of background dialogue. Time distorts. My attention span wavers. Stuff happens, but it all smudges into one, long, half-remembered barrage of good advice I resentfully do my best to ignore.

"So let me get this straight, and make sure it wasn't a comm issue," Sita Frost started in on me right away. She was my best friend, and sometimes more than that, so she felt comfortable laying into me as soon as our feet hit the pavement at the end of our 'Mech ladders, both wearing vests, boots, and a layer of sweat. The field patrol was over. The lecture was just getting started.

"John Hillson, legendary grouch, who has kicked up his grouchiness since even before this deployment began, has managed to be *extra* grouchy tonight," she lectured, her long-legged stride easily keeping pace with me.

I stomped off to the showers, past the technicians swarming our way to take over our 'Mechs. We were on a medium-threat assignment, which meant rigorously maintaining technical readiness, even just after a patrol.

"You've been in a bad mood all day." The lecture droned on. We toweled off post-shower as MechWarriors milled about, snapping towels, cracking jokes, shaving, and getting dressed. Comfortable stuff, don't get me wrong; our Kell Hound Class Cs, our combat uniforms, are little more than flight suits, just our everyday wear. But still, *work clothes*. That rankled. I topped mine off with my favorite jacket.

"And you are now staunchly determined to be in a bad mood all night." The lecture was relentless. She and I milled around outside, waiting for Ramirez and Conrad to finish getting ready. Conrad was gonna be five minutes late to her own funeral, I swear. You'd think being lieutenants in the Kell Hounds 123rd—specifically our Amphibious Warfare Unit—would mean those two might be better at water-adjacent tasks like taking showers, drying off, or navigating slick floors, but no.

"And all of this moodiness is…because we got invited to enjoy the latest Solaris fights at a party?" She continued the lecture as we headed across open tarmac toward the main HQ building beneath the setting sun. Frost finally just *stopped* in her tracks, cutting me off, forcing the issue. Ramirez and Conrad ambled ahead a few steps so they could pretend not to be listening in. Right that second, I was insanely jealous of their ability to just walk away.

"It's not that we got invited to a party!" I stuffed my hands into my jacket pockets, shoulders down, collar up, sulking a bit. Great jacket! It was a classic MechWarrior neo-bomber, high waisted, high collared, highly armored, high-vis reflective stripes. Super cool, but not the best for sulking.

"It's that we got invited to a party *today*, when we had late patrols, and they *know that*, and we got invited by a *major*, and then *our* major reminded us of the 'invitation,' which basically turns it into an order. So, we in Second Battalion had a—"

"*Wild Dogs!*" Conrad and Ramirez, triggered by the magic words, eagerly called out over their shoulders. They were *apparently* still close enough to be listening in, and not shy to show it.

"Ahem!" I glared at them while they pretended to be far enough away to ignore me. "I'm just saying, *Second* had a long duty day while First was back here on base, and still we've got to clean up, dress up, and haul our butts across base to go hang out with officers and the boss's nephew—"

"—at a party, yes. Invited to the office of the legendary hero, Daniel Allard, by the legendary hero, Akira Brahe. And you're right, legendary hero Morgan Kell's nephew, Christian, our fellow officer, will be there, too! It's awful! Senior officers inviting junior officers to socialize, oh noooo!" Frost struck a melodramatic pose, back of her hand against her forehead, a dainty damsel in need of a fainting couch.

"I'm just saying I could be in my bunk right now. Because, again, Brahe *knows* Second Battalion—"

"*Wild Dogs!*" This time, Frost sang it out, too.

I pressed on. "—he knows we had late patrols today, and we've got early patrols tomorrow. And Brahe *knows* that, because Brahe *decided* that, and while our whole unit always bends over backward to accommodate First and their schedule, they still throw us a curveball like this?! It's *bullshit*, man!"

None of the three lieutenants I was ranting at were "men," but I didn't let that stop me.

"Why not just watch the stupid videos tomorrow? While First is on patrol, and Se—" I caught myself as I saw all three of them sucking in air to holler the usual call-and-return, "—and *we're* back on base, with all day spread out before us?"

"We watched the fight vids the next day last time, Hillson." Ramirez grabbed Conrad by the hand and tugged her away, very pointedly.

"And *you* punched a techie 'cause unit gossips spoiled the winners!" Conrad made a what'cha-gonna-do face at me and let herself be hauled off.

Oh. Right. Crap. In my defense, I hated spoilers.

I sighed. The pair left me with Frost, meat for the beast. No witnesses. No mercy. Just earnestness, the worst kind of low, honest, talk. She was Sita, not Frost, for a minute. My best friend, not a peer. *More* than a friend, not just a fellow lieutenant.

"Johnny, you have *got* to get over this whatever-it-is you've got toward First. We're all Hounds here. First Regiment! Look at us! We're officers in *First Regiment,* Kell Hounds, best of the best, devil dogs in red and black! Do you have any idea how many mercs would, I dunno, *kick a baby*, for the chance to be either of us?"

"I know, but—"

"Do you know how lucky we are, how damned *good* we are, to be Kell Hounds at all, plus, you know, to be officers? In *First Regiment*? No matter what battalion? Hell, random mercs, nothing, I know guys right there in Second Regiment who'd *at least* push a baby down to get our spots this close to the big dogs..."

I couldn't help but snort and grin at the mental image of Scott Bradley shoving a baby. Solid hit. Rumor was Bradley and the rest of Second Regiment would be on their way to the Periphery soon, pirate hunting. Honest work, but only after a long, long ship ride. I didn't envy 'em. They were right to envy us.

I smiled weakly at her and nodded.

She'd gotten me to break, so she smiled brightly in return. She *didn't* give me her usual celebratory punch in the arm, though. She'd learned better when I had this jacket on.

"So really, what *is* your problem with First Batt, Hothead?" She used my callsign to rub it in, even as she sounded exasperated at asking me for probably the hundredth time. That hurt more than a punch in the arm. I knew I'd earned it, and not just because of my violently red hair.

She was right. I knew I'd been grouching more than usual lately. I knew why. I knew I could trust her; she was my best friend. I knew anything I told her would stay between us, or *maybe* with a unit chaplain, at worst, but it would never make its way up the gossip grapevine or the chain of command.

But I also knew I wasn't sure how to put it into words, or ready to try. Yet.

"Just jealous," I said, broad shoulders of my jacket exaggerating my shrug, which exaggerated my lie. "Normal stuff. Tired of feeling like we're second fiddle, y'know, with refit assignments, upgrade requests, and…"

I trailed off. One of the best ways to not finish a lie was to just ease off and let someone's imagination fill in the blanks they wanted to hear. Sita wouldn't be able to help but think about the "and" I left hanging for her, she'd tell the rest of my lie to herself for me.

I knew how to lie when I had to. I'd practiced a lot lately.

"Yeah, well, get over it." She reached up and grabbed the lapels of my jacket, hauling me in for a kiss.

I returned it, but sputtered and cast around a wide-eyed look as we finished. Fraternization wasn't against Kell Hounds regs, but it was still faintly frowned on. Ramirez and Conrad had already gotten a stern talking to from the major, Old Lady O'Cathain. I didn't want Frost and I to get a similar lecture. I was tired of lectures. Sita didn't let me worry for long.

"C'mon. Let's go. There's worse fates than relaxing with senior staff to watch Solaris fights." She turned away and sauntered off without me, no hand-holding after the risky kiss. "I hear Major Brahe's busted out the *sake* and is being downright reckless with the bets. Decent odds against the kid!"

I snorted again. Major Akira Brahe would never actually get drunk enough to be reckless about anything, and he'd certainly never get drunk-drunk, genuinely drunk, when we were in a yellow zone like this. Heart of our assigned base or not, with the Capellans on the prowl, Brahe wouldn't stop being a stone-cold killer.

"There's no such thing as decent odds if the kid's in a *Panther* again." I chuckled as I trotted to keep up. We'd all taken a keen interest in a Starlight Stables up-and-comer, slicing his way through ranks in the Class Two matches, the Solaris Lightweight Division. "Thanks, but I think I'll keep my…my…"

*Huh.* We hadn't been on-world for long, and I'd never been in the St. Ives Compact before. In my defense, the place wasn't even as old as I was.

"Hey, what money are we getting paid in again?" I hollered after her.

## KELL HOUNDS TRAINING AREA
## AMBERGRIST
## ST. IVES COMPACT
## 10 FEBRUARY 3048

The voice was as stern as any my mother had ever used on me, and the enunciation was something right out of any sitcom holovid where a husband, brother, or boyfriend was getting scolded.

"Lieutenant Jonathan Laurens 'Hothead' Hillson, are you *seriously* back on your bullshit right now?" She'd busted out my middle name, so I knew she was mad. Sita, "Frosty" when we were on the clock, was back on *her* bullshit, only now she was lecturing me on a tight-band, short-range, comms beam instead of face-to-face. "In the middle of a goddamned training sim?"

Her Heavy Scout Lance and my Strike Lance were forward and on the flanks, while Captain Pattie O'Lochlainn lumbered along behind us, leading the 122nd's big dogs in her Heavy Assault Lance. Banter aside, we kept a tight formation. We were a well-oiled machine; one I *knew* was the equal to any of First Battalion's companies. We were about to show them.

"If by 'back on your bullshit' you mean 'making verifiable observations of favoritism within the regiment?' then yes, Frosty, yes, I am, in fact, back on my bullshit."

I scowled in my neurohelmet, but my hands stayed steady on the controls, my *Wolfhound*'s pace was undisturbed (unlike my mood). I knew my 'Mech's head had a snarl that matched my own, though. A savage crisscross of pointed teeth had been painted onto the canine cockpit, ancient Terran nose art with a modern flair. It always looked grouchy. Most of the time, so did I.

"C'mon, they're just *giving* him a 'Mech!" I was worried I might have let a little too much whine into my voice and not enough disgust. Oh, well. Best to press on. "First Christian Kell gets a *Thunderbolt* for, I don't know, for just existing, and now *this*? For getting kicked *out* of Nagelring and sent back to the Hounds, tail between his legs, they're giving Phelan a *'Mech*?!"

Phelan Kell, the boss's kid. Word around the mess hall was that he'd pulled some cockamamie stunt and gotten booted from one of the best academies in the Sphere, and he was getting rewarded for it?!

"Yeah, but just a *Wolfhound*, that barely counts," Ramirez quipped, because *of course* she'd been given the comm code by Frosty, despite being in a different company. Snug in the cockpit of her *Thunderbolt*, she rubbed salt into the wound. "I mean, a light?"

"Right? Really, is it still a gift if it's just a *Wolfhound*?" Conrad cut in too, clearly enjoying herself, *also* not from the 122nd, but still dogpiling on.

Out of our broad class of junior lieutenants, I was the only one with a light. Heck, I was the only MechWarrior in my own *lance* with a light. I was used to taking a little crap for it, but, c'mon...did *all* my friends need to join in, smug at the controls of a *Kintaro*, a *Thunderbolt*, and a *Rifleman*? Sita's *Kintaro* wasn't even a heavy, and still she poked fun! And why wasn't anyone making fun of Conrad's *Rifleman*?! I had as much armor as she did!

Teasing from Sita was one thing. I mean, Frosty and I had basically grown up together, we'd been best friends and partners in crime for almost as long as I could remember. Since '27, when Morgan Kell had reconstituted the Kell Hounds, we'd been inseparable. Our mothers were best friends, both single moms, both aerospace jockeys. They'd dumped the two of us together for most of our lives, and things had grown from there. So fine, fine. I was used to her pecking. But getting Conrad and Ramirez in on it? Getting dogpiled? That stung.

"Hardy har, real fu—" I started, but then I saw a sensor blip. Bullshit time stopped. We were back on the clock. I thumbed my comm over to battalion-wide with a flicker-quick motion. "Contact, one o'clock," I barked.

My lean *Wolfhound*'s anthropomorphic "ears" weren't just for show. They housed a top-end Digital Scanlok 347 Targeting and Tracking System, some of the finest electronics in the regiment. I could grouse and do my job at the same time; I was an expert at it. I got back quick confirmation clicks as more hostiles appeared, then swapped myself back over to just my 122nd Company channel.

My console lit up as I saw active comm lines from our battalion leader, Old Lady O'Cathain, to her company commanders. There was Major O'Cathain's own daughter, Captain *Maggie* O'Cathain, who was Ramirez and Conrad's boss, there was Captain Kevin Connor, and finally me and Frosty's CO, Captain Pattie O'Lochlainn. The call was quick, and from my own experiences with the major, I knew whatever orders she gave were swift and sure.

A moment later, the captains relayed orders down to us lieutenants, each running our own four-'Mech lance. From the moment I'd spotted a hostile contact to the time each of us lance commanders had our orders and begun to execute them was well under ten seconds.

Kell Hounds, baby. We know our work.

But, man, did I not *like* my order. Holding sucked.

"Lima, Lima, Lima! Let's get 'em," was the six-word order I got from Captain O'Lochlainn.

"Break right, then hold," was the four-word order I relayed to the rest of my Striker Lance. I tried, like every junior officer ought to, to sound confident. Firm. Excited. I wasn't feeling it, though.

A "Lima" go-code meant Frosty's team moving up and drawing fire while the captain's own lance double-timed it to get into range, as well. My Striker Lance? We moved to one side, crouched or knelt in whatever cover and concealment we could find, and waited. I hated waiting.

Enough about the rest of Second Battalion (Wild Dogs!); right now, it was *my* lance I had to focus on. I flashed a low-energy yellow light to each of my shooters, a silent communication, reminding them to hold and be patient.

Speirs blinked green back at me. She and her *Griffin* were rock-solid. She was older than me, thirty and still not an officer, but mostly because she didn't want to *be* an officer, at least not yet. I respected that she saw a purity to her work, just the fighting. Her GRF-3M, hot off the lines in Oliver, brought a long-range punch to our mostly short-ranged lance, and she was an absolute expert with her jump jets.

Singh and her *Crusader* had jump jets, too, and she also flashed me a green light. Her machine was new, and she was still getting used to it. The Kell Hounds had accepted a subcontract to field test a potential variant coming out soon, a CRD-5M. It was a pleasure to set up Singh with the new prototype and run it through its paces.

Tomas "Driftwood" Tereshkova was the last green wink I received. Driftwood and his *Axman* matched Singh and her *Crusader*'s top speed, weight, jump profile...and new 'Mech smell. His was a cutting-edge affair, 65 tons of fancy-pants ferro-fibrous armor, an extralight engine, CASE protection for ammunition, a big malfing autocannon, and an even *bigger* malfing axe. The *Hatchetman* had impressed enough people that the *Axman* had been created to improve on it. Driftwood complained about wanting more lasers and less ammo-dependent guns, but despite the grouching, he was dangerous as hell in his new ride.

We packed some punch, my Striker Lance and I, and we were eager to use our fancy new toys. Training simulator or not, we wanted off the leash.

Instead, a Lima order said we waited.

We watched—anxiously, hungrily—as Frosty's lance engaged the enemy, sensors flaring and flashing, comm channels lighting up as questions, answers, and warnings rang out as swiftly and reflexively as our Second-Battalion-Wild-Dogs call and returns did. Smooth as clockwork, Frosty and her team engaged the enemy, Captain O'Lochlainn and her lance moved up to provide their own tremendous firepower... and then...they began to fall back.

Under withering hails of fire from all three OpFor lances, O'Lochlainn and Frost's advance slowed, stalled, and reversed itself.

"Strikers, ready up," the captain tight-beamed me, and even in the background of that quick little transmission, I heard her getting buffeted by missiles.

I refused to blink, staring at my sensor display. The nearest red 'Mechs were getting close enough I could make out distinct makes and models, and my imagination could fill in exactly what weapons they were using to hammer my captain and her lance, and my best friend and *her* lance, too. Pinging red came a *Crusader*, a *Griffin*, a *Trebuchet*, and a *Vindicator*, pouring on the fire.

The captain sent me a yellow light, blinking twice. She and Frost pulled back farther.

"Guns up," I said over my lance comm, and our hundreds-of-tons of 'Mechs shifted their weight, tensed, coiled like springs ready to launch. I got a hard lock on the *Trebuchet* and tight-beamed my target data to the rest of my team.

Yellow, blinking faster. Yellow. Yellow.

Green.

"Sic 'em!" I barked, redlining my engine and throttling forward beyond suggested factory specs. On streams of plasma, the rest of my lance matched my energy and speed, if not my precise path. We hit, together and hard.

As one, we fell on the *Trebuchet*, our nearest target. My lasers flashed and flayed and armor streamed away from our enemy. Speirs' *Griffin* matched my beams of light and added a volley of long-range missiles. Singh's new *Crusader* upgrade more than doubled that barrage of LRMs, then hammered with short-range missiles, heavier, with heavier warheads, as we closed the gap. Driftwood's scintillating beams of light found something deep in the OpFor 'Mech's chest and touched off the ammunition stored there. The *Trebuchet* blossomed into a simulated fireball.

One down.

*Sorry, Serge*, I grinned in my helmet and flicked my lance-wide target toggle over to the *Vindicator*.

The remaining members of the Fire Lance moved crisply, professionally, swiftly, to meet us. They pivoted smoothly, turning their guns on the new threat, backing away on plumes of fire as they triggered jump jets to try and create distance from their savage attackers.

We lived up to our Wild Dogs nickname as we pressed the attack, though. Another tremendous flurry of energy flew from the four of us to the *one* target, focused, brutal, and as precise as any Kell Hounds you could name. As the wave of missiles left smoke and shrapnel in the air, I thumbed my firing studs a second time. Brilliant spears of energy poured from my trio of chest-mounted lasers and probed the *Vindicator* until I found its ammunition stores, and a massive secondary explosion cleared it from my sensors for good. Andre de Pontcing going down was a good trade for the blasts of hot air assaulting me as my heat sinks struggled to keep up with my aggressive pace.

We kept it up. Billy Kantor in his *Griffin* went down. Then, last, their lieutenant, Fitzmartin in her big *Crusader*. Four up, four down. Fire Lance swept clean.

Trading shots, O'Lochlainn and Frost's lances had taken a beating, sure, but nobody was down, nobody was out. Meanwhile, four opposing 'Mechs had been pounced on by my lance, pouring on fire to exploit their weakened armor, focusing, picking them off neatly. Sweat plastered me and I was breathing heavily—like I'd gotten a face full of air opening an oven—but I couldn't help but smile even as I panted, watching my *Wolfhound* struggle to cool down after the brutal fight.

'Cause so far, we were *smoking* First Battalion.

"Second! Battalion!" someone hollered triumphantly over company comms.

"WILD DOGS!" every MechWarrior roared back.

Then I had to cut in, because my *Wolfhound* helped me spot trouble coming despite the sweat in my eyes. I tagged inbound opponents and ruined the moment of good cheer.

"Back on the clock." I hated how the heat made it come out as a croak. I was trying to play the lieutenant, the firm officer, the no-frills commander in the field. "Guns up!"

A *Catapult* pivoted at the waist to lob a volley of missiles our way, followed by an alpha strike from a *Centurion* coming at Singh, and the broad torso of a *Quickdraw* turning our way. Worst of all, a *Wolverine* came at us, impossibly nimble for all its armor and guns, roaring aggressively toward us on wings of fire. We had earned the ire of Major Salome Ward, Colonel Morgan Kell's own wife, Phelan and Caitlin Kell's mother, and one of the longest-serving, most lethal members of the Kell Hounds, the best damned unit in the Inner Sphere.

*Let's do this.* I felt my frustration, my anger, my Hothead callsign, well up in me. I tamped it down. I focused. I was an officer and a Kell Hound, not a berserker.

I toggled my Striker Lance's priority tracker to the *Wolverine*, then throttled up and led the charge. My *Wolfhound* was the fastest thing in my lance. I had to show them I deserved every square centimeter of that engine.

I slipped under a sheet of LRMs. An autocannon burst glanced off my armor instead of hitting clean. More laser beams missed me than hit. Another autocannon burst flew high. I closed the gap, and, for a moment, a trio of laser beam umbilicals lanced out from the chest of my 'Mech and slashed at the armor on the chest of the major's *Wolverine*, joining us together in a savage display while I was still running straight at her.

Then, in close, I lowered my *Wolfhound*'s shoulder and leaned into it, charging.

Ward met my rush with an extended boot, a straightforward front kick that checked my momentum hard. I stumbled as she hit, twisting at the hips, kicking up turf and nearly falling as my simple, brutal attack was handily foiled. It was all I could do to work my *Wolfhound*'s heat-knotted muscles to stay upright. She had twenty tons on me and decades of experience. A fair brawl wasn't going to go my way.

An *unfair* brawl, though, just might work out. After all, I brought friends.

Driftwood and his axe crashed down scant meters from Major Ward's *Wolverine*. Even as his *Axman* landed, 65 tons of steel, myomer muscle, and mean-spiritedness, Driftwood brought his axe into play. Major Ward pivoted almost as nimbly as I just had—even with twenty tons on me—and avoided the worst of the blow. What caught her caught her hard, though, and her *Wolverine*'s left hand was cleaved messily off, Driftwood's heavy axe blade not even slowing as it hacked through her upraised limb. Singh and Speirs were pouring on fire as they rushed to join us, and in a four-on-one fight, even Salome Ward would have to lose.

Ward's *Wolverine* reeled backward, sparks flying, and she raised her autocannon to blast it—point-blank—at Driftwood's cockpit. Her GM Whirlwind bucked and barked and spat fire and tungsten our way, muzzle flashes and reports like lightning and thunder. In this close, though, with a weapon calibrated for longer-range fire, even Salome Ward couldn't hit more often than miss.

*She knows that.* I ramped up my speed again, circling, twisting my 'Mech at the waist to line up shots across the thin armor of the *Wolverine*'s back even while my mind raced.

*What's she playing at? What's she distracting us from?!*

The other shoe fell.

A *Thunderbolt* fell from the sky atop Driftwood's *Axman*. Not the near-miss Driftwood had opted for with his dramatic entrance, no, but literally *on* him, a 65-ton machine falling from the sky like the fist of an angry god and, angled *just so* by jump jets and a skilled pilot, crashing down, feet first, onto my lancemate's simulated 'Mech.

So, let's see, this velocity, that mass, this height, that kinetic energy, quantified by the gravitational accuracy of our Ambergrist-calibrated simulator pods, factor in the application of conservation of energy, include the work-energy principle, carry the seven, and...and...yeah, no.

Driftwood was hosed.

One *Thunderbolt* landing later, our *Axman* was *down*. Hard.

Standing over the twisted wreckage of my lancemate, leg armor streaked here and there with flashing metal scars, the *Thunderbolt* straightened up from the crouch it had landed in. It immediately started blasting unerringly at Singh and Speirs, hitting them with waves of laser fire and sheets of missiles. Uncannily accurate, tremendously powerful, lashing out with weapons, fists, and feet alike, it tore into us. Another prototype being tested out, this time some fancy damn-new Wolf's Dragoons something-or-other. Still, the *T-Bolt* had a red on black paint scheme, just like all of us Kell Hounds. First Regiment, just like all of us. No markings giving away the MechWarrior, but I knew just who piloted it. I knew the lineup First Battalion had, and who would leap heroically to the rescue of Major Ward in that particular 'Mech.

Major Ward, who started to clean my clock as my lance's attention was suddenly divided.

I knew on a rational level our smart play was for my lance to focus fire on her injured *Wolverine*, to finish her off, then to fall onto the *Thunderbolt* as a pack, and wear it down. But the *T-Bolt* jockey expected it, and so did Ward, and they just...wouldn't...*let*...us. Working in tandem, coming and going from the fight, they interposed their broad 'Mechs between us, rammed us in-close, hammered us at range, made themselves impossible to ignore, aggressed and defended as we all struggled against waves of heat, and they soured our shots on their partner while the larger fight raged all around us.

They fought like hell. They fought like Kell Hounds.

Eventually, Ward's tonnage won out against my *Wolfhound*. Brawn, skill, accuracy, and an SRM launcher will solve a lot of life's problems, especially inside a hundred meters. I went down swinging, but I still went down.

In the end, when the scores were tallied, the training simulation was declared a First Regiment victory by 0.9 percent combat efficiency.

Of course I bitched about it in the barracks. The officially "soothing" pale blue color scheme of the room did *not* work on me. Because oh-ho, yeah, I knew who the mystery *Thunderbolt* pilot was, all right. Lieutenant Right-Place-Right-Time himself.

"Christian malfing Kell!" I threw myself backward onto my bunk, wearing boxers and a scowl, furious about points we'd *almost* earned. "We had Ward! We *had* her!"

"Johnny, you have *got* to get over this." Singh cleaned her sidearm at a nearby table. "Sir."

"Don't 'sir' me! Listen to me!" I sat back up again, still scowling. "So this guy, years ago, he comes in *out of nowhere*, years after Patrick died, right? He just waltzed up to us on Arboris, you guys remember that? I sure do, June of '43, this kid, he just—"

"'42," Speirs piped up, not looking up from her Solaris Games 'Mech-mag. "And you were just a kid, too."

"Whatever, shut up." I didn't let her superior memory get me down, I had a good rant going. "He waltzes up to Morgan Kell, supposedly shows something to him, and then it's bing bang boom, the colonel takes another leave of absence, and off he goes to Outreach?! To train with Wolf's malfing Dragoons?! I mean, really? What are we, chopped liver?"

"Not last I checked," Driftwood said. He was in a better mood about being drop-kicked from low orbit than *I* was having seen it happen.

"Like, what, he's too good to train with the Kell Hounds? Oh, the rest of us Hound pups, sure, *we* can get trained in-unit, but not a Kell?"

There were a *lot* of us Hound pups. Sita Frost and I were close because we'd grown up in the Kell Hounds, children to Kell Hounds parents, but we weren't *special* because of it. Hell, I wasn't the only second-generation MechWarrior in my *lance*, bunking in my barracks right then.

"The rest of us, we come up the hard way, the honest way, we earn it, right here. We cut our teeth *right here*, with the other Hounds, but Christian, no, off he malfs to Outreach? Then comes back all Lieutenant Perfect? You, hey, you know what he said to me today after the exercise?"

"Was it 'Hello, Lieutenant'?" Driftwood asked rhetorically.

"No, he—shut up—no, he looks me in the face and he says, 'I look forward to testing myself against you again,' and he gives me this little Kuritan bow. Like, talk about smug?"

"I don't know, Wolf's Dragoons training makes you a little crazy. I think he just honestly *likes* to fight people who are good at fighting, and I think he complimented you." Singh raised an eyebrow at me, looking my way through the barrel of her disassembled pistol. "Sir."

I gave her a long, suspicious look. I wanted to take her argument apart, but maybe she was on to something, and she *had* kind of complimented me, too, so...

"Okay, but, what about his cousin, huh? Phelan, off he goes to the Nagelring where, in case you forgot, he—"

"Oh, hey, did he get kicked out?" Singh barely raised her voice. I might have mentioned this once or twice before. "Sir?"

"—he *gets kicked out*, shames his father, shames his mother, shames his whole family, shames all of us, and he—"

"I don't feel ashamed," Speirs said.

Driftwood shrugged. "Me neither."

"—and he gets rewarded for it with a 'Mech and—"

"I'm actually kind of proud." Speirs nodded.

"Me too!" Driftwood agreed.

"Second Battalion!" Singh sang out.

"*Wild Dogs!*" The others returned the call enthusiastically.

"—and now all of a sudden there's Phelan in a damned *Wolfhound* he gets as a reward for failure, and he paints it up in—"

"Let me guess, your paint scheme?" Singh not-quite-muttered. "Sir?"

"—paints it up in *my* paint scheme, copies *my* cool fangs and stuff, he *names* his 'Mech! '*Grinner*'?! I mean, come on, who *names* their 'Mech?" *Lots of people*, I knew, but ignored my internal voice.

"Lots of people, but, I mean, naming a light?" Speirs scoffed, louder than was strictly necessary. "That's weird."

"Right? Is a *Wolfhound* even really a reward?" Driftwood kept a straight face. Barely.

I ran out of steam and petered out, glaring from one MechWarrior to another. It was no use. I'd left my dignity behind long ago, maybe when I'd tried to shower angrily. I shook my head and sighed.

"You know what? I could write all of you up for insubordination." I glared around the room.

"Uh-huh." Singh sounded terrified as she *click-clacked* her sidearm back together.

Sometimes I really hated the family-casual atmosphere the Kell Hounds kept in private. We could spit and polish with the best of them when we had to, don't get me wrong. We were utter, ruthless professionals when it counted. Best of the best. Tip of the spear. The elite. But on our own? In our barracks?

No. No, I wasn't pulling rank any time soon. Not to complain about the Kells who'd created us, who'd made us all a family in the first place.

Not when my heart wasn't actually in it. Not when my beef wasn't really with *them.*

"Look, all I'm saying is, if I never see that malfing Christian Kell again, it'll be too damned soon."

**DOWNTOWN**
**WUHAN CITY**
**AMBERGRIST**
**ST. IVES COMPACT**
**17 FEBRUARY 3048**

"Well, thank God for Christian Kell, huh?" a tired Kell Hound from Sita's lance said, offering me a cigarette I waved away. In the distant background, explosions rang out.

I groaned, shook my head and sighed, exhausted. I didn't want a cigarette, not with all the smoke already in the air.

"Christian Kell." I sighed again.

Today had been no sim. It had been no battalion-on-battalion scrap to stay sharp and earn bragging rights. Today had been real. Capellan counterattack to take the world real. City fighting real. The realest fighting we'd seen, on the grandest scale, in a long time. The Kell Hounds had pulled out a win. Chris Kell had made a name for himself.

The radios had been all filled with how the young officer had finally been properly blooded, how he'd taken over just when he'd been needed, how he'd led what remained of his assault lance to victory and glory. Crucially, radio chatter had mentioned how he and his company had tangled up a whole battalion of House Liao reinforcements. That holding action had kept them from turning the tide here in the capital city. That's where the Ambergrist Militia and the Kell Hounds Second Battalion, Wild Dogs, had been grinding against the main body of the Capellan attack all day, especially against an elite force from Warrior House Hiritsu. The siege of Wuhan, they were calling it.

That siege of Wuhan had been where I'd spent *my* day. Being a Kell Hound, not a glory hound.

"The man of the hour." I spat grit and smoke and a little too much blood standing, my *Wolfhound* looming nearby, in the wreckage of Wuhan, the capital city that had been turned into a battlefield.

"Really?" Driftwood gave me a pained, plaintive look. He wasn't in the mood for my exhausted bitterness.

I let his exhaustion stop me before I could get going.

We had only a precious, tiny break. We'd been given time to regroup and see to our wounded. We'd been given a moment's rest, and nobody wanted me to spend it bitching. Honestly, even I didn't want that. Not really.

I filled my mouth with tepid, plastic-tasting water from my cockpit canteen and passed it his way with an apologetic shrug. He nodded and took it, apology and all. Rather than take a drink, he poured a drink's worth over his head, then swiped a hand over his face, wiping away grit and grime. He'd taken a cockpit hit and had fought half the day in a cloud of smoke and sparks.

He passed the canteen to Speirs. She, our veteran's veteran, took a drink, rinsed out her mouth, swallowed it anyway, and washed it down with a second drink. She knew dehydration was a soldier's worst enemy.

Well, maybe the enemy was a soldier's *worst* enemy.

Singh *didn't* get the canteen passed to her. She was in a field hospital a dozen meters away, here at the crossroads where we were resting for a minute. Most of her arm was still in her cockpit.

"She's gonna be okay," Speirs said, handing me the canteen back. She sounded older than me. Wiser. Rank didn't matter, sometimes.

"I know." I didn't know shit.

I sighed after I gulped another mouthful of warm plastic and used it to wash down blood from a split lip. My *Wolfhound* had been battered to the ground by a close-in flight of SRMs. I'd gotten back up, but as I'd done so, deep inside my neurohelmet, my own face had matched the bloody teeth of my *Wolfhound*'s paint job. I'd let that start a bad mood that carried me through the rest of the fighting.

I finished off the canteen and looked around. A dozen 'Mechs in various states of disrepair stood nearby, only a pair of them fully powered up and still wary. A dozen 'Mechs. Less than a dozen MechWarriors, though, shell-shocked, dehydrated, bumped and bruised, exhausted. Victorious.

We'd broken the siege and liberated a city. Second Battalion—Wild Dogs!—had come crashing in on the Capellan besiegers from behind, House Hiritsu and all, and we had hit them, hit them, hit them, ground at them until they'd broken and scattered. The front had moved past us. The Capellans were in retreat. Other lances were nipping at their heels, keeping them moving. Our company had done our share. We'd had a long day. We were dirty dogs licking our wounds, given a few moments to catch our breath.

Frosty wasn't far. I did my best not to stare, not to worry too obviously in her direction. She was okay. Captain O'Lochlainn, too. Our whole company was gathered 'round. The Kell Hounds, First Regiment, Second Battalion, Second Company. The 122nd was supposed to be twelve MechWarriors. Only nine of us were *outside* the field hospital, though: three were in there, in pieces. The ratio could have been worse. Spirits could've been lower. But they could have been higher, too.

Me grouching about Chris Kell wasn't helping. I was a Kell Hound. An officer. I had to do better. I had an idea. Everybody liked a toast, right?

"Hey," I said to nobody in particular as, in the half distance all around us, smoke rose and ash fell, sirens wailed, children cried, and medics rushed.

"Hey! One-Two-Two! We did good work today!" I half stumbled over to climb on top of my *Wolfhound*'s foot, raising my empty canteen.

"Hey! To the Kell Hounds!" A few canteens were raised in response, returning my toast.

"To the Ambergrist Militia!" I waved my empty canteen like a crazy person. They'd done a hell of a job, holding this place until we could arrive. A yell answered me.

"To the St. Ives Compact!" I toasted to the freedom of the former Capellan worlds, now Capellan battlegrounds. A louder yell came back.

"And to Second Battalion!" I grinned like a *Wolfhound* and threw my canteen into the air.

*"Wild Dogs!"* a few called back, voices hoarse from cockpit waste heat.

"What?! Second Battalion!" I croaked against the smoke and death in the air.

"*WILD DOGS!*" It was louder this time, and even Captain O'Lochlainn smiled.

"Second Battali—"

"Contact! North, north, north!"

I'll never know who it was that shouted the warning. I mean, it wasn't *me*, but other than that? No telling. Enough fighting behind you in one day, enough bouncing around in a sweltering hot cockpit, enough chafing from a neurohelmet worn for enough hours, enough smoke in the air, enough fear to crack a voice just right? Speirs could sound like Frosty could sound like Tereshkova.

When the adrenaline and the training kick in, one of them filling your veins with lightning and the other turning your blood to ice, the last thing you pay attention to is someone's voice.

Nobody feels as naked and alone as a MechWarrior outside their 'Mech. We all scrambled for our machines, desperate for their guns and armor in equal measure. We clawed at our ladders and hatches. We slammed our neurohelmets back atop our heads. We went back to work.

I'd had a head start, since I'd already been on my *Wolfhound*'s foot for my dry-canteen toasts. I regretted how quickly I made it into my cockpit when my sensors came online and I found my viewscreen centered on the field hospital while the rest of my 'Mech came online.

It was a standard prefab building, a few red symbols for medics against white paint, the sort of thing meant to be used in disaster relief programs, made of recycled plastics that had been press-boarded into the right shapes to let them be transported in the most common of civilian trucks, assembled onsite, almost like a child's toy. A few squirts of some kind of foam sealed the gaps well enough, regular spray-downs kept them sanitary enough, and all in all they did their job. This one, in the heart of downtown Wuhan, had done admirable work at holding off the rains and letting doctors, nurses, and volunteers do good, godly, work. It had held up well against the Ambergrist wind, the rain, the humidity, for who-knows-how-long.

It didn't hold up well to sustained 40mm automatic fire, though. No. No, they weren't built for that at all.

The last of my preflight warmups finished and my *Wolfhound* came fully online after I'd had to spend seconds that felt like centuries watching the white plastic panels of the field hospital get torn to shreds, watching the red cross and red crescent on the sides get blasted into nothing, watching 40mm anti-tank autocannon rounds come out the far side of the field hospital amid sprays of splintered plastic, shreds of meat, and a fine, pink mist that hung in the air far too long.

We'd had an *Enforcer* on guard duty to the north. Galway, good MechWarrior. She did what she could to protect the rest of us while we were out of the saddle. She held them off, matched her autocannon and laser against their bigger guns, their longer range. Later, our techs—Kell Hounds techs, best in the business—counted eight PPC hits her *Enforcer* took before it went down...but down it went. One to the cockpit. The street was open, crossroads vulnerable, fire raining down on civilians from the north.

I filled the gap, feet sliding on the pavement, throttle wide open, *Wolfhound* driving up the broad street and demanding attention.

I faced off against a scratch company almost two clicks away, a mixed-weight bunch of regular Capellan 'Mechs that didn't know when they were beat. They were led by—the scattered MechWarriors had no doubt been rallied by—a pair of their elite Warrior House Hiritsu killers, notable in their green and black, always in the worst of the fighting. I'd read somewhere back on base that House Hiritsu was supposed to fanatically follow the teachings of Confucius. They were supposed to value courtesy. They were supposed to respect life, at least Capellan life.

In losing and deciding Wuhan was ours they had, apparently, changed their mind on that last bit.

The lead Hiritsu MechWarrior was in a *Blackjack*, firing not one, but two never-ending streams of shells at the field hospital just out of spite. They were aiming their autocannons low, like skipping rocks. Some of the chattering autofire ricocheted off the pavement, others hit the field tent straight on, all of them threatened civilians further down the way, some were being walked side to side as the MechWarrior chased scattering survivors with their crosshairs. People were still running back there. People were still alive. Even this malfhead's misses were killing people. Bullets and missiles and laser beams don't just magically stop in an urban fight, they hit *something*. They do damage. A city's one living, breathing backstop, just waiting to get shredded by careless fire.

*Damn it!* I snarled inside my neurohelmet and yanked at my controls. *You want to shoot? I'll give you someone to shoot!*

I hurled my *Wolfhound* into their line of fire and splashed an unignorable large laser shot off green paint. I got their attention. A flight of missiles from a *Catapult* just barely sailed over my head. A pair of *Vindicator*s tracked me, and after a reluctant, murderous moment, the killing *Blackjack* pointed its Whirlwind-Ls my way, too.

*Fine.* Racing right into their fangs, I throttled up. They started firing.

I saw red and let the rage take over. No fighting it this time. No thinking like an officer. I went absolute berserker. All Hothead. Pure Wild Dog, off the leash. All anger, all instinct, no brain. Maximize damage, damn the heat, kill the bastard in front of you. Run. Shoot. Repeat.

Long minutes later, I found myself panting in mouthfuls of air that felt like fire and tasted like copper. One of my eyebrows was split, fresh blood painting the interior of my helmet and pouring down the side of my face, and all I could hear in the whole world was my pulse pounding and overheat warnings coming at me from all around my cockpit. My *Wolfhound*'s right arm large laser was a heat-twisted mess. Later, a look at my battleROM would show me wedging its muzzle into the *Blackjack*'s belly from behind, punching right through the 'Mech's thin rear armor, and just leaning on the firing stud until it finished dying and falling apart.

Frosty's *Kintaro* stood nearby, practically rippling in the air from the furnace raging inside, but it stood. Captain O'Lochlainn's *Catapult* was missing one of its huge, boxy missile pods, nearly a fourth of the 'Mech just...gone. She was alive, though, my comms board lit up with her as she checked in on who was left. Driftwood was wishing out loud he had more lasers, as his *Axman* had lost its namesake right arm and some breakdown had his massive autocannon just clicking and clicking and clicking on empty, trying to fire but jammed. Speirs and her *Griffin* had hurled themselves skyward and stood atop a nearby vantage point, balanced on one good leg, one PPC-fused leg, and a lifetime of training.

Our counter-counterattack had taken out nine more 'Mechs, despite the sucker punch. Two Hiritsu killers had browbeaten, bullied, and ordered seven regular MechWarriors from three different regiments back into the fray. They'd had over a dozen infantry with them, some of them also Hiritsu warriors, manning anti-'Mech weapons.

The death squad had decided to take a stand. They'd decided to make a statement. They'd decided to go down making Wuhan and its defenders pay for daring to stand against them. They had done a good job at bad work; in time, local authorities gave up trying to tell where one corpse ended and another began, because 40mm rounds weren't made to shoot people with. It was wasteful. Extreme. Grotesque. Due to the overkill, we never found Singh's remains.

Between the ambush and the fight itself, Frost had lost two of her people, too. Captain O'Lochlainn's heavy lance was down to just her and her most-of-a-*Catapult*.

We were beat to hell, but we were mad. In the near-silence after the fight, there was no banter. No playful chatter. No cross-channel teasing, no kvetching about stray Kells playing gloryhound, no sing-songy "Second Battalion" and "Wild Dogs!" call-and-answer.

No, we didn't joke. We took stock. We contacted Major O'Cathain. We pretended not to hear her declare us combat ineffective and disobeyed a direct order by chalking it up to radio interference. We went back to work. We stalked the city, a pack of limping, hungry, rib-showing hounds, kicked one time too many, looking to bite and not let go of the throat this time.

## KELL HOUNDS HQ
## WUHAN
## AMBERGRIST
## ST. IVES COMPACT
## 20 FEBRUARY 3048

Sita and I shouldn't have slept together, probably. Physically, I mean, it had been a bad idea. We'd suffered through it, don't get me wrong, but we had done so acutely aware the whole time that we might tug some stitches loose, might pull a muscle, might exacerbate a sprain. Bad idea. Stupid of us.

But sometimes, in your early twenties, alive when other people have just died? Sometimes, making a living as a soldier, a merc, a MechWarrior, iron for hire and steel for rent, a Kell Hound, best of the best? Sometimes, after making it through something awful, seeing a city torn apart and only just barely held together by hands soaked in blood, sometimes, you've just got to do some *living*. You've just got to be close to someone, feel their heart beating with yours, feel their breath on your skin, grab ahold and feel meat and bone and *another human being*, about as close to you as two people can get. Sometimes.

Afterwards, we lay there, in a pale blue barracks room that felt so. Damned. Empty.

Almost everyone we worked with, what felt like almost everyone we *knew*, was either dead, in the infirmary, or still handling clean-up work. Wuhan had chewed us up and spit us out pretty damned good. My Striker Lance had lost Singh forever, and Speirs and Driftwood were both in the infirmary, still. Ramirez and Conrad were fine-ish, at least; not exactly in one piece, technically speaking, but Ramirez was trying to be upbeat about her new leg, and Conrad was just glad she was alive. None of our captains had died. None of our majors. My mom, in the Bird Dogs, was fine, and so was Sita's mother. Aerospace pilots tended not to get battered around like MechWarriors; theirs was a more binary pass/fail type of fighting.

All in all, Second Battalion had taken a beating, but we were coming out the other side of it. The ambush at the hospital had been the worst of it. And I had to admit it would have been even *worse* without Christian Kell and his delaying tactics. If the Liao forces had gotten companies of reinforcements at a time, not lances. If we'd gotten flanked as hard as we'd flanked them. If Kell hadn't been there, tangling up and distracting their assault force.

"I can't believe he refused it," I said, lying there, next to Sita. Fire and ice. That was us. "Wolf's Dragoons training, man, it makes you crazy. But, I mean, he's not turning down the promotion, at least?"

"Well, Old Lady O'Cathain sure isn't refusing anything. The major's saying Second Battalion's—"

"Wild Dogs," I said reflexively, but couldn't bring myself to holler enthusiastically.

"—getting the St. Ives Order of Heroism. All of us." Sita nestled into the crook of my arm. I didn't have the heart to tell her how badly my shoulder hurt while she did so. The screwing wasn't the only closeness that counted. Not by a long shot.

"Huh. But, really, he's just...he said no?" I wanted to squirm enough to look at her face while we talked. I didn't want it badly enough to actually do it, though.

"He said he's humbled by the rank increase, and it's more than enough recognition for doing his part." She shrugged against me. I hid a wince.

"Huh," I said again.

We lay there, in the quiet, feeling alive. Thinking too much. Feeling too much. Seeing too much as we stared up at the nothing of our field barracks' pale blue ceiling. Eventually, the silence got to her. The silence, and my too-long bad mood.

"What's your..." She paused, gathered herself, and sat up. Half-wrapped in the sheets, she reached down, hand on my heart, fingertips trailing through the curly red hairs of my chest. She bit her lip. "What's your problem with the Kells, Johnny? You weren't like this when we were kids."

It wasn't easy for her to ask. It wouldn't be easy for me to answer. I owed her a try, though. The week had been too big for me not to let some of it out. The grief, the shock, the exhaustion, the hurt. I could...I could let some of it go, right? Just some of it.

Just some of it.

"It's not...it's not with them. Not really. I don't hate them—hell, how could I, I'm a malfing Kell Hound!—and I respect the hell out of them. I do! I just..." I didn't sit up. I leaned back, in fact, not looking at her. Not making eye contact. Not trying to read her responses, not trying to practice my lying. I stared up at the ceiling. I stared up at nothing.

"You know I'm a stray, same as you," I said, using regimental shorthand for those of us, second-generation, who'd been born after what the Kell Hounds called the Defection. For a time, Morgan Kell had broken the regiment down to just a single battalion, and malfed off to a monastery. The Kell Hounds he'd cut loose to do so scattered. Some had kept doing merc work together, as a lance or an aerofighter wing. Some had kept doing merc work with reputable companies. Some had just kept doing merc work.

"If Morgan hadn't fired Mom, she'd never have gone to the Periphery, you know? Never have been a pilot for hire. Never have *met* him, much less anything else."

"'Him'?" she asked, softly.

"My dad," I said, not smiling, not frowning. Doing my best not to feel much. Doing my best to ignore my heart suddenly pounding in my chest, and to just answer. "I, uh, I know I never talked to you about him. I've never talked to anyone about him, except Mom. When I was just a kid. I'd been real young, she'd been real careful. Hadn't shared details with me, you know? But then later, I, we, I, uh, talked to her about him again. This was a...a long time ago. Almost a decade, now. I don't know how much she told your mom, or if she told you, or..."

My stomach hurt. I swallowed. Sita shook her head.

"Sixteen. Remember being sixteen?" I couldn't help but smile. "You feel so smart. So sure. Everything you feel is so big. I don't know...I don't know how our parents don't kill us. I don't know why our friends don't hate us. We're awful, you know? It's so easy to be awful."

I took a slow, deep, breath. She didn't interrupt me. She listened.

"This one fight we had, this fight I started at sixteen? I made her... sob. Not just cry, you know? But *sob*. We yelled so much, slammed doors so loud, some of Captain O'Brien's MPs had come to our flat along with the regular Arc-Royal cops. Before they got there, hell, then again after they left, we just...we really went at it. It was bad. I was... awful. Me and her, we said things, you know? Things you can't unsay. Things you can't take back. Even if you talk about them later, apologize for them, whatever. Shots fired that you just can't, you know, you can't put the bullet back in the mag."

Words said in anger, like weapons fired in a big city's downtown, don't stop. They hit something. They do damage.

"Sixteen." I shook my head. "At sixteen, Phelan Kell'd been at Nagelring, doing all right, right? At sixteen, Christian, he showed up on Arboris, got there gods-know-how, and he stared down Morgan Kell."

I snorted, couldn't help it. Ignoring the heavy wetness in my eyes, ignoring the sniffles I was fighting, ignoring the tightness in my chest, I *snorted*. Hell, almost giggled.

"Crazy, right? *Stared down Morgan Kell*, at sixteen years old."

I shook my head, swallowed, and choked down a lump in my throat.

"At sixteen, me? I found out who my dad was, and I confronted my mother over it, and I almost hit her, and she almost hit me."

"Oh, Johnny..." she whispered. I was giving her more than she'd wanted. "You don't have to—"

"No." I shook my head again, not letting her stop me. "No, it's okay, it's on me, not you, okay? You asked, but I didn't have to...didn't have to answer."

I licked my lips and forced out words that had never passed them before.

"So. My, uh, my dad was a DropShip captain. Mom met him flying security, doing merc work along the Aurigan-Taurian border. She'd ride along on some trips, certain runs, things that were expected to get nasty and they wanted a few extra guns. A *Slayer* can pay a lot of bills if you know how to fly one and you know when to shut up."

Sita's mother, Kim Frost, flew a *Slayer*, too. She'd been temporarily cut from the Hounds, too. She'd made ends meet for a while, too. Sita didn't remind me of any of that. She knew she didn't have to.

I had to say it. I had to *say* it.

"My father's name was Samuel Ostergaard Junior." I lifted my head, then. Had to look at her. Had to watch her face.

Her brow furrowed. It was tickling at her. She almost remembered the name.

*"Newgrange,"* I said like it was a curse, then *"Iberia."*

It took her a second—she didn't remember the events, she'd been too young, but she remembered our history lessons—then her eyes widened slightly. Her frown deepened. Her hands knotted a fistful of sheet.

"Yeah," I said softly, letting my head fall back down. "Yeah, that's him."

Periphery villains. War criminals. Taurian Concordat nationals. My father had been an arms dealer, Captain Samuel Ostergaard II of the *Newgrange*. His *Union*-class DropShip had been operating nominally as a civilian merchant vessel, but had been a disguised Taurian Defense Force ship flying undercover, smuggling ammunition to feed the hungry, brutal guns of the tyrannical Aurigan Directorate. He'd been on the wrong side of a civil war, in more ways than one. He had been killed expressly on the order of the great galactic heroine Kamea Arano, High Lady of the Aurigan Coalition, Sword of the Restoration.

After his son had died on an ugly moon notable for nothing so much as his death there, my grandfather, Commodore Samuel Ostergaard, had stormed into Aurigan territory in the *Iberia*, a massive *Fortress*-class DropShip. He'd run rampant in war-torn Arano space, unrivaled there, a bull in a china shop. He'd brought more than a battalion of BattleMechs with him, and he'd used them, and the *Iberia*'s guns, ruthlessly. Mercilessly. He'd wiped out an entire noble house. He'd killed thousands of people on a planet whose population had peaked in just the millions. Even after being ordered home, he'd refused, he and his crew and his ship and his 'Mechs, and he'd loomed large, the threat of death, an axe hanging over the capital world of Coromodir VI. He'd been ready to glass a city, a planet, to get something that tasted like revenge.

After they desperately took him down, he then killed untold thousands more in the starvation that ensued after the crash. The impact itself, the environmental damage that followed, the economic devastation of the whole affair. He'd almost done it, even in death. My grandfather had almost killed a whole world to avenge my father.

The Aurigan Reach had been on the brink of collapse, torn by a civil war. The *Iberia*'s crash had very nearly been the killing blow. The Ostergaard family had almost killed the Aurigan Coalition, *had* killed or helped kill two of the founding families, had pushed sixteen different local animal species to extinction, and had killed the very skies over Coromodir and brought about a short, brutal ice age that had lasted for years.

The Ostergaards did all that.

And I had their red hair.

I could be as stubborn as my father, who'd refused an order to stand down, who'd stared the Sword of the Restoration in the face and killed his commlink to force her hand. I could be as angry as my grandfather, whose rage had ended bloodlines, clawed open skies, and turned city blocks to ruin and glass.

I lay there, staring up at the pale blue ceiling of the barracks, and I imagined what the people of Coromodir felt when they saw their pale blue sky disturbed by the *Iberia*. When they saw death coming for them at a high-g burn, saw a madman threatening to kill thousands, *millions*, over the death of one.

"I, uh..." I licked my lips again, swallowed, felt suddenly thirsty, suddenly tired. Suddenly stupid. "I think about that a lot. About them. I think about...I see..."

"Johnny, no, it's—"

"No, just listen, okay? I look around the Kell Hounds, right, and I see, like, I see Colonel Allard's kids, and looking at them, I see how good they are, I mean, how *decent*, how good with the other kids. I see Major O'Cathain and *Captain* O'Cathain, and just how damned amazing they both are, right? I see Major Brahe's kids, I look at 'em, and see how smart they are, how dedicated, how focused at whatever they're doing. I see Chris Kell, and I see the stories, my mom's, your mom's, I see everyone's *stories* about Patrick Kell, and I see the courage and the, the, the nobility of him in Chris. I see Salome Ward, and I know how great she is at what she does, and I see that in them, in Phelan and Caitlin, in those kids she and the colonel have, the, you know, the legendary Morgan Kell."

I was ramped up. Kvetching, but inside out.

"I don't—I'll admit it, okay?—I don't know what Phelan did to get kicked out of Nagelring. But I know he wouldn't be getting a *Wolfhound* from his folks if it hadn't been...right. Decent. If he hadn't meant well. Because I know his mother and father, and I look up to them, and I *look up* to people that look up to them, and...I just know. I know that Kell compass, it got passed down to Phelan. Knowing which way's up. Right from wrong."

I let out a long, low, sigh.

"I see other pups and strays coming up here in the Hounds, and I see them following in their parents' footsteps, maybe even surpassing them. Being their mothers and fathers but *better*, but *more*. I see how damned good you are in that *Kintaro*, it's like, like watching you dance, you're *so good* in that malfing thing, Sita, your mom is so damned proud, and I see how she looks at you, but then I remember my mom looking at *me* that night when I was sixteen, and I, I, I..."

I swallowed.

"And I see my red hair. When she sees me, especially since that fight, I know she sees my father, my grandfather. I look around the Kell Hounds, and I see the stuff other people are made of, and then I see the stuff *I'm* made of, and it makes me so mad, and so scared, and so anxious about what I might..." I trailed off, then shook my head, then made myself, finally, *answer* her question.

"I guess I'm just hoping someone could agree with me when I bitch—just once. Ever. I wish someone could confirm it, that just one of them is as bad as I complain about! Phelan or Christian or Caitlin or Megan or Tempest or Yorinaga or just, I mean, just *one* of them, just *any* of them! I wish I'd see one of them not just be their parents but better, their parents but *more*, I wish I'd see them stray from their parents' path, go south instead of north, so that..."

I petered off. My chest hurt. Something inside it hurt worse.

"So that..." I was so, so, tired.

"So that you feel like you can go north instead of south," she said softly.

I choked on a sob as I nodded. Just the one. I'd been saying things that hurt to say, it only made sense that they'd torn me up a little on the way out.

"You hate your dad and his dad," she said, even more softly. "And you're scared you'll be like them."

"I *am* like them," I said, spitting the words like a curse. "I look just li—"

"You idiot," she punched the mattress next to me out of sheer frustration. "You *idiot.*"

I blinked, like an idiot would, and sat up, bewildered as she started in.

"What's wrong with you? You got, you think you got, like, *evil* genes, to, to, to match your malfing hair?" She looked like she might strangle me, or hug me, or maybe a little bit of both. "You think you look like some dead guys, so you're as bad as those dead guys? Huh? You think you inherited their, what, their sins? Their fates? You think you got handed down the moral compass of some guys who've been dead since, what, since like '25, right? What were you, *one*?"

"Well, '25, it was—"

"Shut up! You were barely even *born*!" She bounced up and down in the bed as she smacked both hands on the mattress again. "You're *not* him! You're not *either* of them! You're not some arms-dealing DropShip captain, and you're sure as *hell* not some rogue commodore raining down terror from the heavens or whatever!"

She scrambled, heaved, crawled her way over next to me, propped up, and held my face in her hands. She forced me to look at her, dead on. Eye contact. No dissembling. No faking it. No looking away. I looked into her big, brown, eyes, and she leaned in and kissed me.

"You're...you," she said softly. "Idiot."

But, I don't know, she said it in a way that says *I love you*.

"Thanks?" I said.

"Your mom doesn't see them in you. She sees *you* in you, dummy. And she's so proud, Johnny. I swear, she and mom talk, and she just won't shut up. 'Her poster boy,' she calls you. You and that hair, and how you look in our Kell Hound dress blacks, and even in that stupid jacket you love so much? She's *so* amazed at how you turned out. She jokes and wonders how she made something so pretty." Sita held me, laughing a little. "And, what, you think our moms are proud of *me*, but not proud of you? Like your aptitude/proficiency scores weren't amazing? Top of our class? Like you're not also a lieutenant in the goddamned Kell Hounds? Huh? Best of the best? Like you're not also leading a lance in Second Battalio—"

"Wild Dogs." I sniffed, eyes wet.

"Wild Dogs!" She laughed, then nodded, then smiled at me, her shining, tear-filled eyes, holding mine. "You're a Wild Dog, Lieutenant Jonathon Laurens Hillson! An officer from the 122nd, best damned company in the best damned outfit in the Inner Sphere!"

She leaned her forehead in against mine and we held each other up. She was done. Enough said. Lecture over. Almost. She smiled.

"And, I mean, jeeze, you think they hand the St. Ives Order of Heroism out to just anybody?"

"I don't know, I hear a whole battalion got it today." I snorted, then snickered, then smiled back. "And some other weirdo gave his back."

"Yeah, well." She shrugged. "Wolf's Dragoons training. Makes you a little crazy,"

We sat for a long time. I don't know how long. I don't care.

"So, you gonna go easy on yourself?" she asked after a while, quirking an eyebrow.

*Never.*

"Yeah," I said, trying to mean it.

"You going to go easy on First Battalion?" she asked, eyebrow still up.

*Yeah.*

"Never," I said, unable to hide a smile. "Unless they offer me captain's bars and a transfer."

# UNIT DIGEST: BLAZING ACES

### ALEX FAUTH

**Affiliation:** Mercenary
**CO:** Duke Gideon Braver Vandenburg
**Average Experience:** Veteran/Reliable
**Force Composition:** 1 Heavy BattleMech Lance (3028); 1 Medium BattleMech Company (3050)
**Unit Abilities:** Overrun Combat (*Campaign Operations*, p. 86). Rather than rolling randomly, one 'Mech per lance may be a *Locust*, *Jenner*, *Phoenix Hawk*, *Shadow Hawk*, *Rifleman*, *Warhammer*, *Marauder*, or *BattleMaster* of any appropriate variant.
**Parade Scheme:** Cyan with a black trim

## UNIT HISTORY

The Blazing Aces were born out of betrayal and conspiracy. In 3024, members of House McBrin conspired with elements within the Draconis Combine to seize control of Ander's Moon, an inhabited moon in the Elidere system. The two hired the Dark Wing, a renegade mercenary lance, to invade the world and eliminate the world's ruling family. The only survivor of the family, Gideon Vandenburg, was framed for treason. Realizing he had no chance against his enemies, he fled the world with the aid of a loyal member of the family guards.

Left with only a battered *Jenner*, Vandenburg swore to clear his name and get revenge for the death of his family. Following the few fragmentary leads he had, he travelled across the Inner Sphere on the trail of the Dark Wing and the conspiracy. Several near-death encounters made him realize not only was he in over his head, but also that he would not be able to take on the Dark Wing (which consisted of a heavy

BattleMech lance) alone. Even though he had gained an ally in the form of Tasha Yushenko, an MI6 agent investigating Combine activities in the region, he needed more physical force.

Using what little money he had left, Vandenburg began building a mercenary lance for two reasons. Not only was he looking for a force capable of facing the Dark Wing, but he also took opportunistic contracts along the way to provide the income he needed to continue his personal war. Through his own charisma, as well as the aid of Yushenko, he was able to recruit a lance of veteran MechWarriors willing to aid him. Over the next three years, the newly formed Blazing Aces built a reputation entirely outside their size.

In 3026, the Blazing Aces achieved their goal, confronting the Dark Wing on Kirchbach and defeating them in a pitched battle. With the pirates seemingly destroyed, Vandenburg was able to gather the evidence he needed to expose the truth of what had happened and clear his name. Returning to Ander's Moon, he reclaimed his title and restored the Vandeburg family rule over the moon. The surviving Blazing Aces became the core of the rebuilt planetary guard, their mercenary days seemingly at an end.

Vandenburg married Yushenko in 3029, and their daughter, Maria, was born in 3031. His reign was ultimately short-lived, as the Elidere became a target of the Draconis Combine counteroffensive in the War of 3039. With the fall of the system, the Vandenburg family and Blazing Aces were forced to flee the system, with Gideon aware he had made powerful enemies within the Draconis Combine who would make staying on the world impossible. Retreating to Benet III, he began to build up the Blazing Aces again in anticipation of a counter-counter offensive to reclaim his home.

Instead, the Armed Forces of the Federated Suns chose to stand down its forces and end the war, effectively ceding control of the system to the Combine. Outwardly, Gideon Vandenburg was furious at losing his ancestral home and title after he had done so much to reclaim it. Taking his rebuilt force and his family, he abandoned his allegiance to the Federated Commonwealth and resumed mercenary work.

Over the course of the next decade, the new Blazing Aces grew to company strength as they took contracts aimed at the Draconis Combine. Through a combination of skill and careful planning, they achieved considerable success during that time, and built a reputation as a reliable unit. However, with Yushenko remaining at Vandenburg's side both as his wife and an agent for the unit, it is possible this was all an act, and the Blazing Aces were a front for intelligence operations by the Federated Commonwealth. Vandenburg also built a relationship with the Kell Hounds, one that was as much about fighting the Combine as it was his future as a mercenary.

Regardless of their planning, they were still not prepared for the Clan juggernaut. In December of 3051, the Blazing Aces were on Kaesong as a part of a private contract when Clan Ghost Bear struck. Realizing they were completely outclassed and that escape would be difficult, Gideon Vandenburg made a tough choice. He hid the Blazing Aces' BattleMech reserves before taking a medium lance to fight the Ghost Bear forces. Rather than engaging head-on, he used hit-and-run attacks to harry and delay them while their dependents, including his daughter, escaped off-world.

While initially successful, time was not on Vandenburg's side. Low on supplies and damaged, his lance was caught by a Binary from the Fourteenth Battle Cluster and forced into a last stand. While the unexpected arrival of the Crescent Hawks saw the destruction of the Clan force, it was too late. Vandenburg's force had been wiped out, while he had been mortally wounded in the battle. In his last moments, he passed a message to the Crescent Hawks' leader, Jason Youngblood, telling him to inform Maria of what had happened and for her to find his cache of hidden BattleMechs to rebuild the Blazing Aces.

## COMPOSITION

Starting out with a single *Jenner* in 3024, Gideon Vandenburg built the Blazing Aces into a heavy BattleMech lance over four years. A team of veteran MechWarriors allowed him to make the most of his small unit and was responsible for their victory over the Dark Wing. Salvage taken from the renegade mercenary band made up for their losses, keeping the Blazing Aces at full strength.

By 3050, the Blazing Aces had grown to a medium BattleMech company through careful management, possibly aided by Yushenko's contacts. While this force touched down on Kaesong, most of it was simply unaccounted for; Vandeburg made his final stand in a medium lance that may not have even been a part of his original force. The rest of his BattleMechs were hidden away, left for his daughter to reclaim one day.

# UNIT DIGEST: HALSTEN'S BRIGADE

### ZAC SCHWARTZ

**Nickname:** The Wall
**Affiliation:** Mercenary
**CO:** Colonel Magdalaine "Big Mags" Halsten
**Average Experience:** Elite/Fanatical
**Force Composition:** 1 reinforced armor regiment
**Unit Abilities:** Halsten's Brigade receives a +2 Initiative bonus when
   acting as defender in a scenario.
**Parade Scheme:** Scarlet with gold piping

## UNIT HISTORY

Ever since that fateful day on Styx in 2443, when the BattleMech ascended to its throne as king of the battlefield, the humbled main battle tank has been relegated to a supporting role. Though they have wrested away the crown, many an arrogant MechWarrior has underestimated their predecessors at their peril and paid the price. One panzer regiment in particular—Halsten's Brigade—has built its reputation on going head-to-head with BattleMechs and emerging victorious.

The Brigade's origins lie in the depths of the Third Succession War. In 2952, Captain-General Thaddeus Marik launched the infamously shambolic Operation Killing Stroke, an ill-advised offensive into the Lyran Commonwealth. Months of squandering MechWarriors, material, and M-bills netted Thaddeus only a single world: Cavanaugh II.

Numbered among the Lyran defenders was the First Cavanaugh Panzer Regiment, a force of heavy tanks fighting a valiant but doomed defense, led by the fireplug Colonel Alois Halsten, second son of the Grafina of Gawain. The colonel's brusque manner and refusal to defer to

MechWarriors rubbed the social generals leading Cavanaugh's defense the wrong way, and when the Lyran Commonwealth commanders withdrew, they conspired to jump away before the regiment's DropShips could dock, leaving them in the lurch. With the Halsten estate now in Marik hands, the colonel's ships boarded a merchant JumpShip at gunpoint and fled for Galatea—if they could not expect loyalty from their liege lords, Halsten reasoned, they could at least command better pay.

After initial stints with the Federated Suns and Capellan Confederation, the regiment—rechristened Halsten's Brigade—ironically would spend several decades in Lyran employ, roving defenders on the League-Commonwealth border. In the lineal tradition of many mercenary units, command remained the right of the Halsten family, and by the time Alois' son Pelegrin relinquished the Brigade to his son Jenico, a formidable reputation had been built. They were a premiere defensive unit, renowned for being so dogged their mere presence was enough to dissuade raids and re-route invasions. If the scarlet flag of Halsten flew over a world, it was said, it stayed there.

By the end of the Succession Wars, only the most fearless or foolhardy raiders dared strike a system held by the Brigade. To keep their edge honed, the regiment added a second specialization: high-level cadre duty. Throughout the middle of the thirty-first century, Halsten's Brigade traveled the breadth of the Federated Commonwealth, training against some of the finest armored corps in the Inner Sphere. Nearly every elite tank crew in the Armed Forces of the Federated Commonwealth had crossed turrets with the Brigade by the time civil war forever split the Commonwealth. Mercenary tankers likewise sought out the Brigade for instruction—countless commanders of merc armored companies learned their trade through Brigadier tutelage, a tradition they carried forward.

Playing a role repulsing the final wave of Marik forces during Operation Broken Fist, Colonel Rosalina "Rosie the Ravager" Halsten thereafter elected to pursue opportunities with planetary governments looking for defense against Periphery piracy, correctly intuiting the unfolding Jihad was about to make the mercenary business far more dangerous. This spared them from the devastation the Jihad wrought on their profession writ large.

The next three decades were spent on Anjin Muerto and the surrounding systems, fending off the perpetual piracy emanating from the Tortuga Dominions and continuing to train those who traveled to apprentice under them. It was not until Rosalina's retirement and the ascension of her son—the flamboyant Raimond "Ravishing" Halsten—at the turn of the thirty-second century that they left the Periphery March.

The Duchy of Andurien, a rising power, paid the Brigade a premium for a combined garrison/cadre contract on the recently absorbed world of Butzfleth. Such was the enduring strength of their reputation for both lethal marksmanship and sangfroid under fire that when the Magistracy of Canopus invaded the Duchy in 3104, they intentionally bypassed Butzfleth, unwilling to test the Brigade's resolve. The years that followed saw them tour the duchy, drilling Andurien Defense Force tankers in the finer points of armored cavalry warfare. They were forced to flee in 3111, however, when Ravishing was caught ravishing both mistresses of the Baron of Shiro III.

Halsten's Brigade has since called the Lyran Periphery its home. A steadfast bulwark against the remorseless corsairs of the Rim Territories, the guns and lives of the Brigade were often all that stood between a bustling frontier metropolis and its bloody sack by pitiless pirates. From Venaria to Viborg, from Kowloon to Karkkila, they were welcomed by the locals with open arms, a source of solace from the vicissitudes of living out on the edge of the Inner Sphere. The brief breakaway of the Buena Collective, followed by the rise of the even larger Timbuktu Collective, has Colonel Magdalaine "Big Mags" Halsten worried: battling bandits is one thing, but even with the Brigade's high degree of professionalism, she is unsure they will be as willing to fight opponents many in the regiment see as fellow countrymen.

## COMPOSITION

Halsten's Brigade is a reinforced tank regiment: three battalions of heavy armor and a reinforced battalion of hovertank cavalry. The unit's core—Hammer, Morningstar, and Roughnecks Battalions—prefers heavy and assault tanks like the Schrek, Kelswa, and Manticore. The attrition inevitable to a high-tempo armor force means they often experiment with newer chassis. During the contract with the Duchy of Andurien, Morningstar Battalion became particularly enamored with the Moltke MBT, maintaining a company each of M2s and M3s to this day. Likewise, Colonel Halsten's command company is presently built around the Testudo Siege Tank, an unorthodox vehicle able to contribute at all engagement ranges.

Peltast Battalion, the hovercraft contingent, similarly hews to reliable stalwarts like the Condor and Pegasus. However, much like Morningstar Battalion, they took a liking to the ADF's iNarc-toting Tufanas. The last half-century has seen them switch exclusively to hovertanks equipped with TAG, so they better leverage the Brigade's sizable stockpile of semi-guided missiles and homing artillery rounds. The exception is their fourth company, which since the detachment's inception has used the diminutive Savannah Master.

# INDOMITABLE

### ROBIN BRISEÑO

**5 KILOMETERS SOUTH OF DE ZAVALA PURIFICATION PLANT**
**BANDERA BASIN**
**CORRIDAN IV**
**LYRAN ALLIANCE**
**10 MARCH 3058**

*"MYOMER CONTROL FAILURE.*
*"WARNING! ENGINE CONTAINMENT FAILURE."*

Captain Luz Villanueva silently begged *Indomitable*, her beloved *Marauder*, to hold together. Its damaged reactor whined, flooding her cockpit with waste heat in protest. Her tactical map showed the fight had drifted dangerously close to the sprawling Water Pure Industries her mercenary unit, the Order of Indigo, had been tasked with defending—a facility the entire planet's economy relied on.

*"WARNING! FIRE, RIGHT INTAKE.*
*"WARNING! COOLANT PUM—"*

"Shut up, goddammit!" Luz slammed a gloved fist on *Indomitable*'s master caution reset to silence the litany of warnings.

*Don't make me listen to these again.*

Another barrage of missiles briefly blotted out the glow of the setting sun before crashing against her 'Mech's upper leg. Luz fought her control stick in a desperate effort to stay upright. Her hands quivered as she brought her one remaining PPC to bear.

She placed the reticule over the slit-like canopy of the *Thunderbolt* that was now bearing down on her and squeezed the firing stud. A stream of azure energy snapped across the battlefield, cutting a deep gouge across the *Thunderbolt*'s cockpit access hatch. The machine staggered, falling to one knee rather than collapsing like she'd hoped it would.

Luz cursed under her breath. Even a meter lower, and she could have ended this. One missed shot had firmly flipped the odds against her. The trembling in her hands intensified as anxiety flooded her body. She wiped a sweaty palm on her cooling vest in vain.

"Ember Two-One, Apex is pinned down. Divert your lance to assist," Lieutenant Haruka Nishimura, Luz's XO, called out with her usual unshakable demeanor. If it weren't for the crackling of her *Shadow Hawk*'s PPC and the staccato beat of enemy fire in the background, one would've assumed her orders had come from the safety of a command bunker.

Luz's map showed the rest of the Indigos pushing back the raiders from the main facility, but the pulsating crimson of their status lights showed the unit was rapidly approaching their breaking point. Haruka was prioritizing her beleaguered commander over the mission, putting everyone's lives at risk. Again.

*Don't you dare get someone killed because of my stupidity. Don't repeat my mistakes.*

Four friendly sensor pips began to pivot toward Luz's position.

"Belay last, Ember Lance. Stand your ground!" Luz barked into her mic, her Whirlwind autocannon roaring overhead.

The *Thunderbolt* pilot had hesitated after their near-death experience, but quickly regained their composure even as their 'Mech's blocky torso was peppered with cannon fire. Missiles spewed from the tubular launcher on its shoulder, falling upon *Indomitable* in a hail of flame. Emerald and sapphire beams cut through the smoke left in their wake, clawing through the remaining scraps of Luz's leg armor. Each laser reached deeper and deeper into the structure, slashing through myomer muscle and foamed aluminum bone alike.

A sudden jolt shook Luz violently as her 'Mech's leg buckled. The warning system activated again, shouting new alerts into her ear.

"*WARNING! LEG ACTUATOR FAILURE.*

"*MYOMER CONTROL FAILURE.*"

*Indomitable*'s nose dipped as Luz struggled to keep her 'Mech upright, her HUD's velocity vector indicator bobbing wildly around the horizon. A chill raced down her spine, despite the broiling heat of her stricken 'Mech's cockpit as she fought the urge to turn and run.

"*WARNING! ENGINE CONT—*"

She slammed the master caution reset again.

"Don't let Gabe down," she growled. "Get it together, Luz!"

*Indomitable*'s HUD bounced one more time before stabilizing as its firing reticule drifted back across the *Thunderbolt*. Luz squeezed off another shot the moment her weapon cycle indicator flashed green.

A PPC bolt screamed forth, smashing into the face of the enemy's shoulder-mounted missile launcher and flash-welding it into a twisted, mangled lump.

The *Thunderbolt* returned fire with another brilliant display of coherent light. A pair of beams raked across her 'Mech's left torso.

*Indomitable* shook again with a single dull *thump*.

Luz writhed in agony as a high-voltage surge of electric feedback ran through her neurohelmet. Her vision swam as she fought to stay conscious.

*Thump.*

The shock blended the past and present as Luz struggled to avoid drowning in a tidal wave of jumbled memories. Her world became a disorienting haze of faint radio transmissions, voices she never wanted to hear, and a gunshot she wished she could forget.

The thumps accelerated, now an unstoppable timer counting down to *Indomitable*'s demise.

"Gabe! Goddammit, no! I'm not leaving you!" The words scraped like sandpaper in her throat. She attempted to jettison her remaining ammunition, her other hand simultaneously reaching for the auto-eject override.

*Just one more second. Please...*

Luz suddenly felt herself crushed under the weight of her own body as she rocketed away from her dying 'Mech. She reached desperately for her controls, refusing to accept the futility of her attempts to hold on to *Indomitable* before instinctively clutching her harness. Darkness faded along the periphery of her vision as the G-forces pushed the blood in her head toward her legs.

She could only watch through tear-filled eyes as her *Marauder* shrank into the distance before disappearing beneath a ball of flame.

The low thrum of a scout VTOL's approach filled Luz's ears. She didn't bother to move from where she sat or shield her tired eyes from the dust kicked up by its prop wash as it searched for a suitable landing zone. The gust tousled her short brown hair like a field of scorched pampas grass above her headband.

Luz knew they'd come for her. Her orange parachute stood out like a beacon even in the moonlight, tangled among the scraggly brushes dotting the sun-bleached landscape. She hadn't thought to hide it. Left for dead by the *Thunderbolt*, she had marked the passing hours by the lingering furnace of twilight sliding into the biting cold of the desert night. She welcomed the numbness.

She leaned forward, cradling her neurohelmet in her lap. A few hundred meters away, incandescent embers flicked through the night sky where the gray-and-purple corpse of *Indomitable* still smoldered. A secondary explosion lit her weathered face with a soft orange glow, brightening the amber of her eyes and briefly washing her with a flash of warmth. She didn't flinch at the noise, nor turn away from the light.

It was painful, yet beautiful. The dancing flames reminded her of a candlelight vigil, of the warmth of Gabe's hand grasping hers as she had mourned the loss of her mother.

The VTOL's rotors slowed, then stopped. Voices broke through the silence of the night, barking short orders in a foreign tongue. The crunch of footsteps approached from behind.

A sharp, familiar voice spoke. "Captain."

Luz remained motionless. Her mind continued to replay a lifetime of memories, watching the tangerine flames shift in the breeze. The hue was a perfect match for the dress she had worn to her *quinceañera*—a dress she should have danced in with her father, who had been too busy to attend. The dress she had danced in with Gabe instead.

A minute passed in silence.

"Luz."

Luz finally glanced over her shoulder, the concern in the woman's voice finally snapping her mind back to the present.

Haruka stood at rest behind her, her appearance uncharacteristically imperfect. Her wrinkled uniform jacket was half-buttoned over her tank top, likely thrown on in haste before joining the rescue team. Bleached streaks in the younger MechWarrior's raven-black hair shone in the moonlight, her ponytail framing her sharp features.

"I'm not ready to leave, Haruka."

"I understand. May I sit with you?"

"Always."

Her protégé moved closer, carefully placing her *daishō* on the ground before gracefully settling into her traditional *seiza* position at Luz's side. In another time, another place, Luz would have teased her for being so unnecessarily formal.

Not tonight. Not while she grappled with the demons of her past.

"I am sorry about *Indomitable*. She was a fine 'Mech."

Luz didn't respond.

"We won, Luz," Haruka continued. "We repulsed the enemy's assault on the purification plant with no damage to the filter plant. Ember Lance cornered and destroyed three hostile BattleMechs that attempted to regroup with the *Thunderbolt* after you..." She trailed off, her gaze drifting to *Indomitable*'s distant funeral pyre. "If I could offer any comfort, it is that we took no other casualties. Your 'Mech was our only loss."

Luz curled further over her neurohelmet, clutching it like a stuffed animal. She turned, unable to hide her distress.

Haruka's tone softened as she flashed the same tender, reassuring smile that had brightened many of Luz's darkest days. "We can replace your *Marauder*. I cannot replace you."

"This isn't about *Indomitable*, Haruka."

"Then what is it about?"

Luz exhaled slowly, flinching as she shifted her weight and found a fresh bruise she'd earned during her ejection. "I don't know."

A lie.

Haruka knew it too. "Is this about Gabe?"

Luz winced. The emotional punch of hearing Gabe's name stung worse than her physical wounds. "Yeah," she muttered. "Of course it is."

"You have never talked about him. Were it not for your utterances of his name in your nightmares, I wouldn't have even known he existed. We have been partners for fifteen years, yet you will not talk about your history with him, or why these thoughts so often chain you to the past."

"What's there to talk about, Haruka? I'm sorry. You deserve better than me." Luz averted her eyes in shame as she pressed the neurohelmet deeper into her chest, her chin now resting atop its carbon fiber shell. She had hugged it just as tightly when Gabe had presented it to her, the day she had first stepped into *Indomitable*.

Haruka sat silently for a moment, as if searching for the right words of encouragement. "The Indigos are a family, and you are its head. I am a warrior, not a teacher or strategist. Without your guidance—"

"My guidance?" Luz sprang to her feet, her voice rising with her body. She spiked her neurohelmet into the ground, sending it clattering across the parched earth. She jabbed a damning finger at her burning *Marauder*. "*That* is what my guidance brings!"

Haruka remained unmoved. "It is a machine. You are not."

"You don't understand, do you?"

"Of course I don't. You never talk about the memories that haunt you. Instead, you try to drown them in whiskey. I came to rescue my captain from the elements, only to find my closest friend locked in a struggle with her past. You cannot keep fighting your battles alone. Let me help you. Please." Haruka's demeanor cracked, the worry on her face revealing an empathetic side of herself that she only shared with Luz.

Luz's scowl withered. She sank down next to Haruka, closer this time. "God, it's been so long. What do you know about the Marik front during the Fourth Succession War?"

"I am a warrior, not a historian," Haruka replied.

Luz nodded. "My family controlled a planet back then. Right along the border, little hole in the stars called Danais." She scanned Haruka's face for a reaction, but if she was shocked by the revelation of Luz's noble heritage, her visage didn't betray it. The worry Luz saw in her emerald eyes gave her the courage to continue.

"When Dad wasn't there for me, or couldn't be, Gabe was. He was like family to me. I wanted to follow in his footsteps, so I nagged my dad until he agreed to put me in our family's old *Marauder*. Guess I was enough of a hothead even he could tell I wasn't cut out for the governance thing." Luz cracked a faint, knowing smile at Haruka before letting it quickly fade.

"My father wasn't a very good ruler. From what I understand, his government damn near crashed the economy half a dozen times in twenty years. Cranston Snord smashing through the Amber Regiment and the aerospace fighter line we'd pinned our hopes on didn't help us any. After that mess, he had to put down popular revolts as frequently as your average person doing their laundry."

"A Free Worlds League pastime, I am told," Haruka said matter-of-factly.

"This time was different," Luz said. "Happened during Operation Dagger, in 3028. The FWLM unit that had been stationed on our planet jumped across the border to conduct a series of raids against the Lyrans."

Haruka raised a perfectly manicured eyebrow. "You were sixteen when you went to war?"

"No," Luz said, her voice growing raw as her mind fully sank into the past. "War came to me."

## 18 KILOMETERS EAST OF OAKMONT CITY
## DANAIS
## FREE WORLDS LEAGUE
## 12 OCT 3028

"Good shooting. Keep that up during these live fires, and I might be able to retire at thirty." Captain Gabriel Ruiz's baritone voice echoed over Luz's comm. His tone walked the usual fine line between authoritative and friendly that he'd assumed since he'd taken his post. Only nine years her senior, he had come a long way from the childhood friend Luz still thought of him as, despite only recently being thrust into the position of captain after his father's passing.

"You think my dad will let it happen? His little princess, a static defense unit commander, just like that? C'mon, there'll be a catch, you know it," Luz said as she flipped her master arm switch off, shutting down *Indomitable*'s weapon systems.

"Well, maybe not that easily. If you want the gig, your dad will probably make you dye your hair back. 'Unbecoming of a royal lady,' as he likes to say."

Luz laughed and turned her *Marauder* to face Gabe's *Trebuchet*. "'Unbecoming,' my ass. Indigo's the color of royalty, you know?"

"Looks more purple to me," Gabe said, his words laced with humor.

"Smartass."

"I heard that."

"Good," Luz said with a smug chuckle.

"You know, anyone else would call that insubord—uh, sorry, standby." The line went silent.

Luz rolled her eyes, assuming Gabe had switched frequencies to field another message from her overprotective father. She watched the local grazers slowly make their way back onto the field while she waited. The setting sun cast a gentle orange glow across the rolling hills of the ranchlands they often used as a firing range.

It felt almost sinful to violate the serenity of a place like this with the plodding of BattleMech feet and the roar of 'Mech-scale weaponry, even if the ranchers allowed them to use the fields for training. The tranquil scene calmed her nerves, a priceless reward both she and Gabe could enjoy at the end of another hard day of work.

Gabe's voice suddenly filled her ears, breaking her reverie. "Luz, we need to move. Now. Setting a new waypoint." His tone had changed dramatically, its usual drawling warmth replaced with a tense, staccato cadence.

"Gabe? What's going on? Waypoint's to the south, to the spaceport. Why aren't we heading back?" Luz's heart began to race. She'd never heard him talk this way to her. Something was very wrong.

"Priority-one order. We're getting you off-planet."

Luz's heart skipped a beat. "What the hell did Dad tell you?"

Gabe continued to speak in the quickened, breathless intonation of a soldier under duress. "Wasn't your dad, it was Lieutenant Lastimosa. We've got hostile mercs hot-dropping 'Mechs right on top of the governor's mansion. SDU's putting up a fight, but getting you out is top priority. I've got point. Let's move." Gabe's *Trebuchet* broke into a hurried trot.

Luz pointed her *Marauder* toward the waypoint and pushed the throttle just enough to catch up as she keyed her mic again. "The hell do you mean 'hostile 'Mechs?' How'd they get the drop on us? Why aren't we going back to support the SDU?"

"JumpShip arrived earlier this week, refused our hails," Gabe said, his 'Mech scanning left to right for a possible ambush. "We sent out a request for support, but got no response. DropShip began its descent earlier this afternoon. Guess we know why they're here now."

"Gabe, for God's sake, that's *my dad* we're leaving to die! We have to go back!" Luz instinctively turned *Indomitable*'s torso toward the governor's mansion even as it continued toward the spaceport. Her muscles tensed as she fought the urge to break formation and join the fight.

"We will. The Gryphons are stationed on Kalidasa. We get you safely off-planet, make contact with the CO, and ride back with the Silver Hawks in tow. All we can do right now."

"Like hell it is, Gabe! We have to—"

"Clear comms, another priority one! All frequencies!"

Luz slowed her 'Mech to a halt, desperately hoping to hear her father's voice through her headset.

The radio crackled to life.

"—beration Front. Decades of tyranny come to an end today. We have seized the Palacio del Sol and put the tyrant Alfonso Villanueva to the sword. Never again will the planet of Danais suffer the indignities—"

The broadcast faded to white noise as Luz's stomach churned and she fought back a wave of nausea. Her hands began to shake. Two sentences had just flipped her planet, her world, upside down.

Disbelief turned to grief.

Grief turned to anger.

The embers of her rage erupted into an uncontrollable wildfire of fury.

"No. No, goddammit, NO!" Luz screamed, her snarling voice almost unrecognizable to her own ears. She shoved her throttle to maximum and wrenched her control stick hard to the left, swinging her nose north.

"Luz, what are you doing? We have to leave! DropShip's waiting for us!" Gabe shouted over the droning of the rebel announcement still playing on the comm line.

"No, I'll kill them! I'll kill them all!" The words hissed through Luz's gritted teeth. Tears stung her eyes, her hands too busy fumbling for her master arm switch to wipe them away. As her *Marauder* barreled along the once-quiet farm road, she caught movement through her blurred vision and brought her PPCs to bear.

*Indomitable*'s arms screeched with energy, instantly turning a civilian car and its passengers to ash. Luz didn't bother to watch it burn. Her throttle dug into her palm as she tried to push it beyond its limit.

She continued firing at anything that moved as she ran toward the governor's mansion, never stopping to identify the victims of her wrath. Danais SDU vehicles, civilian transports, and the corpses of incinerated livestock smoldered in her wake.

"Luz, damn it, we need to leave! We'll avenge your dad, but we can't do that if we're both dead!" Gabe shouted over the comm.

Luz blocked out his pleas in her channeled fervor as she rampaged across the fields and into the outskirts of the city. A *Stinger* in unfamiliar colors crested a hill in front of her, immediately firing its jump jets in an evasive maneuver.

*Indomitable* unleashed both of its PPCs at the 'Mech now in her sights. The *Stinger* writhed under the impacts, its limbs torn asunder like branches in a storm. As it fell to the ground, a *Locust* bearing the same colors also trotted into view, stopping mid-stride to observe its dead lancemate as if in shock.

*Rookie move.*

A predatory grin crept across Luz's lips. She pressed her firing stud again and watched a pair of sapphire bolts smash squarely into the birdlike 'Mech's pronounced torso. It staggered briefly before a small figure rocketed out of its head in a dying flourish. Secondary explosions engulfed the abandoned *Locust* in flames, sending its remains flying over and through the streets. Burning armor panels and myomer bundles rained down upon the roofs of nearby buildings, setting them alight.

"Goddammit, Luz, enough! We gotta go, NOW!"

Even with two kills, bloodlust continued to gnaw at her. No amount of Gabe's fretful begging would stop her. His sensor trace faded out among the clutter of the burning city.

Luz watched the *Locust*'s ejection seat climb, then fall away before the MechWarrior deployed his parachute. She carefully dragged *Indomitable*'s crosshair toward the ejected pilot and steadied her aim.

She wanted her vengeance today.

The pilot's eyes locked with hers for a brief moment before Luz pulled the trigger. Her dorsal autocannon belched a stream of 120mm HEDP shells at the diminutive figure, its distinctive report reverberating in her cockpit. The enemy MechWarrior disappeared in a burst of crimson.

Luz proceeded over the hill, leaving the blazing inferno behind her as she watched the wilting parachute dance in the wind as if searching for its lost anchor. She spitefully raked a single laser across the fluttering orange chute, setting it ablaze. Her trigger finger twitched against her control stick, eager to continue the bloodshed.

*Indomitable* suddenly rocked violently to the left as alarms began to whine in her ears. She turned to face her would-be assassin and froze.

Standing to her right was a massive 'Mech, one she'd only ever seen glimpses of in holovids and technical readouts scattered around the ready room. A 'Mech she'd been told was only found in the employ of Wolf's Dragoons…or mercenaries skilled or lucky enough to take one by force.

The *Marauder II* adjusted itself on the side street it had ambushed her from, widening its animalistic stance like an apex predator making an agonistic intimidation display.

A chill ran through Luz's body. She froze at her controls, giving the advancing 'Mech time to fire again. *Indomitable* shuddered under the force of PPC bolts crashing against its right arm, flash-boiling massive chunks of armor away from her shoulder and weapon housings.

Luz pulled the throttle into reverse and whipped her reticule across her target. She pressed the firing stud a millisecond too soon, causing both of her PPC shots to go wide. Her autocannon rounds stitched a shallow line across the *Marauder II*'s shoulder, but failed to penetrate the armor.

The enemy 'Mech continued to bear down on her and fired again. A stream of energy crashed into *Indomitable*'s leg, and Luz heard a sharp *crack-pop* over the din of her autoloader cycling.

*"WARNING! LEG ACTUATOR FAILURE."*

*"MYOMER CONTROL FAILURE."*

Luz watched her viewscreen dip rapidly toward the ground, causing her to instinctively wrench her controls backward. *Indomitable* stumbled about drunkenly in the street as she struggled to regain her balance. As her 'Mech stabilized itself, the *Marauder II* again appeared in front of her, only to quickly disappear beneath a tidal wave of missile plumes and explosions.

"Luz! The waypoint! Go! NOW!"

Luz turned her 'Mech to the south and spotted Gabe's *Trebuchet* barreling toward the *Marauder II* before smashing into it at full speed. Both 'Mechs tumbled across the pavement, their armored hides chafing and sparking against the ferrocrete. The *Marauder II* flailed helplessly, rolling onto its stomach before it came to a halt. Its massive legs kicked wildly for purchase behind it, nearly decapitating Gabe's 'Mech as he rose from the ground.

As the two 'Mechs stood to face off behind her, Luz limped toward the minimum range of *Indomitable*'s weapons. In her compressed 360-degree viewscreen, the *Marauder II* fired its weapons at point-blank into Gabe's *Trebuchet*, severing its right arm. His 'Mech lurched at the sudden loss of mass before unleashing a torrent of missiles in return. Luz twisted her *Marauder* around, extended a single arm to the rear, and snapped off a desperate PPC shot in support.

"Damn it, Luz, *run!*" Gabe shouted over the wailing of his 'Mech's systems.

Another salvo from the *Marauder II* passed over Luz's head. She broke into a cold sweat as fear devoured her rage and her survival instincts took over.

The sounds of battle quieted as her 'Mech fled along the long road through the countryside to the spaceport. Gabe continued yelling into his mic, his words muffled and indecipherable through the sounds of Luz's panicked breathing and racing heartbeat.

Minutes felt like hours as Luz ran. She forced herself to concentrate on putting one foot in front of the other, careful to avoid losing her balance each time her damaged leg made contact with the paved road. Focusing on her 'Mech's balance helped her block out the hellscape of burning vehicles that dotted the landscape on the route to the DropShip—casualties of her rage and despair.

As she entered the spaceport and spotted a silver *Leopard* DropShip on the tarmac, her rapid breathing began to slow, matching the beat of her 'Mech's gait. Luz carefully picked her way around the small army of support personnel in fluorescent uniforms preparing the DropShip for takeoff, its engines reverberating through her cockpit as she limped toward its cavernous cargo hold. The moment *Indomitable* entered the 'Mech bay, the door closed behind her, silencing the cacophonous noise of the spaceport and plunging her into darkness.

Faint radio chatter soon broke the quiet of Luz's cockpit. She pressed the side of her neurohelmet to her ear, straining to hear the distant transmission. A stranger's voice could be heard through Gabe's microphone.

Someone had pulled him out of his *Trebuchet*.

Luz struggled to make out the words being spoken. The stranger mentioned a downed *Locust*, screamed about a burning parachute, and snarled a final insult about "honor among MechWarriors."

The gunshot that followed rang in her ears for what felt like an eternity.

## 5 KILOMETERS SOUTH OF DE ZAVALA PURIFICATION PLANT
## BANDERA BASIN
## CORRIDAN IV
## LYRAN ALLIANCE
## 10 MARCH 3058

"I still hear it in my nightmares."

Tears had begun to trickle down Luz's cheeks as she told the story, her head now cradled against Haruka's shoulder. She paused to wipe away her tears, only for them to immediately return. "I left him, Haruka. I should've stayed with him. Should have stood and fought and died."

Haruka placed a consoling hand on Luz's opposite arm, pulling her in closer to where she sat.

"Every night for the last thirty years, I've thought about the fact that when I saw his status light go dark, I should've been there to go into the dark with him," Luz said, the words barely escaping her lips.

"After everything I did that day, all the innocent people I killed, all those people I got killed? I don't deserve to be here."

The warmth of Haruka's arms surrounded her, squeezing her tight. "Luz..."

Luz's voice trembled, her tears now an endless rivulet spilling down and under the tubing of her cooling vest. "*Indomitable* was all I had left, the only thing I had that still connected me to Gabe. And now I...I..." Her words died in her throat, giving way to a long, anguished cry.

"You were just a child then. You can't allow yourself to be held prisoner by the mistakes you made in your grief."

"I don't want to! But I just can't let go! Everything I've ever cared about in my life is something I've had to let go! My hopes, my dreams, my friends, my family, my 'Mech—it all keeps being taken from me! Why hold onto my life if I'm always forced to let go of all the things that matter?"

"You don't have to let go of everything, Luz."

Luz remained silent, her body slumping dejectedly against her partner. Haruka's fingertips brushed along her back in a soothing caress.

"We formed the Indigos from a group of lost souls who lost their homes as we did. You know our stories. Sergeant Chang's political persecution on Gei-Fu. Lieutenant Delgado's failed insurrection on Gillingham. Miss Ryong's exile from McComb. The lives we once knew died when we left our homelands. But this adversity, these experiences, are the strength that bonds our family together."

Luz nodded, rubbing the dampness of her tears into Haruka's jacket.

"There is a difference between holding onto the past and being a prisoner to it. A key principle of *bushido* is *yū*—courageousness, fearlessness."

"You know I don't subscribe to the whole *bushido* thing," Luz said, mumbling into Haruka's shoulder. Her head rose and fell softly as Haruka shrugged.

"Perhaps you should. *Bushido* teaches that to live a life without risk is akin to not living at all. It is clear that losing *Indomitable* meant losing the one thing you had left which you believed truly mattered. But Gabe is not gone with her."

"He cannot be taken from you, because he lives on in your memories. Gabe would not wish to see you live life as you do now. He would not wish for you to become a husk of a woman in his absence, nor do I wish to see you be held back by your past." Haruka's voice wavered with barely constrained emotion.

The warmth of Haruka's body left as Luz pulled away, no longer wanting to burden her both physically and emotionally. Her heart ached at the idea of failing not only Gabe, but her partner as well. The daunting task of letting go after so many years cast a long shadow over her thoughts.

Haruka placed a reassuring hand on her thigh, her other palm gently lifting Luz's chin until their eyes met. Her gaze felt as if it pierced into Luz's soul.

"You do not need to let go, but you must *move on*. It will not be easy, but if you cannot move on from the past, then you have already died. My coming here will have been for nothing. Honor Gabe with your words and deeds. Choose to live a life worthy of his sacrifice. Be the leader I know you can be."

Luz sat quietly, the corners of her lips slowly lifting with her spirits. The words were a proclamation of faith, a reassurance Luz had once given to Gabe, now being spoken by her closest friend.

Her student.

Her light.

Luz took a deep breath, her gaze drifting back to her *Marauder*. "I have to say goodbye."

A kind smile spread across Haruka's face as well. She gave an encouraging nod, wiping her own tears away. "Then I will walk alongside you, as always."

Luz rose and began a solemn procession toward the husk of *Indomitable*. The sound of Haruka's footsteps followed close behind.

Luz stopped once the warmth of the dying flames embraced her. Haruka's hand slid into hers and gave a comforting squeeze as she took a final, wistful look at her fallen 'Mech.

She needed to move forward, if not for herself, then for her new family. Luz took a deep breath and slowly shut her eyes, committing the sight to her memory.

Consigning it to the past.

Minutes passed as Luz whispered a hushed eulogy, the heat from the fire waning while she said the farewells she'd never had the strength to give before.

When she opened her eyes again, she watched the last embers of her 'Mech's wreckage finally surrender to the night. *Indomitable* faded away with them, becoming one with the darkness.

Above it, a billion new dawns glimmered brightly in the heavens.

# GETTING PAID IN AN UNCERTAIN AGE

## LORCAN NAGLE

**Originally published in the July 3135 issue of *Mercenary Commander*, MRBC press, Galatea. Accessed from aboard *CSF Naglfar*, 13 February 3152**

The collapse of Pax Republica has been a mixed blessing. On one hand, it has seen an increase in conflict and hardship across the Inner Sphere, especially in the rapidly collapsing Republic. But on the other hand, the mercenary business is booming in a way we haven't seen in decades, with many lucrative contracts and an increase in the number of companies to fill them.

However, the financial situation is also incredibly chaotic, with the value of both the Republic stone and the C-bill plummeting. Here at *Mercenary Commander*, we've heard of many small units forced to disband when their fee was worth only a fraction of what they expected by the time they returned to Galatea, and were unable to meet their regular expenses.

With that in mind, we've been talking with some experienced and business savvy unit commanders to get their insights into the options available to mercs these days and their advantages and disadvantages.

### Local Currency

This is what you'll get offered very often as a first option, especially by the Great Houses. The big advantage is that that money spends right away. If you're on a garrison contract, you can purchase services and supplies locally and pay your troops and staff with money they can spend, which keeps everyone happy. It can, however, be the first step to being caught in the company store. Don't get too attached to that comfortable stream of cash, or you could well end up a mercenary in name only.

"It can be tough when you jump a border," said Captain Ron Maloyi of Best Defense, a combined-arms company just returned from the Regulan Fiefs. "With interstellar banking what it is right now, we're carrying a lot of physical money, and got paid in rupees by the Regulans. We'd negotiated a raiding contract with the Lyrans who have little interest in a currency used by a nation they don't share a border with. So when we jumped to Manihiki we started hitting up free traders, checking the exchange rates on recharge stations and so on to find someone who'd give us Marik-Stewart eagles in exchange, which we could then convert to kroner. We ended up having to do three deals because no one was willing to take all of our Regulan cash. Each broker takes their cut of course, cutting into the profit margin. Still, we've got a good administrator, they've got a good nose for where we can get better exchange rates. I can only imagine how much harder it is for green commands."

### Precious Metals, Minerals, and Industrial Products

Legend says the Gray Death Legion took payment for their first contract in the form of a briefcase full of vanadium—this isn't actually true, but it's the kind of thing that's becoming common for small, resource-rich planets to offer mercs instead of cash. Access to a planet's natural wealth or industrial output can be very profitable, but you need to be able to carry that material with you when you leave and then sell it on the open market.

It's not all bad, as Frida Gustavson, a self-described troubleshooter for Mullen's Grenadiers, can attest. "We did a job for...let's say a major manufacturer of military electronics on Donegal and got paid in product. I was able to offload them two jumps toward Clan space at full price because somebody there desperately needed them and couldn't afford to wait for an order to make it to Donegal and back. I get the feeling paying for shipping was a concern too, and we happened to be there. Hell, we're just back from Alrakis and got paid in metals there. While the guys were garrisoning the planet, I was talking with local traders and arranged to get enough spare parts and supplies to get us through a good six months in exchange."

### Stocks, Bonds, and Futures

Say it with us: "The value of your investment may drop as well as rise." Investing in the stock market, especially the defense industry, has long been a mainstay of mercenary finances, but generally, this type of investment is done by taking profits from contracts as opposed to being your payment. This can be a minefield due to various types of stocks and bonds offered, and it's very easy for a smooth-talking corporate exec to bamboozle a merc who doesn't have any first-hand knowledge of investment.

"Stocks and bonds are arcane at the best of times," says Shotaro Kanzaki, a financial adviser on Galatea who specializes in helping mercenaries invest. "I have a client right now who took payment in stock options, and when they went to cash them in was shocked to discover there was a vesting period; they can't do anything with them for three years, and even then, it's just the option to buy at the price they are now and then keep or sell them. The corporation essentially took a bet that this unit would be gone by the time the vesting period concluded, and the reality of the mercenary trade is that this will likely be the case."

## Military Supplies

This can be a mixed bag in many ways. Obviously we all need spare parts and consumables to keep operating, repair damage and maintain operational capacity. Getting that handed to you means you don't need to go on the market to purchase them, but what if your employer doesn't have a specific part to give you? You wind up bartering with other units, jury-rigging or making do. It also doesn't help you pay your employees, which can be very bad for morale.

Eileen Fox, an infantry trooper looking for work, spoke with us briefly: "It's a wretched way to live. I was signed on with Williams' Winners. Never heard of them? Well let's just say it wasn't a clever name and they won't be missed. We wound up on a garrison job where we were paid in supplies and in all honesty, I'm not sure who was more desperate, the planetary government or Captain Williams. Three months we were on that planet, our gear was in decent shape but morale was in the toilet. Our only food was rations, you couldn't go for a couple drinks when you had liberty without counting out your money because God alone knows how long it had to stretch and cover stuff that wasn't included in 'essential supplies,' but sure was essential personally, if you know what I mean? Anyway, the Swordsworn hit us hard and we folded like a book. Nobody cared enough to put up a strong fight, and the survivors managed to make it back here. If my next unit signs up for that kind of contract, I'll walk. Never again."

To help deal with these issues, the Mercenary Review and Bonding Commission announced a new training course, offering guidance to mercenaries on what kinds of payment to accept and when, and how best to make them work for you. This course will be available in-person on Galatea and other MRBC-approved training centers, as well as a pre-recorded version for commanders and administrators to review or learn at their leisure. Pricing options, availability, and booking details will be in the next issue. We do have one last option to talk about, however, and we've kept that separate from everything else for reasons that will become clear.

## Fox Credits

Clan Sea Fox has been roaming the Inner Sphere for more than fifty years now, buying, selling, and trading everywhere they go. And as a result, the Fox credit, their self-issued currency, has a wide reach across multiple nations—assuming the hyperpulse generators don't come back and the Republic can't reclaim their lost territory, the Fox credit is the most likely option to replace the C-bill and the stone. So why aren't we all-in on recommending getting paid in Fox credits?

The Foxes have slowly pushed themselves into so many parts of Inner Sphere commerce—we use their fleets for shipping, they sell us advanced weapons and equipment, and they've become part of the informal Pony Express that passes news around since the fall of the HPG network. And they're still a Clan! Have they given up on their dream of taking Terra and becoming the ilClan? The Jade Falcons have been one of the forces assaulting the Republic, how long will it be until the other Clans follow suit? Simply put, we can't trust the Sea Foxes.

Now, we're not saying don't do business with the Sea Foxes—that genie isn't going back in the bottle, and they're the easiest way for mercs to get their hands on ClanTech. But relying on them even more is dangerous; where does it end? Would they set themselves up as a separate mercenary bonding institution? If so, what happens after you've been relying on them for financial services and they change the terms? [*Appended comment by ovKhan Samson Rodriguez: Damn right we would!*]

# BEHIND THE STICK

### JASON HANSA

**GALATEA CITY**
**GALATEA**
**GALATEAN LEAGUE**
**31 JULY 3151**

*We need work, we need work, we need work,* thought Philip Ausburn as he pumped the steel off his chest in time to the words, again and again, letting frustration fuel his workout.

Born and raised in Terra's ancient city of Barcelona, he had short dark hair and light brown skin that glistened from the sweat running from his left wrist down to his triceps; his silvery prosthetic right arm, however, reflected the workout room's fluorescent lighting. He was already bracing himself for another long day at the mercenary hiring hall, hours spent trying to arrange meetings with agents just to be told they weren't interested in hiring him and his wife, Nevada.

After slowly putting the bar back into place, he cleaned all the equipment and closed the door behind him before heading up the stairs toward his apartment. The owners and their two sons took up the entire second floor above the Highlander Bar, and on the third floor were six apartments, one of which he was renting for the foreseeable future.

"Unfortunately," Philip growled under his breath. He stared up at the ceiling for a moment, calming himself down before jogging up the stairs. Hitting the third floor, he walked down to his apartment and quietly opened the door, trying not to wake his family. It was small, a one-bedroom flat with—thankfully—a decently sized living room and both a well-equipped kitchen and a washer-dryer combo that was in almost constant use because of the kids.

As usual, he needn't have bothered with stealth. Nevada was already in her usual chair, one fraternal twin on a breast, the other gurgling on her lap and batting at her brother's feet above her. She was of average height, had skin the color of stained oak, and dark hair she kept in the close-cropped style common among MechWarriors. Between the caloric demands of the twins, the almost endless maintenance her BattleMech required, and working in the bar downstairs, she'd lost almost all her pregnancy weight—something her physician was already concerned about.

Philip walked over and kissed his wife on the forehead.

"Thought they'd still be asleep," he said as he stripped off his shirt and shorts. Balling them up, he spun on a heel and did a fade-away overhand shot, the clothes landing perfectly on the washing machine. He'd hit a growth spurt in middle-school and led his team to multiple championships before his growing suddenly stopped, leaving him a talented but average-sized guard in high school. But between basketball, baseball, and rugby, Philip could put a grenade just about anywhere he chose to throw it; a useful skill for an infantryman. At his wife's raised eyebrow, he added, "I'll throw in a load after I shower, I'm not leaving them for you."

"I know," she said, then yawned. "I'm just wiped, and I really appreciate you picking up a lot of the slack, even if I forget to tell you." She chuckled lightly. "Momnesia is no joke. I'll probably have forgotten this entire conversation by the time you get out of the shower."

He looked at her, and then at his own body. Even though the scars from his top surgery and hysterectomy were invisible after so many years, he knew where they were. He frowned slightly. "Sometimes, when I see how exhausted you are, I wish I'd delayed, wish I'd held off until I met you—"

"*Stop.*" Her gentle tone switched to one of command, an officer of the Republic Armed Forces that would brook no disagreement. "You had to be true to yourself *then*, and I will not listen to you beat yourself up about it *now*." She smiled slightly to take the edge off, but her tone was still flat and serious as she asked, "Check or hold, Sergeant?"

He smiled slightly, walked forward and leaned over to give her a kiss. "Yes, ma'am, sorry to get too deep into my feelings, ma'am."

She laughed. "Getting moody on me when I can't have coffee is a risky choice, love," she replied. "Keep your head in the game, okay?"

His jaw set. "Absolutely." He leaned in for another kiss and her nose crinkled.

"Good. Remember, I love you for who you are, but...you *reek*. Hit the showers, Sergeant."

Philip smiled and threw a salute as he headed off. "Yes, ma'am."

Eleven hours later, Nevada was behind the bar as he entered, and she could tell by his body language it'd been another unsuccessful day job hunting. She pulled him a locally brewed pilsner, glancing to her right.

"Put this one against me, Christos," she said, and the large man waved it off as he wiped down a pitcher. Christos Makridis was a large man, a native Galatean who'd inherited the bar from his father and grandfather before him. Named the Highlander Bar, it had the front faceplate of the namesake BattleMech mounted on the side wall of the tavern, a large mirror where the cockpit windscreen would be, and drinks arrayed in front of it. Stretching around it was a solid wooden bar, polished and gleaming: by a well-known rule, anyone damaging the bar would get charged for repairs, anyone deliberately defacing the wood would get defaced in turn by the bouncers.

There was a well-lit stage over a small dance floor: sometimes with dancers, sometimes live music, but otherwise a tall, skinny man of Korean descent referring to himself as "Wolfman" kept the tunes lively from a corner DJ booth. The ceiling was red velvet, the room was lit so customers could see each other and have a good time, but dark enough for canoodling in the corners, and the walls and columns were all a deep slate green, covered in chalk signatures. From the bar—or floating around on tables—were sticks of chalk, and customers could sign their names, write messages, draw their unit icons: about every five years or so, Christos would wipe the slates clean, except for a few small spots he'd circled with a "do not erase" tag.

Lovers, friends, notes to missing comrades: they covered every square centimeter around the tavern, and it was that graffiti, that linkage to units and friends gone by, that made the Highlander Bar a staple among the "I'm between units" strata of unemployed mercenaries. Mercs under contract would be too busy trying to get underway to socialize at the Highlander—and wouldn't want to flaunt their good fortune, anyways, lest Lady Luck decide to make an example of them. The truly desperate and broke mercenaries—the ones a few meals away from piracy—kept to the dives and slum bars at the outskirts of town, or simply drank the pain away wherever they stayed.

The Highlander, though, was patronized by mercs in transition. Ones who found themselves unemployed for one reason or another, but had enough socked away and a solid enough reputation that regaining employment wasn't so much an issue of *if* but *when*.

Watching Philip approach, Nevada wondered how much longer this could go on. She gave him a quick kiss when he sat down at the left side of the bar, his right arm against the wall. The opposite side was one of the most popular seats in the bar, many mercs unable to relax without watching the door. Philip wasn't as paranoid as some, he just preferred to see the door; being left-handed, he was able to grab the stool less straddled.

He ordered a cold-cut sandwich, and Christos smiled and said, "Go take a break with him at a table. It's quiet now." He nodded at the empty room for emphasis.

She smiled and thanked him—it was just after dinner time, and their normal rush didn't come in until later, staying until after one on weekdays and three on weekends. After Christos' wife Phoebe had tripped down the basement stairs on her way to swap out kegs, she'd offered to babysit the twins in exchange for Nevada subbing for her behind the bar. Nevada had agreed, slipping upstairs throughout the night as necessary for feedings or in case of emergencies, and she was thankful of the extra cash bartending was bringing in to counter the otherwise constant drain on their savings.

Philip followed her to a corner table. Her husband, as usual, was quietly reading the chalk signatures while sipping the beer. "How bad was it today?" she asked as they sat next to each other.

"Same as usual," he replied with a shrug, then looked at his right hand, the bar lights reflecting off his metallic prosthetic. He made a fist, the thin myomer musculature silent as he clenched, unclenched, clenched, then relaxed it as he took a sip of beer from the mug in his left hand. "I'm just a sergeant from a no-name RAF company who lost an arm to the Falcons while they wiped his unit from existence."

She frowned at his despair. "You know just surviving Mad Malvina is a miracle in itself."

"I know that, and you know that, but all the recruiters on this rock?" He sighed deep. "They don't care."

"Why not?" came an energetic voice, and the Ausburns looked up. Carter Makridis, youngest son of the owner, was bringing their sandwiches. Eighteen, skinny, and often naive about anything not involving bartending, he held two plates with their food. "If you don't mind me asking?"

Nevada watched Philip use his foot to slide the chair opposite from him out, and Carter sat while they took bites. "Now that the Republic of the Sphere is gone, this world is swarming with ex-RAF soldiers, all of us looking for work with any unit that'll sign us on. They have their pick of troops, why should they choose me? My unit lost, I got hurt, we didn't matter. It's not a résumé that rises to the top."

Carter looked sad. "No one wants to hire you? Or Nevada—I mean, she has a BattleMech! That has to be worth something?"

Nevada shook her head. "You forget, my *Paladin*'s an ultra-rare, hard-to-maintain heavy that's an outsized burden on small technical staffs. More than that, we have twins—that's two dependents to add to the insurance, two dependents who can't chip in with maintenance, two more dependents to guard while we're on mission, dependents who need doctor's visits and check-ups and a million little administrative issues that isn't really the unit's problem but, then again, why hire me when they can get some young 'Mech jockey half my age with a common ride and no kids?"

"But...but you're experienced!"

She leaned forward. "I am, and I expect to get paid like it, too. Phil, did any of the units offer anything worth my time?"

Her husband shook his head. "No one offered you a captain slot, and the ones that offered a lieutenant position offered rock-bottom salary for it."

Carter shook his head. "But...that's not fair!"

Nevada took a big bite of her sandwich, glanced over to the bar to make sure Christos was okay—he nodded at her, then turned to help the only customer sitting at the bar—then glanced at the door. She smiled when she saw who walked in.

"If you don't believe me, ask the Dvorskys. They're just as skilled as I am, but they're all working for your dad just to make ends meet."

Carter spun around—it was an open secret he was madly in love with Emily Dvorsky, the youngest of the three siblings.

In the lead was Wynn, his cybernetic right eye glowing a gentle red. He helped as a bouncer, so he was in work pants and a T-shirt, his entire prosthetic right arm and pectoral muscles reflecting the bar's light. He was forty-three and bald, olive-skinned, and worked out constantly to maintain the all-around athletic build of a career soldier.

Behind him was Hester, five years older than him and the eldest of the Dvorsky siblings. She was in khakis and a button-down shirt, leading Nevada to believe she'd probably had interviews today as well. Tall, just as athletic as her brother, with shoulder-length salt-and-pepper hair, she'd change into a midriff-baring tank top and short-shorts before her shift: both of Hester's legs were prosthetics, and she would sashay around the tables on the shapely metallic limbs.

In the rear, two decades younger than her siblings at twenty-four, was Emily, whom Hester had once jokingly called their mom's favorite surprise. Emily, like her siblings, had been injured in the ruthless fighting between her home—the Magistracy of Canopus—and their neighbors in the Marian Hegemony. She was missing her entire left arm and her right leg from just above the knee, but unlike her siblings, her limbs were a milky mother-of-pearl that seemed to change colors with every step she took. She was slim, with long, bouncy hair she dyed red, and her every movement attracted attention.

Wynn fist-bumped Philip and Carter, hugged Nevada, snatched another chair from a neighboring table, and straddled it backward while yelling at Emily to pull them a pitcher—something Christos had already started the moment they'd walked in. Hester rustled Carter's hair like a kid brother, gave a peck on each cheek to Nevada—the three siblings tended to show their affection with physical touch, and it'd taken Nevada a few days to get used to it—before Hester walked around the table to take the last open seat.

Emily, carrying a pitcher of beer and glasses, sat down in Nevada's lap, threw her heels onto Carter's thigh—pulling an instant blush from the teen—and kissed her on the cheek. "Hiya, sexy, miss me? Whatcha talking about?"

Philip grabbed the pitcher, topping off his glass and then pouring for Wynn. "Hester, your sister's hitting on my wife again."

"Run away with me, my darling," Emily overdramatized, throwing her flesh-and-blood arm around Nevada's shoulders and staring into her eyes. "Let's leave this ill-begotten world and live in sin on the distant frontier."

"Tempting," Nevada replied just as theatrically, stretching out the word before breaking into laughter. The table joined in as Philip continued to fill glasses.

Emily stole a French fry from Nevada's plate. "Seriously, what were you talking about? It looked kinda intense."

Nevada's face fell. "How hard it is to find a spot in a merc unit right now, between the twins and Philip's prosthetic."

The table got quiet, and Emily splayed out her prosthetic hand over the table, studying her almost translucent fingers, moving her hand back and forth to pick up different colored spotlights from around the stage. "Yeah. It's been hard for us, too."

"But why?" Carter said. "It's not your fault you guys got injured. You were doing your jobs!"

Emily reached over, stole Philip's glass—ignoring his "I poured you one!" protest—and took a deep swig.

"Carter, I..." Emily looked away for a second, took another deep drink before putting it back down in front of Philip. "I never told you how I got hurt. We were attacking a *Calliope* the Hegemony probably stole from us, and our major wanted it back, and so our battle armor platoon—" She waved a hand to include Hester. "—went after it while Wynn's unit distracted it."

"My commander was an idiot," Wynn chimed in, his red eye burning like pooled lava. "As dense as this table!" he said, smacking it with his artificial hand for emphasis. "She saw the *Calliope* as just another 'Mech, but they're *designed* to kill infantry. I got lucky, just caught some shrapnel. Most of the platoon ate plasma."

Nevada shuddered, and he paused and turned toward her.

"Sorry, Nevs," he said sincerely. "I know you MechWarriors hate fire."

"It's a horrible way to die," Nevada replied, and Emily shifted on her lap slightly as she also nodded in agreement.

He nodded back, his human eye distant and unfocused as he raised his glass. "Yes, yes it is," he quietly agreed.

Emily looked at her brother for a second and then turned back to Carter to continue. "While they were buying time with their lives, we snuck through the trees and flanked the 'Mech. When we finally jumped at him, they caught me!" Emily used her left hand to demonstrate for emphasis, snapping her fingers over the table. "They snatched me out of the air and squeezed! I could feel my own armor ripping me apart! I just remember screaming before the meds kicked in, and they threw me off to the side to step on Hester."

Nevada—and the rest of the table—slowly looked at Hester.

"Right across both thighs," Hester said coldly, little emotion in her voice. "Instant amputation. I don't even remember it—I passed right out—but the pressure on the armor also shattered both of my hips. Thankfully my organs were only bruised, but my entire pelvis is polymer."

"Sometimes I still wake up in a cold sweat from that damn battle," Emily said. "We're damaged goods, the lot of us, but this is what we do. We're not bartenders, though I'll love your dad forever for giving us some temp work and a lot of free beer. We're soldiers, but on a world busting open at the seams with fit and healthy crunchies, why should a unit take a chance on us?"

"Crunchies?" Carter asked.

Nevada chuckled. "A slang term for infantry. It's the noise they make when a BattleMech steps on them—no offense, Hes," she said, and chuckled again when Carter blanched.

Hester chuckled mirthlessly into her beer. "If I was offended, Emily would just say it twice as often."

Emily smiled. "I would. I'm evil that way." The table—save Carter—chuckled, the mood lightening slightly.

The young man was still glum, and shook his head. "It's still not fair."

"Life usually ain't, kid," Philip agreed, finishing off his beer. "It usually ain't."

The next evening, Philip was sitting at the bar next to Wynn when he noticed a pair of tough guys making their way toward them through the crowd. It was after dinner, but before the night rush, so the smaller man in a cheap suit and his better-dressed muscle had to weave around a few couples to get to them. Philip nudged Wynn with his elbow, and the large man turned around, still holding his beer.

"You the Dvorsky brother?" the short one asked.

Wynn's real eye narrowed, and, out of sight of the two men, Philip slowly dropped his hand toward a knife he had tucked in the small of his back.

"Depends on who's asking," answered Wynn.

The smaller man put up his hands. "Hey, we're all friends here. Your sister missed her link-up with me, but I figured you might be good for it."

"Good for what?"

At this point, Hester had slipped through the crowd to be on the man's right elbow, and the bodyguard shifted but didn't stop her.

The smaller man pulled out a small envelope and passed it to Wynn, who opened it, looked inside, then passed it to Hester. Philip watched the situation carefully as she looked inside, and only relaxed when he saw her nod at the man.

"We're good for it. Wynn, please settle up for Emily," she said. As the muscle and Wynn got together to pass some bills back and forth, she asked, "Where's Em, though?"

"Don't know. I told her to meet me at McKinney's Pub, and she never showed. But she did me a solid a while back, so I figured I could swing by here and deliver it to you."

Hester quirked an eyebrow. "A solid?"

He smiled slightly. "She introduced me to my girl."

Hester looked at the big man, who looked away for a second and then quietly said, "My kid needed braces, and Em said she knew a guy. The doc's great."

Hester smiled. "Yeah, that's our Emily. She never showed at the pub?"

Carter interrupted from behind the bar. "Wait, McKinney's Pub?" He looked at Hester. "When she left, she said she was headed to McKinney's *Tavern*. A lot of off-worlders mix them up."

The smaller man narrowed his eyes. "That's Vory territory," he said, naming the organized crime group that ran much of the underworld along the League-Confederation border and even into near Republic and Alliance space. "If she went over there looking for me, she could be in trouble. If they knew she was looking for black-market pheromone implant refills, she could be in *real* trouble." He glanced at the big guy, then turned back to Hester. "Your kid sister's good people, and I don't know many of them. Let me make a few calls."

When Emily didn't return within the next few hours, Hester and Wynn grew anxious. The group, including Jamal—the smaller man—migrated to the corner table. He was constantly stepping outside to meet with contacts, while the bigger man, Ahmed, sat at the table with the two Dvorskys, all three nursing sodas. Philip switched to soda as well, and Nevada was checking for updates every time she could slip away from the bar. Couples danced and partied, and the group got more and more solemn until, finally, Jamal came to the table with a deep frown on his face. Philip put his glass down and waved at Nevada for her to join them.

"Well?" Hester quietly asked.

"She got snatched, but I know who did it and where they are."

Wynn's artificial hand smashed the glass he was holding into shards, and Hester put a hand on his arm to calm him. As heads turned at neighboring tables, Philip—and Nevada, on her way over—convinced them everything was okay.

"Please. Tell us everything," Hester asked just loud enough to be heard over the music.

Nevada took a seat next to Hester, putting her hand on the older woman's shoulder. Hester smiled at the gesture, and then the four focused on Jamal as he sat and said, "She's been snatched by the Vory, working for someone recruiting for the Marian Legion."

Wynn hissed, and Hester growled.

Nevada frowned. "The Hegemony? Why?"

Jamal shrugged. "It has to do with what she was shopping for—those recharge cells and the catalyst agents for her pheromone implant. When she showed up in League territory, the regulars were willing to ignore her—but apparently a Hegemony recruiter was down there. When he found out what she was waiting around for, he called for backup and grabbed her when she left."

"I still don't understand why," Wynn said.

Jamal paused, taking a deep breath and looking at Wynn and Hester before going on. At Hester's nod, he said, "I'm getting this second- and thirdhand, but as I understand it, the recruiter was injured during an Ebon Magistrate raid a few years ago. The Canopian sleeper agent used a pheromone implant on him, convincing him to pass over the credentials she needed to get into his facility." He shrugged. "That's the word I got, anyways. They took Emily out to a safe house they have outside city limits to..." His voice faltered for a second, remembering he was talking to Emily's family. "...to work her over because of it."

Wynn shook his head in disbelief. "That wasn't us. We were still in the Magistrate's training program then."

Hester nodded, her face still solemn. "But Em was close to the agent, remember? They dated for a while. She'll die before she gives up her name."

"Then she'll die painfully," Jamal said quietly. "It might take a couple hours, but I think I can put you in touch with the recruiter. Maybe I can convince them not to hurt her until you talk to them?"

Wynn shook his head. "They won't stop. They're Hegemony. They'll agree to a meet-up and keep going anyway. We have to go get her."

Hester nodded.

"There's only the two of you," Jamal noted.

"Three," said Philip.

"Four," added Nevada, "and I'll pull *Mukden* out of storage."

"Five," said Carter, who'd come up behind them.

The entire table immediately responded in various forms of "*No!*" in multiple languages.

Carter crossed his arms in front of his chest. "She's my friend, too, guys. And if you're all kitted up to kick in doors, who's going to get you there and stay with the truck? I'm a great driver. You need me."

"Absolutely not," Hester said. "Carter, we all know how you feel about Em, but this isn't a job for civilians. I'm sorry, but Emily will kill us if we get you killed rescuing her."

The table fell silent a moment before Ahmed said, "I'll drive. I owe Emily that much."

Hester stood. "Let's take this upstairs—we can keep planning while I swap legs."

Just after 3 a.m., Nevada led the way through the darkness in *Mukden*, her 60-ton *Paladin* PAL-3 BattleMech. The heavy 'Mech had been hand-built by Innovative Design Concepts on Solaris VII almost a century prior. When the Word of Blake invaded the world, her grandfather and the other IDC test pilots had escorted their families out of Solaris City, running alongside a convoy of civilian vehicles that carried their dependents out into the countryside and to safety. He then fought alongside Jessie Watson, Jim Arnold, and a few other IDC MechWarriors against the Word's occupation of Solaris. Once the Word left, he immediately joined the Lyran Alliance Armed Forces, unable to rest until he'd helped throw the Word off Terra.

Accepting the Republic's offer to resettle on Terra, he also accepted a commission in the RAF, as it was the only way to keep his beloved *Paladin* during those early years of disarmament. It had passed down to Nevada's father and then to her; however, unlike when her grandfather and father piloted it, she no longer had the full backing of a Solaris company or a state army to help with the maintenance burden.

The *Paladin* was kept upright by an extralight gyro, powered by an outsized extra-*extra*-light engine, and wrapped difficult-to-find light ferro-fibrous armor around an incredibly dense reinforced chassis. It was a design IDC painstakingly engineered to eke every possible gram of lethality and survivability out of the weight available, but the backend maintenance chores were oppressive. Renting bay space, finding the right tools to rent, hunting down spare parts—and then often having to customize them to fit the all-but-extinct frame—was both physically and mentally exhausting, especially knowing it was a burden no mercenary unit generally wanted to shoulder. Between the *Paladin*'s upkeep and hospital bills from having the twins, Nevada knew she'd soon have to make a choice on keeping *Mukden* or swapping it for something far less expensive, but it wasn't a decision point she was at...*yet*.

She shook her head to clear her thoughts. *Focus*, she reprimanded herself. *Jamal told us they employ a pair of MechWarriors, but his contact didn't know the models.* She grimaced. *I've gone into battle with less information, but I still don't like it.*

When Outreach had served as the central hub for "legitimate" mercenary employment for a few decades, Galatea had dipped from being "the Mercenary's Star" to "the other one." Recruiters with sketchy reputations offering contracts of questionable morality and legality weren't welcome on Outreach, so they remained behind as the reputable employers departed. Many smaller units, as well, soon realized the comparatively clean and prosperous streets of Outreach were no place for warriors that simply wanted paychecks and weren't incredibly choosy on who they had to kill to earn them.

Galatea was soon overwhelmed with criminals, pirates, thugs, and those that wanted to hire them: it got so bad during the FedCom Civil War that battles between rival mercenary units raged unchecked across the world, requiring an entire mercenary regiment to come in under contract and clean up the situation. Not long after, the Word of Blake occupied Galatea during the Jihad, leaving over 80 percent of the population homeless on their own world.

It took the Republic decades of pumping capital into the planet to get it rebuilt, and though it once again served the Inner Sphere as the center of mercenary employment, it was now a hybrid of the two versions that came before: the legitimate businesses and recruiters located in Galatea City, and the less reputable ones scattered across the world in dark bars, seedy hotels, and other shady locals far from the oversight of the Mercenary Review and Bonding Commission.

Far to the north and just outside Galaport were the Hangdorf Proving Grounds, the only certified training facility for units to rent and show off their skills for legitimate employment. Unofficially, just as it was during the dark decades, that left the rest of the world as "unofficial" training grounds—though an unwritten rule was to keep any so-called live-fire exercises outside of populated areas, lest it draw official notice. It was through one of those unofficial but often-used tracts of barren wastes Nevada led the delivery van containing her husband and their friends.

An hour outside Galatea City lay a small, riverside town that catered to whitewater rafters due to a particularly treacherous stretch of river nearby. The Vory, apparently, used the river as a smuggling conduit, sending illicit goods downstream on small watercraft to dock at their front business north of the rapids, a rafting company just outside town. While the Vory did run a legitimate business taking tourists downstream, it was solely to provide a cover for their massive warehouse dedicated to "raft maintenance."

Jamal's information told them Emily had been taken to the small administration building adjacent to the warehouse where the mob kept rafts and canoes up front and drugs in the back. He'd also learned they kept a pair of MechWarriors on the payroll, ostensibly to "protect the town from criminal elements," but really to ensure other criminal organizations thought twice about stealing their illicit goods. Nevada and her friends didn't care about anything in the warehouse, but a pair of BattleMechs could bring their rescue mission to a quick end.

The van entered town—Nevada obeying the unwritten rules and cutting the corner cross-country to meet them outside city limits on the town's north side. With her back in the lead, about five minutes later and a kilometer shy of the property, her BattleMech sensors pinged for attention.

She clicked open her microphone. "Team, I've got two BattleMechs powering up—looks like they're just watching us for now, but the good money says once you make that left toward the river, they'll pop out of hiding. Ahmed, you need to punch it once you make the turn. I'll cover you."

"Understood," came Philip's solid voice. "Good luck, honey," he said a minute later as the van turned and accelerated, its headlights cutting deep into the Galatean night and leaving no illusions as to its destination. The two BattleMechs, still obscured a half kilometer away behind hills and boulders, headed toward the van.

"You too, babe," she said, then clicked the microphone off. Swinging her targeting pip over the closest enemy, she felt her nerves calm and her focus sharpen. *Philip needs more luck than I do,* she thought. *After twenty years of fighting Wolves, Falcons, and Capellans, whatever scrubs these bastards managed to put on their payroll,* Mukden *and I can handle them.*

Once they made their turn, Philip confirmed the interior lights were off and then opened one of the rear doors, moving to the side to let Wynn out. As the asphalt streaked by underneath, Wynn swung out onto the rear of the second door, where an aluminum ladder leading to the roof was bolted on. Philip heard Wynn lock his artificial arm into place, ensuring he wouldn't let go.

With a nod to the big man, Philip closed the door and went back to his seat just as they approached a small guard shack on the edge of the barbed-wire fenced property. The guard held up a hand to block the glare from their headlights: as Wynn had said during planning, it was an old trick to make sure the guard couldn't see who was in the van until the last second, but the old tricks stuck around across the centuries because they *worked*.

Pulling up right in front of the rolling gate, Ahmed rolled down his window and shouted at the guard, "Let us in, there's a BattleMech back there!" As if on cue, the distinct sounds of 'Mech combat started in the distance.

The guard, a surprisingly fit and alert man with the bearing of a fellow veteran, frowned at Ahmed, and glanced over at Hester in the passenger seat. He shifted, trying to see who else was in the van.

"Who are you?" he demanded. "We never get deliveries this late." He frowned again and was about to ask another question when he started, dropping a hand down to his holstered pistol.

Before he could turn around, however, Wynn's steel fist clamped around his neck from behind and squeezed, crushing any noise he might have made, before yanking him backward into the dark. Five seconds later, Wynn stepped into the guard shack, hit the gate button, and sprinted for the back door of the van.

"Go quick but not too fast, Ahmed," reminded Philip. "As far as everyone inside is concerned, the guard cleared us. Let's keep pretending we're their friends right up to the door." The big man nodded as Hester, Wynn, and Philip conducted final checks, all three racking bolts and double-checking their gear.

Philip glanced at Ahmed. "Keep the engine running, no telling how hot our evac might be."

The big bruiser grunted in agreement, and, with a final turn of the wheel, took them around the well-lit tourist entrance and to the employee entrance in the rear. A hard brake on gravel and they came to a stop. Philip threw open the rear doors, Wynn aiming a combat shotgun at the entrance while up front Hester jumped out and swung the barrel of her light machine gun toward the roof.

"Good luck, guys," Ahmed said as he killed the lights, the three veterans running to the door with their weapons at the ready. They quickly stacked up, and with a tap on Wynn's shoulder, the big man blew the lock off the door with his Morrigan Stormsweeper, the shotgun's blast echoing off the buildings in the darkness.

Nevada studied the map on a secondary monitor as she closed the distance. The town was about three kilometers south, and a kilometer to her left was the river, warehouse, and the office her husband was heading to. Half a kilometer ahead of her, behind a low ridge that ran from the road all the way back to the river, were the emissions indicative of BattleMechs, types still unknown. She pushed her throttle open with her left hand, the *Paladin* hitting its top speed of 97 kph within seconds. The acceleration also sent a wave of heat into the cockpit: everything a BattleMech did generated heat, and XXL engines were well known to run even hotter than their smaller cousins.

To fight the heat, she wore a full cooling suit over a full body stocking made of thin, sweat-wicking material woven of thousands of tiny, flexible cooling lines. The tubes grew in size over her chest and vital areas, and when the suit was plugged into the BattleMech, pumps circulated the coolant and helped protect her from the worst of the heat. Resting on her shoulders was a neurohelmet, the interface between her mind and the BattleMech's internal software. Neurohelmets weren't full mental connections: they were only sensitive enough to translate a sense of balance and intentions to a BattleMech's gyro and musculature.

In this case, her intentions were to close the distance. The engineers had used the weight savings gained from the high-tech engine, gyro, and small cockpit to arm her *Paladin* with arguably the most dangerous weapon to grace modern battlefields: an Ultra Class-20 autocannon. Able to chew off two and a half tons of armor at its maximum rate of fire, it was capable of dispatching many BattleMechs with a single, solid hit. However, she only had two tons of ammo, and it was a close-range weapon. Whatever came over that hill, she needed to be in knife-fighting range before they realized what she was armed with and tried to back off.

The enemies crossed over the hill almost simultaneously, one almost directly to her front and one almost 300 meters to her left. She turned her BattleMech left to run along her side of the ridge while keeping her arm-mounted autocannon pointed at the closer enemy. She almost laughed when she recognized it in the green-tinted night-vision setting of her 360-degree monitor: a 35-ton *Panther*, a centuries-old, sturdy workhorse of a light BattleMech, almost every variant of which carried a particle projection cannon on its right arm. Some PPCs were less accurate at short ranges, some weren't, but at the end of the day, it was a light 'Mech slower than she was.

The Vory MechWarrior fired first, a pair of quad short-range missile packs reaching out for her and then the PPC. With that, she saw her computer finally tag the *Panther* as a -10K2, and five of the missiles slammed into the *Paladin*'s arms and legs, followed by the distinctive *slap* of a PPC blasting off over a half ton of armor. The discharge of a PPC always played havoc with a BattleMech's sensors and targeting pips for a second, so she waited a moment for her crosshairs to settle back into position and gleam gold before firing.

She squeezed her main interlock trigger, and both her autocannon in her left arm and the medium extended-range pulse laser in her right arm fired simultaneously. The laser stitched up the *Panther*'s right leg, melting armor but doing no visible additional damage. The autocannon, however, started on the *Panther*'s left arm, eating away at it with a series of explosive impacts before separating it from the torso at the shoulder. Her rounds continued chewing through the *Panther*'s left side, gutting it from shoulder to hip before finally spending itself mauling the light 'Mech's center torso. Belching fire because of an internal ammunition cook-off, the *Panther* fell hard to the ground, and remained motionless.

She gasped as heat flooded her tiny cockpit, the life-support straining to bring the temperature back down. The second BattleMech paused in its advance toward the warehouse and turned to face her. Sweat ran down her face and beaded on her lips as they pulled into a feral grin.

*Good*, she thought. *Running you down would just piss me off.*

Hester kicked the door open and immediately swung back out of the way, allowing Phillip to lean in and check for enemies. He signaled *clear*, and Hester headed in, taking the lead with her machine gun tucked tight into her shoulder, the ammo belt leading down into a cloth magazine underneath it. While they'd planned the rescue back in her living room, Hester had unbolted her standard legs from her body and reinstalled her combat limbs. She now stood on two thick, massive legs. Resembling the blocky, splayed-toed legs of a 70-ton *Archer* BattleMech, the legs were constructed of heavy armor and commensurately powerful myomer musculature. She'd told them that, had the doctors not also reinforced her backbone when they replaced her pelvis, the combat legs were powerful enough to break her own spine.

Philip followed her into the hallway, his Republic-built J17 submachine gun set for left-handed operation; Wynn brought up the rear with his shotgun at the ready. All were wearing light, torso-covering body armor that wasn't the full level of protection they'd have received on the battlefield, but it was better than nothing.

Hester hit the first intersection, whipped around the blind corner, and fired a long burst. A short scream was cut off as a body hit the floor. She looked back at them, and, using silent hand signals, ordered Philip to continue down the original corridor while Wynn held the intersection and the route back to the truck. During the planning, they'd agreed on Hester commanding the operation: not only had she been a Star Corporal when the family fled the Magistry—outranking Philip by a full grade—but it was her sister they were there to rescue.

Nevada kept her throttle open, trying to close the distance as the odd-looking BattleMech started backing up along the ridge, clearly leery of her autocannon. She glanced at the identifying tag: the computer finally marked it as a 45-ton *Eisenfaust*, though it couldn't confirm the configuration until it fired.

She frowned slightly, trying to remember what she knew about the Lyran medium-class BattleMech: it was as slow as the *Panther*, she remembered, trading mobility for armor and weapons.

*Plasma rifle and extended-range large laser*, she cautioned herself. *Centerline pulses I need to watch out for and what the hell?* She tilted her head questioningly as the *Eisenfaust* aimed its torso-mounted main gun at her, an over-under laser configuration she wasn't sure she'd ever seen before. It activated with a loud *zot* sound, both barrels firing simultaneously.

"A blazer cannon?" she shouted incredulously as the *Paladin* rocked from the impact. "Are you bloody *kidding* me, a *blazer*?" She fought the controls to keep *Mukden* upright after losing three-quarter tons of armor from her right torso, her wire-frame damage display instantly dropping it from green to bright amber. Belatedly, the computer updated the enemy configuration to an -8X.

Nevada counted down the seconds until she was in range, but before she could fire, the *Paladin* surged forward, struck from behind. Her monitors danced, telling her exactly who'd shot her and with what; when they stabilized, she could see the damaged *Panther* standing behind her. Her schematic showed the entire rear left torso armor as destroyed, but luckily the PPC had spent itself on her reinforced structure without causing any system damage.

"Fine," she growled as she saw the *Eisenfaust* set itself to fire. "We'll do this the hard way."

The *Eisenfaust* waited until she closed within fifty meters and hit her with an alpha strike, three pulse lases and an extended-range small laser melting away armor across her arms and left torso before the blazer fired with its distinctively loud *zot*. The twin green blasts dug deep into her right torso again, melting off the remaining armor and a bit of structure. She rode out the blasts, keeping *Mukden* upright almost by sheer force of will.

*My turn.* She pulled the main interlock trigger: the laser ate into the *Eisenfaust*'s right arm, knocking it backward. This, unfortunately, moved it out of the way of about half of her autocannon rounds, flying uselessly through the air where the arm had been just a second before tracking in and chewing into the 'Mech's right torso. Her computer told her she'd destroyed all of its armor and a chunk of its internal structure; mashing her thumb trigger, the four machine guns in her left torso spun up, spreading fire across much of the enemy's center torso and left arm, but doing little real damage.

The cockpit's internal temperature soared, and warning lights began flashing, indicating her 'Mech was starting to slow down because of the heat.

*But we're still fast enough, aren't we,* Mukden? Sliding to her right, Nevada brought the *Paladin* into a tight turn to get behind the slow-moving *Eisenfaust*. A near-miss from the *Panther* scrambled her sensors for a second, and she tweaked her movement a hair to avoid a blast from the variable-speed pulse laser in the *Eisenfaust*'s left arm.

Her targeting pips flashing gold; she let them slide an extra half second off dead-center to just below the right shoulder before she pulled her main trigger again. The laser in her left arm struck the *Eisenfaust* dead center in its back, but her autocannon once again hit its beleaguered right side. Easily carving through the thin back armor, it destroyed the remaining internal structure in the right torso before cutting through the last of the back's armor and ripping deep into the 'Mech's guts. There was the distinctive sparking-explosion of a damaged gyro sending pieces of itself whirling through space, and the *Eisenfaust* fell forward, its right arm falling to the right and rolling down the hill.

Nevada gasped, the heat in her cockpit ripping the moisture from her lungs. The *Paladin* felt sluggish, its speed cut by a third as the 'Mech tried to cool itself down, and she could see the *Panther* 300 meters away, aiming at her. *Ammo bin's at less than half,* she noted. She flipped her radio to an unencrypted channel.

"I don't want to destroy your 'Mech," she managed to say before her mouth went dry. She swallowed to get moisture back in her throat again and then added, "But I will."

"You can try," an arrogant, gruff voice replied, just before hitting her dead center with his PPC.

She growled as she fought the computers glitches caused by both the heat and the PPC to bring her pips back on the *Panther's* center of mass.

"Rookie mistake," she replied, and fired her autocannon again. The rounds chewed straight up the *Panther* from groin to forehead—slicing through the armor and shattering the gyro—before continuing up to eviscerate the cockpit. "You should've walked away." The *Panther* fell backward and slid down halfway down the ridge.

Checking her sensors one last time for any other foes, Nevada sighed, sagged in the heat to catch her breath for a second, and then started trudging her BattleMech toward the van.

Philip moved down the corridor to a corner, swung around it, and found a darkened stairwell heading toward the basement. Slowly crouching to look down it, he saw the stairs double-backed on themselves once, opening on an empty corridor about ten meters long with a door to either side.

The only light in the hallway was provided by the large glass windows to the left and right. Philip quickly realized the windows were one-way mirrors: to the left, there was a sparse room with nothing but a pair of stainless-steel chairs and a matching table with open manacles. To the right, though, muffled by the glass, he heard a scream, a sob, and then another, longer high-pitched scream.

He looked in: Emily was strapped to a stainless-steel table, her prosthetics piled in a corner, and a pale, rail-skinny man with a pencil-thin mustache was lowering a red-hot poker to her plaid skirt just above her amputated knee. Philip could already see the blister and scorch marks on her clothes and body where he'd already tormented her: the skirt caught fire, and then the poker burned through to touch bare skin. Emily clenched her entire body, Philip saw a wisp of smoke come up from her burning flesh as she held her scream in for a moment, and then she let loose, her head thrashing in pain. The man lifted the poker away and then roughly slapped the skirt's flames out, drawing another moan of pain from his victim.

Philip's jaw clenched and he almost yelled at the man to stop, but held back when he noticed a shadow in the corner. Moving slightly to his left, he identified a large, scarred woman wearing a trench coat over street clothes to the left of the entrance, where she could easily strike anyone entering, while a right-handed intruder would have to attack with a cross-body shot. Philip nodded in appreciation of her tactics.

Philip double-checked his J-17 to ensure it was on semi and watched Emily sag in relief as the man went to reheat the poker in a brazier in the far corner. Swinging in front of the door, Philip kicked it in. He immediately entered with his barrel facing left: the guard was fast, he noted, a large bowie knife almost magically appearing in her hand, but three quick shots into her chest dropped her to the ground.

"Who are you?" the man yelled at Philip from the far side of the room, red hot poker in his hand. Instead of responding, Philip went to Emily and ripped the straps away with his cybernetic hand.

"Thanks," she gasped, then, "Behind you!"

Philip turned, his right arm up in a block, barely catching the downward thrust of the large knife. The woman's charge crashed her into Philip and the table itself—he heard a shriek from behind him as Emily toppled to the floor—but he couldn't give her a moment's attention. The knife was large enough to reach well over his arm, and as the woman put her full weight behind it, his arm gave just a little, and he felt the blade graze his cheek and draw blood.

The woman smiled, a horrible sight, her face a mess of scars and raised areas he realized were stylistically applied branding. Glancing down, he could now see the bulge of light ballistic body armor under her overly large T-shirt.

"I'm gonna cut your eyes out," she whispered.

Philip hooked his left heel behind her right leg and twisted, flinging her backward. At the last moment, she grabbed him, so he tumbled forward as well. Before he could bring up the submachine gun, she charged again, crashing both of them into the mirrored wall.

Behind her, Philip could see Emily shakily raising herself to her knees. The man approached her and tried to hit her in the face with the heated poker. Grabbing it with her right hand and pulling it toward herself to throw him off-balance, Emily swung a kick into his stomach, and suddenly the two were tumbling on the floor.

Releasing the J-17 to hang loose at his side, Philip managed to get a hand on his knife, but his cybernetic hand was still trying to hold back both his attacker's arms as she pushed the knife toward his unarmored throat. He tried to head butt her, but missed; she barked a laugh, and then viciously kneed him between the legs.

Philip grunted in pain; in the split-second she was slightly off balance from her knee-strike, he slid his prosthetic hand up her knife arm to her wrist and squeezed, hearing the satisfying crunch of her bones under his grip. She yelled in pain, but by then his knife was already clear of the scabbard and into her trachea.

The thug fell away, holding her throat as arterial blood coursed out between her fingers, and he staggered forward to go to Emily's aid.

They were still fighting on the floor, and the torturer flung her off him and to his right. Grabbing the poker, he swung it at her again. Avoiding the hit, Emily grabbed his wrist with her hand, trapped his arm between her full left leg and the meat of her right thigh, and, arching her back so only her shoulders and hip remained grounded, she hyperextended his elbow with a loud *pop*. He yelped in pain, and wrenching the poker from his hurt arm, she swung up to her knees and smashed his throat with it three times.

She sat back onto her haunches, catching her breath as her torturer flopped on the floor, holding his destroyed throat and drowning in his own blood. She slowly turned her head at Philip's approach.

"You good?" he asked.

"No."

He grunted. "Yeah. C'mon, let's get you out of here." Slinging his submachine gun over his back, he grabbed her limbs from the corner and handed them to her. He then scooped her up, taking care to not touch the burns he now saw covered far more of her skin than he'd realized. "Take the Sturm Eagle," he said, nodding to the pistol in his shoulder rig. "In case we run into company."

Adjusting her prosthetics so they rested in her lap and wouldn't fall while they walked, Emily drew the Eagle and checked to make sure the safety was off. Then she swung it toward the now-motionless man on the floor and fired once. The man's head exploded; then, aiming at the woman, Emily fired twice more, hitting the head on the second shot.

Philip quirked an eyebrow.

"Making sure we're not followed," Emily growled.

With an approving nod, Philip adjusted her in his arms and headed for the door.

**GALATEA CITY**
**GALATEA**
**GALATEAN LEAGUE**
**7 AUGUST 3151**

"More beer, everyone, and some appetizers," Hester announced.

Philip smiled as she dropped a small basket of chicken livers in front of him. She was back in her waitressing legs, her artificial thighs gleaming in the reflected lights of the stage as she placed more food and fresh pitchers around the table before sitting down herself.

"Those are gross, babe," said Nevada, sitting across from him.

They were back at the round table in the corner, where they'd anxiously awaited word on where to find Emily only a couple days ago. This time, though, the mood was of cautious celebration: Emily was wearing a loose, bright-green set of coveralls, with antibiotic-soaked bandages scattered across her body. Because the torturer had focused so much on Emily's amputation sites, the doctors recommended she not use her prosthetics until she healed. Her entire left shoulder and right thigh were wrapped in antibiotic-gauze; she was once again sitting in Nevada's lap and generally making a drunken nuisance of herself.

Philip grabbed a pair of chicken livers, popped them into his mouth, and dramatically chewed, before he theatrically swallowed and rubbed his stomach. The table laughed, and Nevada shook her head.

"You better brush your teeth twice before you try to kiss me later, love," she said.

"The offer to run away with me is still on the table, Nevs," said Emily. Her bandaged left shoulder propped up against Nevada, she woozily leaned over, grabbed Wynn's drink—a local variant of the Davion PPC, with four shots of moonshine and a shot of bourbon—drank half, and then pulled his fried squid rings in front of her. Wynn rolled his eyes as he finished the drink, and smiled gratefully as Hester slid her basket in front of him. Wynn had quietly told Philip and Nevada that Emily was still waking up every night screaming, but she was down to once a night now instead of every time she closed her eyes.

Philip refilled Hester's glass, then checked to see if Nevada had plenty of water. "Trade you a couple livers for some of yours," he offered Wynn, nodding at the big man's fried squid. With a nod, they traded a handful each. Popping one into his mouth, he said, "Okay, so Wynn, you were saying? Jamal doesn't think the law's going to search for everyone?" Wynn shook his head, and Philip's mouth turned down. *I'm happy to hear that, but I feel like there's another shoe waiting to drop.*

"Why not?" Hester quietly demanded from Nevada's left.

The table leaned in to listen.

Wynn signaled Carter at the bar for another PPC before turning to them. "Jamal said, because of its history, the authorities on Galatea are often running behind the criminals. In this instance, as far as the authorities are concerned, a smuggling ring was shut down and they're not going to investigate too closely into the reasons why. In their eyes, as long as this doesn't start a turf war, they consider the case closed."

Philip locked eyes with Nevada, who bit her lip, studying the chalk signatures some ambitious patrons had managed to place on the ceiling long ago, then looked at Wynn. "But the Vory will figure out we were involved sooner or later, right?"

The table got quiet, and Wynn shrugged slightly. "He's not sure." A fresh PPC appeared at Wynn's elbow and Philip's eyes flicked up, thinking it was Carter, and started so abruptly his chair squeaked on the floor.

"That one's on me." The rest of the table turned to the beautiful, tall, and pale woman standing behind Wynn with a tumbler of her own. Philip moved a hand slowly toward a concealed pistol, but she shook her head and tossed a glance at a large man carrying a pair of chairs toward the table with just one hand while his other hung suspiciously near his hip,

"Don't," she said, gently shaking her long blond hair. "James doesn't like it when people draw on me. Besides, I come in peace," she finished with a smile.

Placing a chair behind the woman—who sat between Wynn and Nevada—James moved slightly off to the side, spun his chair around and straddled it. Philip studied them: the man carried himself with the obvious bearing of a professional soldier, while she was...*different*. Attractive, but under the stylish-but-not-noticeably-so outfit, she had the wiry look of an experienced martial artist. *Intel?* he thought.

"And we should believe you, why?" Nevada asked, frost in her voice.

The woman sipped her triple whiskey on the rocks before setting it down.

"Shh, sexy," Emily said in a playful tone. "She's pretty and buying drinks. Let's hear her out."

Nevada rolled her eyes as she shook her head, and the table chuckled as the tension lessened slightly.

"Forgive my sister," Hester said. "She's drunk, and considers strangers just ex-lovers she hasn't met yet."

The woman laughed gaily. "Well, the night's still young," she said, throwing a wink toward Emily. Her face then cleared, and she turned to Nevada. "And yes, I come in peace. Your...*associate*, Jamal, isn't wrong: the authorities aren't looking for you. For what it's worth, the Vory aren't looking for you either, *yet*, partially because of some calls I've placed and some money I've passed to the right hands. But you're right to be concerned: the Galatea Vory aren't stupid, and if they identify you, they will hunt you down."

The table was silent for a moment before Wynn grumbled, "Well, tell us something we don't know."

The woman smiled tightly, sipped her whiskey, then put the tumbler down. "How about this—it's a bar, let's play a drinking game." Emily smiled broadly, but before she could say anything, the woman cut her off. "One where the clothes stay *on*, First Ranker."

The table chuckled at Emily's overdramatic sigh.

*She knows our ranks*, Philip thought. *She did her research.*

"No, this game's a classic called 'two truths and a lie.' You can call me Gwendoline, though you've probably already guessed that's not my real name."

"Hi, Gwen," Emily said instantly, while the rest of the table threw glances at each other.

*Truth*, Philip thought.

"I'm a secretarial assistant at the Lyran embassy, and James here is just a humble security guard," she continued.

Hester snorted, barely suppressing a laugh, which caused Nevada to chuckle and even Wynn to smile a hair at Gwendoline's obvious falsehood.

*There's the lie*, thought Philip.

Emily ate a squid ring and then reached over to swipe Gwendoline's drink; the blond smacked Emily's hand, pulling a *yipe* from the young woman and full-out laughs from both Hester and Wynn.

Gwendoline smiled slightly as Emily theatrically shook off the hit; she drank about half of her whiskey in one easy motion and studied the glass for a second before looking around the table.

"I believe you've all been overlooked by everyone, including myself, because not only were you hunting for employment separately, you three—" she said with a look around the table at the Dvorskys, "—are running under fake dossiers missing most of your history. Working together as you did, though, displays an entirely different, intangible set of skills." She threw back the rest of her drink and put her tumbler upside down on the table.

"Annnnnnd," she said, drawing the word out, "as it so happens, I'm in need of a *team*."

# PLANET DIGEST: LE BLANC

### ERIC SALZMAN

**Star Type (Recharge Time):** G0V (181 hours)
**Position in System:** 4 (of 11)
**Time to Jump Point:** 10.43 days
**Number of Satellites:** 2 (Jessen, Orones)
**Surface Gravity:** 0.82
**Atm. Pressure:** Low (Breathable)
**Equatorial Temperature:** 24°C (Arid)
**Surface Water:** 15 percent
**Recharge Station:** Nadir
**HPG Class:** B (3151)
**Highest Native Life:** None
**Population:** 60,216,000 (as of 3151)
**Socio-Industrial Levels:** D-D-B-F-D (3151)
**Landmasses (Capital City):** Continent Alpha (Port Paix)

Le Blanc was colonized in 2164 as a mining world, with surveys showing a thin but breathable atmosphere and ample supplies of antimony, bismuth, cadmium, zinc, and tin—all in great demand during the settlement boom of the 2100s. A French mining consortium designated the barren, water-poor world "Le Blanc," after the predominantly white color of its surface, and established an ore extraction and processing operation at Port Paix, on the shores of the world's largest sea. Though the colony was initially totally dependent on imported foods to meet its needs, it was clear interstellar shipping rates would make this cost prohibitive as the colony grew, necessitating substantial investment in hydroponic gardens.

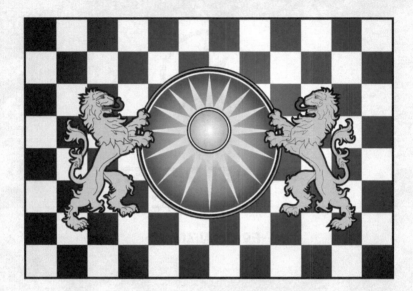

Le Blanc remained loyal to the Terran Alliance during the Outer Reaches Rebellion, and even dispatched troop levies to support the Alliance's marine expeditionary forces in putting down insurgencies on nearby worlds. When the Expansionist government fell and the Liberals issued the Demarcation Declaration in 2242, Le Blanc found itself cut off from its parent company on Terra and alienated from its more independence-minded neighbors. After David Sandoval of Robinson seized control of that world and declared himself Lord Protector, Le Blanc's planetary administrators reached out to secure a mutual defense pact with their more powerful neighbor. When Robinson joined with New Avalon to form the Federated Suns, Le Blanc came along as one of Robinson's protectorates.

During the First Succession War, both Le Blanc and Robinson were overwhelmed by the unexpectedly strong Kuritan offensive in 2787, falling under Combine control. The Combine made extensive use of forced labor to keep the mines operating and the Dragon's quotas filled. The occupiers also controlled access to the hydroponic domes, using the world's output to keep the Arm of the Dragon fed, and limiting the miners to starvation rations. When the Federated Suns' Third Counteroffensive liberated Le Blanc in 2811, they found more than half of its original population dead and the rest skeletally starved. Combine forces had heavily damaged the domes during their retreat, hoping to tie up Davion resources.

The Combine returned in force in 2830, targeting Le Blanc with a hit-and-run raid as part of Operation Red Wind. The shattered world offered little organized resistance, and the attack undid most of the recovery work done since liberation. When it later came out that the Ministry of Information, Intelligence, and Operations (MIIO) had learned of the Combine's attack plans but chose to concentrate its forces on more strategically valuable worlds, anger and resentment against the Federated Suns government surged, and a pro-independence movement began to gain traction, seeking to declare the world a neutral non-combatant.

Faced with widespread anger among Draconis March citizens following the New Avalon regime's failure to protect its border worlds, House Davion radically reconstructed its border defense posture. Rather than abandoning the ravaged world, the Federated Suns brought its still significant resources to bear, not only rebuilding the hydroponic systems, but also expanding them to support a substantial garrison. As the Draconis March was reorganized from Combat Regions into polymorphous defense zones (PDZ), Le Blanc was designated as the capital of its own PDZ, making the once sleepy mining backwater into a bustling hub for military traffic and civilian shipping.

Recognizing that vast fields of hydroponic domes made an easy target for raiders, Armed Forces of the Federated Suns engineers made the systems as self-sufficient and recyclable as possible, concealing them underground and scattering them across the wastes. Though Le Blanc continued to rely on imported foodstuffs for variety, these hydroponic facilities ensured it would never again face the risk of mass starvation.

By the time of the Combine's Marathon Offensive, in mid-July 2854, the Draconis Combine Mustered Soldiery invaders faced the Second Robinson Rangers, the Robinson Draconis March Militia, and the Le Blanc Planetary Guard Unit. Kurita forces blockaded the system, secured a landing zone on the outskirts of Port Paix, and crippled the city's visible local hydroponics. As the fighting continued, they were shocked by the Davion forces' dogged defense, unaware that their foes were being resupplied from the hidden underground gardens. By year's end, it was the Combine's reserves that were running dry, and the surviving DCMS troops retreated off-world on New Year's Eve, 2854.

Mining continued to dominate the planetary economy, with all investment channeled into maximizing output. The planetary government made the educational system purely vocational, ensuring there would be sufficient miners to keep their profits flowing. The only alternative employment was in hydroponics and in the service industries supporting the PDZ administrative structure and the garrison forces. Given the harshness of the mining sector, large numbers flocked to a booming service industry to cater to the needs of military personnel stationed in Port Paix.

Learning that the similarly barren world of Galatea had transitioned from a struggling mining world to a major economic hub by establishing itself as a neutral world for contracting mercenaries, Le Blanc's planetary government (a council of mining firm CEOs) decided to leverage the existing military service support infrastructure and follow in Galatea's footsteps. Their highly controversial decision, announced in 2867, declared Le Blanc as officially neutral in the Succession Wars, and offered its services as a free port for mercenaries and hiring agents from any employer.

The court on New Avalon was aghast at this show of disloyalty, but was legally constrained by the provisions of Article XII, which granted Federated Suns' member worlds complete internal freedom. So long as the government did not actively collude with the Combine or other enemies of the Federated Suns, House Davion could not intervene. Seeking to take advantage of the world's open status, the MIIO greatly increased its footprint in Port Paix, keeping an eye on their counterparts from rival Houses and the expanding network of freelance informants who made Le Blanc a hub of interstellar information brokerage. Moreover, Le Blanc proved a convenient source of mercenary assets for missions against the Combine without having to send emissaries all the way to Galatea, in Lyran space. Units taking Combine contracts against the Federated Suns often ended up infiltrated by MIIO agents posing as freelancers, greatly aiding House Davion's intelligence gathering throughout the Third Succession War.

Criminal enterprises also took advantage of Le Blanc's "open world" status, setting up smuggling networks and gray markets for *lostech* and stolen military equipment. The ruling merchants turned a blind eye to such activities as long as they received their cut. Throughout the early 3000s, bombings regularly rocked Port Paix as the Wobbe Cartel battled with the Griez Syndicate and encroached yakuza clans for control of Le Blanc's underworld.

By the 3030s, the yakuza were firmly in control, placing them in position to support the Combine counteroffensive—Operation Orochi—in the War of 3039. Coordinator Takashi Kurita's 3028 Death to Mercenaries edict had greatly reduced local demand, leaving a glut of unemployed mercenaries stranded on-world. *Tai-sa* Tomoe Sakade traveled to Le Blanc in secret, smuggled in along with elements of the Fourth Ghost regiment. She hired enough local mercenaries (paying up front) to outfit three battalions, which then joined the Fourth in an attack that drove the Robinson Draconis March Militia from its headquarters at Fort Mason. The DMM fell back into the wastes, leaving the Combine in control of Port Paix, from which Sakade staged stunning strikes against Davion rear-area worlds. *Sho-sa* Horman Chokei held Port Paix with two battalions until the Second Ceti Hussars regimental combat team arrived in October 3039, leading a massive assault that convinced most of the mercenaries to surrender. Chokei and his core Ghost company died in combat by year's end.

The combined yakuza/mercenary attack convinced the merchant council to rethink their ways. Under intense pressure to close the security holes that had facilitated the Combine counteroffensive, the government tightened its "open world" policies and subjected mercenaries and employers to far greater official scrutiny. Following the events of the Clan invasion, the Federated Commonwealth/Draconis Combine détente and the mercenary market's shift in focus coreward toward the Clan occupation zones rendered the once bustling hiring halls virtual ghost towns.

Le Blanc's star began to rise once again after the Jihad, with the dominant mercenary hub of Outreach reduced to an irradiated cinder. Demand for mercenaries surged amid renewed low-level clashes throughout the so-called Draconis Reach from the 3080s to 3139. Nearly all the mercenary units that fought there, on both sides, signed their contracts on Le Blanc, only two jumps away.

Le Blanc fell to the 3144 Combine offensive that also captured the nearby March capital of Robinson. With much of Le Blanc's garrison forward deployed in Duke Sandoval's failed bid to secure the Draconis Reach, there was little to stop the Nineteenth Galedon Regulars from seizing control of the world. The occupation force closed all hiring halls and scattered any mercenary units still present. Having taken significant losses in its follow-on attack against Doneval II, the Nineteenth's commander, *Tai-sa* Hideki Hendersen, fell back to Le Blanc to dig in and await reinforcements in 3145.

He was still waiting when the First Kestrel Grenadiers attacked Le Blanc as part of Operation Perceval in 3147. Mercenaries that had gone into hiding (mostly at concealed wasteland hydroponic centers) emerged and attacked the Nineteenth from the rear. The distraction enabled the Grenadiers to destroy the Galedon supply bunkers, then depart, taking as many mercenaries as possible to replace losses. Those unfortunates left behind were hunted by the vengeful Nineteenth, while the Internal Security Force coordinated a parallel purge of the planetary underworld, rooting out subversives and anti-Combine elements.

The heavy-handed crackdowns swelled the numbers of anti-Combine partisans, and the still-hidden hydroponic gardens in the wastes proved perfect bases for a well-coordinated guerrilla movement centered around surviving mercenary formations. The Nineteenth's hunting expeditions into the badlands proved largely futile, and increased oppression in Port Paix (particularly the decision to reserve all food for the DCMS garrison) led to widespread rioting. When the Third Davion Irregulars landed in early February 3150, they linked up with pro-Davion partisans and the mercenary-led resistance movement, pushing the already struggling Galedon Regulars into a full retreat from the planet.

As of 3151, Le Blanc has fully and proudly rejoined the Federated Suns. Recruiters for House Davion are filling contracts at the re-opened hiring halls to take the fight to the Dragon, and the inhabitants of Le Blanc are firmly committed to ensuring units operating out of Port Paix have everything they need to wreak vengeance on the Combine. The Mercenary Review and Bonding Commission has reopened its offices and has been joined by representatives of the Mercenaries' Guild and Clan Sea Fox in offering bonding and contract support services.

## TERRAIN TABLES

To randomly determine the mapsheets for a battle set on this planet, roll 2D6 and select the map matching the result. The maps in this list can be found in the noted map pack (MP).

### Continent Alpha

**Note:** Most population centers are concentrated around several large inland seas and scattered lakes, but small mining communities, fed by concealed hydroponic gardens, dot the outer wastelands. Aside from small greenbelts around the seas, the surface of Continent Alpha is a barren, whitish expanse of jumbled rocks and windblown dust.

**2:** Desert Runway (MP Deserts)
**3:** Sand Drift #1 (MP Deserts)
**4:** Desert #1 (Beginner Box)
**5:** Washout #1 (MP Deserts)
**6:** Badlands #1 (MP Deserts)
**7:** Mines #1 (MP Deserts)
**8:** Mines #2 (MP Deserts)
**9:** Badlands #2 (MP Deserts)
**10:** Washout #2 (MP Deserts)
**11:** Sand Drift #2 (MP Deserts)
**12:** Oasis (MP Deserts)

# LONE WOLF AND FOX

## BRYAN YOUNG

### PART 3 (OF 4)

### CHAPTER THIRTEEN

**ALYINA MERCANTILE LEAGUE HEADQUARTERS**
**EXCHANGE PLACE TOWER**
**NEW DELHI**
**ALYINA**
**22 OCTOBER 3151**

"It happened again, ma'am," Merchant Li said, her voice filled with exasperation.

Sitting at her desk going over reports, Syndic Marena had hoped for some good news, but it seemed to her building your own empire free of the Clans and the wasteful ways of the warrior was fraught with nothing but bad news. She didn't even know *what* had happened again, and it worried her that Li's tone could indicate a repeat of any number of problems she had been having since she had made her move.

She stopped scrolling and looked up at Li, standing opposite the desk, hands behind her back. "Is it the warriors or the mercenaries?"

"It is both, but mercenaries instigated in this case."

"Which ones?" Marena had first lauded her own decision when the Lone Wolves, who had been largely professional, arrived and fended off the most recent pirate attack, but the rest had only caused her headaches. "Since Merchant Helen returned from Kandersteg, Alyina has been crawling with them, and I can hardly keep track."

"An armor unit. Rekenzie's Everswored."

"What happened?"

"What always happens. A fight broke out. A *solahma* warrior and one of the Everyswordded. Words were exchanged, a challenge called, as though that matters. They beat each other bloody."

"Anyone dead?"

"No."

"Thank..." Marena almost said *Kerensky*, but caught herself. If anyone died in one of these conflicts, it would only escalate. And that felt like the least of her problems. "Thanks be."

"It was indeed fortunate. But they are getting worse. It will not be long before things escalate." Merchant Li held a breath at the top of her chest, as though she were holding back another thought.

But Marena knew exactly what it was, though she gave Li no leave to say it.

Perhaps bringing the mercenaries here was a mistake.

But they solved problems. It was just a matter of whether they solved more than they created.

Marena turned her mind to what she viewed as the largest problem before her. "Have you made any progress on the leaks?"

Merchant Li lowered her head, breaking eye contact with Marena. *"Neg."*

"You understand that is the single largest problem we have, *quiaff*?"

*"Aff."*

"If we cannot find who is selling information about our operations to pirates, we will never be able to bring enough mercenaries to Alyina to defend us. They are a necessary evil, for now."

Merchant Li frowned. "How do we deal with the unrest in the meantime? Many of the older *solahma,* and even members of lower castes, still view themselves as Jade Falcons. They have been raised as such for generations, and do not agree with a merchant leading the planet, let alone an entire interstellar government that cuts out the Clan caste and style of rule completely. This is all they have known."

Marena tried her hardest not to sigh or roll her eyes. Frustration filled her. "They will learn better."

But Merchant Li knew as well as Marena did that it was impossible to change the hearts and minds of an entire planet, generation after generation, without having some malcontents.

That, however, was not the point. Marena rose from her desk and looked out over the twinkling night lights of New Delhi, spread out below her. "The point is that we do not know if it was a single warrior or an entire organization. We need information. And we have nothing."

"The Watch left with the Jade Falcons to Terra."

"The Watch has elements everywhere," Marena said. "You would be a fool if you thought there are no Jade Falcon Watch agents left on

Alyina. And we have reports that many elements of the Watch stayed. They were masking the disappearance of Malvina's *touman*."

"Could the saboteur be a Clan Jade Falcon Watch agent?"

"What advantage would they have in disrupting us?"

"They have every reason. If they are loyal to Khan Jiyi Chistu and his pitiful little nest of Falcons, it is to their advantage to disrupt us so they can annex us. If they are loyal to Malvina Hazen and the regime, old, likely dead and gone on Terra, then they could simply want to punish us. Cruelty was policy in Malvina Hazen's Falcons. Especially with lower castes, was it not?"

*"Aff."*

"And if they are Watch agents from another Clan, say Hell's Horses, perhaps, then they would have obvious reasons to want us weakened. But this does not feel like that. This feels like internal dissidence."

Merchant Li's frown deepened, as though she was finally starting to understand just how difficult a position the Alyina Mercantile League was in. "We need an intelligence apparatus of our own."

"We do. I want a proposal for the creation of such an apparatus on my desk tomorrow."

"Of course, my Syndic."

"And come hell or high water, I will figure out how to solve the unrest between the older thinkers and the mercenaries. There has to be a middle ground. If this happens again, see to it they are all arrested. We will see how a stay in the stockade might cool their heads."

*"Aff."*

Marena waved Merchant Li away, dismissing her. Li faded back to the elevator and disappeared, leaving Marena to stare out into the bustle of New Delhi, wondering who out there would betray them, and who out there was simply going to cause trouble.

Had she made a mistake?

She hoped, more than anything, that she hadn't.

Marena and the whole Alyina Mercantile League stood on a knife's edge. The very future of everything she hoped to build hung in the balance.

# CHAPTER FOURTEEN

**AML MILITIA TRAINING COMPOUND**
**CORLEONE**
**MONTESSORO**
**ALYINA**
**ALYINA MERCANTILE LEAGUE**
**22 OCTOBER 3151**

Arkee Colorado's *Quickdraw* hung on the hoist lifts above Katie Ferraro, its arms raised wide like a steel scarecrow, separated from its feet because Dexter Nicks and Rhiannon Ramirez couldn't leave well enough alone.

Katie had begun by disassembling what was left of the ankles—that is, after they had hauled Arkee and his damned *Quickdraw* back to the base in the first place. There was nothing more infuriating to Katie than a 'Mech that couldn't walk itself back to the bay.

Most of the ankle had been blown away by the far-too effective sticky bombs. Dexter and Rhiannon had spared no amount of destruction. The explosive force had torn through most of the smaller bits and peeled open holes in the larger bits. Once she had everything cataloged and figured out what she had, she realized it wasn't much. Almost none of it was salvageable. That meant, if Arkee wanted to go into battle on his feet instead of crawling around on his belly, she'd need to source more parts, fast.

Not even just for the *Quickdraw* either.

For Evan's *Locust,* too.

If she didn't know how much the two of them loved piloting 'Mechs and pulling their weight in the unit, she would have thought they were trying to organize their own second honeymoon or something by the way they kept getting their 'Mechs almost destroyed. But that didn't track with how Arkee had been acting over the last little while. Something was up between them, but Katie really couldn't tell what.

Besides, she had bigger things on her mind than worrying about her two lovesick MechWarriors. The words of Major Bugsy Heidegger—the spokesperson for the Lone Wolves—echoed in her mind. He had suggested she find an XO, which was all well and good, but where the hell was she supposed to find an XO deep in Clan space?

Frankie walked up beside Katie, doing her best mental list of all the parts of the ankle actuator. All the myomer pieces, all the housings and casings, the gears, the nuts, the bolts, the hydraulics, motor control units, all of it.

There was just no way to make all of it into something functional.

Katie was at a loss.

Frankie stood beside her and looked at all the pieces, just as she did. Almost as if they were doing their own mental catalog, too. "You asked me to come by, boss?"

"Yeah." Katie tore her eyes from the mess of *Quickdraw* parts and the foot assembly and looked up to Frankie.

Frankie was a really great person, and the best mechanic in the Fox Patrol that wasn't Katie. They kept their hair cut short, mostly, but with a bit of a floofy point in the front in a way that highlighted their thin, angular face. They always hid their frame beneath the loose-fitting standard issue Fox Patrol maintenance coveralls in rust red. The feature Katie might have liked the most about Frankie was their steely blue eyes that had a way of seeing through all of the bullshit and cutting right to the heart of a problem. They'd joined the Fox Patrol when they got the *Fox Den*, and Frankie had become instantly invaluable.

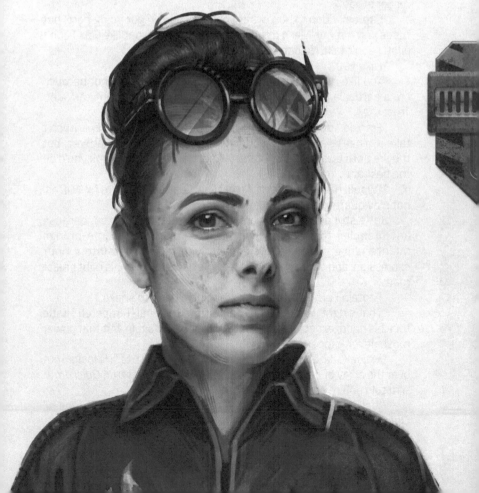

"What's up?"

Katie sighed. "How would you like a promotion?"

"To what?"

"XO. Of the Fox Patrol."

Frankie made no move for a moment. Just standing there. Waiting. They narrowed their eyes and pulled their head back just a bit.

And then they laughed.

Not a small laugh.

No. A great big belly laugh that made Katie feel small.

Frankie got ahold of their breathing. "You almost had me there for a second, Captain. Me...XO. Ha."

"I was being serious."

The laughter stopped.

"I can't source all these parts, Frankie. I don't even know how to start, especially on a planet like this. You're resourceful, and everyone respects you."

"Captain, I don't know what you think you've got going here, but that's just not my 'Mech tread. I'm a mechanic. I'm not like you. I don't pilot. I don't talk. No one even likes me."

"I like you."

"You like me because we speak the same language, not because I'm a particularly good people person. I'm not the person you want. Trust me."

"Frankie, I don't have anyone else. You know Arkee and Evan won't take it. They're allergic to work work. I'd ask Nicks and Ramirez, but they're both busy training infantry. And, frankly, I really think you'd be the best at it. You're it."

"I would have to respectfully decline, Captain. I want to fix 'Mechs, not play quartermaster."

Katie stopped herself from growling. Just in time, too, because an unfamiliar face approached. He wore black-and-flame-orange maintenance coveralls, a clean-shaven face pulled into a dour expression, and dark aviator glasses. The nametag over his right breast read KADE.

"Captain Ferraro?" he said, extending a hand to shake.

"That's right. You must be the XO from the Foul-Tempered." Katie took his hand, expecting it to be tightly squeezed again, but that power move never happened.

"Major Kade. Correct. I'm here to talk about the parts." He looked out over the array of parts before them from Arkee's shattered *Quickdraw*. "I'm told you're having a bit of a problem."

"Well, I was looking for *Locust* parts, but I need some for the ol' *Quickdraw*, too."

"I see."

Katie smiled. A great big, devious smile. She had an idea, and she didn't have a choice.

"Well, Major Kade, thank you for coming over here. The Fox Patrol got hit pretty hard in that first engagement, and our trainers in the infantry exercise were a little more zealous than I would have liked. Those responsible have been thoroughly tongue-lashed. So, we are definitely in need, and sourcing these parts on Alyina has been difficult."

"And your XO has tried the other mercenary commands?"

"Not quite." Katie looked over to Frankie and couldn't quite make eye contact. "Let me introduce you to Lieutenant Frankie Fischer. They're the XO of the Fox Patrol and our chief 'Mech tech."

If Katie could have brought her eyes up to Frankie's, she would have seen the bright fury of PPC beams in them.

But Frankie took it in stride when Kade extended his hand to them as well. "Pleased to meet you, Lieutenant Fischer."

Frankie took the major's hand and clamped down their jaw. Resigned. "I'm sure the pleasure is all mine."

Katie's broad smile turned into a nervous grin. "So, yes. Lieutenant Fischer will be your main point of contact, Major Kade, and any help you can give them would be greatly appreciated. We really need to get our 'Mechs back into working order, and they'll know best what we have in trade to help with the effort. Isn't that right, Lieutenant Fischer?"

Frankie, with a glare that would wither flowers on a perfect spring day, turned to Katie and put on their most inauthentic smile. "Of course, Captain Ferraro. I would be delighted to help in this effort."

"We do have some *Locust* parts in our DropShip, the *Black Mood.* But you'll need to show me what you need. And I have a manifest of some parts I'm in constant need of myself."

"Walk this way, Major Kade, I'll take you to the *Locust.*" Frankie extended a hand and led the major away from the *Quickdraw* and toward Evan's *Locust* on the other side of the bay.

Before they left, though, they turned and mouthed something to Katie. With wide, glaring eyes, the picture of anger, they said, *"I am going to kill you."*

And Katie thought it was a distinct possibility, but for the moment, all her problems were solved.

# CHAPTER FIFTEEN

**THE FALCON'S ROOST BAR**
**CORLEONE**
**MONTESSORO**
**ALYINA**
**ALYINA MERCANTILE LEAGUE**
**22 OCTOBER 3151**

Ignoring the swirling lights and melotronica music thrumming around him, Arkee Colorado nursed his drink as though it were the only thing in the world.

"Would you just talk to me?" he heard Evan say, off to his right.

But Arkee didn't want to respond.

There was a knot of jealousy in his chest, fury and fear all tied together into one big Gordian lump.

Arkee shrugged.

Not only did he not want to respond, he didn't know what to say.

"He's just a friend," Evan said.

But still, Arkee did nothing but sip his House Davion PPC—four shots of pure grain alcohol and two shots of bourbon.

He figured a couple of PPCs and he wouldn't be able to feel anything anymore, and that was exactly what he wanted. But no matter how much he drank, that knot wouldn't go away. Not after what he'd seen. Not after what he'd felt.

"He was holding your hand," Arkee said finally.

"What if he was just checking my pulse? He's a nurse."

"Was he?"

"Was he what?"

"Checking your pulse."

"No, but—"

"See?"

Evan groaned and gripped his chest with his good hand. He was out of the hospital, but he wasn't completely recovered. To be honest, Arkee was a little surprised he'd even followed him to the bar.

"I thought I'd lost you."

"You're not gonna lose me, Arkee."

"That's not how it feels."

Evan sighed. "You know we take risks every day, right? Every time we get into our 'Mechs. Me most of all. I pilot a *Locust*. A *Locust*, Arkee. I take my life into my hands every time I strap myself into my command couch. If you lose me, it's going to be there. Not with some nurse."

Arkee took another sip of his drink, pointedly not looking at Evan. "What's his name?"

"Dev. Dev Caponigro."

"Soft hands?"

"God damn it, Arkee."

Arkee felt like he was watching a battleROM of himself, outside his body, sitting there at the bar, tuning out the music and tuning into the burning inside of him. Like a 'Mech, he was powered by a fusion reactor, and he'd overheated it, and that heat spread to every corner of his body and started shutting down systems. Like logic. And compassion.

All he could find were the missiles of his hurt and sadness.

He could risk the ammo explosion in his torso, or he could fire it all elsewhere.

And Evan was the closest nearby target.

"You said he was cute."

"He is. There are plenty of cute people around I don't want to leave you for or cheat on you with."

"Right."

"He's just a nurse."

"History is full of war-torn stories of nurses and wounded soldiers falling for each other. It's a trope because it happens all the time. Why not now?"

Evan said something else. But Arkee couldn't hear it. He couldn't hear much of anything. The music changed songs; another rapid-beat electronic power ballad came on. Something from a decade prior. Then Arkee looked over to the door and there he was.

The object of his rage.

The nurse.

Dev Caponigro.

He wore a fashionable shirt with a V-neck collar and skinny pants, all topped with a wide smile when he made eye contact with Arkee.

He didn't even know he should be ashamed of himself. And he didn't know he should have stayed away.

Arkee vowed to himself that he wouldn't move. That he wasn't going to be the one who had to run away. This was his spot. This was his watering hole. He wasn't going to be chased away by this tourist in his life. He was going to stay right there.

"Please don't do anything stupid," Evan said as Dev approached them, waving.

"Me?" Arkee downed the rest of his drink and scanned the bar for the tender so he could order another one. "I'm a perfect gentleman, Evan. Always have been."

There was an implicit accusation in his voice, though, and he knew it. Arkee couldn't help it. There was so much more he wanted to say but couldn't.

"Hey, fancy seeing you two here," Dev said when he arrived at the bar.

Arkee said nothing.

What could he say?

"Yeah, how wild," Evan said. Nervous and polite.

"How are you doing? It's been a couple of days. Is the leg okay?"

"It hurts when I walk on it, but that's to be expected."

Arkee wasn't looking at Evan, but knew from the affable enthusiasm in his voice he was smiling wide. A wide, bright smile. Magnetic. Alluring. Attractive.

"You'll get better. You'll be piloting your 'Mech again soon."

"I know, Dev. You've been such a great help this whole time."

Dev turned to Arkee, talking to the side of his face. "I wanted to return him to you in better condition than I found him. He talks so much about you."

Being talked to by his rival, Arkee wanted to shrivel up into a hole. He felt three centimeters tall, a human standing at the foot of an assault 'Mech. "I bet he does." Arkee looked out across the bar, hoping for something to distract him while he had to endure this hell.

"It has been so lovely to get to know you, Evan. You are such a wonderful person. I hope everyone who visits Alyina is just like you."

"Yeah, this is a very beautiful planet. And I'm so glad I've been able to see it."

On the other side of the bar's circle, a fight was brewing. Arkee could see it and feel it. Maybe he was just being oversensitive, but he could see it starting. And it was easier to focus on that than struggle through Evan and Dev cooing at each other like lovesick idiots. Especially since a fight might mean trouble, and that was the last thing he wanted.

With Evan, he was in enough trouble already.

The guy at the bar was just drinking and minding his business, dressed in Alyina Mercantile Blues. Arkee couldn't quite tell, but the patch seemed to indicate he was infantry. He was big, too. If Arkee had to guess, given his size and uniform, the guy was a Clanner, or former Clanner, or something. The others were clearly mercs from an outfit Arkee didn't recognize. Their emblem had tank treads writ large on them, though, so he assumed they were tank operators with classic feelings of needing to prove something. Fights like this had been breaking out a lot, as far as Arkee had heard. Tensions and tempers were running hotter than his jealousy.

These clowns also looked drunk. Based on the shouting the smallest one was doing, it seemed a pretty safe bet.

The larger of the two mercs held the little one back, but he kept pointing and screaming. Arkee couldn't quite make out what he was yelling about over the din of the crowd, but the Clanner was not interested in taking the bait at all. Something about finishing what their friends had started.

For Arkee, this was a welcome distraction from everything he was experiencing and all of the feelings of inadequacy he had.

In his mind, he put money on the Clanner.

The Clanner spun around on their stool to regard the merc and merely smirked. The merc screamed something Arkee couldn't make out when the music stopped abruptly and then everyone could hear it.

"—that's what it's called, isn't it? A *batchall?* Answer my *batchall,* damn it!"

The AML infantryman just laughed. He didn't even dignify that with a response.

"We need to do something." That was the nurse. Of course it was. "Someone's going to get killed."

Arkee rolled his eyes, but before he could even think about doing anything one way or the other, Dev was already on the other side of the bar trying to mediate.

It made a certain sense, a guy in nurses scrubs seems to be as neutral as a person could get, but that didn't change the tempers and the alcohol.

"We should all just take a break," the nurse said, raising a hand between the merc and the militiaman. But that only seemed to make things worse.

"What is he doing? He's going to get himself killed," Evan said.

And Arkee said the most cutting thing he could think of. "Let him."

He hated himself for thinking it. Doubly so for saying it. That wasn't like him, and he knew it. It was as though some deep, dark part of him had crawled from some deep crevice and was using him as a puppet to be mean.

He loved Evan.

He didn't deserve to be treated like this.

But Arkee couldn't help it. That last thing he wanted was to lose Evan.

"That's cold, Arkee. Especially coming from you."

"It would solve a lot of problems."

"He's just trying to help. Where is this coming from? You've never been the jealous type."

"I never had to worry about you cheating before."

"I'd never cheat on you. He was my nurse and is my friend."

Before Arkee could offer another cutting response, the fight triggered across the bar.

The angry, flailing merc broke free of the grip of his mates and Arkee's eyes widened at the glinting flash of a knife in his hands. He shoved Dev down to the ground, moving past him like a shot. The Clanner wasn't even looking in the direction of the merc, so he didn't see the knife slide into him.

Arkee saw it, though.

The Clanner's eyes widened as he turned to remove his attacker. The much smaller merc looked like a *Locust* going for a *Kodiak*, but the *Kodiak* had been caught entirely unawares. It wasn't very honorable to make an attack like that. The Clanner tossed the merc to the side and stood, getting ready to fight back. The knife wound in their back bled, the blood looking black as night under the dance lights of the club.

The crowd of mercs formed a ring around the fight as though they were marking off a Circle of Equals. Arkee couldn't figure it out. Why were they all egging it on? Was it just the booze and the mood?

The nurse stood up from the blow and tried to intercede again, but he couldn't stop the knife from slashing the Clanner once more, this time across the chest.

"Stop it, this is not the way to handle things!" Dev said.

But he got shoved off to one side again, both by the Clanner *and* the merc, slamming into the bar.

He looked up and Arkee could have sworn he made eye contact with Evan, as though that was who he was trying to impress. Of course he was. This whole thing was a show to steal Arkee's husband. Why else would you toss yourself into a fight like this?

But it wasn't much of a fight.

The Clanner parried the clumsy knife slash with his wrist. With his other hand, he leaned in for a punch that landed squarely in the merc's face. A second merc came for him and he pushed his arm out of the way. But that's when the first merc struck, his arm flying high, plunging his knife right into the Clanner's head, just above the ear. The Clanner collapsed to the ground, blood pooling around his head.

The merc backed up, almost shocked by what he had done.

For his part, the nurse turned and immediately went to render any aid he could to the Mercantile Militia Clanner.

A whistle shrieked at the front door of the bar. Arkee and Evan both turned to see the local police force marching in. A woman led the cadre of cops, half a dozen of them. They came in like they owned the place and started shoving people out of the way and tromping toward the scene of the scuffle. Maybe the bartenders had called them in. Or maybe there were cameras everywhere. Arkee didn't know.

The merc who had done the stabbing tried to run for the back door, but tripped.

By the time he got back to his feet, the cops were on him, restraining him and pulling his hands behind his back. He was screaming at the top of his lungs. "It was a trial! It was a fair fight! Why are you arresting me? We settled this like warriors!"

One of the police put a hand on the nurse's shoulder and pulled him away from the dead Clanner.

There was no coming back from that.

It was murder. Plain and simple.

Arkee had never seen someone die up close like that before. He'd seen people die, sure, but in his 'Mech. It all seemed so far away at that point.

That guy was bleeding out of his head.

And that nurse ran headlong into it, trying to help him.

And Arkee sat there and did nothing.

No wonder Evan was so taken with him.

Evan said something to Arkee, but he was lost.

"Huh?" he asked, trying to catch up.

"I said, are you okay?"

Evan put a hand on Arkee's shoulder, and Arkee bucked beneath it, trying to get away. He didn't want to be touched.

"No." Arkee took another long swig of his PPC. Maybe it was the alcohol talking. And maybe it was an even more foolish thing to drink a depressant when he was already depressed. "I'm not okay."

Evan eased his hand back onto Arkee's shoulder, soft and soothing. "What can I do?"

Arkee didn't try to get out from under it this time. He let it sit there and remind him of all the times Evan had been able to comfort him. "Nothing. I don't think there's anything you can do, Evan. I'm broken."

"No, you're not. We can fix this."

And before Arkee could respond, a pair of cops were in their face, asking for statements.

Arkee told them exactly what he thought of the "trial." That it was murder. Plain and simple.

"This place is a tinderbox," one of the cops said, probably not realizing she was talking to a mercenary. "All of these mercs and old warriors are going to blow this place sky high."

Merc or not, Arkee couldn't argue.

## CHAPTER SIXTEEN

**LONE WOLVES HEADQUARTERS**
**GARRISON WAREHOUSE**
**FACTORY ZONE 4**
**NEW DELHI**
**ALYINA**
**24 OCTOBER 3151**

Sitting in the common room with a half-dozen other Lone Wolves watching the tribunal play out on the holofeed, Bugsy Heidegger could admit he did not like this one bit. He'd watched all of the tribunal himself, but as they waited for the final arguments and a verdict to be read, others from the Lone Wolves had gathered in the common room to see what the fuss was about.

"How do you think it's going to go?" Jackie Darwin of the WhipIts asked, kicking her feet up onto the desk. She piloted a pink *Wight* and took no guff from anyone.

Bugsy shrugged. "Not well. I mean, by all accounts this guy murdered that AML freeborn in cold blood. The guy wasn't trying to pick a fight and just kept drinking when he got stabbed in the back. These guys were like bringin' snowballs to a fight in hell."

"Who are these guys that did it?" That was Bien Canonizado from the Moa Hunters. He rolled in a tank and sat in the back corner of the room, a big guy with brown skin, darker than most Capellans Bugsy knew, and a dragon writ large on his shirt.

Bugsy Heidegger seemed to know everyone by their 'Mech and unit. "Tread of Doom. I don't know much about 'em. They're an armored unit. Tanks exclusively, no 'Mechs at all. Bunch of hotheads, it sounds like."

"Not one of ours, then?" came another voice. Stephanie Chowdhury. The CO of Stetson's Big Booties. She fought in an *UrbanMech* that looked like it had been covered in bird plumage; a parakeet that started blue at the bottom, faded to green, and up to yellow by the top.

"God no. If they were one of ours, we'd have run them out of the Lone Wolves right quick. All our people know how to behave better than that."

"I dunno," Jackie Darwin said. "We've pulled in a lot of green units before this job."

"Naw," Bugsy said. "The greenest is the Fox Patrol, and it sounds like one of their guys was a witness and someone with them even tried to break it up. No, I think we're okay here, but this place is like a powder keg. The Syndic is calling for the heads of these Tread of Doom fools, and this tribunal is going to be make-or-break for a lot of folks."

Bien Canonizado nodded. "What mercenary's gonna want to work here if they can get sent away for a bar fight?"

Stephanie Chowdhury said, "I mean, they stabbed the guy in the back. I wouldn't qualify that as a bar fight."

"That's my thinking, too," Bugsy said. "These folks are burning down the house and ruining it for the rest of us."

"Leave it to tankers to screw it all up," Jackie Darwin said.

"Hey," Bien said.

But Bugsy couldn't quite disagree.

There was something about tankers in a world full of MechWarriors where, for the most part, they all thought they had something to prove. And on a former Clan world, against an AML militiaman who had been a freeborn Clanner beforehand, what better way to prove their mettle?

It was just plain foolish, though. And this guy was going to hang for it.

The holofeed squelched back to life and the leader of the tribunal, a gruff-looking man with white hair, called the proceedings back into order. The text at the bottom of the feed named him as Merchant Wagner. "We will now hear final arguments from the accused and the prosecution before rendering a verdict. Derby Halloran, commander of the Tread of Doom and officer in charge of Gary Hooper—the accused—you may plead your final case."

Derby Halloran stood. The tri-vid cameras on the holofeed offered a clear view of him. To Bugsy's eyes, he looked like a hothead and, with the first words he spoke, Bugsy knew his temperament matched his looks.

"With all due respect, all I see from this tribunal is hypocrisy." Halloran could barely contain the rage in his voice. "If my man, Sergeant Hooper, had been another Clan warrior, this matter would have been settled right there at the bar. This was a fair fight. A *batchall* was issued, and all the witnesses agree to that view of events. You have heard their testimony. How can you murder someone in a fair battle? This Clan warrior died in battle, and that's all there is to it. If this court finds Sergeant Hooper guilty of adhering to the local customs and the ways of the Clans on a planet controlled and populated by Clan warriors, then there is nothing but a mockery of justice being made. I submit to you all a final time, do justice in this tribunal. Sergeant Hooper is here to defend you all against threats foreign and domestic, he fought in a fair fight after his honor had been impugned by your Clan warrior, and he dealt with it in the ways of your people. Don't make a decision you will regret."

Halloran took his seat next to Sergeant Hooper and nodded to him like it was all over. An open-and-shut case.

But Halloran didn't seem to get that he wasn't on a Clan world. And that was exactly what the prosecution said. "Your Honor," the prosecutor began, standing up and pacing between the dais and the desks for all to see. "There is no dispute over the merits of this case. In a drunken scuffle, the accused admits to putting a knife in the back of Frederick, a freeborn of the Alyina Mercantile League Militia. There was no provocation and, indeed, thanks to witness testimony from the defense, there was no need for this murder to occur. Where the defense is gravely mistaken is that this is no longer a Clan world, and no longer operates under Clan laws. The Jade Falcons died on Terra. What is left here on Alyina is a strong system that no longer kowtows to the whims of overzealous warriors. This aggression cannot go unchallenged. We cannot allow the ways of the past to dictate the new future we intend to forge. And, by convicting the accused, we will send a clear message to the world and the entire Inner Sphere that the Alyina Mercantile League is something new and something different. More civilized than the ways of the Clans, a force to be reckoned with."

Wagner nodded. "And what sentence does the prosecution request for this trespass against the Alyina Mercantile League and the life of the freeborn militia fighter, Frederick?"

The prosecutor sighed heavily, and Bugsy knew it was going to be bad before he even said it. "On behalf of Syndic Marena, we would ask that the accused be sentenced to death. It seems only fair, a life for a life."

There was a gasp in the courtroom. Halloran and Hooper hung their heads in incredulity. A matching gasp came from the assembly of 'Mech commanders in the room with Bugsy. Not in a million years did he think they would go to kill the guy. At the most, he figured they would lock him up forever and throw away the key.

"They're gonna kill him?" Jackie asked.

"I mean, the verdict and sentence isn't final yet," Bugsy said.

But he might have spoken too soon.

The merchant leading the tribunal banged his gavel, silencing the gasps and whispers in the room. "At the point where the accused has admitted his guilt and the state asks for the death penalty, this tribunal has no recourse but to grant it. The execution will be held in seven standard days. So it is said, so you have been sentenced. So it will be done."

The murmurs in the court grew, but Merchant Wagner hadn't finished. He banged his gavel once more.

"Does the condemned have any last words for the court?"

Sergeant Hooper had to be held back from leaping over the table, screaming a string of expletives at Merchant Wagner. "You son of a bitch, how dare you? I'll kill you for this! You hear me?"

The bailiffs had only begun to restrain him when the holofeed cut off, leaving Bugsy to stare at the group of Lone Wolves before him. "Well, that could have gone better."

"It's sad," Bien Canonizado said. "Aside from that first attack, this is the most action we've seen on this deployment. All interpersonal drama. No 'Mechs. No pirates. Is this job even worth it?"

Bugsy laughed. "Would you prefer us being shot at every second? Yeah, it's a little boring, but we're doing our drills and working more cohesively as a unit. We've heard nothing but good reports from the other pieces of the unit elsewhere in Alyina space. And it's not our folks getting sentenced to death for barroom brawls. So, I'm gonna say we're winning on this one."

"This place just needs one match to light it up," Stephanie Chowdhury said. "They don't even need pirates. Or these new Jade Falcons. Or the Hell's Horses. Or anybody gunning for them. They're just gonna go up in flames all by themselves with everything they have right here."

Bugsy shrugged. He couldn't argue with that.

And it left him wondering if there was somewhere better the Lone Wolves could be right now.

## CHAPTER SEVENTEEN

**AML MILITIA TRAINING COMPOUND**
**CORLEONE**
**MONTESSORO**
**ALYINA**
**ALYINA MERCANTILE LEAGUE**
**29 OCTOBER 3151**

"Absolutely not, Captain!" Arkee pounded his fist on Katie's desk. "If you let him join up and come with us, you can absolutely count me out!"

Katie took a deep breath and tried to get her bearings, but Arkee was coming in hot. "Whoa, what is going on, Ark? I haven't seen you this tense since we fought that *Kodiak* on Kaesong."

"I can't do it. I will flat-out resign if you take him on as a medic!"

"I mean, we need a medic." Katie kicked her boots up onto her desk and put her hands behind her head, trying to adopt a more conversational and casual tone. Maybe that would simmer Arkee down. "What happened to Evan is proof of that. I'm impressed we've gone this long without a ship's doctor anyway. That seems like a ridiculous oversight on my part, given how much trouble we get in on every job."

Arkee growled and pointed a finger at Katie. "He's a nurse, not a doctor."

"I know that, but it's like...a battlefield-medic sort of situation we need. I don't expect our ship's doctor to be treating cancer or anything. We'll stop into a real port for that sort of thing, heaven forbid."

"I can't do it, Captain! I won't!"

"Evan speaks very highly of him, Ark. What's really going on?"

"Oh, Evan speaks highly of him, does he? Was this his idea?"

"I don't know if it was his idea, but I certainly asked him what his opinion of this guy was. I mean, he did take care of him during his hospital stay. And I thought it was a great idea because it's definitely a gaping hole we have in our crew, especially since Frankie's promotion."

"That's not gonna last long."

"It's going to have to last, at least for now. But...like, what else is going on here? Dev Caponigro is a hero, he tried to stop that fight and just seems like a really nice guy, overall."

"He's a little too nice if you ask me."

"Arkee."

"What?"

"Sit down."

Arkee hesitated for a moment, but collapsed into the chair on the other side of Katie's desk, hiding his face with an open palm.

Were those tears he was hiding?

Katie lowered her head, trying to get a view from beneath his hand, but he kept his face covered. "Tell me what's going on."

"Nothing."

"This isn't like you."

He wiped his eyes again and took a measured breath. "You ever think to yourself that it's not like you? That someone else must be feeling for you because it's not like you at all?"

Katie furrowed her brow. "What do you mean?"

"Like, you ever watch yourself in battleROM footage and think it can't be you in that 'Mech because it's not moving or shooting or operating on a level you know you're capable of? Like they put you as a child in the command couch or something."

"Is this about your *Quickdraw*? Because Rhiannon and Dexter have already apologized for the damage, and you didn't do anything wrong. You did exactly what I would have done."

"No, this is about..." He choked on Evan's name, but Katie could see what he was trying to say.

"Arkee, buddy, what's going on between you and Evan?"

Arkee looked away, staring out toward the door.

"And the nurse... Is this... Do you think...?"

Arkee nodded.

"Arkee, Evan hasn't cheated on you. He'd never do that. You know he'd never do that. He worships the ground you walk on."

Casting his guilty eyes, big as a hound dogs, back to Katie, she saw all the shame he felt weighing him down. "I know it doesn't make any sense."

"Is it just because this nurse looked after him when you couldn't?"

"It's more than that."

It pained Katie to see him hurting so badly. She wanted so badly to help, but didn't know what she could do. "What is it then, Ark? I hate seeing you like this and I don't want to cause you any more heartache. But we do need a ship's medic."

"It's because I'm not good enough for him. You see that?"

"For Evan?"

Arkee nodded, choked on another round of tears, and then it all poured out at once. "And if this nurse, who is such a good goddamn person, is hanging around, Evan's going to see he's wasting his time with me."

Katie froze.

She wanted to walk over to him and put a hand on his shoulder. Let him cry on her shoulder, even. Because that wasn't going to happen. Evan wasn't going to leave him. From the day she met them both, she'd never known anyone else who had ever been that in love with each other. Over the moon. The vague recollections she had of her parents in love when they were alive before the accident didn't even match up to the levels of these two.

She just couldn't get over the idea there was trouble between them. Katie couldn't stand.

All she could do was lower her voice to almost a whisper. "Arkee, you're one of the best guys ever. If Evan's gonna leave, it's not gonna be because you're not good enough."

Arkee looked back up to her, his eyes wet with sadness. "So, you think he would?"

"I didn't say that."

"I just don't know what to do, Captain. But I know if you bring this guy on, I don't think I can continue. I can't walk around the *Fox Den* thinking he's coming after my husband. And even if he's not, I've had the most horrible thoughts about him. Every time I see his face, I just get irrational. Like, I see myself behaving this way. I don't trust him. Men are the worst, y'know?"

"Are we talking romantically?" Katie had no experience with them in a romantic capacity. She had no experience with women in a romantic capacity either. She didn't really *have* a romantic capacity she could find, which also suited her just fine.

"In all ways. Even me. When that nurse was trying to stop the fight, all I could think of was how much easier it would be on everyone—me especially—if he just got killed right there."

"Ark, that's horrible…"

"I *know*. But I couldn't help it. That's not me. But somehow it was. It just…filled me up, this hot rage and inadequacy."

"I'm thinking maybe we don't need a Fox Patrol medic as much as a therapist. Have you talked to anyone else about this?"

"No."

"Evan?"

Arkee shook his head. "Sort of. He knows I'm upset. He thinks it's just me being jealous."

"Isn't it, though?"

"I don't know."

"Listen, Arkee, I'm not going to accept your resignation if we take Dev in as our medic. But I'm going to talk to him and Evan and see what I can do to settle this. You're a grown man, and this behavior from you—frankly, it's shocking. Evan's a grown man, too. And neither of you are in any danger of losing the other. I promise you."

"The nurse will make it so much harder, though."

Katie realized Arkee couldn't even bring himself to use Dev's name. "Ark, I understand you're hurting. And I understand you have some stuff going on. But you need to get a grip. There is so much going on around here, and it's so much bigger than any of us."

"Like what?"

"Like the fact I still have to fix your *Quickdraw* and Evan's *Locust*, and I still don't have any idea where I'm going to get the rest of the parts. That I have to hire new crew to fill out our support roles. That we're in the middle of a conflict where I have to answer to someone like Bugsy Heidegger instead of to myself, which is the way it's been since we started, which I don't mind because I can focus on working on 'Mechs. Like the fact this place is ready to explode with tension between mercs and former Clanners and, somehow, we got caught in the middle. Arkee, there is so much going on right now I think you just need to take some time off and think about all of this. I'll see about finding a therapist to put on the payroll. We might do well enough on this job to afford it—"

"Would that mean we couldn't afford the medic?"

"Arkee."

"Just asking."

"I know the work we do is hard. It's traumatic. And the invisible wounds we face in our well-being are every bit as real as the physical wounds when we get shot down. I get it. And we need to acknowledge that. I'm here for you. I'm listening. I will do what I can, but I still need you to pull yourself together. Talk to Evan. Have a real talk with him. Clear the air."

Arkee slumped in his chair.

Maybe he didn't want to go?

Likely, he didn't want to face Evan.

But the polite knock on the door interrupted them.

Katie looked up to see Frankie standing halfway in the doorway, their fist still on the door.

She smiled wide and was grateful for a change of subject. "Frankie, what's the word?"

"Good news or bad news first?"

"Good news?"

"You've got all the parts you need for the *Quickdraw* in the bay, ready for you."

"That's terrific, how'd you do it?"

"Well, I played XO. But that leads to the bad news. I'm resigning from the Fox Patrol. You can take this XO job and shove it. I won't do it anymore, and you'll just have to find someone else."

The life drooped from Katie's face and her mouth fell open. Before she could even respond, Frankie left. As though that was that. Never to be seen again.

# CHAPTER EIGHTEEN

**DOWNTOWN NEW DELHI**
**ALYINA**
**ALYINA MERCANTILE LEAGUE**
**30 OCTOBER 3151**

As night settled firmly on Alyina's capital, Derby Halloran knew his plan was dangerous, but the Tread of Doom never left a man behind. Especially not a ride-or-die guy like Sergeant Gary Hooper.

"Distance to the jail?" he asked the driver of the heavy tank—a Manticore—he rode in, rumbling along the downtown city streets of Alyina.

"Another klick and a half."

Derby Halloran looked down at his command panel and saw the other five heavy tanks in his command rolling in a tight formation. These Clanner bastards would learn to fear men like the Tread of Doom, not treat them with the disrespect they'd been shown. Gary Hooper was a goddamned hero, and they were going to make damn sure he didn't die like a punk at the end of a Jade Falcon firing squad.

"One klick left," Sant, the pilot, said. "We're almost there."

Halloran pulled up the comm and spoke to everyone in his command; the Tread of Doom would not be put down, and he wanted everyone to know it. "Gentlemen, this is our hour of truth. We are going to free our comrade and make this a night the Jade Falcons won't soon forget. They dared to challenge us when we came here to defend them, and we will not let that challenge go unanswered."

"Half a klick," came Sant's voice again. Good old reliable Sant.

"As I said before. We crack open the jailhouse. We bust out everyone we can. As soon as we get Hooper, we roll out. And there is so much more than that planned with the Romeo unit. But what I want to know from all of you from Alpha is this: Are you ready?"

Over the comm, a half-assed smattering of responses came back. "We're ready..." and the like.

But that wasn't good enough for Derby Halloran. "I said, are you ready?!"

They all came back in unison this time, with a verve and volume that pleased Halloran. "*We are ready!*"

"Damn it, that is what I like to hear!"

"Here we go," Sant said.

And, indeed, there in front of them was the stockade in the heart of New Delhi. It took up a whole city block, built up at least six stories in brutalist concrete and grayscales. Halloran didn't get the impression it had always been a prison. Maybe it was a residential district or something, but Marena, their employer—*former employer after this*, Halloran thought—had converted it quickly into a prison to house all of the malcontents her leadership had created.

Halloran didn't mind working for a woman. He didn't mind working for a Clanner. But when they were as bad at leading as he thought Marena was, there was no common ground to work with. He thought Clan space would be a great place to work, because they would have a firm grip on what it was a good mercenary team could do. But they were just like everyone else. Since the Tread of Doom wasn't MechWarriors with a cadre full of oversized 'Mechs, they didn't get the respect they deserved. But Halloran would put his tanks up against any one of their damn BattleMechs and not feel bad about it at all. He'd take those odds and bet them long every day of the week.

If this was their last day on Alyina, they were going to make it count, one way or the other.

Halloran gripped the butt of his pistol, well-worn in the holster at his hip. Even in a tank, he didn't go anywhere without a gun. None of his men did. It wasn't worth the risk.

"Shall I open fire, sir?" the gunner asked.

Halloran looked at the blank slate of a wall they'd staked out for the break and nodded. "Do it."

The Manticore unleashed its short-range missiles, smashing against the ferrocrete wall.

"Again," Halloran said.

And the gunner complied, firing another volley of SRMs, cracking the jail open like an egg in a blossom of flame. The concussive blast was enough to rock the tank back, but that wouldn't stop them.

"Roll in," Halloran commanded Sant. "The rest of you, create a perimeter. We'll go in and do what needs to be done."

Sant nodded and drove the Manticore right through the wall and into the center courtyard of the makeshift prison.

Halloran burst out of the hatch, squinting through the ferrocrete dust, pistol drawn. "Yee-haw!"

One of the guards, dressed in the blues of the AML, coughed in the smoke and tried waving away the particles from her face. Halloran shot her right in the chest with his pistol.

She collapsed to the ground as Halloran looked around for anyone else that might be in the way and needed to be shot. Seeing no one, he crawled from the hatch of the tank and bounded to the ground. He didn't even pay the woman a second glance as he stepped over her body, looking to make the rest of the prison break happen.

His cadre of Treaders had left skeleton crews in the tanks to help him swarm the jail and release everyone they could find.

At the first cell he came to, Halloran blasted the locks on the sealed door with his pistol and swung it open wide. He didn't even care who was inside.

"You're free now. Do your thing. Fly!"

The man inside, big and tattooed across his face, grunted his thanks and fled into the bedlam.

Halloran shot another pair of guards—one in the face and another, fleeing, in the leg—before freeing another prisoner. By the end, the Tread of Doom freed half the prison before Halloran finally found the death row cell he wanted; the one belonging to Gary Hooper.

"Hooper!" he said finally, swinging open the door of his comrade's cell.

Hooper looked around, incredulous. "Major Halloran! What are you doing here?"

"We're busting you out of here. You know we don't leave anyone behind. And these Clan bastards aren't going to have the last word with the Tread of Doom."

"We getting some payback? Nice..." Hooper said.

But Halloran grinned. "In spades, Hoop. You don't know the half of it..."

## JADE DEPOSITORY
## UPTOWN NEW DELHI
## ALYINA
## ALYINA MERCANTILE LEAGUE

"Ready?" Sergeant Matt Shurtleff asked the rest of his command, a contingent of swift hovercraft and a cadre of VTOLs, all barreling toward the Jade Depository in uptown New Delhi.

According to his mission briefing, Sergeant Shurtleff knew the Jade Depository was a massive, guarded vault wrought of dyed green ferrocrete and iron bars. He was assured they were not going to expect the attack, especially not with the prison break occurring on the other side of town. On their way to the depository, all of the flashing sirens of AML hovercars headed in the opposite direction, giving Shurtleff the boost of confidence he needed to think their little operation could work.

"They're not going to take this from us," his CO, Major Halloran, had told him. "We are going to get what we're owed, and we're going to get Hooper out while we do it."

Shurtleff had no reason to doubt him.

As much as everyone liked Hooper as a person, they all liked getting paid more. And since the former Falcons certainly weren't going to finish paying on their contract after that business with Hooper, it was time to take what was owed right from them.

That was Shurtleff's job.

The hovercraft favored by the Tread of Doom—converted Bandits— were equal parts infantry transport and modest tank, all the right ingredients to inconspicuously crack into a fortified structure, get in, and get out. And that was essentially the plan.

"I've got eyes on Elementals at the front," came Hector's voice over the comm from another hovercraft.

"How many?" Shurtleff asked.

"Four I can see. I think there are more on the far side."

"Keep your eyes peeled and wait for my mark." Shurtleff switched his comm to another channel. "Apex Alpha, this is Doom One, do you copy?"

"Apex Alpha. We got you, Doom One."

"You see the target?"

"We got the Depository locked in and are circling from an inconspicuous distance, waiting to move in."

"Perfect." Shurtleff took a deep breath.

It wasn't every day they committed a smash-and-grab against their former employer. Hell, it was the first time in Shurtleff's entire tenure with the Tread of Doom. But he had a mission and he wanted to get paid. Wasn't that the first rule of being a mercenary?

"Doom One, this is Doom Two. We are in position."

"Excellent. Doom Three?" Shurtleff asked.

"Locked and loaded."

"Doom Four?"

"Right with you."

"On my mark, then." As soon as he said go, they would all zoom in on the target, crack open the vault, and make away with what they could.

It wasn't an elaborate plan, but Major Halloran wasn't the most tactically minded fellow. Shurtleff knew the biggest problem would be the Elementals, but he remained optimistic. It wasn't like they were going up against BattleMechs. And maybe the AML folks *weren't* really Clanners like they kept saying, which is why they wanted to kill Hooper for that little scuffle in the first place.

"Mark," Shurtleff said, and everything flew into motion.

Shurtleff's hover pilot tore around the corner and there they were: the Elementals in full armor as promised. Shurtleff knew it took a lot of brass to put on a suit of Elemental armor. The stories told of massive Clanners, twice the size of a normal human—real gorillas—cramming into the tin cans of powered armor and laying waste to armies.

But nothing he'd seen on Alyina made him think any of these Alyinians were proper Clanners.

So, he had nothing to be afraid of.

"Open fire."

His Bandit—Doom One—had approached the Jade Depository from the side, rather than head on, so he could only barely make out the elaborate Jade Falcon mosaic rendered in tiles on the front of the building. Shurtleff *could* see the Elementals standing guard, though they were facing out with their backs to the building. The street lit up red, bathed in the light of an oncoming laser. It slashed against the front Elemental's power armor and sliced the arm right off it, clattering to the pavement in a pool of slag. The other two Elementals went to work, fending off Doom Two and Three, which were coming straight at them. Maybe they didn't notice Doom One taking potshots at them from the side, but it didn't matter.

Doom One's gunner missed, but the lasers flashing down the darkened street added to the chaos and confusion, which was just as well for Shurtleff and his mission.

One of the Elementals turned to face Doom One, and a chill ran up Shurtleff's back when he thought for a moment the Elemental was making eye contact with him. Staring him down. Telling him to stop. To go. To run the other way.

"We're gonna hit him," Hector said matter-of-factly.

Shurtleff agreed. "Do it."

Hector built up even more speed, and in a blink, they were within striking distance of the Elemental, but they leaped up into the air, right over the hovercraft.

"I lost 'em."

"Damn it."

Hector skidded the craft around, angling up to the front of the Depository, guns pointed right at it.

"Forget the Elementals, just get us in."

"Got it."

Looking down at his command console, Shurtleff watched the feed of the battle overhead, piped in from one of the Apexes, and it wasn't going well, but it wasn't going horribly either. "They don't want us in there," Hector said.

"Of course they don't, but if it were up to them, we wouldn't even be here. Just stay on target, and we'll pull this thing out fast."

Hector blasted the building once more, but then redirected at Shurtleff's command, angling the hovercraft around the corner to get a better shot at the back of the Depository.

"We've got to get inside," Shurtleff commanded. "Now."

"Working on it," Hector said from the inside. But as they went to work, the voices over the comm only got more desperate.

"Doom Five is down!"

"—He tore it right in half!—"

"—where'd he go?"

"—they're over here!"

Sweat beaded on Shurtleff's temple, listening to the rest of his fellows get massacred in their heist attempt. Hector remained resolute, carving holes into the ferrocrete side of the Jade Depository with the craft's small laser. "Let's get through this."

"I'm doing the best I can," Hector said. "This isn't easy work. I'm not exactly the right tool for the job."

"Just keep your mouth shut and keep going. We're running out of time."

"Yes, sir."

"Just think, on the other side of that wall is enough money to make us all rich and get us out of this stinking system ahead of where we were when we got here."

"Yes, sir."

The comm flared up again, a solid mix of panic and professionalism. Shurtleff smirked. Maybe that was the best way to describe the Tread of Doom: a solid mix of panic and professionalism.

The sound of shearing metal shook them from their concentration. Something on the outside of the hovercraft. Something big.

"We've got an Elemental incoming!"

"How close until we're in?"

"Just a few more seconds."

"Damn it." Shurtleff thought fast. "Doom Two, this is Doom One. We need help."

"What's the sitch?"

"Elemental."

"What's your twenty."

"North side."

"On it."

Shurtleff turned back to Hector. "That should buy us a minute, easy. We're gonna need to move a lot faster, though. Get the tow cables ready."

"Got it."

Looking out the side window of the crew compartment, bouncing up and down with the Elemental on top of Doom One, Shurtleff looked out and saw the other Bandit—Doom Two—tearing around the corner. They had their own Elemental to deal with, tearing a hole in the roof of their hovercraft like someone opening a tin can, but true to their word, they came to help with the objective. That was the best part of the Tread of Doom: you could always count on them to stay on objective, no matter how dangerous that got.

Doom Two fired its laser at the Elemental on top of Doom One, and that only temporarily got the bouncing in the hovercraft to stop. But that was when the ferrocrete wall collapsed in front of them, billowing dust in a voluminous cloud.

"Okay," Shurtleff said. "We're in! Fire the tow cables!"

Staying in the same spot, Hector cranked the control yoke and spun the hovercraft around quickly. Shurtleff hoped that would shake the Elemental on top, but they had no such luck. That Elemental was on there good, and unless Doom Two blasted them off, they weren't going to give up that easily.

Hector smashed the buttons that released the tow cables and whooped. "We got it!"

"Then let's go. Now." Shurtleff braced himself in his chair, holding on to the handle next to him as Hector punched the accelerator. "Doom Squad, we have the package. Apexes, plot an intercept course."

Myriad affirmative responses came from the other teams. Now all Shurtleff and his crew had to do was get to them.

Hector was a helluva driver, and Shurtleff had all the confidence in the world in his skills to get them out of there, but those Elementals were no joke, and they weren't going to let them get away alive if they could help it.

The Elemental's massive claw pierced the roof of the hovercraft, and Shurtleff ground his teeth. "Somebody needs to kill this guy."

"We're having our own problems," Doom Two called from their position.

Shurtleff looked back beyond the vault they were dragging behind them to see Doom Two down on the ground, the lift skirt showering sparks where it scraped the pavement. The Elemental had taken them down completely. And that was the same position he was going to be in if they didn't do something.

He pulled his bulky laser pistol from his holster—twice the size of a ballistic pistol to house the battery—and aimed it up at the Elemental's fingers. He fired a steady beam, hoping he could cut right into them.

"Maybe not the best idea, sir," Hector said as he cornered a tight turn, shoving Shurtleff, the Elemental, and the laser beam off course. The laser ate into the ceiling like a cutting torch.

Shurtleff stopped firing, not wanting to cause more problems than he already had. "Where are the damn whirlybirds?"

"They're on their way," Hector said. "I'm clearing the path."

"Step on it."

"I can't go any faster."

Shurtleff wondered if they could get any more help. "Doom Three, anything you can do?"

"We're trying to intercept, sir."

"Anything you're gonna do, do it fast."

Shurtleff checked once more on the cargo, dragging in the street behind them. The vault was massive and dropped their top speed considerably, but they had it. That was the important part. The vault itself was a great metal box that contained who knew what treasures. They hadn't really had a chance to pick. But Major Halloran had assured them his intel said any single vault they could capture, big or small, would be worth their fees and any lives it cost.

Beyond the vault, lit up by the shower of sparks in the road, was another Elemental bearing down on them.

"Turn that gun around and open fire," Shurtleff commanded, and his crew complied as best they could, but they couldn't get the gun to turn. The Elemental on top must have disabled it.

That was when Doom Three burst through the intersection, crashing into the Elemental in pursuit of them.

"Well, that's one down." But Shurtleff wasn't sure if he was talking about his comrades or the Elemental, because their fight continued.

"Doom One, this Apex Alpha, approaching the pickup zone."

"Hector," Shurtleff said, "How close are we?"

"I need to get to the outskirts for the VTOLs to have room to get in."

"Distance?"

"Two more klicks."

With the buildings of New Delhi so bright and reaching high into the Alyina night, Shurtleff couldn't imagine there being a clearing enough for a VTOL to get close within two klicks, but he had to trust Hector to know what he was doing.

The claws of the Elemental slammed into the top of the hovercraft again, the tips of the armored fingers cutting through the reinforced roof for all to see. Nothing about it made Shurtleff feel safe. Two centimeters of lightweight armor was all that kept him safe from a very pissed-off Clan Elemental.

Hector jerked the controls again and turned a corner, forcing the Elemental's fingers to grip harder into the hovercraft. Shurtleff hoped one of those harsh turns would shake them off at *some* point, but it just didn't happen.

"We're close," Hector said.

And up ahead was a clearing between buildings, an empty parking lot near the outskirts, lit with old, yellow streetlights.

"There's our spot."

"If we can make it..."

The VTOL's spotlight lit up everything around them, and then so did their weapons, firing at the Elemental.

"Careful, Apex!" Shurtleff shouted into the comm. The last thing he needed was their rescue to turn lethal.

"Elemental down," Apex Alpha reported. "That makes three total."

Shurtleff's chest heaved in relief.

"Okay, let's get this vault transferred to you, and we'll get to our DropShip. We'll meet up with the major and Hooper, and we're getting the hell off Alyina forever."

"Roger that."

Shurtleff wanted nothing more than to stay true to his word never to return.

# CHAPTER NINETEEN

**ALYINA MERCANTILE LEAGUE HEADQUARTERS**
**EXCHANGE PLACE TOWER**
**NEW DELHI**
**ALYINA**
**30 OCTOBER 3151**

The fire inside Syndic Marena matched the fires in the streets below. One at the converted stockades where she'd been holding prisoners who had disrupted the order of Alyina. The other at the Jade Depository, where she'd been keeping a planet-bound stockpile of their wealth.

The Tread of Doom could not handle the justice they had been handed for the murder of one of her militia. And in the process, they had shattered her stockade and let out hundreds of prisoners who had already proven they could make her life difficult by sowing dissent during this transition. And to add insult to injury, they made away with one of the smaller vaults from VaultShip Beta.

Three Elementals had been killed.

Yes, they had done their fair share of damage back to the Tread of Doom, but that was not justice.

This could not stand.

And the mercenaries roaming free across the Alyina Mercantile League—hired by her own hand—were going to have to be controlled with a much more iron fist. Or she was going to have to kill them all herself.

Standing there, gazing out the window from so many stories up in the Alyinian night, Marena knew what she had to do.

It would not be easy.

But she knew her path never would be.

Not only would she have to hunt down the Tread of Doom to the ends of the Inner Sphere, she needed to crack down on Alyina and use the fist of a warrior in ways she never wanted to.

"Damn it," she said under her breath to no one in particular. "You're going to force me into the warrior's ways, aren't you?"

But the night did not respond.

The only thing that burned brighter than the fires below her was her fury.

The mercenaries would answer for this.

All of them.

## TO BE CONCLUDED IN SHRAPNEL #16!

# THE TRUTH
# ABOUT THE BOUNTY HUNTER?

## LORCAN NAGLE

**Excerpted Transcript of 23 April 3134 edition of *Around the Sphere*, TruNewsNetwork, Atreus**

**Marcus Adeboye (Host):** Welcome back to the show. Reports have reached us from the Republic of the Sphere to indicate the Bounty Hunter has been seen again, having been observed on Quentin in June, and then in the heavy fighting on Irian last November. The Bounty Hunter is, of course, an enigmatic and infamous figure in the Inner Sphere mercenary business, always seen in public wearing a customized suit of powered armor. Having first appeared in the early thirtieth century, the Hunter has a long history of disappearing and reappearing, and there are many theories as to what happened in each case. To discuss this topic tonight, we have Agnieszka Vitkus, from Arcadia University College; Damon Rundall, author of *The True History of the Inner Sphere*; Eric Mason from MechWorld publishing; and Frankie Pinestone, a popular media commentator on EagleNet. Professor Vitkus, I'd like to turn to you first.

**Vitkus:** Thank you, it's a pleasure to be here again. I think it's worth establishing a few ground facts, or at least commonly accepted speculations about the Bounty Hunter. Clearly the identity of the Hunter has been passed from person to person over the years, given the figure has been active as a mercenary in the Inner Sphere for over two hundred years. While many of the people are a mystery, a common belief is that a man named "Vic Travers" was wearing the armor by no later than 3035.

**Rundall:** Oh come on, the Travers theory is common, but I debunked it thoroughly in my book *Mercenaries of the Thirty-First Century*. It's a conspiracy theory for people who are obsessed with linking Wolf's Dragoons to every event since their arrival in the Inner Sphere.

**Vitkus:** [*speaking faster and more agitated as she continues*] The Bounty Hunter is clearly connected to the Dragoons at that time, though! Even ignoring his long-standing rivalry with Natasha Kerensky that coincidentally stops shortly before their feud with Kurita begins, a pair of Wolf's Dragoons officers are seen in the Hunter's company following the Fourth Succession War, and then they show up in the DCMS in time for the War of '39, and *then* they return to the Dragoons after Takashi Kurita's incredibly suspicious death before he was meant to duel Jaime Wolf? Their time with the Hunter corresponds with the disappearance of Michi Noketsuna, whose movements between the Combine and Outreach perfectly match up with those two Dragoons! There's clearly a link here! Clearly!

**Adeboye:** Agnieszka, please. We've had you on to discuss your theories around the Dragoons before and may do so again, but this episode is meant to be about the Bounty Hunter. Let's turn to Eric for his opinion on the Bounty Hunter's return.

**Mason:** I feel like investigating the Bounty Hunter's "true" identity is futile. What we should be looking at is the atmosphere and the ambiance of the Inner Sphere between their prominence and obscurity. What is happening when the Hunter appears and disappears? The ebb and flow of the universe? I'm far more interested in the primal spirit the Bounty Hunter represents and the chthonian urges they're responding to. The political maneuvering and the conflicts that come as a result of them.

We can see this clearly in how the Bounty Hunter first appears. It had become clear that the Third Succession War was going to continue indefinitely, and while it was not as destructive as the first two, it became a further normalization of war as a political tool, similar to the Age of War itself. This sort of generational trauma will create people who self-martyr, who feel they need to take it upon themselves to represent the psychic pain we as a species feel. How better to critique the rampant greed of the Successor Lords and their indifference to the plight of their citizenry than to become a faceless, soulless avatar of violence and greed?

Consider the events since then: The Fourth Succession War, the Clans, the Jihad, and now all these new wars. We even had wars during Devlin Stone's so-called peace! A never-ending spree of death and violence and hate! The Bounty Hunter needs to be there as a focus for our existential dread, a reaction to the decisions made that we can never influence. No face, no morals, no identity but the desire for profit.

**Adeboye:** [*flustered for a second*] Right. Damon, I hear you have some ideas on the Hunter's comings and goings?

**Rundall:** Yes, I'm not going into too much detail—

**Vitkus:** [*barely audible*] Thank God...

**Rundall:** *Because* I have a book coming out about the Hunter, but I have an interesting thing I'd like to share. Can you bring up the slides please?

[*An inset appears, showing a green Leopard-class DropShip on a landing pad in a battle-damaged DropPort.*]

**Rundall:** This is the DropShip *Headhunter* on Hall in 3078, shortly after the planet was liberated from the Word of Blake. This ship has been linked to the Bounty Hunter on multiple occasions, and it was tracked taking off and heading toward the Zenith Jump Point a few days after this picture was taken.

[*The inset image changes to an image of the planet Hall, which zooms out to show more and more of the solar system, with a dotted line extending out and upward, continuing past a sphere labeled "ZENITH."*]

**Rundall:** Damage to the tracking network meant contact was lost around three days later, but there is no record of it docking with any JumpShip known to be in-system at that time. In fact, the next time it appears on publicly available databases is when it lands on Van Diemen in 3109.

**Adeboye:** What are you suggesting?

**Rundall:** I think it's possible that this ship accelerated to a significant percentage of the speed of light and took almost thirty years to travel the eighteen-odd light years between those two systems. If this is the case, it's entirely possible that the Bounty Hunter has traveled between systems at relativistic speeds to age at a slower rate, and while the person inside the Bounty Hunter armor has changed, the number of times it has changed may have been significantly fewer than is currently assumed, or it might even have been the same person all this time. It would help to explain the Hunter's sometimes lengthy absences.

**Vitkus:** You can't be serious! A ship that small couldn't possibly keep a crew alive for decades! And you think he did this repeatedly over the course of centuries?

**Rundall:** It's possible the ship had suspended animation facilities aboard, or rendezvoused with other ships en route.

**Vitkus:** Or it could have linked up with a JumpShip and the records were lost in the chaos of Operation Scour.

**Rundall:** Yeah, maybe Wolf's Dragoons made the records vanish?

**Vitkus:** You son of a—

**Adeboye:** Yes, yes, thank you! It's certainly a fascinating theory, Damon, and your book will go into more detail?

**Rundall:** Among other theories, yes. It'll be out from TruMedia Books, hopefully next year.

**Adeboye:** I'm sure it'll be a hit with our audience. Now Frankie, we haven't heard much from you tonight. Do you have any ideas you'd like to share?

**Pinestone:** I don't have any solid proof for this theory, but the evidence I've found is unnerving. The first thing I'd like to show you is a photograph from ancient Terra...

**Adedoye:** Excuse me?

**Pinestone:** Yes, this photo is dated to the late nineteenth century, but what's interesting is that there was an actor who was prominent around a hundred years later who looks identical to him. But then—then someone else with incredibly similar features was caught in gun-camera footage retrieved from Tintavel during the massacre in 2412 pulling civilians out of the line of fire...

[*The camera cuts to Rundall and Vitkus, who are side-eyeing each other in mutual embarrassment.*]

**Pinestone:** Even since the Age of War, we have photographs and holographs of this man in the Rim Worlds during the Reunification War, and then as a Gunslinger during the First Hidden War, piloting a shuttle out of Calcutta on Bolan in the First Succession War just before the bombers struck...and...and in a café on Glenmora in 2917! And nothing since then—it can't be a coincidence that he stops showing up only a short time before the Bounty Hunter first appeared in 2920...

[*Pinestone's audio cuts out while he continues to visibly talk, getting more animated by the second. The camera abruptly cuts to Adeboye.*]

**Adeboye:** ...And we have to leave it there, I'm afraid. Join us after the break, when we'll be looking at some Unexplained Aerial Phenomena seen in the skies over Tamarind last month, checking in on the developing police violence scandal from Wallis, and we'll also have a panel discussion on some newly unearthed documents calling the true identity of the Master into question, with shocking implications for the future of House Marik...

# ACE DARWIN
# AND THE SECOND TRY FIASCO

## JAMES BIXBY

*For Gudge...*

**GREEN FAE STEAKHOUSE AND BORDELLO**
**HARDCORE**
**MAGISTRACY OF CANOPUS**
**20 APRIL 3049**

I stared across the table to the other three MechWarriors, who should have been celebrating their victory as members of my WhipIts. The look on their faces could only be described as a mixture of shock, confusion, and in the case of poor Swampy Marsh, visible pain.

"Look, it could have gone much worse," I said, and signaled a well-rounded waitress to bring us another round of well-chilled drinks.

"Yes, there was the riot, and our employer is now in a coma, and there was that truck carrying all the exotic animals that got knocked over, and of course the glow weed field caught fire." I took a long draw from my mug of cold beer. "But the Mercenary Review Board considered the contract fulfilled. It could be worse!"

Every set of eyes all turned at me in disbelief. Andrew Sevrin lit his habitual cigarette, this time of local variety. Through the faintly luminescent smoke puffed out he simply said, "This time we got paid."

## MCMURDO FIELDS
## SECOND TRY
## 29 AUGUST 3047

Despite having attended the Nagelring for a hot minute, I was never really one for cold climates. So, whatever possessed me to take a contract on Second Try without looking at the planetary survey is beyond my ability to comprehend. The world met the barest definition of "habitable," given it had a breathable atmosphere and a ridiculously hearty collection of equatorial conifers to maintain it. But the planet was so far away from the sun that equatorial temperatures only got to about 5 degrees centigrade in local summertime.

I was not stationed around the equatorial regions. That joy belonged to a detachment of the famed Twentieth Avalon Hussars, who had taken this planet from Maximillian Liao almost two decades prior. The more northerly and southerly settlements, however, were so sparsely populated they rarely merited the attention of military patrols, and the planet itself was still recovering from its conquest under the Steiner-Davion alliance. So towns, mines, and other various localities had to hire schmucks like me to defend themselves from partisans, pirates, predators, and other pissants who think that by hurting people who just want to live their lives, they will somehow bring back whatever "good old days" they seemed to value.

That's how Ace Darwin's Whiplts was officially paid by the small township of McMurdo Fields, subsidized by the Armed Forces of the Federated Commonwealth, to look tough and prevent ne'er-do-wells from running off with the sundry belongings of ordinary folks.

I was accompanied in this endeavor by Phillipa "Pip" Marcus, a young woman of indeterminate national identity. She claimed to be from the Lyran world of Drosendorf, but her accent fit her purported heritage about as well as the *Hermes II* she operated. Conrad Mladenoff was just the opposite, with very dark-skinned features best described as more angular than the armor of his *Quickdraw*. Finally, there was the Trell called Guthrie, who, heaven help me, was his real and only name. When not sitting in his yellow tartan-coated *UrbanMech,* he spent his time with Andy Sevrin and the subcontracted techs, sipping whisky and seemingly only speaking in grunts.

For a three-month contract, it went by decently enough. I took one of my more mobile companions out on a patrol to stare at a vast field of nothing, making sure we made our presence known to one of the three small communities of farmsteads tending to their underground greenhouses. We would then stop back at the titanium mine that also served as our base of operations and warm up. The MechWarrior I went on patrol with in the mornings would repeat with the other one about four hours later. Guthrie's 'Mech, being significantly less mobile than the rest, was stuck walking between the mine and the adjacent town. On weekends, the Twentieth would send a lance of 'Mechs, or a couple of platoons of snowcat-equipped infantry that had pissed off their CO, to fill in for us.

Aside from freezing my gonads off when I got out of my 'Mech and into the barracks, it was a pretty easy gig. It reminded me of my time finishing my legally required stint in the Kooken's Reserve Militia. Given it was a mining town that only respected people who could get hot and dirty despite local conditions, we were welcome in the bars, gambling dens, and other entertainment venues that supported the mining community. I only needed to answer for bad behavior once or twice as a commanding officer, where I assured the aggrieved party that their son or daughter's honor would be satisfied and I would see to it the offending MechWarrior's pay was cut before closing the door and laughing with the crew, resolving that the offending party should make themselves scarce in town for a week or so. Advice I had to take myself in the second week when back-to-back liaisons with what turned out to be a brother and sister in town led to panic, confusion, and threats of a shotgun wedding, before realizing my *Panther*'s PPC was bigger.

It was that last week of the contract, before the Eighth Federated Commonwealth RCT was to assume responsibility for the whole planet, where things went south.

Saturday, around 0800 by the universal clock, I was roused from my usual lie-in by the local communicator's buzz. Rolling off the bed so as not to disturb the redhead I met last night, I grabbed the phone, expecting one last civil disturbance. "Go for Ace."

"Commander Darwin, could you report to the local sheriff? We have some video that needs a MechWarrior's eyes."

The grainy black-and-white video showed the same handyman moving from place to place. He looked around as though he felt he was being watched, a distinct irony given the cameras. At every stop, he pulled what looked to be an emergency flashlight from his toolbox and used it to replace one that was already mounted.

"So, why is this sketchy?" I asked.

The sheriff and the mine's chief of security and chief engineer stood around the table. "That's the damnedest thing, we have no idea," the sheriff replied. "The lights are the exact same ones that were already mounted. Combination LED and infrared handhelds. Charged by solar panels on the poles they were mounted on."

"Why infrared?" I stared confused, flipping on the example torch that was brought in.

"The IR beam can be used to mark for Fire and Rescue aircraft or as a supplemental spotlight for IR goggles used inside the mine," said the chief engineer.

"Neat. So, why concern me with this? I am here to protect against Capellan and Free Tikonov Partisans," I said, walking over to the coffee maker and pouring myself a cup.

"Well…" The chief of security drank his coffee down in one gulp, wincing a bit before moving on. "To be honest, Commander Darwin, we have no idea why this happened. There was no work order to replace these lights, and no trace of the workman or the original flashlights we had installed. As best as we can figure, everything about this is completely innocuous."

I drank my own coffee and shrugged. "Dunno what to tell you guys. You found no electronic trackers or anything, can't find the workman who installed them. Could it be some paperwork was just lost?"

"I guess it's possible…" the chief engineer replied. "Sorry to bother you, Commander, we needed another head on this. Glad to know we weren't missing something."

**WORKMECH REPAIR BAY 3**
**MCMURDO METALS TITANIUM MINE**
**SECOND TRY**
**31 AUGUST 3047**

I had mentally discarded the whole "mystery flashlight" incident by the time the next piece came into place. I walked into the WorkMech service bay that served as the WhipIts' central staging area. Guthrie was asleep on a lawn chair next to his *UrbanMech*'s leg, a cooler draining wastewater next to him.

My reliable technician, Andrew Sevrin, was joined by Pip and Conrad over a model aircraft of some sort. The broad flying wing marked it as a miniature *Shilone* replica, though the fiberglass frame was unpainted. I saw Sevrin was pouring a can of some sort of fuel into a funnel in the back while Pip was screwing in some sort of camera where the cockpit was supposed to go. In deference to the potential accelerant being dispensed, I made sure to take a few steps back toward the mounted fire extinguisher by a support column.

"Well, Andy, I did say I would like to hire an aerospace pilot full time. This seems a little small, though."

Sevrin didn't even look up from his work, his mouth clenching the habitual cigarette as he muttered. "Pip apparently has a thing for model aircraft. I was just helping her with the FLIR module before she test flew it."

"FLIR? Not familiar," I replied.

"Forward Looking Infrared. It's an IR sensor supplementing the optical camera. A lot of traffic control is controlled by IR beacons, and this makes those visible so it doesn't fly where it ain't welcome."

I looked at Pip and raised an eyebrow. "Like aerospace, eh? How come you're not a pilot?"

"Oh, I hate flying, I spend most of my time on DropShips conked out on tranquilizers. Building models is a fun little hobby, though. Too bad around here. I had to take a day pass out south to find a shop with the parts I needed for this puppy."

"That much of a niche?" I asked, curious.

"Not as much as you think," she replied as she wiped down the protective dome over the cameras, "but the three hobby shops along our patrol routes were all sold out of engine and optics parts. Heck, there was hardly a fixed-wing kit in sight. Plenty of rotary-wing drones, though."

"Engine I get, but why optics?"

Sevrin piped up. "Without an onboard camera, you're limited to visuals for the plane's range. An onboard camera allows you to maneuver farther from your runway and eases any maneuvers you want to do."

With a grunt of approval and a shrug, I went back into the office for a few hours, reviewing possibilities for the next contract to take on the way out.

A couple hours later, I was called out to watch Pippa push her mock *Shilone* into action. The makeshift jet engine shoved it off its launch ramp, and once it was clear of any ground-based obstruction, I was treated to an airshow of S curves and Immelmann turns.

"Can you do a barrel roll?" I asked.

Guthrie chuckled as Sevrin and Pippa just glared at me.

"Dumb question, I know." I smiled and went back to the office. Before entering the glass-lined cubicle, I looked out and witnessed Guthrie hauling the now-empty cooler off to get refilled with snow for the team's beverages.

"Don't drink too much, Guthrie," I warned him. "Our last patrol run is in twenty hours or so, and I want all hands on deck before the Eighth FedCom takes over for us."

"Just water bottles and soda today, bossman. Will save the distilled stuff for our ride out."

"Good man, Guthrie, get some rest."

"Sleep well, Ace."

## HENRIKSON ICE FLATS
## SECOND TRY
## 1 SEPTEMBER 3047

To say my last day on Second Try was ideal would have been an irony, the way things turned out. I rolled out of my cot, no deference to the lady or gentleman who was there next to me. To be blunt, I couldn't be bothered to remember who or which they were. The skies were clear, the local star shining bright, and there was no wind blowing the loose powder that dominated the space between settlements. It was still cold enough I didn't want to go outside without a parka, but snow goggles were optional if you didn't mind facing the bluish-white light of snow reflection.

As had been the usual routine, Guthrie stayed close to the McMurdo titanium mine in the unlikely event some partisan dared roll up in an armed snowcat thinking it could withstand his *Urbie*'s 75mm cannon. Conrad, Pip, and I rolled our BattleMechs due east, heading to the farthest-out settlement in unison to reassure the locals who had complained of some pro-Capellan demonstrators while I was consulting on the great flashlight mystery. Apparently, the so-called mayor of that town thought BattleMechs could intimidate any protestors into submission. My recent experience on Anywhere taught me just how foolish that hope could be.

"All right locals, the farewell show of Ace Darwin's WhipIts is on stage," Conrad called over the general frequency. "Get a look at your heroes before they are gone!" His *Quickdraw* struck a series of extravagant poses that reminded me of some old bodybuilder that would look heroic in an *Immortal Warrior* program.

"Always striving for love and adoration, Connie?" Pip replied as her *Hermes II* headed for the southern outskirts of the town, getting ready to peel off on her patrol route.

"Well, I get nothing from you sweetheart," Connie replied. Laughter flooded the airwaves at the inside joke.

"All right, lovebirds, knock it off, unless you want to reveal whether you did or didn't, for the betting pool."

The two MechWarriors got suddenly quiet at being called out for their months of back-and-forth, and I was suddenly grateful 'Mech-to-'Mech communications were encrypted from the general bands used by the sheriff. As much as I am one for levity, I wanted to leave a good impression with our employers. It made the post-contract after-action reports from their perspective flow so much better.

"Okay, boy and girl, you know the drill. Make for waypoints Sierra and November, wide serpentine pattern. Once you get there, make contact with the locals. Stand around and look tough for about an hour, and then you can dismount and grab some lunch. Another hour of dismounted duty and then RTB. After that we can get paid, get laid, and get the hell out of here."

Pip and Conrad waved acknowledgments from their 'Mechs and broke off to their assigned routes. I decided to play a little late twenty-fifth-century death metal over my 'Mech's internal speakers: "Small Laser of Doom," by the Blue Wömbats. Bringing my neon-pink *Panther* back to full power, I marched out on what would hopefully be the last long, boring day of a long, boring contract.

And that was exactly how it went for the first two hours. I was sitting in an enclosed deck, nibbling a sausage roll and sipping my fourth cup of coffee, when the radio chimed.

"Go for Ace!" I said, and my indelible partner Sevrin replied:

"Ace. We have a problem."

"Couldn't wait till we got off-world, could it?" I sighed and walked over to my kneeling *Panther*.

"Guthrie is reporting a lot of small aircraft blips on his radar. He thought they were birds, but there aren't any on this planet."

"Weird," I said. "He tried radioing them?"

"No response, but there are about a half dozen of these things, and we don't know what to do about them."

"Sevrin," Pip chimed in. "Can you take my drone toy up and do a visual flyby? Might tell us what is going on."

I was about to object, thinking about things like how long it would take to intercept the contacts and how close the drone could get to even identify the things, but Andy jumped ahead.

"On it, stand by!" Sevrin replied.

"Well, at least that's the only weird thing to happen," I said to myself.

It was that moment when things went straight to hell.

"CONTACT, CONTACT. I READ TWO BRAVO-MIKES BY LUCAS RANCH!" Conrad shouted loud enough to make my eardrums bleed.

"Calm down, Connie, I am powering up and moving toward you," I replied.

"Contact," Pip called out. "One Bravo Mike and an indeterminate number of snowcat technicals. At least one has a recoilless!"

"Crap, both patrols marked at once—" I said before a volley of missiles impacted around the feet of my parked BattleMech. "Make that all three. You are on your own, boys and girls. Draw away from the homesteads and make for McMurdo. Guthrie, get ready for guests!"

"Copy."

And with that, I turned to face my own problems.

"IT IS MY LAST DAY, YOU INSOLENT BASTARD!" I screamed as I chucked my coffee mug at the incoming, vaguely pod-shaped BattleMech.

The squat, armless form of a *Hornet* was running north along the town's outskirts, its missile pod still reloading. On its own, the thing couldn't pose much of a threat to my *Panther*. Clearly it was here to keep me pinned down, hoping I would cause as much damage to the settlement as it would. That was not my style.

I ran through the full startup sequence, ignoring the tinnitus from slamming my neurohelmet in place, and slammed the foot pedals of my controls down. The 35-ton monster beneath me leaped into the air on pillars of blue-white flame and landed clear of most of the town square. Far too many yokels ran out of buildings to get a gander at the real-life 'Mech battle going on.

"GET THE HELL INSIDE *NOW*!" I screamed through the external speakers as I lined up the PPC in my *Panther's* arm. The *Hornet* pilot kept running flat out, popping off poorly aimed laser bolts to try and disrupt my aim. I let fly with the PPC just as it stopped to turn around. That stop saved the pilot's life, as the beam went wide to disperse God only knew where.

I pushed the throttle forward and my 'Mech settled into a gentle walk, hoping to pressure the *Hornet* farther from the town's outskirts. That way, I could bring my missiles to bear and aim lower without risking the houses and buildings. The enemy pilot had other things in mind, however, and hit their own jump jets, landing firmly back in the town square.

With nothing for it, I lined the shot up again as the *Hornet's* small laser opened up on the local sheriff's office. The bolt of lightning connected our two 'Mechs briefly before the hole left from its impact saw boiling green liquid erupting from its jagged edges. Realizing the trouble it was in, the *Hornet* hit its jump jets again and arced skyward. Taking advantage of the clear line, I loosed a volley of short-range missiles, one of which clipped the 'Mech's leg. The cumulative damage wasn't enough to make the 'Mech stumble, though, and the *Hornet* ran flat-out westward toward McMurdo.

"Whiplts, report!"

"I took care of mine, everyone is cooked," Pip replied.

I winced, thinking of the results of a BattleMech flamer used on unarmored infantry.

"One *Cicada* toast, the other running toward McMurdo," Conrad called out.

"Same with my friend. Form up in the middle, setting waypoint Mike. Guthrie, get ready for guests."

"Copy," the Trell replied.

"Andy, any updates on those air contacts?"

"Taking off now! Should have a report in ten minutes."

"Copy that. Everyone be careful. Remember, we have civilian structures to watch out for." I turned to look at the sheriff's office that had been hit by the *Hornet*'s laser. Some deputy was waving a green flag and gave a thumbs-up. Good, no injuries. "Deputy, I presume you got things under control here? I got terrorists to hunt." Without waiting for a reply, I turned my *Panther* and moved off.

Several minutes of hard running later brought McMurdo up on the horizon. Guthrie's *UrbanMech* was maneuvering as best its stubby legs could carry it, popping autocannon bursts at the *Cicada* Conrad had reported. A smoking pile told me what happened to the *Hornet*.

"Keep 'em busy, Guthrie, we got you!" I called out.

Missiles, autocannon shells, and my own PPC lashed out at the 40-ton scout, shredding the 'Mech's left side. A second particle beam connected the left side of the *Cicada* and Guthrie's *Urbie*, causing the pod carrying its large autocannon to go limp.

"Guthrie, you still in this?"

"Negative, bastards bit me good. I am falling back to the mine."

"Copy that. Watch your back!" I said as the *UrbanMech* lit its jump jets and hopped over a windbreak to the mine on the other side. The *Cicada* took the hint and turned to the trio of us still in this fight.

"Keep the gunline up! We outnumber it!" Another volley of fire peppered the light sniper and jostled its return fire. Steam rose up from a PPC bolt hitting the snow and clouding the line of sight between us and it.

"Ace, we have a problem!" Sevrin called out. "Those aircraft are hobby drones, and they just—"

I never got to hear what Andy said the drones did. A series of explosions covered the horizon, sending thick black smoke into the sky and shaking the ground so much that Conrad's *Quickdraw* lost its footing and fell hard enough that both ankle actuators shattered. The *Cicada* also fell, more smoke pouring from its rear.

"Pippa, get to the mine! Make sure Guthrie and Andy are okay. Help search and rescue as much as you can!"

Pippa's teal-and-white *Hermes II* bolted off without a word as I checked on Conrad. The radio antenna that ran parallel to the *Quickdraw*'s shoulders was shredded, but he managed to give a thumbs-up through his opened canopy.

"McMurdo, McMurdo, do you copy?" I called out, relieved the fighting was at least over. "Large explosion in the vicinity of the mines. Can you send search and rescue?"

"Commander Darwin, we are already assembling for rescue and recovery. Any help you can provzzzzzzzzzzzzz..." The radio fuzzed out just as lasers lashed my *Panther*'s left side. Hitting the jump jets by instinct and turning my 'Mech to bring the PPC to bear, I saw

a BattleMech I had never seen before. The entire torso and head assembly looked like a giant bird's head mounted on reverse-canted legs. A double-barreled laser hung off a right-side stub wing, while a boxy antenna and a radome hung off the left. Tucked underneath those sensor pods was a missile pod of some type, though I could not get a count, given the thing was shooting at me.

"What the hell are you?" I wondered as I loosed a flight of my own missiles at the matte-black machine. The bird machine ran headlong at me and replied with its own missiles before banking hard to the left, away from my *Panther*'s PPC. Lasers flashed between my 'Mech's legs as I snapped the Lord's Light and more short-range missiles back at it. Haste caused the shots to go low, and wide enough that it scored against the 'Mech's back leg, but luck was with me as the back-canted knee locked up and sent the whole thing tumbling face first to the ground. The pilot must have tried to eject as it fell, because the cockpit glass blew out just as the top of the head hit the snow. The bluish smoke of smoldering electronics gently wafted from the avian 'Mech.

"And stay down!" I said to no one in particular, then headed off to help the rescue effort at the mine.

**MCMURDO FIELDS**
**SECOND TRY**
**2 SEPTEMBER 3047**

It was the long-delayed ending to a perfect day. Andrew Sevrin, God bless the crazy bastard, was in town rather than at our now thoroughly destroyed base of operations. A bent cigarette dangled from his mouth, and his beard was covered in soot-contaminated snow as he drove a light crane to haul off debris. About twenty black bags were lined up by the drive leading to the mining complex. One of those was Guthrie, the body bag draped in his yellow tartan blanket by Conrad. His *UrbanMech* was mangled by impact and concussion from the exploding volatiles.

His was the first death under my command. If I am honest, up to the events of today, I had only ever been responsible for one death in my life, and that was the previous owner of my *Panther*. Now that number had gone up to a higher degree than I felt comfortable thinking about.

Pippa Marcus walked up in a dun long coat, coffee mug in hand. "It turns out those hobby drones were loaded with pentaglycerine. Nearly a dozen of the things took a nosedive at points illuminated by those emergency flashlights that were mysteriously replaced a few days back."

A surprisingly low grunt of pain puffed out of her mouth as she sat on a crate next to me. "It turns out the IR beams were set to be always on while they were charging. It was like having a big sign saying, 'Shoot me, I am here.'" Her hands shook around a thermos. From the cold or the rage, I could not tell.

"First time you lost someone you worked with?" I asked, and she nodded. "Me too. I'm not sure what I am feeling, beyond everything all at once." I took a deep breath and stood from my perch, putting on the brave face a commanding officer was supposed to show his troops.

"Pip, it's all over for us but the crying. Get your 'Mech to our ride out of here. Andy and I will see to our salvage and Guthrie." She let out a deep exhale and dragged her feet back to the parked *Hermes II*, still laser-scarred from fighting and stained with smoke.

My *Panther*'s normally neon-pink paint was thoroughly covered in greasy black soot, on account of hauling girders and debris into various industrial haulers. Off on the horizon, a new lance of BattleMechs was marching to the mines. A signal pierced the wind and into my radio headset. "Commander Darwin, this is Major Fronhoeffer, Twentieth Avalon Hussars, Third Battalion. We are here to assist and relieve you!"

"Thank you, Major," I replied, making no effort to hide my fatigue. "The rest is all yours!"

A *Hunchback* was leading several gray, tan, and green medium and heavy 'Mechs with hand actuators, a horde of their combat engineers driving behind them. The ad hoc effort was now in more organized hands.

By the time Conrad's *Quickdraw* was loaded onto a flatbed, I was more than happy to get going. Sore, tired, and angry, I barely noticed when my personal noteputer chimed with a new message with the subject line: *Contract Dispute: Failure to Complete Mission.*

By then, I was too tired to care. I could resolve it on Galatea.

"Andy, tell the DropShip captain to prepare for dust-off. I have had enough of this planet," I said as I started marching to the DropPort.

**GREEN FAE STEAKHOUSE AND BORDELLO**
**HARDCORE**
**MAGISTRACY OF CANOPUS**
**20 APRIL 3049**

"So, despite that this was a small terrorist action that 'officially'—" Venom dripped freely from Sevrin's lips as he gave air quotes around the obvious lies. "—did not involve any 'Mechs or heavy vehicles, the MRB decided we were only entitled to a contract minimum. Barely paid for our expenses." Andy sipped his tequila.

"Even after our AAR was submitted, MIIO came in and redacted the holy hell out of it. Couldn't get any corroborating statements from the Twentieth, since they hadn't witnessed the fighting. So, a mining corporation attempting to swindle us essentially got the Federated Commonwealth seal of approval. It was like I was being headlocked by Hanse Davion himself." I finished resting a cigar on the tray. "All 'cause of that damned Death Commando *Raven*."

Everyone looked at me funny. Clearly, I had to explain.

"We were hauling Connie's *Quickdraw* onto a recovery vehicle when I saw a bunch of engineers surrounding the *Raven*. Except for the leg being blown off and a self-destruct charge in the cockpit misfiring and turning it into a barbecue instead of a bomb blast, it was reasonably intact. I'll be damned if that was not a skull on a green triangle painted on the side of it, though. By the time we were ready to haul it off as hard-earned salvage, an MIIO attaché was waving us off as politely as an implied threat could manage."

One of Andy's technical crew belted out in disbelief, "That *had* to have been the worst Death Commando in the galaxy." Which caused everyone to laugh.

Andy lit yet another cigarette. "But, when you think about it, terrorism against the very planet you are trying to liberate is counterproductive. You are crippling your own planet's economy to make a point. It was lashing out for the sake of lashing out instead of actually striking at the foreign presence."

Swampy looked agog. "Tactically, the method is kind of brilliant, when you think about it. Low intensity, minimal training, difficult to counteract."

"It's what I kept saying to the lawyer, and they said to the MRB. Someone out there either did not know or does not seem to care. We were screwed. On the official side of things, anyway. 'Mechs fight wars; they cannot pacify terrorists.'"

Sevrin continued the story. "Unofficially, we got a nice thank-you check from the AFFC. Turns out that *Raven* was packing some super-secret squirrel EW tech generations ahead of the junk they used in the Fourth Succession War. The AFFC paid us a handsome bounty for it. Almost as much as the contract and bonuses we could've earned had there been an invasion."

A bar wench rolled up with more drinks and rolls of smokables, and I gladly accepted a glass of amber liquor. "One more for the historians, I guess." I had been holding in some pithy remark about manmade climate change and the burning chemicals unleashed. But when I reached inside my jacket pocket for my wallet, the yellow tartan pocket over my left side held my tongue.

I tossed a credit chit on the barmaid's tray and downed the whisky cocktail in one go. "So, my next contract is on Irian. Does anyone want to extend and join me?"

# THEY WALK ALONE:
# MERCENARY FREELANCERS

### ERIC SALZMAN

"Freelancers. I seen 'em come and go—mostly dumbass punks raised on *Immortal Warrior* reruns, ready to take the Inner Sphere by storm all by themselves. Most times, they end up Dispossessed, broke, or dead. Sometimes all three. But the ones that make a go of it...they're some of the best damn mercs in the business. If you wanna be a legend instead of a kill marker on some other MechWarrior's cockpit, check out my book and take my advice. And when you make it big, look me up. I'll be wanting my cut."

—Syndicated MercTalk Interview with Kevan "Kronerhound" Ortman, author of *Profiting from the Suffering of Others: A Ten-Step Guide*, 14 September 3149

"What unit are you with?" is the question whenever mercs get together. Most will flash their colors and state their allegiance, but some will proudly proclaim they're independent, applying an assortment of labels to their status. Loners garrisoning isolated Periphery colonies once styled themselves "errants," while some ex-gladiators attempted to claim the title of "gunslinger" after the Blackout. (As if anyone believed they had graduated from the Star League Defense Force's dueling program.) Most, however, take the title coined back on pre-industrial Terra: "freelancer."

Every freelancer has their reasons for going it alone: personal mission from the Unfinished Book, lone survivor who can't face losing more friends, a record of screwups and dereliction that means no sane unit will take them, or an ego convinced lesser mortals would only hold them back. Regardless of motivation, the successful ones figure out how to get work and stay functional without a built-in support structure. Let me break down how that works for you.

## FINDING WORK

If you're a fresh-faced lieutenant in, say, Horlick's Haberdashers, you typically rely on unit specialists to run down contract leads and slog through the back and forth of contract negotiations while you tend to the fighting end of things. Freelancers don't have that luxury. Trying to negotiate your own deals can lock you into garbage contracts, and there are better options available.

### Contract Brokers

For a fee, independent brokers find assignments that match your capabilities and preferences, negotiate a contract, and only require you to sign the final paperwork. Do your homework, though. There are lots of brokers out there, and some of the shadier ones will rob you

blind. *Never* trust the Mercenary Review and Bonding Commission's in-house service; their negotiators' incentive package depends on how cheaply they can deliver you. Get the highest quality broker your rep and budget will cover, one that will match you with career-enhancing missions, not hang you out to dry on some backwater planet.

### Subcontracting

Sometimes a merc unit takes on a job that turns out too big, and they try to boost their numbers quickly by putting out a call for freelancer support. Depending on your rep and how dire the unit's need is, you can command a substantial premium on these short-term gigs. For example, after the rest of Team Venom was wiped out in 3044, Grady Kiefer got back on his feet by briefly subcontracting with Hansen's Roughriders.

### Bounty Hunting

Your other option is to take work on a "bounty" basis—doing missions on spec with the promise of a payout on completion. These bounties offer no support or contract negotiation—they just offer a reward for a result, whether it's securing a fugitive, killing a noble, or blowing an ammo dump. Most sanctioned bounties are posted at hiring halls and circulated on planetary newsnets. Unsanctioned bounties also exist and can pay well, though you need to develop an informant network with the right connections to get into that information stream (see Chapter Six, "Navigating the Underworld"). Since bounties aren't exclusive contracts, you'll likely have to deal with competing claimants in addition to whatever defenses the target's hiding behind. Just hope you don't run up against the infamous Bounty Hunter himself (or herself or themself, depending on who's wearing the armor this week), a proven master of such missions.

## TECH SUPPORT

Back in the Third Succession War, it was accepted that maintenance, parts, and repairs were rarely available, forcing even House Regulars to go into battle with barely functional equipment held together with duct tape and prayers. It's been over a century since the technological renaissance, however, so that doesn't fly with employers these days. Mercs need to fully repair damaged gear after combat actions and perform regular maintenance between missions. Big units will have technical crews for this, but freelancers need to find alternatives.

### Do-It-Yourself

Some try to fall back on pre-renaissance techniques, making patchwork repairs themselves. There's precedent: even Teddy Kurita was said to tune up his own ride when he ran the Legion of Vega. More often, though, such efforts result in ramshackle wrecks that are more modern art than military hardware. Unless you're a certified technical prodigy whose family owns a parts factory, attempting your own repairs is a shortcut to the scrapyard.

### Employer Provided

Many brokers build technical support into freelancer contracts, relying on employer-provided maintenance and repair services, as well as replacement parts. This can be convenient, but also can put you at their mercy if they jack up the prices or "lose" your parts, forcing you into debt through a "company store" scheme that delays compensation and encourages in-house supply purchases on credit until you owe so much interest you'll be paying for the privilege of running your own 'Mech. Avoid at all costs!

### Third Party Service

Your best bet is to outsource maintenance to independent "speed shops" that have the technical know-how and equipment to properly service your gear. Though such places were rare back in the Succession Wars, there are now many competing chains, such as Mech-it-Lube, C-Fix (pricey, but capable of servicing ClanTech), Jake's Discount Equipment Warehouse, and Triple-S (Synguard Support Services), all of which have outlets at mercenary hiring hubs. Competition keeps the rates low and quality high, and several run customer loyalty programs.

## FINAL WORD

Have no illusions: freelancing can be risky. Nobody's there to watch your back. On the other hand, come payday, you get to keep all the money. The choice is yours, MechWarrior.

# PICKING THE BONES

### ALAN BRUNDAGE

**REPUBLIC CAMP**
**RUINS OF NEO-TOKYO**
**SHOKAKU**
**YORII**
**RASALHAGUE DOMINION**
**12 APRIL 3151**

The ocean washed up what had once been a central boulevard, the clear, slightly irradiated water steadily eroding the foundations of the long-abandoned high-rises. Nature was reclaiming the area, and one day the buildings would topple, vanishing beneath the waves as if they had never existed. The works of humanity, even those of the first Star League, were fragile and ephemeral by comparison.

The crunch of footsetps on gravel drew Major Rikisha Tamarack out of her melancholy reflections about fleeing the fall of the Republic, returning her to grim and broken reality.

"There's another group of droppers touching down outside the city limits, Major," said Soo Lien, the only other high-ranking officer in the collection of soldiers Rikisha was optimistically calling a combat command. "Not sure who they are yet, but I doubt they're allies. So that's two we know of."

Rikisha threw a stone, watching it plunk into the waves. "As long as it isn't the Ghost Bears, we should be okay. How's morale?"

Barking laughter escaped from Soo Lien. "Shot all to hell. And then stomped on, spit on, and buried in a latrine hole. Blake's Blood, sir, we lost *Terra*. We lost the Republic. We *ran*!"

Rikisha's hands balled into fists, and she thumped them into her legs just for something to do with the anger. "I know. But what were our other options? Stay and die? Surrender and join the malfing Wolves? Retire and spend the rest of our lives under a Clan? There were no good options, Soo."

"Sir, we know that, but we need to know what's next. We've been on the run, but now we have a tiny amount of breathing room. That's good, but it's also giving people a chance to think. That means time to dwell. We need orders, a direction. Purpose."

There it was again, reflection. What was your purpose when everything you'd stood for was gone? The Republic of the Sphere had been a grand and noble dream, but that dream was dead, throttled by the ruthless ambitions and machinations of Kerensky's misbegotten children.

"Let's start with survival. After that? We'll just have to try to figure it out."

They walked back to the mostly intact stadium serving as their temporary base. Her highly skilled and expert pilots had gingerly maneuvered the DropShip under the still-intact half of the dome using a combination of hovering and lateral thrust. They'd set fire to the wild vegetation of the field, but that actually served to provide a clearing for the camp. The dome provided some shelter from detection, serving to hide the DropShip and its precious and secret cargo. The only ace they held. And wasn't that a sad state of affairs?

Inside, a makeshift camp surrounded the heavily modified *Overlord*-class DropShip *Aurelius*. The 'Mechs and vehicles that had been crammed in the DropShip were now parked around it in a loose formation, grouped by their original units. Her warriors lounged, tinkered, and performed calisthenics and maintenance that had been impossible in the cramped travel conditions; she allowed them the freedom to do whatever necessary to get through these trying times.

"Any progress on how we were tracked down?"

Lien shrugged. "No, sir. Best guess is one of the deserters."

*Deserters*. The word hung between them. It rankled Rikisha, for how did one desert something that was already dead? More, how did one abandon their companions in such trying times? A handful of her warriors had done just that in the hours after landing here. It had been their first opportunity to do so, given this was their first landfall.

"Doesn't matter. We need to be prepared to fight our way out."

"And then what?"

Rikisha sighed. "I'll have to think of something."

**UNION-CLASS DROPSHIP *ROSENCRANTZ*
GREY HEART IRREGULARS LANDING ZONE**

The sun gleamed off panes of shattered glass in the ferrocrete maze of the city. Colonel Keir Amberson, commander of the Grey Heart Irregulars, marched his ancient and much-loved *Warhammer* forward. If family legend was to be believed, this 'Mech had been taken from the Star League Army during the first phases of the Periphery Uprising in the Taurian Concordat, but it had been rebuilt so many times over the years no one could prove it. Still, he loved the old workhorse.

Looking out over the crumbling city, Keir could only marvel at the magnificent decay. It brought home the inherent rot of the core worlds, the source of so much of the misery visited on his beloved Taurian people. The generational trauma of those decisions plagued his people to this day. For those reasons, he felt some glee at the ruin of the city.

He was still human enough to feel guilty about that.

For now, the hunt continued. After months of chasing them, he knew his quarry was nearby. He'd managed to chase off their JumpShip and force their DropShip to ground after the jumper blew a seal. Delays in launching his own DropShip meant they had only a rough idea of where the former Reps had gone. Their vector had led here, to this crumbling city. It truly was an excellent place to hide. Recon sweeps hadn't located them yet, but it was only a matter of time. After all, they had nowhere to go.

Behind him, the rest of his short 'Mech company fanned out, storied models that had been available for generations: a *Shadow Hawk*, a *Thunderbolt*, two *Locust*s, two *Stinger*s, and his pride and joy, a pair of *Toro*s. They were good, solid Taurian 'Mechs a long way from home, but then, so were their MechWarriors.

He toggled on the company frequency. "You've all got your search vectors for today. If you find the Reps, send up a flare. No playing hero. They're desperate, and have one hell of an ace in the hole."

"Roger that, boss," said Nicolletta, one of his *Toro* pilots, followed by a flurry of acknowledgments from the rest of the company.

Keir cruised forward at a leisurely pace, making for the warehouse district. The booming thumps of his advance scared off a swarm of tiger raptors, the striped reptiles that infested the ruins.

Concealed high in the debris-choked remnants of an apartment complex was a small team of specialists from the Third Fides Defenders.

Section Leader Darrian, designated Cobra, watched with interest as the mercenaries spread out for a third day of searching. Their antiquated gear was easily spoofed by the Fides' equipment, allowing them free rein to observe.

He pulled out his radio pack and ensured the scrambler was on. "Cobra for Defiant. The vultures have left the nest. Expected search pattern should leave you in the clear. Out."

A muffled growl came from beside him, and he turned to look at Specialist Tatiana. "What is it?"

"We could take their dropper right now. Why won't the major let us?"

"She's keeping our options open."

"She's indecisive!" Tatiana snapped.

Privately Darrian agreed, but he was realist enough to know that was a product of his training. "She has to weigh all the options. Now, focus on your duty."

The heated nylon scent of the field tent crept deep into Rikisha's nasal passages, making its presence known at the back of her throat. It was almost enough to make her leave, almost. She needed a plan to present to her unit before they realized she no longer had any authority—and she didn't have one. The Republic they'd fought for was gone. The Wolves had never been an option, especially after conquering Terra. She could appeal to the Rasalhague Dominion, but with half of the Dominion being Ghost Bears, they might sell her out to the Wolves. The Capellans and Combine hated her people. The Davions might be an option: their desperate wars with both the Combine and Confederation meant they were always hungry for troops.

There was one more alternative, and that was to go mercenary. She mulled it over, turning the idea around in her head. In the Inner Sphere, the armies of fallen nations often went mercenary. The Rim Worlds Republic had done so. The original Star League Defense Force had as well. Even some fallen Clans had followed that path. It was something of a tradition.

And there was always comfort in tradition.

"Enemy in the field!" Grey Six, Lieutenant Aaron Baxter, shouted over the common frequency.

The transmission energized Keir, despite also startling him. He slapped his transmission button. "This is Grey actual, confirm!" While waiting, he called up Aaron's search grid and began angling that way.

"Confirmed, boss! I'm taking fire from a *Shen Yi* and a squad of Fa Shih. Pretty sure I saw a Zahn dodge around the corner too. I don't recognize the paint, but they're definitely not the Reps. I could really use some backup."

The grid came up. Aaron was a good distance away. "We're en route. Can you hold?"

"Not sure, boss." A reverberating *bang* sounded through the channel, like something had slammed into the cockpit. "I'll do my best, just get here fast."

"We're on it."

The next several minutes were tense. They could hear Aaron's losing battle. Support was too far away, but he ordered his *Locust*s to close at maximum speed anyway.

The sudden silence spoke volumes. Aaron was down; the only question that remained was how badly.

Long, desperate minutes passed as he pushed his *Warhammer* up to its maximum speed. As he approached, he could see the *Locust*s of Sherman and Hess standing guard. The area was cratered with the stray shots of a running firefight. The entire frontage of the nearby warehouse had collapsed, its glass and ferrocrete strewn chaotically everywhere.

Bits of shattered armor formed a trail to the downed *Shadow Hawk* Aaron had piloted. The damage the 'Mech had suffered was catastrophic: the upper torso and head were completely missing, probably as the result of a chain reaction of ammo explosions.

"Any sign he managed to eject?" he inquired of the *Locust* pilots. He didn't expect a positive answer, but the question had to be asked.

"No, sir, not unless whoever he was fighting managed to snag him before they hightailed it out of here," replied Hess, his premier light-'Mech jockey.

That thought put an unexpectedly worrisome spin on things. "Whoever they are, we need to find them. They put down one of our own. That marks them as competition that needs to be eliminated. I want you two scouting the area again, but focus on finding our attackers. We need to confirm Aaron's death, and I won't let these mystery mercs get away with it. Understood?"

"Yes, sir," said Sherman.

"You know it," Hess acknowledged.

As the *Locust*s angled away on their new tasks, Keir grimly marked the location of the wreckage. At some point, he'd get a salvage crew out here, but that was a minor concern for when he was no longer facing two hostile forces.

Captain Augustin Zhou, commander of the Bronze Blades, found himself offended by this world. It was ruinous, it was too bright, and it stank. He couldn't say exactly what it was, but the odor in question climbed up his nose and stabbed the back of his eyeballs. The sooner he could leave, the better, but that first required him to locate his quarry, and now there was an unanticipated complication.

The members of his command lance were gathered around him at the field table with its miniature holo-display. The feed from the augmented scout team was being fed to his terminal via a relay from Verity's *Cyclops*. On it was a looping recording of the surprise arrival of the *Shadow Hawk*.

"Thoughts?" Augustin asked as he gazed at those around him.

Dmitri Turlov was, predictably, the first to reply. He was given to quick responses and little thought. "Mercenaries," he spat.

Augustin allowed the dismay to show on his face. "It may be a polite fiction devised by the Maskirovka to fool the rest of the Inner Sphere, but *we* are mercenaries, deniable assets, and given this one last chance to serve, or had you forgotten?" He stared coldly at his subordinate.

Turlov visibly paled. "No, sir."

Augustin allowed himself a sharp, satisfied nod. "Now then, does anyone have any cogent thoughts?"

"My guess is that word has spread of what the Reps carry, so most likely these other mercenaries are in search of the same prize. Is there any chance our employer hedged their bets by hiring additional forces to secure the asset?" Nadya, on the other hand, was precise with her words.

"It is possible, but I was told we were the only ones dispatched. These other mercenaries could have been hired by another interested party with sources close to Terra, acting on the same or similar intelligence."

"Is it possible we could we cut a deal with them?" asked Morai.

"Before our encounter perhaps, but now that we've drawn blood, I find it unlikely."

Nadya offered her blunt assessment. "Then we must destroy them all."

A heavy silence fell.

"Is it even feasible to do so?" asked Morai. "Have we the strength?"

"We know we can take the Republic force, unless they field the asset against us. The other mercenaries, now..." Augustin paused in thought. "I am unsure. It depends on their available resources, but let us not forget they're already down a 'Mech."

Dmitri grinned. "Then it's a race,"

"It is," Augustin agreed. "To that end, we need a sense of this city. Send out all VTOLs. Have them locate any structure large enough to conceal the asset. We'll investigate them one by one. If they happen to locate our rival mercenaries, so much the better; we'll shift focus to eliminate them. No one will take the prize but us."

A night that had started out rough and uncomfortable had only gotten worse. While attempting to sleep, Soo Lien had come to find her. Her expression had been grim, her face pale. She hadn't said anything, just gestured for Rikisha to follow her. Together, they had gone to the tent of Sebastian Metz. That had been twenty minutes ago.

Viewing the scene, Rikisha fought the urge to vomit. It wasn't that she hadn't seen blood before; it was the sense of hopelessness and quiet despair that pervaded the tent.

She didn't know much about Sebastian, much to her dismay. She knew most of his family had been killed when the Jade Falcons conquered Ryde. Arriving on Terra as a refugee just before the Wall went up, Sebastian had finished his education on Terra before joining the RAF. He had trained for the chance to take the fight back to the Falcons and save the Republic. Instead, he had been forced to watch as the Republic was devoured. He had seen the Jade Falcons land on Terra, his new home, and been unable to defend it, too. Then came the order to run. Like most of those in the camp, she knew he had been facing his demons as best as he could.

Unfortunately, his demons had won, the result being a tent drenched in blood, and a single sad and lonely corpse on the ground.

"Coward," Soo Lien whispered.

Rikisha's head snapped around in shock, unsure of what she'd heard.

Soo Lien's expression hardened, and her voice became firm. "He was a coward. Did he think the rest of us didn't understand? That he was the only one left untethered? Bastard looked around, knew what we were facing, and still took the easy way out. To hell with him."

Rikisha took a deep breath, facing grim reality. "I disagree, but that's beside the point. This leaves us short a MechWarrior. Who have we got among the techs that might be a serviceable replacement?"

Soo Lien's sneer faded as her brain shifted to focus on the problem at hand. "Chloe Dirge might be a good fit. She's logged plenty of time in lights and mediums during maintenance, so her piloting is acceptable, but her gunnery is the problem. She can't hit the broad side of an *Overlord.*"

Rikisha frowned. "All right, we'll move Oyelowo into Sebastian's *Griffin* and put Chloe into the *Roadrunner.* In the worst case, we can use her to scout and harry. In the meantime, get her started on some training simulations. We need to get her up to speed yesterday."

"And what do we do about this?" Soo Lien gestured at the corpse.

"He was a soldier of the Republic. We'll bury him with the respect he deserves."

**DOWNTOWN**
**RUINS OF NEO-TOKYO**
**SHOKAKU**
**YORII**
**RASALHAGUE DOMINION**
**13 APRIL 3151**

*It's too quiet*, Keir thought as he maneuvered his *Warhammer* with care through the shattered neighborhood.

This area of the city had suffered more than most. At some point since the Jihad an earthquake had rocked the area. Great rents had been torn in the ground, exposing subterranean levels that had been further expanded by the sea. Many buildings had collapsed, while several more were on the verge. It was through this apocalyptic obstacle course a lance of Grey Heart Irregular 'Mechs travelled, still in search of the Republic landing site.

He had just finished crossing an overgrown park when the target lock alert chimed and missiles began raining down around him. Fortunately, a *Warhammer* was a sturdy machine.

"All units, heads up! They're coming in hot!"

Keir rounded the collapsed remains of a residential tower and was confronted by the opposing force. It was the other mercenary force with their distinctive bronze paint scheme. His sensors fed him the daunting information as he threw his *Warhammer* into reverse, giving himself space for battle.

"It's an augmented lance again! Watch for battle armor and try not to trip over their vehicles!"

He spied a *Calliope*, a medium machine originally built for the Magistracy of Canopus, but instead split his focus between the more immediate dangers of a hard-to-hit *Shen Yi* and a *Victor*. Whoever these mercenaries were, they favored Capellan gear and tactics, but he didn't recognize their paint scheme. Not surprising in these communication-hindered times. New units cropped up by the dozen and disappeared just as fast. Most before they made any kind of impact.

Another heavy, a *Catapult* this time, joined the fray. All told, his lance with its *Thunderbolt* and two *Stinger*s was grossly outclassed. That meant there was no option but to cut and run.

"Irregulars, withdraw. I'll provide covering fire."

His two *Stinger* pilots paused in their headlong rush forward and grudgingly began falling back.

Andrea Tor shouldered her *Thunderbolt* in beside him as she spoke, raking the enemy position with an impressive amount of fire from her large laser and long-range missiles. "Sir, given the two missile boats they're using, I strongly advise you to leave. I'll cover the withdrawal."

Keir snapped off a shot with his PPCs, managing to hit the *Catapult* with one while the other went wide to inflict further destruction to a derelict building. "That's not how this works, Lieutenant. We're all getting out of here."

Andrea's sigh was purposefully and theatrically audible. "That's damn stubborn of you, sir."

"I know."

Together they moved up, bathing the *Victor* in their combined fire. The constant barrage from one side or the other denied the enemy MechWarrior any chance to react. That was the plan, at least.

The MechWarrior in the *Victor* was good, damn good. They let the assault 'Mech absorb the damage before snapping off a shot with their Gauss rifle. The streamlined metallic round flew too fast for the eye to see, threading the gap in between Keir's *Warhammer* and Andrea's *Thunderbolt* to punch through the weak rear armor of one of the retreating *Stinger*s. Severing vital connections, the Gauss round continued its journey, blasting out through the front armor and continuing on to be lost in the field of ruined buildings. Gutted and inoperable, the *Stinger* collapsed to the ground.

Keir checked which *Stinger* had fallen, then called the pilot of the remaining one. "Lillian, I need you to rescue Kaur. Andrea and I will cover. Once you've got him, you run like hell. Got it?"

"Absolutely, sir, pick up and run."

Keir switched over to Andrea. "We're going to buy Lillian a few minutes, then withdraw. We're not in a good position to win against them right now."

"No problem, sir."

The two Irregular 'Mechs spaced themselves out to maximize their firing zones and waited for the enemy's next move. It didn't take long.

Long-range fire poured in from the *Victor* and *Catapult*. The *Shen Yi* and *Calliope* closed in order to use their closer-ranged weapons. More annoying were the infantry-crewed support PPCs fired from positions inside the abandoned buildings. The damage was light, but constant, like being nibbled at by flies.

"If things keep up like this, we're going to have to demand a hazard bonus," Andrea quipped.

A hail of medium-range missiles fell around the two Irregulars, the *Shen Yi* announcing its presence in style. Keir watched as his spotlight and one of the machine guns went dark on his damage display. They were minor losses he could live with. His armor loss was of more concern.

"I've got him! Withdrawing now!" Lillian called out.

"Excellent work," Keir replied. "We'll see you back at the ship."

A moment passed before Andrea asked, "How are we going to do that, sir? Everything they've got can pace us, and that *Calliope* is faster."

"I'm working on it," he snapped.

"Lucky for you, I've got an actual idea."

"That is lucky. Will we both walk away?"

"Well..."

"Right, okay."

Andrea kept her *Thunderbolt* reversing, snapping off the occasional shot to discourage the bronze-painted enemy 'Mechs. Before long, they were near one of the most precariously perched of the collapsed buildings.

"You're not..." Keir began in sudden realization.

"I am," she returned. He could hear the manic glee in her voice.

She triggered an alpha strike, risking the heat curve to facilitate their escape. The missiles and energy beams wracked the side of a crumbling structure that was just barely supporting a half-collapsed tower. Once Keir saw what she was shooting at, he added his fire to hers.

With a groan more felt than heard, the tower finished succumbing to gravity, the debris of its final collapse filling the street as a veritable wall. A cloud of dust billowed out, obscuring virtually everything from view.

Ferrocrete bounced off the hull of his *Warhammer* as he turned to Andrea. "You're crazy, you know."

"You say the nicest things. Besides, it's the only way I'd take the job, sir."

**REPUBLIC CAMP**
**RUINS OF NEO-TOKYO**
**SHOKAKU**
**YORII**
**RASALHAGUE DOMINION**
**15 APRIL 3151**

A virtual insect swarm of techs worked against the clock to complete the decidedly nonstandard add-ons Rikisha had requested be made to their cargo. She held on to the slim hope they'd be able to achieve her goal and grant her an actual advantage for a change.

The sound of crunching gravel alerted her to someone's approach. She turned and spied Soo Lien. It took her a moment to realize what seemed different. The other woman no longer looked ground down, instead looking optimistic for the first time in weeks.

"You look like you have good news," she said by way of greeting.

"You could say that. Our field teams are reporting the mercenaries are fighting each other. This could level the playing field in our favor."

"Indeed it could. What have we learned about them?"

"The first group, the ones who chased us here, are called the Grey Heart Irregulars. Most of their people are from the Taurian Concordat or Calderon Protectorate. So is their gear. They have plenty of older, serviceable designs, all rugged and simple. No word on their employer yet.

"The other group are called the Bronze Blades. They're more of an enigma. Gear, force structure, tactics, all point toward Capellan regulars, or former regulars. We can't pick out their employers yet either, but I'll give you two guesses and the first doesn't count. For what it's worth, I'd say they're deniable assets for whatever shady shit the Capellans want to try on any given day."

Nodding thoughtfully, Rikisha turned, staring in the general direction of the city center as options began to form in her mind. The defensive play wasn't going to work anymore. It was time to go on the offensive.

And she knew just how to start.

"Wait, say that again?" Tatiana said with undisguised surprise in her voice.

Resting uncomfortably with his back against a pillar, Darrian gritted his teeth in an effort to calm himself. Tatiana continued to grate on his nerves. She was as stubborn as every other member of the Fides, but that didn't mean he appreciated it. "Orders came in from the major. We're to redeploy and attempt to locate the staging location of the other mercs."

"Bah. More cloak and dagger. More hiding. Give me something to shoot."

"That might just be the goal."

"Oh?"

Darrian warmed to the subject as he was talking. "Yeah. These new mercenaries are a bigger unit, with newer tech. They'd spot anything the major and her 'Mechs could do, but we might be able to slip in and cause some damage that gives her an advantage."

A feral grin creased her face. "So, a sneak and break? Works for me."

## BRONZE BLADE LANDING ZONE
## RUINS OF NEO-TOKYO
## SHOKAKU
## YORII
## RASALHAGUE DOMINION
## 16 APRIL 3151

Finding the Bronze Blades landing field had proven to be easy. They'd grounded their DropShip, an *Overlord*, at the remains of the DropPort, using the most intact landing pad. It made sense. The Blades weren't the ones trying to hide. They were the ones on the hunt.

But now the Fides were on the hunt as well.

Darrian and his squad rushed forward. This was the type of mission they were meant for, a desperate gamble of an attack that would save the rest of the unit.

His squad was small, only five individuals, but they were equipped with heavily modified stealth Kage power armor. If anyone could accomplish this, it was them.

Everything seemed quiet as they approached the DropShip. This was either exceptionally good luck or exceptionally poor luck.

Turned out it was the second.

Fa Shih and Amazon power armor popped out of nowhere as the Fides approached, crossing the invisible threshold of making an easy escape. Darrian cursed. Of course, the totally not Capellans would be equipped to counter stealth armor. It was one of their specialties.

"We've been made! Scatter!"

As the Kage-equipped troops began to break for cover, a *Calliope* emerged from the lee of a building. That was when Darrian knew they was doomed. Knowing the end was near, he bounded in to do what damage he could, darting straight at the *Calliope*, firing his Gauss rifle as quickly as it would cycle.

The light 'Mech turned to face him, and the last thing he saw was the glow of the plasma rifle firing.

## NEAR REPUBLIC CAMP

The endgame had come. The Bronze Blades had found them. To buy what time she could, Rikisha had ordered everything she had into the field in a desperate attempt to fend off capture, defeat, or death. Her soldiers strode forward, knowing the stakes were the highest they'd been since the escape from Terra.

Above the overgrown maze of what had once been a park, opposing VTOLs clashed. The lightweight Gossamers of the former Republic soldiers and the Yashas of the Bronze Blades ripped into each other without mercy.

Cobalt PPC bolts speared out into the aptly named Gossamers, shredding the virtually nonexistent armor of the light machines so fast they almost didn't have time to explode. Their shattered wreckage rained down to be lost in the wild foliage below.

The pilots of the Gossamers refused to give up, intent on clearing the skies for their ground-based companions, though it might cost them their own lives.

Pairing up, the Gossamers darted in, spewing a flurry of green daggers from their medium pulse lasers. The spirited attack took down several Bronze Blade Yashas, but not enough to give an edge to the Republic. Despite their efforts, the last Gossamer exploded while attempting to ram a final Yasha from the sky.

Rikisha watched from the tangle below, the cockpit of her *Lament* isolating her from the sounds of the aerial battle, but failing to protect her from the radio. She listened to the aborted screams and shouts of her pilots, each one another mark of failure. She squeezed her eyes shut and pushed her emotions aside for later. Now she had to figure out how to extricate everyone from this debacle.

"Major, scout teams are reporting enemy 'Mechs on approach." Soo Lien's voice was low and devoid of emotion.

"How many?"

"At least two lances, with probable vehicle support. They'll be here before we can prepare."

Resolve hardening, Rikisha sat up, straightening her back. "Then we fight. Soo Lien and Oyelowo, position your *Griffin*s on my flanks. Chloe, hang back, but be prepared to harass the enemy when you see a chance. The goal is to get away, so if a gap opens up we can use, take it. There're too many dead already. Move!"

They had barely taken up position when the Bronze Blades approached. Two *Raven*s, a *Yinghuachong*, and a *Men Shen* made up the vanguard. Lumbering some distance behind was a lance of heavies and assaults: a *Cyclops*, *Catapult*, *Shen Yi*, and *Devastator*. Farther behind was a second lance of heavies.

Quite simply, it looked grim.

The missile boats fired first, lock on alarms screaming for her attention. Weathering the battering explosions as best she could, Rikisha breathed out and ordered, "Concentrate fire on the *Catapult!*"

One PPC lashed out from each of her paired *Griffin*s, while she triggered her own pair of heavy PPCs, aiming by eye thanks to the enemy's ECM. The powerful energies scoured the *Catapult*, the impacts crackling across armor it didn't melt, but not enough to put the machine down. Instead, it sagged drunkenly with probable gyro damage, one missile pod almost seeming to droop. She'd call that a win.

Less of a win was the withering barrage of return fire. A Gauss round slammed into her torso with a resounding *gong* that shuddered through her spine and lit up amber all across her damage schematic. Missiles erupted around her in near misses, but by far the most damage was done to her lancemates.

Oyelowo's light-'Mech thinking led to his *Griffin* managing to leap out of the most devastating fire, by luck more than anything else. The *Griffin* took too many shots to its elbow actuator, and the arm dropped away, taking the PPC in the process, hampering its effectiveness.

Soo Lien was considerably less lucky. Enemy missiles broke through the armor still damaged from the retreat from Terra. Her ammo reserves detonated, blowing the *Griffin* apart in a sphere of golden fire. An argent pulse of plasma blew out of the front of the wreckage, a sure sign the fusion reactor had been breached, releasing the superheated plasma within. Chunks of the 'Mech rained down for several seconds afterward. She was gone without even a scream to mark her passage.

Rage boiled up. Rikisha pushed forward. "Chloe, withdraw and stay out of range. I only want you approaching if you see a sure kill. Oyelowo, you're with me, we're going to inflict as much damage as possible. Can you manage?"

"We succeed or die in harness, Major," Oyelowo responded in a deceptively mild tone.

"Then choose your target, and good luck."

Rikisha pushed her *Lament* to top speed and angled off toward the bulk of the *Devastator*, while Oyelowo took his damaged *Griffin* against the heavily damaged *Catapult*.

The two battered 'Mechs exchanged fire, missile contrails passing by each other to rain down on their respective targets. Oyelowo did an admirable job of dodging, but enough got through to further damage his armor. The *Catapult* lost its balance and crashed to the ground as Oyelowo's missiles succeeded in finishing off the drooping missile pod. The angle of the fall snapped the 'Mech's left knee off, meaning the *Catapult* was effectively out of the fight for the moment. Next, Oyelowo bounded after the *Yinghuochong*, a typically bold decision.

At that point, Rikisha could no longer pay attention; she had her own fight to worry about. The *Devastator*, though distant, loomed large on her screen. It was a 'Mech of the same design school as her *Lament*, but even more powerful. Her advantage lay in speed, by comparison at least, and initiative.

Rather than wait, Rikisha fired her PPCs and began a zigzag closing pattern. The azure bolts struck true, but the assault machine shrugged them off, seeming to lose little more than paint.

The return fire from the *Devastator* lived up to its name. It fired its own PPCs, the energy crackling through the air like lightning, pairing it with a double shot from its Gauss rifles. One PPC missed, but the other scored the center of her *Lament*'s chest. Both Gauss rounds impacted, throwing her stride off-balance. One destroyed her left medium laser while the other shattered armor on her left arm and lodged in her elbow actuator, limiting the mobility and targeting on that side. She'd have to be more thoughtful when using it.

Lining up her own shot, Rikisha had her aim thrown off as the *Devastator* immediately followed its first barrage with another. Her teeth slammed together from the impact, and she tasted blood, but managed to keep her 'Mech on its feet despite its loss of armor. She fired again, close enough now to use the two medium lasers left to her. Both green beams connected, but did no visible damage.

The *Devastator* fired its Gauss rifles again. Again, the pilot demonstrated their skill as both shots hit true. This time she couldn't keep her feet under her, and the *Lament* crashed to the ground. She was a sitting duck.

A signal came in from the *Devastator*. "Republic warrior, this is Captain Augustin Zhou of the Bronze Blades. Based on the markings on your 'Mech, I suspect you are the leader of your forces. I demand your surrender. Do so, and I will deliver the members of your unit to a world of your choosing, less your equipment. Deny me, and I will have my prize regardless, but you will be dead. I require your answer immediately."

Rikisha snarled. There was no way she was going to surrender to these not-so-secret Capellans. She reached out to transmit her reply, but didn't get the chance. Paired PPCs slammed into the *Devastator*, slagging armor along its left side.

The *Devastator* torso twisted to face its attacker as a new voice came in over the channel. "Not to be all schoolyard, but I was here first."

A *Warhammer* entered her field of vision, flanked by a *Thunderbolt* and a *Toro*. It was an impressive team-up, one that might be suited to taking down the *Devastator*.

"You would be my competition," Zhou stated.

"That would be correct. Colonel Amberson, at your service. I'm going to give you one chance to withdraw, out of the goodness of my heart."

"I'm disinclined to agree to your request," Zhou replied. "I have superior forces, Colonel. It is you who will withdraw."

"I see. So that's a no? But I have stubbornness on my side," Amberson retorted.

Taking advantage of the distracted Bronze Blades leader, Rikisha levered her *Lament* back to its feet. The mercenaries were discussing the future of her soldiers, so there was no way she was going to sit it out.

On the plus side, listening to the mercenaries bicker gave Rikisha time to think. The Bronze Blades had clearly slain some of the Irregulars, in addition to members of her unit. *The enemy of my enemy*, she thought. With that, she knew what she had to do, and there was only one bargaining chip. She just needed things to hit the right tipping point, which came with a signal from the base camp.

She activated her comm. "This is Major Tamarack for Colonel Amberson. It appears we've both suffered at the hands of the Bronze Blades. I propose an alliance. Assist me in driving them off, and we can come to an arrangement over what you've all been seeking."

Seconds ticked by and silence was her only answer. At last, a reply came. "Agreed, Major. We'll fine tune things later. Pull back and use your forces to take that second incoming lance. I'll focus my troops here."

Seeing the wisdom of the request, Rikisha began retreating several hundred meters. "All Republic forces, rendezvous at Nav Point Kappa. *Aurelius*, reposition to Beta. Good luck."

"All forces" sounded more impressive than it was: her *Lament*, Chloe's *Roadrunner*, Oyelowo's *Griffin*, which had picked up a stray girder from somewhere to use as a club, and a trio of JES III missile carriers. The Morningstar Mobile HQ was remaining behind in the stadium for obvious reasons.

A dull rumble shook the ground. A humorless grin creased Rikisha's face as she watched as the *Aurelius* launch in a plume of smoke, bound for a secondary site far enough away from what was about to happen here. It would preserve the crew and the valuable information they carried.

The wall of the stadium shattered outward in a shower of dust and debris. Ponderously emerging from the cloud was the lodestone she'd been carrying since the flight from Terra. It emerged like a demon of legend, all 135-tons of the *Ares* colossal-class superheavy 'Mech. It stomped forward awkwardly, its tripod design granting it a unique gait. Its bulbous upper torso bristled with enough weapons to equip a lance of heavy 'Mechs, and of course, the special modifications her techs had been hurriedly adding.

She had never supported the superheavy concept of an intimidating mobile fortress, preferring mobility, but the *Ares* was an asset to be used, and she would use whatever was available to save her people.

The presence of the *Ares* proved a magnet. The Bronze Blades scout lance raced in, blinded by their prize and heedless of the firepower they were about to face.

"Lance, fall back toward the *Ares*. Jessies, fire a few rounds for effect to discourage them."

The JES IIIs, medium-weight vehicles equipped with a quartet of LRM 15s, responded by firing two racks each, sending a total of ninety missiles at the approaching Bronze Blades. The missiles scattered, spreading out their damage, but it was enough to put down one of the *Raven*s and batter the rest of the lance.

Rikisha stalked forward, targeting the *Men Shen*, the heaviest of the approaching 'Mechs. It was an ungainly, strangely articulated machine, with a broad, forward thrust head that made for a perfect target, so that was where she targeted her PPCs. The heavy energy bolts crashed into the cockpit and upper body, melting armor and shorting out systems. The 'Mech wobbled and crashed to the ground, the pilot overwhelmed. They struggled to rise, but Chloe raced in beside Oyelowo. Her medium lasers melted furrows into the armor and Oyelowo's LRMs peppered its body. Oyelowo then leaped in on his jump jets and swung his improvised girder weapon down to shatter the *Men Shen*'s left leg. The pilot wisely opted to shut their 'Mech down after that.

With two of their number down, one of which was their strongest 'Mech, the remaining *Raven* and *Yinghouchong* turned tail and ran. Rikisha let them. There were bigger problems to deal with now.

Dueling was not something Keir usually found all that wise, but that was exactly what he found himself doing with Zhou's *Devastator*. If only it hadn't been with the larger cousin of his 'Mech. Trading shot for shot with an assault 'Mech wasn't a wise idea, as his damage display could attest. But there was no chance he'd stand down.

While he was doing that, Andrea and Nicolletta had combined their efforts and taken down the *Shen Yi*. That left them with just the *Cyclops* and *Devastator* to contend with until the third Bronze Blades lance arrived, though his own second lance was harrying it in hopes of delaying its arrival.

The two assault machines were attempting, in their ponderous way, to skirt around his lance and get closer to the *Ares*. He was tempted to let them, but instead, he fired on the *Devastator* again.

"Enough of this," Tamarack transmitted. "Withdraw your forces now, Captain Zhao, or I destroy your prize. The choice is yours."

To his credit, Zhao knew how to multitask. He fired both PPCs at Keir, while responding to Major Tamarack. "You're bluffing, Major. That monstrosity behind you is an engineering marvel, and the only bargaining chip you have. You won't destroy it, certainly not while it's crewed."

"Try me."

Keir was impressed by the fact her conviction survived being transmitted through the comm distortion. He certainly believed her. He wished he didn't because it would deny him his prize as well. He zoomed in on the *Ares* and saw something strapped across every part of its body. Explosives. More specifically, spoiling charges.

Zhou either didn't hear it or chose to ignore it. His pair of assaults continued on their path.

"Remember, you were given a choice."

A small sun blossomed in the distance, followed moments later by a tremor through the ground. The *Ares* vanished from his sensors.

"What have you done?" Zhou's question came out in a strained whisper.

"What I needed to do for my people. You're welcome to sift the wreckage, but I promise you, I was quite thorough." Only silence greeted her. "I trust we're done, then.

"Colonel Amberson, we should talk privately."

**POINT BETA**
**RUINS OF NEO-TOKYO**
**SHOKAKU**
**YORII**
**RASALHAGUE DOMINION**
**19 APRIL 3151**

Rikisha watched with satisfaction as the DropShip of the Bronze Blades finally launched, climbing into orbit and taking as much charred wreckage from the *Ares* as it could carry. She had recommended letting them. It ended the fighting, and the Blades were getting nothing of value anyway. Additionally, the Dominion forces on-planet had finally noticed their presence. It was past time to leave, now that she had recovered the *Ares* crew that had ejected before the 'Mech detonated.

She stood with arms crossed, hands seeking the Republic unit patches she had torn from her uniform just yesterday. She had finally admitted the reality of their situation. The Republic was the past. It was time to look to the future. She glanced beside her where Keir stood, hands casually thrust into the pockets of a rumpled uniform.

"I'm glad you and your people are joining us, Major," he said.

"It's not without its growing pains, but my people are glad to have a purpose again. I'm also glad you're letting me stay a major. It's eased some tensions."

Keir shrugged. "A colonel still outranks a major."

They began walking back toward the DropShips.

"Tell me," Rikisha began, "who was your contract with? Not the Capellans, I trust."

Keir scoffed. "Not likely. The contract was with the Free Worlds League, their Clan Protectorate, to be specific. Which means Sea Foxes, I guess. They'll sell anything."

"The terms were favorable?"

"They were more than favorable, they were downright generous. But that doesn't matter now. You, justifiably, destroyed the *Ares*; the contract is void."

A sly smile appeared on her lips. "I destroyed the *Ares*, it's true. I did not, however, destroy the technical manual or spare parts that came with it."

He gaped at her in shock.

Rikisha couldn't help needling the merc leader just a bit. "Do I get a bonus for fulfilling the contract?"

As Keir closed his mouth and nodded, Rikisha felt an easing of the burdens she'd been carrying. A mercenary life wasn't what she'd expected for her and her people, but it gave them a chance to build something for themselves. The Free Worlds League better embraced the lost ideals of the Republic. She could make a home there...for now.

# UNIT DIGEST: TWENTY-FIRST CENTAURI PEREGRINE LANCERS

### STEPHEN TOROPOV

**Nickname:** The Peregrine Lancers; Rosin's Repulsers
**Affiliation:** Mercenary
**CO:** Captain Rosin Douglas
**Average Experience:** Elite/Fanatical
**Force Composition:** 1 Medium BattleMech Company and 1 Combined Armor and Mechanized Infantry Company
**Unit Abilities:** The Twenty-First Centauri Peregrine Lancers have the Special Command Ability Shielding (see below).

> *Shielding:* Any opposing unit must fire on a 'Mech before targeting a vehicle or infantry Unit, as long as the 'Mech is closer and in Line of Sight.

**Parade Scheme:** Initially using a distinctive teal and gray paint scheme, the Peregrine Lancers adopted the same royal blue scheme as the rest of the Twenty-First Centauri Lancers while operating in the Hinterlands to underline their local authority.

## UNIT HISTORY

Set on the wing amid the fire and rubble of the early Dark Age, the Twenty-First Centauri Peregrine Lancers have risen above the chaos and built a reputation of honor and excellence befitting the storied legacy of the Twenty-First Centauri Lancers.

Serving as the Lancers' independent operations force, akin to the Black Widow Company of Wolf's Dragoons, the Peregrine Lancers' story began on Towne in 3133. Hired by the planetary government

to bolster the defense of one of the few hyperpulse generators still functioning after Gray Monday, the Lancers dispatched a light support lance headed by Lieutenant Rosin Douglas weeks before Landgrave Jasek Kelswa-Steiner's renegade Stormhammer militant group raided the world. Douglas' lance performed with distinction during the defense, first spearheading the operation to eject the Stormhammers from the HPG compound, then coordinating with local Republic Armed Forces units under Knight-Errant Kristoff Erbe to end the three-day Battle of Port Howard that followed. Arriving to relieve Douglas and her lance with an expanded task force of Lancers, Captain Chak Rasbid was deeply impressed with the lance's performance. He recommended Douglas' executive officer, Thos Cardella, for the promotional fast track and convinced Lancers command to grant Douglas a different honor—the right to form a subordinate company and operate it autonomously.

Scarred by the brutal urban combat and civilian casualties on Towne, Captain Douglas set about building her roaming command from the ground up with an ironclad drive to protect the innocent. Recruiting troops with reputations for outstanding moral rectitude from the broader Lancer organization, the newly constituted Twenty-First Centauri Peregrine Lancers quickly found themselves with no shortage of good causes in need of their assistance as the Fortress Wall went up and the Republic abandoned whole prefectures. In particular, the Peregrine Lancers built their reputation by offering discounted services to planetary governments beset by pirates or unscrupulous freelancers. Such pro bono work would be ruinous to most units their size, but drawing on the greater resources of their famous parent command kept the Peregrine Lancers solvent. In return, the Twenty-First Centauri Lancers further burnished the upstanding reputation that allows them to charge a premium for their services.

When the Twenty-First Centauri Lancers took up a long-term contract with the Lyran Commonwealth, Captain Douglas' lingering horror at the conduct of the Stormhammers caused her to balk at joining the move to Lyran space. The unit remained in now-former Republic territory, where defensive operations like deflecting pirates on Deneb Kaitos in 3136 gave way to more harrowing missions like the evacuation of Alkalurops' government in the face of wrathful Jade Falcons in 3143. The heroic reputation of Captain Douglas' stalwart band solidified, but the growing scale of warfare forced the Peregrine Lancers into extended periods of rest and refit between missions, during which relentless news of unprevented atrocities would agitate Douglas to no end.

Battered and battle-hardened, the Peregrines eagerly reunited with the main body of the Twenty-First Centauri Lancers on Galatea when the Lyran contract lapsed in 3151. As the brigade weighed competing offers from House Kurita and the upstart Tamar Pact, the whole roster of the Peregrine Lancers lobbied to heed the call of undefended peoples in the Hinterlands. In turn, Governor-General Sarah Regis of the Tamar Pact saw propaganda potential in sponsoring Douglas' selfless chivalry, and immediately sent the Peregrine Lancers on a conspicuous mission to clear out the pirate colony of Almotacen. Within months of arriving, Captain Douglas had not only ended the pirate threat, she also collaborated with local powerbrokers to establish a new hub for small scale mercenary contracts in the Hinterlands. This upstart venture now operates under the strict moral supervision of the Peregrine Lancers, who lead by example and continue to take jobs with half their force while the other half oversees law and order on Almotacen.

## COMPOSITION

Operating as a general showpiece for the Twenty-First Centauri Lancers, the Peregrine Lancers have their pick of equipment and personnel from the larger unit's rolls. Rotation through Captain Douglas' command is considered a mark of honor among the Lancers, as she subjects candidates to a rigorous battery of tests, interviews, and background checks before approving them for a billet. A successful tour of duty with the Peregrines marks a warrior for promotion upon returning to regular duty, and Rosin Douglas' voice carries more authority within the Lancers' overall command structure than her stagnant rank would imply.

Maintained as a reinforced company, the unit's operational organization is strictly defined with one BattleMech company supported by two platoons of mechanized infantry and one lance of light combat vehicles. The BattleMech forces tend to favor mobile medium and heavy 'Mechs, while the infantry forces have access to both hover and tracked APCs depending on the needs of the mission. Drilled extensively in coordinated operations, the BattleMech forces are particularly skilled at delaying and drawing away the main body of an enemy force while their support elements secure a threatened objective.

While they rely on hired transportation to get their full roster to and from contracts, the unit maintains a modified *Lung Wang*-class assault transport called the *Peregrination*. Dropping the aerospace fighter bays for light vehicle transport capacity, this DropShip allows the Peregrine Lancers to quickly respond to emerging threats while on contract.

# SILENT PLANS

### DANIEL ISBERNER

**INDUSTRIAL HUB
SUMARIS PLAINS
CARNWATH III
LYRAN ALLIANCE
30 OCTOBER 3068**

General Anori McFaris sat down at her desk and sighed. The rebuilding process after their raid on Laurieston was almost over. The Silent Reapers had been betrayed and forced into hiding, and the Laurieston operation was supposed to be their first contract after coming out of hiding, but they had been betrayed *again*, from within *and* without this time. The losses in equipment and people had been heavy. Her father— Juan McFaris, the Reapers' former general—had been assassinated by one of their own, and many others had been lost in the fighting.

The Silent Reapers had been on the brink of total destruction when ComStar had clandestinely intervened, pulled them out, and recruited them to take the fight to the Word of Blake, the cause of all their trouble. Their mission was to disrupt the Word's hunt for some Star League-era bio-weapon data on Caph. Her troops had managed to win the battle, but she had no idea if they had stopped the Blakists before they could transfer the data to another facility.

*With our luck, we were too late.*

Nevertheless, ComStar had set them up in an old campground they used as a safehouse.

*We need something to do.*

The Silent Reapers were all set up. Their equipment had been repaired, and they had even managed to find new members by using recruiters on Galatea. With the unit's name still connected to the destruction of the hyperpulse generator on Capra, they had needed to use some backchannels, but it had worked.

Their battle-armor forces were back at full strength, and they had found new MechWarriors for their OmniMech lance. Selling off some of the Lyran 'Mechs they'd captured on Laurieston had helped pay for everything without having to use their existing accounts, making it impossible to track them down.

As much as Anori loved to see the Silent Reapers grow again, all the new faces out there reminded her of what they had lost. Her father, founder and former general of the Silent Reapers, had been murdered by a traitor in their midst, someone Anori had considered a friend. Others had died during their escape from Laurieston.

*So many dead...*

One of the files in front of her was an analysis of the data they had recovered on Caph. They had managed to find a professor of virology at the Judge Christian University on Laurieston that Peter Brantling, the Reapers' computer expert, said they could trust. Professor Mason had had the files for two months now, and Anori had started wondering when she might hear back. And now, here it was.

The analysis was straightforward, and as frightening as she had expected. What exactly the Star League researchers had intended to achieve on Caph was unknown, but they had sought out a secluded area of the planet for a reason. They had tried to modify the Terran *hantaan orthohantavirus*—hantavirus, for short—possibly for use as a weapon. Most of the research had stopped when Caph was attacked with chemical and biological weapons during the Amaris Civil War, but Anori noted that the hantavirus research had seemed to continue even after the area around the lab had become uninhabitable.

*They stayed in the lab and died there. Probably starved to death. But they kept going.*

Anori wasn't sure if she should be impressed or horrified by the thought. These scientists could have escaped. They had all the hazmat equipment available to get out, but they had stayed instead. She made a mental note to look into the lab's personnel records to find out why. While it all happened 300 years ago and would no longer have any impact on today's events, finding out why people would stay and die instead of saving themselves could potentially help her on a mission.

Of course, it could have been the boring way, with soldiers there, forcing the issue. But it might have been something psychological she could use.

Anori pushed strands of blond hair away from her face and reread what she had just skimmed over while in thought, trying to wrap her head around the analysis Professor Mason had written.

*It looks like this was only one part of the project, with the second part being researched elsewhere for security reasons. If this was supposed to work as a weapon, additional modifications would be required, something impossible to do with the equipment available to these researchers at this location. In my research, I have come across rumors about such a research station hidden somewhere in Lyran space, but it has never been found. The data presented here points to those rumors being true.*

Anori read it again. And again. And again.

*Shit!*

She jumped to her feet, throwing her chair backward as she ran out of her office. On her way, she ran into a few Reapers who didn't expect their general to race through their base without giving a damn about who was in her way, but most of them managed to jump aside, if only barely.

When she reached Peter's room, she forewent any semblance of social nicety and just used her command code to override the lock on his door.

The hacker sat at his desk and looked in her direction as if he had been expecting her.

"I figure you've read the report by Professor Mason?" she asked.

He didn't even try to hide that he had in fact read it, despite her not giving him clearance. Anori ignored it. She had long suspected Peter was doing a lot of things he wasn't supposed to. "Laurieston was the second base."

Peter nodded. "I think so."

"Can you arrange for the professor to come here?"

"I already prepared a message for her. I figured you also didn't want to risk sending her the research data from Laurieston. You give the go-ahead, and I'll arrange for her to come here ASAP, no matter the cost."

"Go ahead."

There was no time to waste. If what Anori suspected was correct, the Word of Blake now had access to a bioweapon so deadly the Star League had compartmentalized the research across multiple locations to prevent it from falling into the wrong hands.

*And the Word of Blake is more wrong than the Star League could possibly have imagined.*

**INDUSTRIAL HUB**
**SUMARIS PLAINS**

**CARNWATH III**
**LYRAN ALLIANCE**
**17 DECEMBER 3068**

Anori greeted Professor Joane Mason when the woman entered her office. She would have preferred to greet her when she had arrived, but there were too many things to take care of here. Besides, Peter had picked her up from the spaceport himself, which made it easier to explain the situation to her.

The professor was of average height, in her mid-forties, and had shoulder-length brown hair combed over to one side. Anori remembered that hairstyle from Laurieston; she had seen it come into fashion shortly before they had run for their lives.

"Thank you for meeting with me, Professor," Anori said. "I assume Peter has already filled you in on most things?"

The woman sat down before responding. "Yes, he has. And I understand why you couldn't send me the Laurieston data. Even on the short ride over here, having both datasets in the same place..."

Anori's mouth went dry.

"So, my fear was correct? This is a potential planet-killer?"

"Yes."

Just one word.

For a moment, no one said anything.

"It's surprisingly obvious if you've looked at both files," the professor continued. "I am not surprised Peter could see it, despite having no actual knowledge in the field. But he always had a good eye for patterns. Both research teams worked on different parts of a project to weaponize what is commonly known as the hantavirus. One team was looking into easing the jump to humans, the other was making sure it could resist inoculation and known medications. If you release it on a planet, depending on population size and proximity, you could render it uninhabitable in *weeks*. Neither team finished, but it seems there is not much work left to be done. With the right equipment, I think I could weaponize it within a month or two."

Anori just stared at her. The Word of Blake had had access to both datasets for much longer than that. "Did...did the Star League look into a counteragent?"

"I cannot say. There might have been a third research facility looking into that, but the data you gave me doesn't show any research into it. Which is remarkable, given that development of a counteragent is usually mandatory if you're working with this kind of pathogen. Of course, I only had a short look into the second set of files, so I might simply not have found it yet. And given the compartmentalization of the project, they might simply not have known about the third facility."

Anori shook her head. Even if there was a third facility that had worked on a counteragent, finding it would take far too long.

The general stood up. "Thank you, Professor. Peter will show you to your rooms. I need some time to think."

"Of course, General McFaris. It was nice meeting you."

"You too, Professor. Say, one more question: How do you know Peter?"

"We grew up together." With that, the woman turned around and left.

*They grew up together... Does that mean she is a ROM agent?*

It would explain how Peter knew her. His family has been with ComStar for generations, his parents and aunt working for ROM, ComStar's intelligence arm. His brother had died on Tukayyid, fighting Clan Nova Cat, which led Peter to leave the Order and ROM. The fact he survived what could only be called desertion showed just how much influence his family held.

*Did we just hand planet-killer data to ROM?*

The thought made Anori shiver, but they needed help. Just because Peter spotted something while looking over the files didn't mean he understood any of it.

Anori stood up and left her office. All she wanted to do was to take a walk outside, but that wasn't really an option. Carnwath was a good place to hide because no sane person visited it. And no sane person visited it because there were insects outside. Not just a few, but uncountable numbers. Not just small ones. Quite a few of them were the size of a fist, and some were even bigger. While the local government had started looking into getting a handle on the insect population, the research would likely take decades to yield any appreciable results.

No one moved outside without donning what was pretty much a hazmat suit. Not exactly a feature that attracted tourists to Carnwath.

Instead of going to the hazmat suits stored next to the exit, she went over to the battle armor stacked on the wall. The berth next to hers was empty. It had belonged to her girlfriend, Sakumoto Miyus. Sakumoto had been her second-in-command, back when Anori had just commanded the battle-armored troops of the Silent Reapers. She had been kidnapped by the Word of Blake and by now, they were certain, she was dead. Still, the Reapers left the berth empty to show their respect. The role of second-in-command of the battle-armor squads had been taken over by Cassandra Farinadis, who commanded Beta Squad.

Slowly, Anori began putting on her own Gray Death Scout armor, which had been heavily modified to serve the Silent Reapers' needs. It had been upgraded to an improved stealth version, the jump booster was gone, reducing the overall jump range, but a flamer and machine gun had been added to provide offensive capabilities. The lack of an active probe had been somewhat compensated for by an improved

sensor package, but she recognized that as the drawback it was. Still, she wouldn't give up the Reaper version of the suit for anything.

*Well...perhaps for a ClanTech upgrade.*

The thought made her smile. No Clan would sell the required parts to them, and the Great Houses used whatever ClanTech they could get their hands on themselves, instead of selling it to third parties—at least as far as battle armor equipment went. The Silent Reapers did have access to Clan-grade 'Mech parts, they even had a *Ryoken* Anori could see when she looked to her right.

Even after having it around for years now, the 'Mech still looked strange to her. It had birdlike legs with knees bending backward, a squat torso, and arm weapons that looked way too big. Since they started working for ComStar, getting their hands on replacement parts for it had become easier, and she could see parts and weapons neatly stacked up around it in its 'Mech bay.

Deep in thought, she had not even registered how far she had come with putting on the armor. Grabbing the heavy chest plate brought her back to the here and now. It was one of the parts that was almost impossible to get fastened by herself, but over the years, Anori had learned a few tricks. She put the backplate on the ground, grabbed the breast plate, and lay down in the back half. Then she carefully positioned the heavy plate over herself and let it fall down about a centimeter.

It snapped into place. Had she been off with her positioning, it could have caused serious injury, or the bolts meant to fasten it could have broken off. The first option could have taken her out for a few weeks, the second one would have been very expensive and a pain in the ass for her techs. Something underscored by the annoyed stare she got from a few of them. They all knew better than to chastise her—they knew she was working something out when she donned her armor by herself—but they also had an eye on her to hurry to help her, had she messed up. Anori was thankful for all of it. It told her they trusted her and had her back, and not just literally.

After she had put on her helmet, she waited for the suit's sealing mechanism to give the characteristic *hiss* that signaled the suit was fully sealed and all the locks were in place, then activated its systems. The HUD in front of her eyes came to life and ran an analysis of her health and the suit's integrity. After all that had been confirmed, the weapons systems and myomer muscles were checked to make sure she could fire her weapons and move. Finally, the secondary systems like the jump jets and sensors showed green.

The whole systems check had taken less than ten seconds. Putting on the armor by herself had taken over an hour. But it had helped her clear her head.

Slowly, she began taking the armor off again.

## 18 DECEMBER 3068

Peter looked at Joane Mason while he ate a croissant. He had not seen her in more than a decade, but having her here felt good. Like they had never been separated.

"So, tell me," she said with a coy smile, "why didn't you contact me when you were on Laurieston?"

He had feared she would ask ever since she had arrived. She had surprised him by not asking last night. But now, during breakfast, his time was finally up.

"I..." He sighed and decided to tell her the truth. "I was afraid of your reaction. When I left ComStar and joined the Reapers, you were furious with me. I feared you didn't want to see me. And once things got out of control, I didn't want to endanger you."

"Oh, Peter. I was never angry with you for leaving. I know Frank's death shook you and I also know what General McFaris offered you—the elder one, I mean. I heard he died."

"He did, yes. For a moment there, Anori thought I had killed him."

Joane just stared at him, and he decided to tell her the whole story. How the general had been murdered by a Word of Blake sleeper agent who had thrown suspicion on him. How they had escaped from Laurieston after the Word had betrayed them, how they had found the second dataset on the planet, the death of his parents... Everything.

In the end, he was crying in her arms, and she was kissing his head while he sobbed.

Four hours later, the two of them were sitting in Anori's office. While Joane had analyzed the data the two datasets provided when combined, Peter had gone to the local HPG to download any messages they might have received.

In theory, their ComStar liaison officer could also get any messages, but Peter preferred to do it himself. That way, he could also access the back-channel transmissions ComStar had no idea he was receiving. Or at least, he assumed they had no idea. He was piggybacking on ROM channels he'd gotten access to back when he was with ROM, using his own protocols to hide data in an already hidden stream.

Usually, there were no messages aside from the data ROM channeled through there, which he had not even tried to access so far. He gave it a 50 percent chance they actually had no idea he was in there and, if they did know, it was better not to access data he wasn't supposed to access.

This time, though, there was a message—and his blood suddenly froze solid.

The Word of Blake had cracked his encryption of the data they had stolen on Laurieston. And they had done so months ago. They must have managed to do so in a secure facility, making it impossible for the trojan he had hidden in there to send its message immediately. But once it had gotten onto a noteputer that had left the facility, it had taken the first chance it got to send its message.

*I'm still thinking of my programs as sentient beings.* Joane had pointed that out to him when they were teenagers; he hadn't even noticed before.

After reading their reports, Anori put down the noteputer and looked at both of them intently. "So, the Word of Blake has managed to weaponize the hantavirus?"

"It seems like it, yes," Joane responded. "Peter's trojan couldn't sneak out enough data without breaking the limits he programmed into it to prevent it from getting detected, but from what he showed to me, they have. It seems like they created different versions, at least two, of it to use in different environments, or to see which one would better serve their needs. Without getting full access to their research data, though, I cannot say for certain."

"Thank you. Both of you," Anori said, clearly dismissing them.

Peter stood up and left the office, Joane followed right behind him.

"What's she going to do?" she asked after the door closed behind them.

"Knowing Anori? She is now probably contacting our ComStar handler, giving him all the information he needs, and setting us up to get moving. Can't be long before the general alarm will start ringing and people will get packing."

"Do you even know where to go?"

Peter looked at her. He loved having her back, but he wasn't stupid. She was still with ROM; he wouldn't tell her everything he knew. Then again, Anori would have to tell ComStar anyway for them to get transportation.

"You know me well enough." He looked at her. "You will know once Anori tells ComStar. And don't tell me ROM isn't going to keep you in the loop. Given your background, they'll probably order you to follow us under some flimsy excuse about research and whatnot."

She laughed. "It is good to be back with you."

That was when the alarm started ringing.

Anori packed a small bag and left her office. She had sent a message to ComStar, preparing them for her immediate arrival, then she had sounded the alarm. She didn't know what ComStar would say, but she needed to contact Demi-Precentor Lóorez immediately to arrange for JumpShip transportation.

Luckily, they didn't need ComStar to make planetfall. Captain Büttner and the *Anja*, a massive *Mammoth*-class DropShip, had arrived back on-planet a week ago, bringing equipment and goods to trade.

The crew had signed on with the Silent Reapers recently after their old DropShip had been destroyed over Laurieston. A *Mammoth* wasn't exactly sneaky, but its massive size offered enough places to hide their 'Mechs, battle armor, and other equipment. The fact the ship had formerly been used by slave traders was actually a bonus, as the hidden compartments were plentiful and well shielded from scans.

In the hangar, Anori sat down behind the wheel of one of their modified civilian cars, equipped with environmental sealing to keep out bugs, and drove off. To get outside, first she had to go through the airlock, which felt even slower than usual.

The inner door closed behind her, then the whole compartment was overpressurized before the outer door would open. The air blowing out made sure no bugs would get in before the outer door would slam shut behind her. In an emergency, she could have overridden the whole process, but while the situation was urgent, they were not under attack. And bugs getting in would potentially cause more problems than her having to wait for thirty seconds.

Once she was outside, bugs crashed against the windshield and forced her to activate the windscreen wipers immediately, while constantly pouring soapy water on it to get all the goo off.

*Why do people keep living here?*


## HPG STATION
## CARNWATH CITY

Anori had driven right inside, only being stopped for a few seconds, thanks to the credentials the demi-precentor had given her. The airlock procedure was pretty similar to what they had set up in their own base. The main difference between coming in and out was that her car had been sprayed with powerful insecticides before it was allowed to pass through the inner hatch. They had the same basic protocol in place in their own base, the main difference being how long it took.

When she entered the demi-precentor's office, located below the surface, away from any visitors, he was sitting behind his desk. Given that he was a ROM agent and not officially on-planet, putting his office below the surface seemed like a good idea. His being a spook was also the reason she had come to him and not the other way around. She didn't like spooks in her base. Bad enough Peter had invited one.

"Ah, Miss McFaris. Your message sounded quite urgent, but without telling me what exactly this is all about. Would you enlighten me?"

Anori scoffed. "Stop playing games. I know the professor already updated you. The Word of Blake has a bioweapon at its disposal, and we need to stop them before they can release it."

"Why is that?" Lóorez looked at her, acting puzzled, like he didn't care.

*Perhaps he really doesn't. All he cares about is defeating the Word of Blake.*

When she had first met this man, she had felt something was off about him. She had later blamed it on the fact that he was black ops, just like them. But she now realized there was more to it. Behind those dark blue eyes lay a coldness. *As far as he is concerned, people could die left and right, as long as he fulfills his mission.*

*I need to make this about him.*

"What do you think the Word of Blake will do with the virus, once they successfully test it? You think they will just sit down and think, 'Wow, that was fun. Let's put it away and never talk about it again'?" She speared him with her eyes. "They will use it against *you*. Whatever it is they really want, they want to get rid of ComStar. They will get to your most important bases, and they will release the pathogen there."

She could tell he was thinking about what she was saying. The way he cocked his head at an angle and looked at her. For the first time since she had entered the office, he really looked at her. Trying to figure out if she really believed what she was saying. Trying to figure out if *he* did.

"Let's assume I agree with you. How will sending you into the thick of it, possibly getting you killed and robbing us of an asset, stop that from happening? Releasing the pathogen will kill people or it won't. They will then use it against us, even if you kill every last one of them on their target world. They will still have all their data in their research location."

"Target *worlds*!" Anori corrected. "They have created multiple versions. What *you* want is the research data so you can defend yourself. They need a copy of it on their target planet to create the plague. *That* data is what I'm offering."

The offer itself was easy. The hard part was that there was absolutely nothing she could do, should they be too late. If the Word of Blake released the bioweapon, it would not just become impossible to access the data, everyone on the planet would die.

Part of her died at the thought.

**MAMMOTH-CLASS DROPSHIP ANJA**
**EN ROUTE TO THE NADIR POINT**
**CARNWATH SYSTEM**
**LYRAN ALLIANCE**
**20 DECEMBER 3068**

Konstanze Kurz looked at Anori in shock. Her XO had been with the Silent Reapers since the beginning. She had helped build them and while she hadn't walked into combat once, she was the one taking care of all the bureaucratic hurdles a mercenary unit faced. Especially one that didn't exactly offer its services on the usual channels.

Black ops, and sometimes even outright illegal operations, weren't something the Mercenary Review and Bonding Commission condoned. They did have a backchannel to offer their services there; Anori was fairly certain it was an open secret, but it had never been their main route for new contracts. Ever since Laurieston, that source had been completely cut off anyway. Besides, they were on a long-term contract for ComStar, who had rescued them from certain destruction and offered them a chance to get their revenge against the Word of Blake.

Anori regarded the older woman before she said anything more. When the whole mess with the Word of Blake had started two years ago, Konstanze, while well within her sixties, had not looked older than in her mid-thirties, but the last two years had taken their toll. Her once platinum-blond hair was now starting to look gray, and she had gotten more and more wrinkles, not just in her face. Her hands had deep craters crossing all over them.

*Not the last two years,* Anori corrected herself. *She began aging once my father was murdered.*

"I know it is horrible," she finally said. "But there is nothing we can do. When we arrive, we will start looking for the Word of Blake immediately. Try to get to them before they can release their bioweapon. But we cannot warn anyone. We simply cannot!"

Anori had to repeat that last part, to convince herself. She knew it was true, but that didn't make it hurt any less.

"I know," Konstanze finally admitted with deep sorrow in her voice. "If we warn anyone, those bastards will find out and they will simply release their bioweapon early."

"Taking away our chance to stop them," Anori finished.

They both agreed that was a correct assessment. Anori could see it in the older woman's eyes.

"What are we going to tell the others?" She wished her father was still alive to make that decision.

"I am not sure." Konstanze looked distraught. "I know you are wishing your father was still here, to let him make this decision."

Anori wanted to say something.

"No, don't deny it. I have practically raised you; I know that look on your face. What I can tell you is he would not have known either. Decisions like this... What to tell the Reapers, or even you. They are never easy, despite what it may have looked like to the outside, or to you. He spent whole nights without sleep over things like this."

Anori looked up in surprise. Had Konstanze just admitted she had spent the nights with her father? Anori had always suspected they were more than just friends...

"Have you...?"

"Been with him on those nights? Yes. But I know you are asking more along the lines of a relationship. And that is not an easy answer. Your father never managed to get over the kidnapping and death of your mother. The Silent Reapers were his answer to it. At first, he founded them to get rid of the pirates that had plagued our home planet and return the hostages they had taken. When that didn't work as he had planned, he vowed the Silent Reapers would train hard enough, become good enough, to never have something like that happen again."

Anori knew all this, but said nothing. She knew Konstanze well enough to know the older woman was making a point and was best left uninterrupted.

"For the first few years, we took on only anti-pirate contracts. Infiltrated them, killed them, and returned what they had stolen or whomever they had kidnapped. As we became bigger, we also took on other jobs to pay the bills. Your father's pain subsided, became less. He watched you grow up, and let me take care of you when he was away. In a way, I became not just his XO, but his partner."

She paused, pain and loss creeping into her eyes.

"I spent nights with him. Took him in my arms when the burden became too heavy. But did it become a full relationship? I really can't say. When the walls around his pain crumbled, it kind of was. But when he re-erected them, it wasn't. I think he loved me. I know I loved him. But his fear of losing someone he loved once again was too great. I had to fight him to let you train to become a soldier. You wanted to become a Reaper, he wanted you to be sheltered and never to risk your life. Whenever we got closer, he pulled back. And I let him."

She sighed wistfully. "I always thought things would change when he finally made the decision to give the Reapers to you and to withdraw as general. But...he was murdered before that happened."

Tears streamed down her face, and she swiped them away. "But to get back to the problem at hand... No, he would not have told the Reapers. Just like he didn't tell anyone when the Word of Blake threatened your life and blackmailed him. In his way, he would have thought that would protect you."

"But it didn't," Anori whispered.

"No, it didn't. It didn't protect you, and it was the reason he was murdered. In his drive to protect everyone else, he forgot that people are able to protect themselves *if* they know what to protect themselves *from*. But, on the other hand, sometimes people can't think clearly when they are afraid."

For a while, neither one of them said anything. Anori pondered what Konstanze had told her. Then she came to a decision.

She would tell the Reapers and have them decide what to do. Whoever wanted to follow her into a mission that could kill them all could do so. Whoever didn't could stay back and catch a ride to the next planet, waiting either for their return or for news about their death.

She would not hold it against anyone who decided to stay back.

Two hours later, Anori knew no one would stay back. Only their dependents and two squads of infantry were staying. Lucas Hammilton, their infiltration specialist and commander of their conventional infantry, had been assigned to remain with them for protection. Anori had noticed the two squads, coincidentally, consisted of everyone who had small children.

Lucas had looked innocent when she had pointed that out to him. She had thanked him anyway.

**CRAIOVA SPACEPORT**
**ALARION III**
**ALARION PROVINCE**
**1 MARCH 3069**

Anori looked at the *Anja* as it ascended into space. Captain Büttner had wanted to stay to provide the Reapers with a base of operations and a potential exit strategy, but Anori had denied the request. She had also denied taking any of their 'Mechs on planet. Instead, they would rely on their battle armor.

All their troops had exited the DropShip over the last hour, disguised as tourists or people looking for jobs. Given the highly industrialized nature of Alarion III, most of those looking for jobs had gotten fake backgrounds in high-tech areas. Almost none of them could actually work in the field they were looking for jobs in, but no one was planning to write any applications. Alarion III had very strict quarantine and settlement restrictions, though. They required specific reasons for why you were visiting the planet and, if you wanted to stay, you had to provide even more details.

Peter and ComStar had made sure they had everything in place. Part of Anori liked the fact that their current employer could simply fake any off-world research someone would send out via HPG. It made things a lot easier than setting up fake companies and backgrounds.

*We don't have to burn a single one of our existing shell corporations.* The thought made her smile.

For now, they had to find where the Word of Blake was hiding and from where they were going to start their plague.

Looking around bolstered her resolve. This would be the most important job the Silent Reapers ever took. They would either succeed or die trying. There were no alternatives.

*Well, we could die while succeeding...*

She accepted that. Death for them was the most likely outcome, no matter what.

"All right, let's do this!" Anori muttered to herself as she strode forward.

# SUCCESSOR LORD:
## A CARD GAME FOR THREE TO FIVE PLAYERS

### KEN' HORNER

"Successor Lord": this phrase can cause many reactions, but in gambling halls throughout the Inner Sphere and Periphery, it means the stakes have just doubled.

This card game cropped up in the mid twenty-ninth century, but has exploded in popularity three hundred years later. It is similar to Spades or Bridge in that each turn every player plays one card and whoever wins that turn keeps the group of cards, often known as a trick. Scoring and winning is based upon the number of tricks taken during each round. It is usually played using the Successor Deck (*BattleTech Initiative Deck*) but can also be played with the ancient standard fifty-two card deck.

Successor Lord can be played by three to five people. Select a suit for each player and remove the twos and threes (for the archaic deck, use the whole deck for four players, and remove the fours entirely from the game for five players). Shuffle the remaining cards and then separately shuffle the twos and threes. Place the twos and threes into a pile, this is the trump pile. Turn over the top card; that suit is trump to start the game. Then deal the remaining cards to the rest of the players. All the players then place their ante wager into the pot; typically, this is money or chips, but games in schools and military units can often involve alcohol or clothing as an alternative.

*Tian Ramirez was a legend at the tables on Dustball, both in poker and Successor Lord. He was not only skilled at knowing the odds, but also reading his opponents. After years of domination, he was in a game with a few familiar faces and a newcomer in Katia Chiraque. Tian once again dominated in the beginning, often doubling up on Katia's errant bids to earn extra tricks. On the tenth hand, they doubled the pot six times in the last few rounds. Katia then played in a bizarre manner the next two hands, often giving tricks to the other players as long as Tian didn't win any. On the thirteenth hand, her strategy became clear as Tian ran out of funds and was sent scrambling to find money to ante up. With Tian away from the table, Katia cleaned up, taking her one hundredth trick minutes before Tian was able to get back to the table with new funds.*

The player to the left of the dealer plays the first card. In informal games, the dealer will pass to the left for each round, while at most casinos, a professional dealer will deal, and a symbolic "dealer button" will denote which player is acting as the dealer. Each player will play a card in turn from the suit that was first played in clockwise order. If the player does not have a card of that suit, they can play any card they wish from their hand. The highest card of the initial suit will take the round unless a card from the trump suit was played. In that case, the highest trump card will take the round. In Successor Lord, aces are high and particularly powerful.

*After Count Kim-Aigo died, his estate was split between his four sons and daughters with the exception of his Martell Laser factory. The will stated that the four would need to decide who would inherit it. Unable to come to an agreement, the four could only agree to a game of Successor Lord, using the rest of their inheritance for wagering. Three of them played well while Lester fell behind and left the game. Sun-Yoo was aggressive toward the end but failed to anticipate how long her siblings could keep the game going and soon found herself nearly leaving without an inheritance. Lupe, up 98 to 94, doubled down the last three tricks of what she assumed was the last hand, but was only able to pick up one, forcing another hand. In the end, Paulo ended up winning 103-101-95 and earning nearly three quarters of the remaining inheritance in addition to the laser factory.*

The player that wins the turn collects the cards in a pile as a trick. All tricks are equal in value, no matter which cards make it up. If an ace was played, the dealer flips over the next card from the trump pile, and that card determines the current trump suit. The player who won the previous trick then plays a card to begin the next round, continuing in clockwise fashion. If a player calls "Successor Lord" (occasionally a current house lord may be used as well), the pot immediately doubles. Unlike other wager-based games like poker, however, this cost is all borne by the player calling Successor Lord. Once the player antes up, the dealer again flips over the trump pile after the current turn is finished, though typically players will wait until the last card of a turn is played to call Successor Lord. Additionally, players may call Successor Lord before the first card of the turn is placed down, each not only doubling the pot by matching the amount currently in it, but also resulting in another trump card turned over. Most rules prevent a player from calling multiple times between turns, but some high stakes games allow it. In the rare occurrence that the trump pile is exhausted, trump is frozen on the last card turned over.

*Legend has it that Duke and Duchess deSummersville met over a hand of Successor Lord. Seated next to one another, friendly banter turned into highly charged innuendo. The future duke was not terribly adept at the game and was in last place, while the duchess was easily crushing four other players. Supposedly on the last trick, he stated, "Lord of Royal Foxx" and placed an exquisite ring in the middle of the pot. The duchess arched an eyebrow, didn't ask for an evaluation of the value of the ring, and merely said, "If you prove worthy." She won the last trick, collected her winnings, and they retired for the night before getting married the next month. If asked these days, the duke will sometimes confess to this tale and sometimes tell an entirely different one, while the duchess always demurs with a pleasant smile.*

At the end of the hand, the tricks are tallied. Most games of Successor Lord are played until a number of tricks are won, such as 25 or 50, across multiple hands, and the jackpot grows until there is a winner. Others may have a winner per hand. The jackpot is normally kept separate from the pot of the current hand, but games on Kooken's Pleasure Pit and Royal Foxx have seen pots spiral into the millions of C-bills.

*Successor Lord gave birth to a new mercenary unit when MechWarrior Holly Gustafson was at a table on Outreach. She was tied at 49 tricks in the last turn with Mandrinn Bau-Ta of Sarna. The pot had grown substantially, to nearly 10 million C-bills while the trump showed diamonds. Holly called Successor Lord and put up her 'Mech as collateral. Trump flipped to spades. The Baron matched the pot with two 'Mechs from his personal guard, and trump returned to diamonds. The Baron laughed heartily and threw down his nine of diamonds even though it was another player's turn to lead. The other cards were placed until Holly gently set down her ten of diamonds, suddenly two 'Mechs richer. Finding two Dispossessed pilots, the Gustafson Rangers were born.*

The basics of Successor Lord are rather easy, mastering it is a different matter. Players of other games often fail to appreciate that it is not similar to their other games. Bridge players will often find the lack of a partner unsettling, while poker players will have to adjust to the difference in making wagers between the games. Successor Lord is a more patient game where each trick and hand is part of a bigger picture, but not to be overrated. Calling Successor Lord can shift the odds briefly in one's favor, but comes at a cost that can only be recouped in victory at the end. Skilled players will keep track of what cards have been played and what is still in other players' hands. The use of Successor Lord can steal a few tricks, but the best players will use it more defensively, removing a trump suit they don't have any or many cards of. The only time to bully is when the end is inevitable; when players fold in Successor Lord, it is typically for the game, not just for the hand.

# SIX MONTHS ON THE FLOAT

## JAMES KIRTLEY

**UNION-CLASS DROPSHIP GROVER'S FOLLY**
**ALL OVER THE FEDERATED SUNS**
**WAY TOO MUCH OF 3025**

"Join a mercenary company, Leo," they said. "Travel to exotic, distant lands, meet exciting, unusual people, and kill them," they said. Only they totally failed to mention just how much of each of those things I'd be doing.

So far? Pretty much just the travel part.

No, I'm serious. It's a thing they don't tend to mention about the mercenary life. I mean, I should have thought about it; it's kinda obvious in retrospect. I'll get more into detail about that later, but let's just say I've been with Lucius' Lancers for about six months, and we've spent almost all that time just trying to get where we're going—before we've seen any bad guys.

You know how interstellar travel works, right? First, you load up on a DropShip. In our case, a *Union*-class DropShip called the *Grover's Folly*. They're the things you see at spaceports everywhere, the ones that look like giant balls the size of a football pitch. *Union*s are common as dirt—I think they used to come in cereal boxes or something. But there's a good reason for that. They're solid and dependable. Which is important, because the way they get you off a planet is by firing plasma out their keisters so hard they can escape a planet's gravity.

Of course, getting off a planet is only half the battle. The other half is getting from star to star. No matter how fast your DropShip can go, it'll never get you to another star in a reasonable period of time. That's what JumpShips are for. JumpShips basically just pass a whole bunch of energy through something called a jump core, and suddenly you're in a different star system. Look, I took high-school physics. I know roughly how DropShips work. JumpShips? No idea. That's some sci-fi magic crap right there.

Thing is, JumpShips are *huge*, even compared to DropShips. Most of 'em are long and spindly and fragile, and they can't do their magic anywhere near sources of gravity like stars and planets and stuff. Mostly. It turns out they can use something called pirate points, where the gravitational forces of planets and the star kinda balance out, but those are risky. You only do it if you're in a real hurry, because if you don't do your math perfectly, or you're missing a planet or whatever in your calculations, you could misjump. Then you wind up God-only-knows-where, and not necessarily with your insides still on your insides. It's some nightmare-fuel level shit, lemme tell you. Fortunately, we're not in a hurry, so it's a standard jump point for us.

It takes, like, two weeks to get to the jump point from Galatea, and that's accelerating at the rate that you would fall if you fell out of bed on Terra. Once you get about halfway there, you gotta turn around and *decelerate* at the same rate so you're not really moving once you get to the JumpShip. Well, not moving *relative* to the JumpShip. *Everything* is moving in space. So, you gotta time everything just right.

Man, I am *really* glad I'm not an astro-navigator, by the way. I'm *really* bad at math.

One thing I'll never get used to is how absolutely *still* in-system travel feels. Once you're out of atmo, there's no turbulence, so other than the thrum of the engines and the air recyclers, there's not much to remind you that you're moving at all. Unless someone's shooting at you or there's something wrong with the ship, it's just like you're in a building on the ground. At least until you see someone coming the other way.

Once we break atmo, our CO, Major Lucius, calls us all together for a briefing in the MechWarriors' lounge. That sounds a lot fancier than it really is. In reality, it's just a conference room with a big lectern, a tri-vid projector, a table, and a few more than a dozen chairs.

Once everyone is settled down, Lucius pipes up. "Okay, boys, listen up! I hope you're all settled into your bunks. As you're no doubt aware, we've completed atmospheric escape from Galatea, and are now burning at one G for the zenith jump point. The current course has us beginning our deceleration burn in roughly one hundred and forty-two hours and docking with the JumpShip *Sojourner* in a little under twelve twenty-four-hour cycles.

"First off, a couple of routine matters. For the duration of this journey, we will be on Terran Standard Time, making it—" He checks his noteputer. "—roughly 1417 hours. You will find your communicators have all synced with the ship's chronometer. If they haven't, please contact Scotty, and he'll figure it out.

"Second, the *Grover's Folly* has a fairly standard layout. The top deck is the bridge and crew quarters. As such, unless you have been expressly invited up there, consider it off limits. In general, you should restrict your activities to Decks Two and Three, which contain our quarters, recreational facilities, the mess, and so forth. I understand many of you are quite attached to your BattleMechs, and I have secured permission from Scotty to allow anyone to visit or maintain their 'Mechs between the hours of 0800 and 2000. If he catches you outside of those hours, he will assume you don't trust him and his astechs to properly do their jobs.

"Third, we're still a small unit, and I'm afraid I haven't had a chance to recruit an XO, which frankly is a good thing, as we're a bit cramped here already. Because of that, for the short term, Captain Archer will be filling that role. She is currently handing out your ID badges. You are to keep them with you at all times, as they will serve as your access cards to various parts of the ship.

"Fourth, your noteputers should all have the current duty rosters. For the first week and a half, I'm afraid we're all going to be quite busy with various tasks that have to be performed while under thrust. When you're not on duty, you are encouraged to familiarize yourself with our assigned areas of the ship. Additionally, Dr. Miller has requested everyone stop by at some point so he can take some baseline readings. You can find the medical suite on Deck Three, Dorsal.

"Fifth. Now that we've broken atmosphere, I can tell you our destination is the Federated Suns world of Memphis."

Someone, I think it's the captain, whistles audibly. She's native to the Fed Suns, so I take it that's not a good thing. Personally, I've never heard of Memphis, so it means nothing to me.

"Before you go looking it up, Memphis is at the spinward edge of the Crucis March. It is approximately six hundred and fifty light years from here."

Now the rest of us whistle.

"I realize we'd all prefer something a little closer to Galatea, but as a new unit, we don't really get to pick our jobs. Think of this as an opportunity to get to know the other members of your company. We will have regular briefings every Monday at 0700, but don't worry—I expect them to be significantly shorter than today's. With that said, I'm going to pass the meeting over to Captain Archer, who will fill you in on the details of your duty assignments."

With that, Mel stands up and approaches the lectern while Lucius steps away and leaves the briefing. Mel then goes into detail about the various things we'll be doing for the next twelve days. There's a lot going on, and she goes into ridiculous amounts of minutiae, but somehow I manage to stay awake.

Once the briefing is over, it's a quick trip to one of the cargo bays on the main hangar deck to pick up our uniforms and bedsheets and stuff, and then an all-too-short fifteen minutes or so to settle into our bunks before we're instructed to change into running shorts and head to "Deck Three, Dorsal."

Dorsal is really just a fancy term for the end of one of the four main passageways that lead off from the central elevators on Deck Three. On a wet-navy ship you can describe directions relative to the direction of travel: the bow is where you're headed, the stern is the opposite, and port and starboard are left and right when you're facing the bow. No problem. But on a DropShip, the direction of travel is "up," so you can't just face that way and look to your left or right, right?

So instead, they arbitrarily pick one of the directions and call it "dorsal," like a fish. It turns out that's the direction folks on the bridge all face. (Again, it's not like they can face the direction of travel—they'd get a terrible kink in their necks!) Then the opposite is ventral, and then you have left and right laterals. Sometimes, locations are listed by times, with noon being dorsal, three o'clock being right lateral, and so forth. And no, I have no idea why times would have any bearing on a location on a circle. It must be some strange leftover from the wet-navy days.

Okay, so anyway, we all show up at the end of the dorsal-leading hallway on Deck Three to discover the outermost circumference of this deck is one long, round corridor. The outside is made of floor-to-ceiling transparisteel windows, which I'm told is some sort of nonstandard luxury modification we're really lucky to have. I wouldn't really know—this is my first military transport. Across from the windows are various offices and living spaces. I don't have long to sightsee though. As soon as the twelve of us have all gotten there, Mel lines us all up and makes us run.

I gotta say, as runs go, it wasn't the worst view ever. At the time we still hadn't passed Galatea's moon (imaginatively named "Galatea Minor"—well done, naming people), so every lap, around three o'clock, we had a gorgeous view. The rest of the circle wasn't bad—lots of pretty stars to look at and all. Problem was, while *Union*s look really big on the outside, they really aren't all that big on the inside—it's about six laps to the kilometer, which means the eight-kilometer run Mel had us on was almost fifty laps.

Let me tell you something. Even the prettiest of views gets *old*. It might have been nicer if we could see Galatea proper, but because we're flying away from it, and we're at the top of a ball-shaped object, you just can't see anything.

I'm proud to say that of the twelve of us, I wasn't the one in the worst shape. Some of the former military folks were the best, obviously, since they've been running professionally for their whole careers. Pat, who is surprisingly spry for a smartass, commented that Mel probably got put in charge not because she was the best pilot or best leader, but because she was the best runner. It really wouldn't do to have the captain huffing and puffing at the back of the pack, would it?

After the run, Mel (Sorry! Captain Archer) had us do a bunch of other calisthenics—mostly body-weight stuff like pushups and jumping jacks. I think that's just what she assumes you're supposed to do in the military on account of all that time she spent in the AFFS. Whatever it was, by the end we were all good and sweaty, and were sent off to our cabins for a quick shower to clean up.

I know what you're thinking: "Leo! How can you take a shower? You're on a *spaceship*." And you'd be right. The *Grover's Folly*, like many other wonders of the Star League, has actual water showers on it. If you think about it, the ship has to carry enormous tanks of water around for a pile of reasons—and it's gotta be able to infinitely recycle it, too. So, occasionally dropping some on people's heads for a few minutes isn't really a big deal.

It will be, of course, when there's no gravity, and thus no "down." But we'll get back to that.

By this point, it's pretty much dinner time. The run aside, this is the first opportunity we really have to meet each other. And I don't know if you've ever tried to chat someone up while running in tight circles and trying not to dry out like a prune, but it's not really possible. So here we all are in the galley, sitting mostly in little clumps (I assume by cabin, I know I was) and, well, not actually talking to each other, silently chewing on whatever mass-produced food we had thrown at us.

I mean, in part, it's awkward because, less than a year ago, some of us were actively shooting at each other. Okay, *I* wasn't—I wasn't active military, but some of us absolutely were. And the major Houses of the Inner Sphere have been fighting each other for so long that everyone has a story about a family member killed in some atrocity perpetrated by their galactic neighbors. Anyway, none of us really noticed at first that one of the other recon lance pilots (I didn't really know him yet), Tristan Didier, had been stewing and giving one of the other pilots the stink eye. So, naturally, we were all quite startled when he got up quite suddenly and stalked over to her. His fists were balled up, and if it wasn't such a cliché, I'd'a said he was itching to pick a fight.

"I was on Hoff, you know."

You know, as pickup lines go, that's lousy.

Didier is the kind of guy you just know has a bit of a complex. He's pretty short, and *wiry*. You can tell just by looking at him that he's wound up tight as a drum, and this was probably not the first fistfight he'd gotten into with people that were supposed to be his friends and colleagues. I'm really hoping at this point that he's not in my lance, since a guy wound up that tight is almost certain to be trouble.

Based on his accent, I can tell he's a Fed, like Mel. The target of his ire was a *Panther* pilot named Sachi Fukuda. As you can imagine, she's Combine. A *lot* of bad blood there. I think more than any other border. I've never heard of Hoff, though, so I'm not sure what he's all pissed about. I suspect he picked Fukuda because she had obvious Asian features; so clearly, she *must* be Combine, right?

That's sarcasm, by the way. There's folks with "Asian" features all over the Inner Sphere. Most have never been to Terra, let alone wherever "Asia" is. Didier is an asshole, however. The kind who probably assumes everyone who looks vaguely Japanese must be a Kurita stooge. Turns out Fukuda actually *is* from the Combine (okay, even assholes are right sometimes), and based on the way she's looking at Didier, I think she's got a chip on her own shoulder, and is seriously considering which of the salt or pepper shakers to use to break his nose.

Before anything really unfortunate could happen, however, the pilot who was sitting with Fukuda stood up and interposed himself. That was Jingyi Song. He's from the Confederation, I forget exactly where—it wasn't somewhere I'd heard of. He's pretty reserved, but nice enough, especially if you get him going on a subject of interest to him. I don't get the impression assholes from the Fed Suns count, though. I'm expecting him to say something to calm down the situation, but he doesn't, he just stands there.

"You stay out of this, *Capellan*."

Wow. I'd never heard the word "Capellan" said with such venom. And I'm from the League. We've had more than our fair share of dustups with them.

Tristan at this point looks like he's trying to decide who he wants to punch more. Song is just standing there, cool as a cucumber. I think he's waiting for Tristan, who is a good ten centimeters shorter than him, to take a swing. Fukuda looks annoyed that Song has gotten in the way. All in all, it's got the feeling of one of my extended family retreats. At least one of those ended in fisticuffs when one of my cousins from Oriente took a swing at one of my cousins from Andurien.

Yeah, we Simonideses get around. Anyway, things look like they're about to get real ugly when suddenly we hear Lucius' voice. "Okay, boys, listen up!"

Everyone goes deathly still. *That's coming from inside the room.* How long has he been here? And how did nobody notice him entering? Everyone snaps to something resembling attention, leaping to their feet (if they weren't already standing) and staring forward—all in different directions. Nobody actually knows *where* to look.

"As some of you may be aware, and all of you *need* to be aware, fighting is not allowed anywhere on Decks Two or Three. Song and Didier, you are to take this outside. I'm thinking you should use the ventral air lock on Deck Five. On second thought, Didier, I think that giant noggin' of yours is gonna need one of the 'Mech doors. Ask Scotty if you need help getting it open."

At this point, people are starting to become suspicious. Some people even look around a bit. I think I'm the only one who has figured it out, and only because I'm sitting right next to Pat: apparently, he does a spot-on Lucius impression. Gravelly voice, somewhat vague, definitely Periphery, probably Taurian, accent, the works.

"Also, I'm a giant tightwad with no sense of humor and a weird rash Doc told me is probably nothing to worry about."

That might have been taking it too far, but as I've learned, Pat doesn't know the meaning of "Too Far." Also, it totally worked. Several of us totally lost it. Sachi grins at him, and I could have sworn Jingyi actually gave him one of those little nods that's really just a slight tilt of the head. Tristan looks over at us and mutters something about "Toaster-humper," but his edge is completely gone.

It's at this point that Captain Archer arrives, carrying a case of beer. The old-fashioned kind, in bottles. "Hey everyone! Look what I found while doing an inventory of Cargo Hold B! It should be cold by now, and we've only got a week or two to drink it before the gravity goes away."

She nudges Tristan with one of the bottles. "Didier, drink this. You look like someone ate your puppy. What?"

It's amazing what a little alcohol can do to the attitude in a room. Quickly enough, everyone is swarming Mel. Over the course of the evening, we go through a lot more than one case, and everyone, MechWarrior Tristan Didier included, winds up having a grand old time.

Honestly, a little "social lubricant" was exactly what the crowd needed. We all got to know each other pretty well. It turns out that, of the dozen of us, we've got quite the range of backgrounds. We've got someone from each of the five major Houses, plus two Periphery nations and my buddy Pat, who's from Terra. Some of us were House military. Most weren't. We've got a couple of military brats, including myself, and some who'd pretty much dusted off an antique 'Mech they'd come by one way or another.

Some of us are assholes. Most aren't. Fortunately, none of us were belligerent drunks. I think if they were, the border tensions would have bubbled up again, and nobody's gonna fall for Pat's "the Major is here" trick more than once. Well, maybe Didier. He's an idiot. And that's no longer an initial gut feeling—that's an impression I spent the entire evening building. One important thing I think everyone realizes is that our backgrounds are a lot less important than having each other's backs.

Well, everyone knows that on paper. It'll be another issue entirely when the shit actually hits the fan.

The informal "BS and beer" session went pretty late into the night, which we all regretted the next morning when we had to get up at what Mel referred to as "oh-dark-thirty" when she kicked us all out of the galley. Of course, the idea of sunrise or sunset is kinda goofy when you're in space. Interestingly enough, they constantly (but slowly) rotate the ship. It turns out it has nothing to do with setting day/night schedules, but everything to do with making sure that the ship absorbs stellar radiation evenly. They use the ship's lighting to set schedules.

See? You learn something new every day.

The next day started the pattern we'd live by for the rest of the flight to the jump point. We'd start with calisthenics and plyometrics, and then move to various duties, which included everything from 'Mech maintenance to cleaning the ship to cooking and laundry. A lot of this is stuff we had to do while we had gravity. Some things are easier with gravity ('Mech maintenance is a lot easier when fluids go downhill and when you can't accidentally shove 500-kilo laser emitters across the room where they might crash into something or someone). Some things just aren't possible—you can't wash things with water, for example, that sort of thing.

Over the course of that week, we all got to meet the rest of the unit as well. In most military outfits they talk about the "tooth to tail" ratio. For some ground units, there's like six to eight support folks for each warrior. In the past, like in the Star League, it was more like twelve or even more. In our unit, it's a little closer to one-to-one, but there's still a lot of folks needed to keep us running.

There's the commander, of course, Major Stephen Lucius. He used to be a MechWarrior but apparently can't (or won't) drive a 'Mech anymore. I'm sure it's related to his limp, although I couldn't say why. You do use your feet while driving a 'Mech, but it's generally not that big a deal if you have a slightly gammy leg. On the other hand, if the limp is due to neurological damage of any sort, then he very well may not be able to use a neurohelmet anymore, and that's definitely an immediate disqualification. Major Lucius also has a secretary named Layton who acts as a liaison when we have to deal with folks off the ship.

There's also the techies. Besides the head tech, James "Scotty" O'Malley, there's half a dozen assistant techs, or "astechs." Yup, us military folks really love to save lots of time by shortening words and smushing them together. In some units, you'd have one or more astechs, per 'Mech, but we only have room for half that many. I'm assured that that's enough to keep us running, at least for now. In effect, we each share an astech with one other pilot so that they can be intimately familiar with our machines. My "astech buddy," as I call him, is Jingyi Song. He drives something I've never seen before but that, like my *Locust,* has backward-canted legs. Apparently, those are somewhat tricky, so we get a specialist. His name is Collins Chandler. Or maybe it's Chandler Collins. I was introduced to him when we met and now I can't remember, and it's been too long now to ask without looking like an idiot.

Fortunately, he answers to either, so that's good.

Finally, there's also Doc Miller, and her assistant, Ioan. I had to go see them to get baseline readings for the trip; heart rate, blood pressure, that sort of thing. They also did various blood chemistry tests. They were saying how, on extended trips in zero-g, people's bodies do strange things, and they'll need to semi-regularly test stuff to make sure we aren't generating vitamin deficiencies or stuff like that. They seem nice enough, but I hope to not deal with them too much in my career of shooting more than getting shot at.

There's also the crew of the ship. They're kinda also members of the unit, but more like independent contractors. Lucius doesn't own the DropShip, he just rents it and its crew out. The captain's name is Nielson, and he speaks English with an accent I can't place, which I've only ever heard over the ship's intercom. I keep meaning to talk to the captain about setting up a mixer with the crew. I'm sure they're regular folk just like the rest of us.

One of the few times I've heard the captain's voice was at the halfway point of the journey. After we'd spent six days accelerating at roughly the acceleration caused by Terra's gravity, we turned around and *decelerated* at the same amount. That's right. We spent most of a week building up velocity, just to literally turn around and bleed it off. This seems like a horribly inefficient way to do things, but it turns out that the only real cost is fuel (which is basically water anyway, so who cares?), and in exchange, you get to have gravity the whole way.

Anyway, the captain comes over the intercom to let us all know that we're about to perform a routine flip-and-burn procedure, and to strap in. After a few minutes, the engines cut out, which is a really weird sensation. You kinda come to block out the noise of the ship's engines after a few hours, but when suddenly that noise is missing the whole universe goes deathly silent. I mean, there's still noise—air circulators, hydraulic lines, people talking and breathing, that sort of thing, but compared with the sound of the engines, it's *really* quiet.

Then the gravity kicks out. Hopefully you're strapped in at that point, as everything you forgot to secure in your cabin starts floating. That's not the real problem. The problem is when they fire the thrusters. This imparts a "gentle" spin in the ship. At least, they call it gentle. It's not so gentle living it, let me tell you. This is when the stuff that was mostly harmlessly floating over where you'd forgotten to secure it goes hurtling across the room.

Yes, technically, the object stays in the same place. It's the room that's hurtling. But that's not what it looks like.

Anyway, once the ship has its new orientation, then they fire up the engines again, and the noise and the gravity return. That's when the object, which is nowhere near where it was when the procedure started, goes crashing to the floor. Or would. If the object wasn't a beer bottle some idiot—let's call him Sam—forgot to get rid of before the flip-and-burn. And also, if that bottle hadn't crashed into you during its attempt to hurtle across the room. In that case, it ends up in your lap below the bruise it left on your chest.

Yeah, Sam owes me big for that. I'm just glad it was a beer bottle and not, say, a big ol' knife or a brick or something much more painful.

So, other than the fact we spent the next six days *decelerating* instead of *accelerating*, time passed pretty much exactly the same as it had before. The direction of travel was now "down" in the ship, and Galatea was now visible if you could look straight up, which is actually basically impossible, and it wouldn't matter because we're several AU away by this point, so Galatea is pretty much just a glowing dot anyway.

Once we got to the actual jump point, our lives actually changed. At the end of the twelfth day, we all were once again sent back to our cabins to secure them for zero-g. Then we strap in for the last set of maneuvers. Once again, the engines kick out. It turned out the crew had been slightly adjusting the engines for the previous few hours to make final course corrections, but none of us really noticed.

At this point, we needed to float for a while. If you think about it, you can't just keep firing the main engines right up until you get to the JumpShip, since while you're decelerating the engines are spitting hot plasma out in the direction you're traveling—which would be right at the JumpShip. So, you need to aim away a bit and do the last bit of steering using thrusters. Again, be glad I'm not doing the math on it. I know I am.

This means the final approach to the JumpShip involves a lot of the ship making minor adjustments. You can feel weird little bits of centrifugal force applied to your body from the straps keeping you in place. The docking procedure is pretty complicated, but at the end, the bottom of the DropShip is connected to the JumpShip via giant docking clamps to something they call a "docking collar" on the side of the JumpShip. So there's a final *clang* that reverberates through the ship, and then we're on the float.

And unlike the flip-and-burn, we're on the float for good now, not just for a few seconds.

We didn't have too long to get used to it, though, as we were the last DropShip the *Sojourner* was waiting for, so it wasn't long after that that the jump klaxons rang throughout the ship. Then we jumped.

You know how I said that JumpShips were magic? Yeah, they definitely mess with things humans aren't really supposed to mess with. I'm told everyone experiences jumps differently. For me, it's like the whole universe gets weirdly tunnel-like and then springs back to normal shape. The whole thing is over in a fraction of a second, but the human brain actually somehow stretches it out so that it feels longer.

For me, there's a period of mild dizziness after, and sometimes I get a little headache, but it's nothing serious. Some people get something called transit disorientation syndrome, which is usually shortened to "jump sickness" or even "TDS." For some folks, the headaches and fatigue and other symptoms can be debilitating—causing them to miss all the excitement that comes from jumping into hostile territory.

That wasn't my biggest worry. For some people, TDS can make them ralph all over their cabins or even worse. Fortunately for me, that's not the case with either of my roommates. Trust me, you do *not* want to have to clean up sick in zero-g. That's nasty.

After the jump? We were just under thirty light years away from Galatea, in the Lyran system of Zollikofen. Here's where the trouble starts. JumpShips need to use an incredible amount of energy to perform a jump. So, when they complete a jump, they then have to deploy these enormous solar sails to recharge the jump engines for the next jump. That takes about a week, depending on stellar size, brightness, color, and a bunch of other stuff. Unfortunately, during that week you're just sitting still—so there's no thrust to generate gravity. That means you're just floating around the ship.

You might think that being on the float would be awesome—flying through the air with hardly any effort to go wherever you want. To some extent, you'd be right. For, like, a day. Maybe. Let me tell you something, however—it gets old. Quick. Yeah, as Pat discovered, the float opens up all sorts of fun pranks you can play on people, like hiding "above" doorways and startling people. But after, I don't know, a day or so—maybe even a few hours—the fact you have to drink everything out of these crazy little plastic bulbs, or that things don't stay where you put them, or heck—you can't even *sit*—well, it gets annoying. Don't get me started on using the john. Sorry—"head." I'm on a ship now, gotta be accurate.

It does, however, offer up some hilarity. For example, at least once Sam thought he'd get Pat back by hiding above a doorframe and jumping out at him. Problem is, Sam forgot the first rule of zero-g: stay near a wall. If you've never been in zero-g, you might think you can just sort of "swim" through the air, but air isn't nearly thick enough for that. If you get far enough away from a wall, you can actually get stuck, with no way to move around.

So anyway, Pat comes through the door to one of the storage bays where Sam is waiting to ambush him. Problem is, Sam had been waiting for quite a while, and he'd kinda drifted away from the bulkhead without noticing it. So, the door opens, and Sam yells "Boo!" and then, suddenly, realizes he's stuck. Pat was still laughing about it hours later at dinner.

There is a solution to this, of course—mag boots. They've got electromagnets in the heel that stick you to the hull (which is conveniently made of steel). You can engage and disengage the magnets when you need to take steps. It's a bit tricky, but once you get the hang of it, you can mostly move around like normal. Problem is they're really bulky, and the batteries don't last all day, so people don't tend to wear them on long hauls.

There's another, very low-tech solution, of course. One that Sam would have known about if he'd paid any attention in high school physics, and that's Newton's third law. Take off one of your regular boots and throw it. You'll go flying (slowly, but you will move) in the opposite direction. If you don't hit a wall soon enough after one boot, well, you've got two. Once you get to the far wall, you can push off it and recover your boots.

Sadly for him, Sam didn't think of this. And Pat didn't tell him. He mostly just floated there laughing for a while before getting what he entered the bay for, and then just left Sam floating there. It was about an hour later when Mel went into the bay for something and found Sam there, all red-faced and swearing.

Fortunately for Pat, even Sam was able to laugh about it. Eventually.

Another problem is that it turns out that *Union*s weren't originally meant for long-haul travel. You were supposed to live on cozier ships and then transfer to the *Union*s when it was time for a planetary assault. Unfortunately, we don't really live in the Star League days anymore, so we kinda have to make do. Speaking of which, I'm pretty sure the *Folly* was built (not just designed) during the Star League. It certainly smells like it was.

Oh yeah—that's another problem with *Union*s. They're notorious for having inadequate air circulation. Not enough that people will get sick and die or anything, just that they aren't very good at scrubbing bad smells out. So not only do you get all cozy with the other members of your unit, but you also get all cozy with all their failings in the personal hygiene department, too.

Remember earlier when I said water showers only work while under thrust? Yeah. There are ways to get vaguely clean that mostly involve dabbing yourself with a damp sponge. But stress on the word "vaguely." So yeah, after a while the place gets more than a little bit ripe.

I know what you're thinking. Or at least, what I was thinking, which is, "Why wait for the solar sails to charge the jump engines? Why not just hook up the fusion reactors the JumpShips use to generate the electrical power to charge those giant capacitors? That's gotta be faster, right?" And you want to know the answer?

I have literally no idea. I mean, Scotty got drunk and tried to explain it to me one night, and I don't know if it was the alcohol or my not being an engineer or whatever, but it made no sense. So I just trust him on that one. That didn't stop him from trying to explain it, though. Honestly, it was kinda cute.

Okay, so a single jump is only good for about thirty light years. Six hundred and fifty light years divided by thirty light years is—let me do the math—about twenty-two jumps. If you could do it in a straight line. Which you can't, for a host of reasons. The main one is that there aren't always conveniently inhabited star systems where you want them to be.

Yes—it is possible to use uninhabited systems. And sometimes you do, especially if you're trying to be secretive, or if you're in a hurry or something. But there's a serious drawback to using uninhabited systems—if something goes wrong, you're almost certainly going to be stuck somewhere until you run out of food or the $CO_2$ scrubbers fail, or something similar, and you die. So, generally, you stick to inhabited systems.

All told, it took us twenty-eight jumps to get to Memphis. Yes, I counted.

Now here's the thing—you don't always have to wait the whole week. Sometimes you can catch an earlier ride. Systems often have a bunch of JumpShips waiting at the primary jump points, and as often as not, they've got a docking collar or two available. So, you detach from one, jet on over to the other, pay them some ridiculous fee, and then attach to them. You can often shave a few days off each jump that way.

Of course, every time you do that, there's another time when something breaks, and you have to wait for a part or something to get shipped up from a planet. Sometimes the JumpShip isn't going exactly where you want to go, so you have to switch to another JumpShip (sometimes one that hasn't even arrived yet!). Either way, in the end it still takes on average about a week per jump.

So yeah, we didn't arrive in Memphis until mid-June after leaving Galatea the first week in January.

Oh, a quick note—did you ever think about where our dates come from? It turns out Sam is this weird font of knowledge. I think he does nothing but watch weird educational vids on his noteputer all day. Anyway, despite the fact that most of us have never even been to Terra, we all keep track of what the date is there all the time. Even when our local system uses days that are nowhere near the Terran standard of twenty-four hours, or years that are nowhere near the Terran standard of 360 or so days.

Did you know that for people who live on Terra (and Pat is literally the only one I've ever met), they tend to have this weird association with dates and weather? Pat, who grew up in someplace called New York, spent the beginning of the journey wearing sweaters and stuff, and by the end had busted out shorts and T-shirts. I know, this is even weirder from someone who lives on a spaceship where the "weather" is strictly controlled, but for some reason it made him more comfortable.

Anyway—when you're on the float, life is very different. There's a lot of things you can't do. You can't do things involving water (okay, you can drink it, but you can't bathe in it, or wash things with it). There's also things you have to do. We don't think about it, but humans aren't meant to be in zero-g all the time. Stuff stops working. Your bones get all brittle and your heart says, "Oooh, this is nice," and gets all complacent. Basically, you'll just die after a while. And that kinda defeats the purpose of traveling somewhere in the first place.

So, you do a lot of exercises. Resistance-band stuff, mostly. There are also these funky exercise bikes they strap you to that you can pedal away to your heart's content, and a few other things. You spend a lot of your time dealing with just trying to stay alive. And that's not counting all the drugs that Doc's got us taking.

It's not always terrible, though. Some JumpShips actually have these things called grav decks, which sound all futuristic and stuff, but are really just giant spinning rooms centered on the spine of the JumpShip. They act a lot like those carnival rides where you get pushed against the outside. Again, Newton to the rescue. The main problem with grav decks is they're limited, which means you never get as much time on them as you'd like. As I mentioned before, any given JumpShip can carry a number of DropShips, and they're all full of folks who'd like to spend just a little while not pooping into a vacuum cleaner.

Oh yeah, I didn't mention that, did I? Well, don't think about it too hard, but even basic bodily function stuff doesn't work the way you want it to in freefall.

Heck, when we do get on a ship with a grav deck, Doc will often prescribe us time on the treadmills they inevitably have. I actually look forward to that, and I *hate* running. Yes, that's what zero-g will do to you after a while.

One thing you can sort of do on the float is train. I think it's pretty standard among BattleMech companies of all flavors, from the lowliest mercenaries to the fanciest of House line regiments. In the days of yore (as Sam likes to call it) you'd spend all your time practicing shooting and stuff. Well, you can't do that in zero-g, but you can strap yourself into a simulator and have pretend 'Mech battles. It's not quite the same as being in a proper 'Mech while under gravity, but it's close enough, and it definitely takes some of the boredom away.

'Mech simulators are really cool, and very immersive, actually. They're typically completely enclosed, with fancy gimbals and stuff that mimic what you'd feel in an actual 'Mech. To make matters worse, they even heat up like a real 'Mech would. Sometimes I think they overdo it—my *Locust*, for example, really doesn't overheat, and yet for some reason I always come out of the simulator sweating up a storm.

Anyway, we spent a good deal of those first few months on the float learning to work together and learning tactics. Whatever he was before forming the Lancers, Lucius definitely picked up 'Mech tactics. He's spent most of the last six months drilling everything from basic tactics ("Try not to get hit," "Concentrate fire") to the psychology of 'Mech combat and getting the other guy to fight on your terms rather than on theirs into our heads.

And then we ran mock battles. Some of them were purposefully unfair. Especially for us in the recon lance. I swear, half of the first six months of training for us was teaching us when to run away. One scenario we ran all the time was to put one of the fire or command lances in big 'Mechs, and then have us in the recon lance find them and bring them back to the other of our fire or command lances, and then work together to take them out. Oh yeah, and that asshole Didier? Yeah, he's in the recon lance with me, so yippee.

Once, they put my bunkmate Sam in a *Warhammer*. Did I mention I had a *Warhammer* poster on my wall as a kid? It was one of the Davion ones where they strip out the missile rack and the machine guns and just add more armor and heat sinks. It's an absolute beast. When we saw the thing, I just kinda froze. I'm not sure if it was that I was scared shitless (which is silly in a simulator), or if I was just geeking out, but either way I just basically stood there while Sam blew me to smithereens with one shot from the arm-mounted PPCs.

One thing I'll say about all of that simulator time, we've all become much better shots. Or at least we've all become much better *simulated* shots. At the beginning, most of us couldn't hit the broadside of an *Atlas* if both it and we were standing still. Now we can actually hit targets while on the run. I suspect this will come in useful once we get into a real fight.

So, that's about it! I've been a merc for a little over six months now, and I haven't fired a single shot at anyone that wasn't a computer image. Fortunately, that's about to change. We're now about a day out of Memphis. We've had a week of glorious, glorious acceleration where we all got to stand on the floor of our own ship for the first time in months. Of course, that time has been spent doing all the maintenance tasks we couldn't do since we first latched on to that first JumpShip back in January, but it was just amazing to finally be doing *something* different.

I will say that one of the things I was most excited about with this unit was the sense of belonging I'd first experienced on that initial takeoff from Galatea. And you know what? I wasn't disappointed. I mean, sure, Didier is an asshole, but he's *our* asshole. He even mostly gets along with Fukuda and Song now. You spend six sweaty, stinky months in a small group and you either go batty or you become really close, and I'm happy to say it was the latter.

I'm sure in a week or so, once we've settled down into our cozy little garrison contract, I'll be once again bored out of my skull. However, for now there's so much I'm actually looking forward to—for example, taking my own 'Mech out for just a simple run, or drinking beer in a glass again. The major's got us scheduled for live fire drills the day we arrive, so we'll get to see if our newfound simulator shooting skills translate at all to the real world. For some people, like Captain Archer, Memphis will be just another world. For me personally, however, I've only really been on two worlds that I can remember, and I was only on Galatea for a couple of months.

"Join a mercenary company. Travel to strange, exotic places. Meet interesting, unusual people. And kill them."

Finally, I'm gonna get to do stuff other than the "travel" part!

# ALPHA STRIKE SCENARIO TRACK: EMBERS OF THE PAST

### ED STEPHENS

**IMSTAR AEROSPACE FEEDER PLANT 2**
**OXBRIDGE CITY LIMITS**
**AMITY**
**WOLF EMPIRE**
**8 JULY 3151**

*With a thundering crunch, the boots of the suit slammed into the roof of the sprawling factory as the roaring jets hissed to a stop. The figure crouched after landing atop the complex, eyes and sensors alike scanning and probing for signs of movement. Three chirps sounded as the corners of a box condensed from the edges of the HUD to form a target indicator, centering around a star of toads trotting down an alleyway. "Bravo One, contact. Bravo, engage, suppressing fire!" The right arm of the suit raised, swiveled slightly, and whined as a laser beam lanced forth...*

The following scenarios take place either in the Wolf Empire after the events of "Strike and Fade" (*Shrapnel #13*) or while continuing an ongoing *Alpha Strike* campaign or during a standalone game. One player assumes the role of Game Master, controlling the Wolf Empire, while the other players undertake the missions with their own mercenary force. Players can alternate the role of GM if they wish to each play a campaign force. The scenarios parallel the events of the Silver Hawk Irregulars 3151 campaign into the Wolf Empire, as detailed in *Empire Alone*, p. 40, though the sourcebook is not required to play the scenario.

Force card lists must be assembled and printed from masterunitlist. info to use the forces suggested below. The scenarios make use of the *Alpha Strike Box Set* contents, miniatures from the *Clan Invasion Box Set*, and vehicles from the *Mercenaries* Kickstarter. For all non-'Mech units in the suggested forces, counters from the *Mercenaries Box Set* can be used if miniatures are unavailable.

## TOUCHPOINT: KICK DOWN THE DOOR

## SITUATION

The Gryphons regiment of the Silver Hawk Irregulars, under the command of Colonel Lucas Cameron-Witherspoon, is continuing its incursion into Wolf Empire territory. Finding many worlds underdefended, they make a push toward Amity, the home planet of the Colonel, birthplace of the Gryphons, and location of the Imstar Aerospace facility. After the Gryphons secure the orbital facility, the player's mercenary company has been contracted to assist them by seizing the component feeder plants on the ground below.

## GAME SETUP

*Recommended Terrain:* Industrial, 36" × 36" play area

Players should arrange an industrial zone in the center of the battlefield. This can be achieved using two or three sets of buildings from the *Alpha Strike Box Set* or *Counters Pack*. Buildings should be clustered in groups of 2–4 with sides touching, forming lines, L, and T shapes. Smaller buildings can be placed on top of larger, and 1" wide flat cardstock strips can be placed connecting roofs as gantries. Three building complexes should be designated as Objectives using tokens— two selected by the Attacker, and one by the Defender.

### Attacker

*Recommended Forces:* ilClan-era mercenaries (250 PV)—all units are Skill 4:

Demolisher Heavy Tank Mk. II
Pegasus Scout Hover Tank
*Gladiator* (*Executioner*) J
*Blackjack* BJ-5
*Puma* (*Adder*) T
*Pouncer* D
*Black Hawk* (*Nova*) C
2x IS Standard Battle Armor [Laser] (Sqd4)

**OR**

250 PV selected from the player's campaign force.

### Defender

*Recommended Forces*: Forty-Second Wolf Garrison Cluster (195 PV)—all units are Skill 4.

3x Galleon Light Tank C
Maxim Heavy Hover Transport (Clan)
Elemental Battle Armor [Flamer] (Sqd5)
Manticore Heavy Tank (XL)
2x Clan Mechanized Infantry
3x Clan Foot Point (SRM)

## DEPLOYMENT

The Defender selects one edge as their home edge and deploys their forces anywhere up to 18" from the Attacker's home edge. The three Clan Foot Points may deploy within buildings using the Hidden Units rule (*AS: CE*, p. 168). To designate buildings, the Defender can slide 3 tokens underneath select buildings in secret.

The Attacker's units move onto the board from anywhere along their home edge during their first Movement Phase.

## OBJECTIVES

**Captured (Attacker Only):** At the end of any turn, the Attacker wins the scenario if only the Attacker has non-hidden units within 6" of each objective token.

**Rebuffed (Defender Only):** The Defender wins the scenario by putting 66 percent of the attacking forces into Forced Withdrawal.

## SPECIAL RULES

### Buildings

Use of the Urban Combat rules (*AS: CE*, p. 72–73) is recommended. Segments of the factory buildings (represented by individual buildings) can be collapsed separately. Use Light/Medium/Heavy Industrial CFs (3/4/12) for the three sizes of building segment.

### Forced Withdrawal

The Attacker's forces operate under Forced Withdrawal (*AS: CE*, p. 126). The *Solahma* Defenders fight to the death.

**Aerospace Support**

On Turns 3 and 5, the Defender gains one Light Bombing Battlefield Support Card to use during the Combat Phase.

## AFTERMATH

The Gryphons quickly seized control of the orbital factory. With support from their mercenary attachments mopping up ground forces, the planet was liberated and returned to the fold of the Free Worlds League.

The Attacker's units persist as a continuing campaign force. Damage suffered by units may be repaired at a price of 1 PV per armor point, 2 PV per structure point, and 3 PV per critical hit.

If the Attacker is victorious, they are paid 60 PV for repairs and to purchase new units. If they failed to complete their objective, they receive 50 PV of Damage Insurance for repairs, but may not purchase new units with these points.

## TOUCHPOINT: SMOLDERING WAKE

## SITUATION

**ELEANOR'S PEAK**
**NAGAYAN MOUNTAINS**
**HELM**
**WOLF EMPIRE**
**12 AUGUST 3151**

The Gryphons are nearing the end of a week-long campaign of obliteration against the Wolf Empire forces left on the planet Helm. Quenching their thirst for revenge for the slaughter of their units here in 3138, they have led a bloody campaign, leaving a trail of destruction in their wake. The player's mercenary company has been contracted to mop up pockets of resistance. A Binary of Wolf Empire Garrison forces has holed up in a treacherous ravine, and the mercenaries must traverse hazardous and difficult terrain to neutralize them.

## GAME SETUP

*Recommended Terrain:* Mountain Ravine, 36" × 36" play area

Players should arrange 4–8" diameter patches of forest all around the battlefield. Between patches should be placed impassable hills, Gravel Piles (1" hills), and patches of Ultra Rough terrain (*AS: CE*, p. 57), representing the treacherous nature of the ravine. The rocky templates

and red liquid pool templates from the *Alpha Strike Counters* pack can be used to represent Ultra Rough terrain. The Defender places one objective token on open ground within 8" of the center of the board to represent the tunnel entrance to their bunker, where reinforcements will deploy from.

## Attacker

*Recommended Forces*: ilClan-era mercenaries
250 PV selected from the player's campaign force
        PLUS
2x IS Standard Battle Armor [Flamer] (Sqd4)
(Force list from Kick Down the Door can also be used if playing standalone)

## Defender

*Recommended Forces*: Provisional Garrison Cluster (222 PV)
All units are skill 4.
2x Elemental III Battle Armor [MicroPL] (Sqd5)
2x Clan Foot Point (Rifle, Energy)
2x Clan Jump Point (SRM)
2x Vedette Medium Tank V9
Mad Cat (Timber Wolf) B
Locust C
Chameleon TRC-4C

## DEPLOYMENT

The Defender deploys their entire force within 12" of the center of the board. The Attacker then chooses a home edge and moves units on from it during their first movement phase.

## OBJECTIVES

**Seal Them in (Attacker Only):** The tunnel entrance can be targeted by Anti-'Mech attacks (Immobile Target –4 TN applies). If successful, the attack removes the token from the game. Otherwise, the token can be destroyed with 15 points of weapon damage delivered at Short range only.

The game ends the turn following the token's destruction.

**Another Day (Defender Only):** The Defender wins the scenario by destroying 50 percent of the attacking forces before the game ends. Else, the Attacker wins.

## SPECIAL RULES

### Wolf Den

Caught unprepared, the defending Wolf Empire troops did not have their entire force readied at the start of the battle. During the end phase, the Defender may redeploy any destroyed infantry units within 2" of the objective token, up to the 6 units they began with. The redeployed units have the damage on their card erased.

### Forced Withdrawal

The Defender non-infantry forces operate under forced withdrawal (*AS: CE*, p. 126) and must retreat toward the objective token. Non-infantry units within 2" of the token in the end phase are removed from the game.

## AFTERMATH

Within one week, the entire garrisoning Wolf Empire force was wiped off the planet. The rapid success of Gryphons and their numerous Mercenary attachments allowed the Silver Hawks Coalition to continue repatriating worlds...for now.

If the Attacker is victorious, they are paid 100 PV for repairs and to purchase new units. If they failed to complete their objective, they receive 80 PV of Damage Insurance for repairs, but may not purchase new units with these points.

## OPTIONAL TOUCHPOINT TRACK: GHOSTS OF THE PAST

If the players wish to flesh out their campaign with more missions, the scenarios from *Turning Points: Helm* can be adapted to represent the Gryphons' campaign of revenge against the Wolf Empire on Helm in August 3151. OpFors can be constructed using the suggested Wolf Empire units from the above scenarios.

The Wolf Empire plays the Defender in all scenarios, except A Cruel Thing Is War.

**Rage:** The player's mercenaries assist the Gryphons with wiping out a sector of Wolf Empire troops.

**Hold the Door:** The mercenaries try to capture some of the few remaining Wolf Empire DropShips.

**Into the Breach:** The Wolf Empire troops desperately defend themselves in the mountain passes.

**A Cruel Thing Is War:** The mercenaries set an ambush for a known movement of Wolf Empire troops.

**Yea, Though I Walk:** The Wolf Empire desperately attempts to halt the advancing Gryphons and mercenaries.

# RAPTOR'S REQUIEM: CANTICLE

## LANCE SCARINCI

**CRESCENT HAWKS BARRACKS**
**PRIMETREE**
**HOOD IV**
**LYRAN COMMONWEALTH**
**31 OCTOBER 3147**

Jezebel had just slipped into dreams when the Devil burst into her room. He danced a jig, shouting and hooting as if she should be happy to see him.

"*Callahan!*" Jez jerked upright, but the drink wasn't done having its way with her, and she fell back into her sheets as the room spun. "Callahan! The only reason I haven't murdered you is 'cause you've never tried to sleep with me."

DevilJack Callahan, all 1.5 meters of him, dropped onto the foot of her bed and slapped her thigh. "Can't tell me you haven't thought about it. Come on, admit it, you've always had a little Devil in your dreams."

Jez fumbled with her nightstand. Somewhere in there was a knife she'd taken off a dead Jade Falcon Star Captain. It would look good in Callahan's stomach, or maybe his neck. *Yeah, his neck...*

"Come on, I thought you'd be happy to have another Youngblood running around." Callahan cackled and tickled Jez's ribs, waving a datapad in front of her face.

She grabbed the pad, grabbed his hand, grabbed his entire scrawny arm and twisted it into a pretzel. With a snarl, she propelled Callahan out into the corridor, introducing him to the door frame on his way. "You will father my children the day Kerensky comes back riding Blake's greased behind. Break into my room again and you'll be introducing yourself as Devil*Jane*, you hear me?"

"You got me wrong!" Callahan choked out, but he was always saying that. The son of a bitch was a criminal, thief, pathological liar... "It's your cousin! Jen!"

"Jen died on Arc-Royal, with most of my family. Don't you say her name again."

"She didn't." Truth was an animal DevilJack Callahan feared above all others. Its proximity made him fidget, eyes darting around for an escape route. Like now. "Got a bit of intel on Callandre's surviving Kell Hounds. She's got a Youngblood on her rolls. Could be a different girl, but..."

He held out his now-cracked datapad for Jez to snatch. It was an Lyran Intelligence Corps brief on the Hounds, what was left of them after Mad Malvina's last rampage. Alphabetized, as always, but it was easy to skip to the bottom.

*Youngblood, Jennifer; BZK-D3 Hollander III, WIA Arc-Royal. Active.* Jezebel read it again, then a third time. *Active.* A little bit of the dead inside her chest died.

DevilJack found enough courage to stand up and brush himself off. "Good news, you said. 'Callahan, why can't you ever find me some good news?'" He waved a hand at the report. "There you go. Maybe it's time we go pay a visit. Kell Hounds and Crescent Hawks are kin, remember? You do remember?"

"Callandre..." Jezebel's lip curled, a Pavlovian response to that name. "Don't you think there's a reason I've kept us independent?"

"Yeah, 'cause you meeting another you might cause a reverse Big Bang. Suck it up, Jezebel."

She looked at the report again. *Active. Alive.*

Suck it up? She just might have to.


**THIRD LYRAN REGULARS HQ**
**PRIMETREE**
**HOOD IV**
**LYRAN COMMONWEALTH**
**1 NOVEMBER 3147**

"Ain't that convenient?"

Jez's fingers involuntarily closed around the hard copy, crinkling it in the way she wanted to crush the sender of the message. *And Callahan, can't forget him. He must have known.* How could he have gotten that info about Jen without knowing this, too? Her lip curled as she read the words again.

*I am enacting Directive KH-09... Any and all Kell Hounds, past or present...make best speed to rendezvous Where it All Began...*

"Who the hell does she think she is?" The words hissed through Jez's gritted teeth.

"I think she thinks she's our CO, or, I dunno, that the Hawks owe the Kell Hounds for our existence or something." Polonius Dog-Kissing Allard, her XO. He was DevilJack with a prettier face, and maybe he didn't steal as much. Maybe.

"Evan Kell gave me carte blanche to run the Hawks as *I* see fit. *He* was the one I reported to, not her. Our debt to the Hounds died with him." Jez hung her head. She'd liked Evan Kell. "I don't answer to Callandre, and never will. This means nothing." She tossed the crumpled paper away.

Pol looked at her in that unblinking way he had. He just stared, waiting for more, but Jez refused to give it to him. He knew anyway. "So, we're gonna go?"

Jez sighed, long and deep. "I can't let her take Jen away to god knows where."

"Jen is her own person, not an extension of you. Maybe she wants to stay with the Hounds. It's not like she's ever tried to join up as a Crescent Hawk. Hell, we didn't even know she was still alive until now."

"She's a Youngblood. Last I checked, the *only* other Youngblood. There's power in a name, a heritage she has to live up to. We both have to."

Pol dismissed her with a *pfft*. "Sounds like Clan talk. I've got Dan Allard and Morgan Kell crouching up in my family tree. You gotta get into a Great House to have worse ancestors staring down at you, but I don't let 'em bother me. A name's just a name. We carve out our own destinies."

Jezebel slammed her hand on a desk. "Jen belongs with the Crescent Hawks, and that's final, Pol!" No one jumped at her outburst, not even the comm officer whose desk she'd hit. They were used to her, even Colonel Cayan's Third Lyran rats.

The words "that's final" would have meant more to Polonius Allard if he hadn't heard them so many times before, and known they weren't always true. He picked up the crumpled missive from Callandre and unwrapped it. "Rendezvous 'Where it All Began'? First Encounter? Do you know what any of this means?"

"I might have, once. Directive KH-09? It was in the packet Evan Kell gave me when he dropped this command shit on me."

"And where's that?"

"Where d'you think? Back on Arc-Royal. I didn't need Evan looking over my shoulder, even metaphorically."

"Well, that gives us a great starting point."

"Arc-Royal's still out of reach, Pol. For now."

Out of reach. Yeah, that was an understatement. Last Jezebel had checked, the Jade Falcons were still squatting on the Hounds' homeworld, shitting on God knew what. And there wasn't a damn thing one company of 'Mechs could do about it. Which was probably why Calamity Kell was regrouping and calling in all the favors in the galaxy.

Jezebel laid a hand on the comm tech's shoulder, not unkindly. "Can you bring up a map for me? Highlight each world we know the Kell Hounds have raided."

A map of Lyran and Jade Falcon-occupied space blossomed in the holo display. "There aren't many, Captain, at least not confirmed." The comm tech hit a few more buttons. "This is all the known action across the Falcon border, all actors included." Many worlds took on a flashing aura, with colors dictated by the attacker. Blue for Lyran raids, orange for Hell's Horses, red for Callandre's unsanctioned assaults. Many were gray, for unknown attackers. And all of it was old information, damn this unending HPG blackout to every last hell.

"Isolate the reds and unknowns. Cross-reference with dates. Remove any grays occurring before Callandre's last confirmed raid."

"You think she's running dark?" Pol asked as he neatly folded Callandre's missive.

"She's going to ground. If the Falcons are out to exterminate her, then she'd be an ass to travel with IFF active. Well, more of an ass. Where did that message originate?"

"Chahar."

Jez tapped the comm tech again. "Highlight all worlds between the Hounds' last known hit and Chahar." The result was a line of worlds that began red, then turned to gray.

"The dates match up with recharge times, Captain."

Pol nodded. "Yeguas, Deia, Chahar...she's setting a course anti-spinward."

"Not quite..." Jezebel pinched her lip, studying the line of worlds. *Damn that Callandre...* "She's hitting worlds with functioning HPGs, so she can send out that message." She nodded. "Somerset. We'll intercept her there."

The comm tech looked around. "That's spinward from Chahar, Captain. Way out of the way."

"Callandre will turn spinward, you watch. Her current path will have the Falcons anticipating her at Clermont, or Kolovraty. You know, worlds we border. Worlds I border! Rile them up and send them at me so she can duck out unnoticed. It's just the kind of shit—"

"Pull up the fastest course from here to Somerset," Pol told the tech. He turned to the still seething Jezebel. "We can't just go. We have a contract."

"We have an escape clause. Time to enact it." Jez heaved her biggest sigh yet, and that was saying something, these past twenty-four hours. "Get the company ready to move. I'll go disappoint Colonel Cayan."

## BEN CLARKE
## GORMLEY HIGHLAND
## SOMERSET
## JADE FALCON OCCUPATION ZONE
## 31 DECEMBER 3147

"Star Captain Bennet, you are twelve minutes overdue."

Falconer Commander M'oko's sharp voice cut through the static filling Bennet's comm. He could ignore it no longer. "*Aff.* Forgive my tardiness, Falconer Commander. The mountains are interfering with transmissions."

"Indeed." M'oko's tone suggested that he would by habit verify that tidbit. "Report."

M'oko wanted progress, but Bennet had little to offer him. Whoever these trespassers were, they moved like the very phantoms laborer caste mothers warned their children about, the ghosts of Star League and Rim Worlds warriors locked in eternal battle in Somerset's hills and marshes, happy to claim any stray victim. But phantoms did not leave BattleMech-sized footprints, walking single file to obscure their numbers, nor did they issue indecipherable microburst transmissions at regular intervals, or stymie Falcon radars with intermittent DropShip flights. Despite three weeks of this cat and mouse chicanery, the intruders had attacked nothing, avoiding all settlements.

Bennet could not wrap his mind around the *why* of it all.

"Report!" M'oko barked again, snapping Bennet back to the present.

"Twelve hours since the last microburst. If they follow their pattern, the next will be right around sundown, local time. My Star has taken position around Ben Clarke, the highest point in this region. It is the best spot to transmit from. When the microburst comes, we will triangulate and catch them."

"Very good, Star Captain. Keep me apprised."

Bennet stretched as best he could in the cramped seat of his *Spirit*. His usual *Thunderbolt IIC* was much roomier, but ill-suited for this chase. Had he taken it, he would be half a day behind the rest of his Star, still futzing around a hundred kilometers southeast in the Dagda Moors, where the last microburst had originated.

He massaged a calf muscle that was trying to cramp. *Freebirth.* His Binary was here to test graduating *sibko* cadets, not spend three weeks traipsing around Somerset's endless highlands.

Bennet thumbed his comm. "Ito, where are you?"

Some two kilometers away through the light mist, Bennet saw movement as MechWarrior Ito's *Stinger* rose from concealment.

"I did not tell you to reveal your position!"

"Apologies, Star Captain." Ito was yet young, but there was a reason she had tested into the Twenty-Second PGC with Bennet instead of a front-line unit. Her 'Mech wavered a bit, as if she were unsure to drop it prone again or not.

"Now that you are up, move three hundred meters farther up the slope. Keep your sensors toggling between infrared and magres. Report anything vaguely man-made."

Bennet could chase down these intruders if he had air power, but Malvina Hazen's war machine constantly hungered, and Bennet's Binary sported only a single Point of aerospace fighters, and even those were gone now. Point Commander Josie's *Issus* had suffered a thrust failure during liftoff and carved a gouge into Somerset's runway. Josie had had the temerity to eject, and now commanded a Point of *solahma* infantry, leaving Bennet with an ancient *Lucifer II* that could be charitably dubbed a hangar queen, though scrap heap was more appropriate. Falconer Commander M'oko could help by loaning his cadets and their fighters, but he was using them elsewhere and chose not to share. Satellite intel was also out. Somerset had thousands of satellites, but every time Bennet positioned one to help, it mysteriously lost contact. Someone else clearly had air superiority, but who?

Twenty-three minutes to sundown, and the next microburst. M'oko's techs thought they had cracked its encryption, but the message was indecipherable. "Gobbledygook," one of the techs had called it. The microbursts were followed by a DropShip hit on radar, taking off from the planet then landing again, but not just landing. Scouts sent to the location where it vanished from radar reported nothing. That meant the pilot was good enough to fly a multi-thousand-ton ship at nap-of-the-earth clear out of visual range. Bennet had nothing but three weeks' worth of charred landing zones, lines of BattleMech footprints, and a single refuse pile, burned into uselessness.

The clock ticked down as the sun ducked behind Somerset's evening mists.

"Microburst detected!" Ito shouted. "Wait...*stravag*... It is not coming from here. It originated from Ben Glainne!"

Bennet groaned. Ben Glainne was the *third* highest point in the area. He had been outfoxed again. Damn it, but they were good. A dozen kilometers away, the mist-shrouded hill taunted him with ghostly visions of BattleMechs marching to their next point like cadets on maneuver.

"Star Captain?" came M'oko's inquiring voice.

"Falconer Commander. Ben Clarke was a failure. They transmitted from somewhere else."

"I see." M'oko sounded oddly satisfied. "Do not pursue them."

"I have failed you, Falconer Commander. I will perform *surkai* when I return."

"You have *not* failed, Star Captain. You have gathered information we can now arm ourselves with. Return to the Academy."

*"Aff."* Bennet smacked the arm of his command couch and glared at the shadow of Ben Glainne. "What are they *doing*?"

"What *are* we doing?"

Even filtered through the wire linking their 'Mechs, Jez heard three weeks' worth of pent-up frustration swirling in Pol's voice, and had to bite her cheek hard to resist throwing it back at him. He'd asked that same question every day since they'd landed. Every day they'd been shadowing and baiting this Star to keep them off Yasmine Takagi's Pursuit Lance. Yasmine's job was now done. That was the last transmission she had to send, and by now, her people would be heading back to the rendezvous point. There really was no need to keep this Star of stubborn Falcons around anymore.

"We can take one Star," Pol said, as if reading her mind. "From ambush, with weight of numbers, it'll be over in seconds."

He was right. Two lances of Crescent Hawks, laying mostly powered down under sensor-blocking tarps at the base of Ben Clarke, could be picking their teeth with Falcon bones within ten minutes of opening fire. "Then what would it be tomorrow, Pol? A Binary? A Trinary? Then a Supernova? There aren't any Mech-it-Lubes on the moors to repair and rearm us."

She could hear Pol rolling his eyes. "Any word from the Devil?" he asked.

"Nothing new. Just what he got off those techs last week." Callahan's new friends among the Falcons' lower castes knew the Twenty-Second Provisional Garrison Cluster had forces on-world, but not how many. He also had leads on foodstuffs and other sundries, and a place where they might find salvage from the Ice Hellion Encroachment of 3071, and that was why she kept him around.

"The Falcons are leaving," Pol said. "And so should we."

Jez gritted her teeth. She was going to grind them down to nubs before the end of this. "We'll wait until they've reached the other hill, then—"

"No, I mean they're *leaving*. Their course is southwest, back toward their base. Looks like they've given up."

"We're not that lucky." Despite knowing the Falcons had been on the wrong hill, Jezebel couldn't help noticing they gave up the chase after Yasmine's very last transmission. It was probably coincidence. Jade Falcons were a lot of things, some of them even positive, but creative they were not. The Crescent Hawks thrived on creativity, and these microbursts meant more than any Falcon could comprehend.

*Right?*

### NORTH GORMLEY
### SOMERSET
### JADE FALCON OCCUPATION ZONE
### 1 JANUARY 3148

Nine hours later, Jezebel stood in the hold of the *Leopard*-class DropShip *Trinity*, watching Somerset's twin moons bathe the empty highlands in silvery light. It reminded her of home, of Grandpa Jerry's vineyard on Arc-Royal, where she played as a girl, with Jen and her other cousins, all scions of the Kell Hounds. Children with names like Wilson, Allard, and Brahe had joined in their antics, stealing a bottle or two of Jeremiah's finest vintage, or teasing the young Wolf pups with their serious frowns. Those days spawned a number of great friendships and rivalries, but no rivalry was as great as the one determining the true alpha female of their group. Not Jen, she and Jezebel were a unit. No, it was Jezebel and Callandre Kell who butted heads and tussled in the grass over and over, neither one a clear winner.

And who was Jen pairing herself with now?

Callandre would come, if only to sort out that question. Even if she just passed through the system on her way to wherever the hell it all began, she'd get one of the Hawks' microbursts. The Falcons had certainly intercepted and cracked it, but they'd never decipher the message without the proper accompanying text. A Crescent Hawk or Kell Hound would cross-reference the message's first and last digits to a list of documents, and find *The Wonderful Wizard of Oz*, a choice that would piss off Callandre Kell.

And a pissed-off Callandre would come.

"Captain?"

Jezebel turned to find her senior staff had joined her. Pol and Yasmine, and Divebomb Engelson, who commanded her air assets. Even the *Trinity*'s captain, an old man named Bloom, stood there with his arms crossed. He'd been taking the most risks lately, launching and landing his ship just to keep the Falcons confused. They all wore frowns and did not flinch from her warning eye.

"Can we have a word?" Yasmine was doing the talking. The reasonable one. Jezebel's silence encouraged her. "The company's running a bit short on faith at the moment, Captain. They might feel better if this was a contract with a real objective, but some of us are wondering how long we're going to be doing this. We can't dodge the Falcons forever."

"You want to go in guns blazing? Squeeze out your frustrations for the hell of it?"

"Not our first choice."

"I'll do it," Pol said. "Headcap a few green meanies, collect the salvage, and run. We have to make some profit from this."

"Is that all it is, Pol? You're worried about getting paid? I have a couple bottles of my grandfather's wine. High-value stuff. Will that shut you up?"

Yasmine stepped between them. "It's been three weeks with no reply. We might need to look at the possibility we missed Callandre."

"Clara and Simon are running out of fuel," Divebomb said, citing the two pilots operating out of their DropShip on the moon of Bull, keeping the skies clear of Falcon satellites. "They've only had one hint of an incoming ship, and were unable to confirm. Falcon fighters keep getting closer to them, too."

"The noose is tightening," Bloom said. "We shouldn't be here when it closes."

All these thoughts had been niggling in the back of Jez's mind for days. She cursed Evan Kell for resurrecting the Crescent Hawks, cursed Callandre for being late, cursed Jennifer Youngblood for not already being by her side. And cursed herself, who deserved it most.

She looked to her senior advisors. Her friends. "We'll give them one more week. Then you can shoot me."

While the others dispersed, Polonius Allard lingered. Him with his damn pretty face and impenetrable gaze, and deep knowledge of Jezebel's soul. He stood beside her and put his arm around her, and she laid her head onto his shoulder. "Who's left, Pol? From Arc-Royal, from our youth? For a while, it was just you and me. Now we can have Jen back. She's the last of my family."

"You have cousins on your aunt's side. The ones running the vineyard."

Jezebel snorted. Yes, there were cousins, children of her aunt Christine, who hadn't kept Grandpa Jerry's name when she'd married. Jeremiah didn't mind, as he didn't mind that branch of the family not choosing the path of the warrior. Jezebel minded. After every argument with her cousin Cliff, who also never backed down, she minded. "They aren't family, Pol. Just relatives."

"I understand you want Jen back. That you *need* her. But there's family right here who need you. You've got to protect them, even if that means giving up. Even if it means running away."

Jez retreated into her bunk. She leaned against the door, and sank down until her knees touched her chest, then laid her head on them. It was easy to shut out the world this way, but even easier with some liquid aid. A bottle of Glengarry Black Label lived in her nightstand, mostly empty. No glasses, though; she didn't need something extra to break. Her hand knocked over some holos on the way to the bottle. It was her forebears, always looking out for her. She took them up instead.

Jezebel was the fourth Youngblood to command the Crescent Hawks. She kept these holos of the others nearby to remind her of her heritage, her duty. Jeremiah Youngblood, her great-great-grandfather. Even with clothing and hair over a century out of date, he was handsome, with a rakish smile that had wooed many a noble lady.

Jason Youngblood. His holo always gave her a chill, because Jason was looking back, staring into her soul across the ages. Intense, smoldering and fiercely intelligent, he seemed to judge Jezebel, and always found her wanting.

Jeremiah the Second, Grandpa Jerry. He had a sad, weary look to him, one that never fully left the old, wrinkled face she'd loved in her girlhood. He was a kind, soft-spoken old soul who had drunk his fill of war during the Blakist Jihad, and wished it on no one. He'd died a decade before Gray Monday, still believing he had won a permanent peace for the Inner Sphere.

"I'm sorry, Grandpa," Jez sniffed. "I'm sorry we threw away everything you fought for."

At some point she had picked up the bottle of Black Label. She set it down, and sat on her bed with the holos, remembering family.

**MILITARY ACADEMY OF SOMERSET**
**SOMERPORT**
**SOMERSET**
**JADE FALCON OCCUPATION ZONE**
**2 JANUARY 3148**

Bennet entered Falconer Commander M'oko's office expecting to wait, but the Falconer was ready for him, standing with hands clasped behind his back, eyes twinkling as brightly as the buttons on his uniform. He nodded crisply to Bennet, then gestured to the map burning in his holotank. "Star Captain. Tell me what you see."

"Gormley Highlands." Bennet had grown very familiar with the area as he traipsed hopelessly through it. "You have marked the spot of each transmission from our guests."

"Very good. And have you noticed what I have?" M'oko had been a Falconer so long he could not help turning everything into a teaching moment, watching Bennet with an appraising frown.

Bennet saw nothing new, but he had been down in that mud for weeks while M'oko was here, collating data. Seeing the bigger picture, from a falcon's perspective. Bennet zoomed the map out and saw what he could not see from the mud. A pattern, formed by the transmission locations. That was why they had stopped, why there had been only one unidentified DropShip flight in the past two days. The pattern was complete, tracing a crest that Bennet recognized, a shrieking hawk's head every Jade Falcon had grown to hate.

He straightened up. "You knew their last microburst would come from Ben Glainne, to complete the pattern."

M'oko beamed proudly. "They confirmed it for me. And by doing so, they confirmed my solution for the larger puzzle encoded within. I have always had a great love of puzzles. They teach a warrior to think creatively."

"I prefer to think with my guns."

"That is why you languish in a garrison Cluster."

That was fine criticism from an unblooded old man shuffled out of the *touman* to train the next generation of warriors, but Bennet held his tongue. "So the decoded microbursts mean nothing after all?"

"I think there may be something yet hidden within them. A code left to crack."

"You could have sent me to the right location and let me crack them personally."

"*Neg.* That way we would only have the part of them sending those bursts. Now we will have the whole. These dots here." M'oko indicated a few innocuous looking spots on the map. "These bursts were different. Longer by fifteen percent. When put together in the correct order, they provide a set of geographical coordinates."

"A rendezvous point. But with who?"

"With us, Star Captain. Prepare your unit, and I will gather some of my choicest cadets for an outing. Instead of your Binary, I will blood them against the Crescent Hawks. Should prove a worthy Trial of Position, *quiaff*?"

Bennet straightened. "Falconer Commander, we still do not know the nature of this intrusion. You could be marching several *sibkos* into a trap."

M'oko paced to the opposite wall, frowning slightly. "The Crescent Hawks are Spheroid barbarians and money soldiers, but they are not without a certain honor all their own. They do not slaughter civilians." He turned back, grinning like a wolf. "Or the young. We can exploit that."

"I am not sure I agree. Respectfully, Falconer Commander—"

"It is not your place to *agree*. Galaxy Commander Tamara Faulk placed you under my command, *quiaff*?"

"*Aff...*" Bennet might have added "for the purpose of trying *sibkos*," but he was not one to engage in needless conflict.

M'oko leaned on the edge of his desk. "You are an older breed of warrior, not only in age, but in philosophy. The old ways led to stagnation, but the Mongol Doctrine has brought us great glory. Malvina Hazen wants Mongols in her *touman*, not traditionalists, and I must train them. They will learn that no challenge to Clan Jade Falcon goes unanswered. These trespassers must be punished with all the ferocity a Mongol demands. Do you believe your Binary alone is up to that?"

Twelve elite Crescent Hawks versus a handful of aging warriors in old equipment? Bennet was not so traditional as to ignore reality. "*Neg.*"

"Then make your preparations, and I will make mine. We move out in two hours."


## NORTH GORMLEY
## SOMERSET
## JADE FALCON OCCUPATION ZONE
## 5 JANUARY 3148

The worst place to be when trouble comes calling isn't the mess hall, or the shower, or in bed. It's in the head, which was exactly where Jezebel was when a loud *BAW!* rang through the ship.

She'd gotten pretty good at identifying various booms and bangs over the years. This sounded bomb-ish, small and hand-delivered. It wasn't hard to guess by whom. Sympathetic vibrations ran up the privy seat into her rump. Jez hung her head long enough to expel one fatalistic breath, then she was up, buckling her belt as she joined a hall full of running, shouting bodies.

In less than a minute, she was out into the open night, donning her coolant vest as she ran to *Gray Lady*. Her *Phoenix Hawk* genuflected in the gloom, chain ladder extended to welcome her mistress so they could address this trespass as one. Lights spilled from the *Trinity*, and from Alise Gogol's *Stiletto* and Sweetbottom's feral-looking *Jaguar*, but no one was shooting yet.

"Someone give me a report!" Jez yelled into her comm before even getting properly seated. A gaggle of voices chimed in. Jez filtered the mess to get the words "sabotage" and "battle armor," along with a few choice swear words.

More 'Mechs began moving. Their unseen enemy had kicked the hornet's nest, and now it was time to sting. Bailey Redgrave jumped her *Gyrfalcon* onto the *Trinity*, giving her long-range guns a vast field of fire. Soon, twelve active BattleMechs ringed the DropShip, but still no one was shooting. There was nothing to shoot at.

Jezebel's scanner pinged distant movement, but it was just some local fauna fleeing the activity. Nothing else moved. "The hell is going on?"

"Smart Falcons," came Captain Bloom's dejected voice. "They snuck in under ECM and planted some charges. Blew a hole in the port hull. Not subtle, but effective. If we leave atmo, the entire cargo bay will be open to vacuum."

"Repairable?"

"Yes, but it'll be a few hours."

"Can we get the other ships here?" Yasmine asked. "Evacuate us in time?"

"Unlikely, but call 'em anyway." The Crescent Hawks traveled in three *Leopard*s, but the *Trinity*'s sister ships couldn't carry everything. Which third of her equipment should Jezebel leave behind? Pol was right: she had waited too long, and now the Falcons intended for her to stay.

Pol's *Scourge* stepped up beside *Gray Lady*. "Well, I guess they'll be here shortly."

Jezebel's neurohelmet prevented her from massaging her temples, so she settled for smacking its bulky side. "Divebomb, get your fighters in the air. At least we can see which direction they're coming from."

"Don't think I can, Captain. We can see a bulge on the side of Piper's *Morgenstern*. The airfield's had visitors, too."

"Looks like they're *really* smart Falcons," Pol muttered.

Alise and Sweetbottom had been on watch, but there was no point reprimanding them. Even the Jade Falcons had stealth suits these days. This sabotage was not intended to destroy, just prevent the Hawks from running. Every point of retreat was probably mined. They had lingered too long, and Jezebel's clever plan wasn't clever enough.

It wasn't too much longer before pings started registering on long-range scans. A lot of nasty, Falcony pings, far more than Jezebel expected.

"Callahan!" DevilJack had returned to them two days prior with a truckload of supplies and one or two illicit items. He was no traitor, but he wasn't exactly careful, either. "Someone get me Callahan."

A moment later, he was on the comm, protesting his innocence. "Nobody tailed me! It was—"

"Never mind that! How big did your tech friends say the Falcon presence was?"

"A Binary. Twenty-Third—no, Twenty-Second PGC. Lambda Galaxy."

Jezebel watched the angry green dots blip into existence on her scanner. "That look like a Binary to you, Pol?"

"Sure. And a Trinary. And another after that. That's a short Cluster, Jez."

Falcon dots kept popping into life on the HUD, representing combat vehicles and a few Stars of battle armor, but mostly BattleMechs. Was a time not long ago when a garrison Cluster only had a handful of 'Mechs, back when the Republic still had power and people respected Exarch Devlin Stone. That idealistic bastard was gone now, and the factories churned out metal death day and night, especially among the Clans. There were no more easy raids, where Jez ran circles around idiot Falcon test-downs in their second-hand trucks. Every other *solahma* had a 'Mech now, and each new dot was like a shiv in her stomach.

"At least their formation is sloppy," Pol said.

"Great, we can kill them with demerits. Load a few when you're out of Gauss rounds."

The Falcons grew more discernible through predawn mists. Some machines wore the beige and red of the Falcon's Lambda Galaxy, but most were primer gray, or a hodgepodge of generic camouflage. Only one OmniMech marched among them, but it was a *Turkina*, a massive machine the equal of any three of Jezebel's.

"Commander of the Crescent Hawks," came a sharp, formal voice over an open frequency. "I am Falconer Commander M'oko of Clan Jade Falcon, and I welcome you to Somerset. You have chosen a very lovely world to die on."

"We have no quarrel with you, Falconer Commander." Jezebel hoped she sounded as calm as he did. "Give us time to repair our ship and we will be on our way."

"You have trespassed on Falcon land, disrupted my schedule, and forced me to expend resources tracking you down. You owe some form of recompense. I will have your ship, your 'Mechs, and whatever personnel survive to become bondsmen."

"Yeah, shove that up your feathered ass." Jez flipped to a tactical frequency. "Striker Lance, onto that outcrop southeast of my position. Hold the high ground and pour on the long-range fire. Pursuit Lance, hang back by the *Trinity*. Use its guns for cover and take targets of opportunity. Command Lance, with me; isolate and destroy enemy command elements. Lance leaders, choose targets and focus your fire."

The Hawks moved. They were veterans and would do their duty until the end. The Falcons halted at three kilometers, still far out of range. Jason Youngblood's anti-Clan strategies poured through Jezebel's head, and she dismissed them one by one. The Crescent Hawks specialized in recon, raiding, and mobile warfare, not stand-up slugfests against numerically superior foes. Running seemed their best option, but the high walls of the canyon that protected their LZ prevented easy escape. There must be a clash, and one side held a distinct advantage.

Small groups broke off from the edges of the Falcon formation, fast 'Mechs and tanks sent to flank the Hawks. That would not be allowed. On the left, Pol's lance positioned themselves for a wide field of fire. Yasmine took her lighter pursuit lance to the edge of the *Trinity*'s covering fire and prepared to meet the flankers on the right.

The Falcons failed to coordinate properly, with the left side coming under Pol's guns before the right side had properly closed. They were small, fast 'Mechs—*Locusts*, *Vixens*, *Baboons*—speedsters that foiled targeting systems, but the Striker Lance's heavy fire intimidated them into a swirling gaggle that would not retreat, but ceased to advance.

Jezebel moved the Command Lance to support Yasmine. A Star of slightly heavier 'Mechs, supported by a pair of Cizin hovertanks, closed with enough firepower to level the Pursuit Lance. "Bailey, pop those hovers. Yasmine, fall back to me."

Redgrave's *Gyrfalcon* loosed LB-X flak rounds at over half a kilometer, sending one of the tanks into a spin with a shredded air skirt. The other juked and dodged, taking cover behind a Clan *Shadow Hawk*. Bailey bathed that 'Mech's torso with laser light. Yasmine designated the closest, bravest, and most foolish Falcon 'Mech, a *Hellhound*, and her lance opened fire. Explosions bloomed like caustic flowers over its left side. Jezebel added a blast from her large pulse laser at maximum range, and the *Hellhound* fell, smoking, onto its back.

The Falcons pulled up, and the remaining Cizin shot around from behind their line, curving across the flank to focus four laser beams onto Romulus Halstead-Kell's *Gambit*. Designed for light fire support, the little 'Mech's armor couldn't hold, and it buckled like a tree about to fall. Romulus' ejection seat puffed him back toward the *Trinity*, and he filled the comm with curses all the way down. Sweetbottom immediately avenged him, unleashing his *Jaguar*'s entire missile armament into the Cizin and rendering it so much useless scrap. Under fire from seven Crescent Hawks, the remaining four Falcon 'Mechs retreated.

Jezebel recognized some Sun Tzu in the Falcon commander's tactics: he had tied up her strongest force with his weakest and struck her weakest with his second strongest. That meant his strongest would be coming for her second strongest, her own Command Lance, and indeed, a Star of heavy BattleMechs was rumbling downfield toward her position. Executed properly, this strategy would have left the Falcons victorious two out of three times, while having lost only their weakest element. However, their timing was off, and the Crescent Hawks would exploit the hell out of it.

"Pol!" Jezebel shouted as she moved her crosshairs onto a *Rifleman*. "Quit playing around with those bugs. Get ready to scissor these heavies. Yasmine, gather your lance for a charge through the ranks."

The Command Lance deployed west, as if to shield Yasmine's three remaining 'Mechs. The Falcon Star turned to follow. The proper counter would have been to halt all forward advance and shift laterally, keeping all the Hawks in front of them, but these Falcons were more eager than smart.

"This is going to hurt, Command. Hold!" Jez scarred the *Rifleman*'s torso with laser pulses. It returned fire, but only scored a glancing blow on *Gray Lady*'s arm. Lasers and missiles crisscrossed the field. Isla's *Mad Cat III* brought down a fat, lumbering *Pinion* with massed LRM fire, but the Falcons stepped over it and kept coming.

Timing was everything in a firefight, and recognizing the opportune moment was a skill no one could teach. It was innate, and Jezebel had honed it to a killing edge. "Hawks, execute!"

Pol's Striker Lance turned as one and fired on the rear of the heavy Falcon 'Mechs. The *Rifleman* exploded as two Gauss rounds tore through its rear armor. The other three 'Mechs staggered under heavy fire, catching their balance just as Yasmine's lance rushed past Jezebel's and into their ranks. It was a dangerous move full of potential friendly fire, but if Jezebel had drilled one thing into her Crescent Hawks, it was to hit your intended target. Yasmine's *Havoc* planted four lasers into a hole Pol had made in a *Jade Hawk*, greeting its SRM ammunition with gleeful abandon.

One Falcon 'Mech, a *Grizzly* in unhelpful arctic camouflage, had the good sense to retreat. Jezebel let it go. It was not a victory without cost. Every Hawk 'Mech showed damage. Black Bart's *Gauntlet* had suffered a smashed hip and couldn't move properly. Alise's *Stiletto* lay in the dirt, its torso blown open. Pol's Strikers fared best, but time and weight of numbers would wear them down, and the Falcons had plenty of both.

Jezebel opened a channel. "Falconer Commander...Mokey, was it? If this was your best, perhaps you should reconsider your profession. Your laborer caste certainly has room for clowns."

A scoff came back, and Jez smiled sardonically. Sooner than she'd like, taunts might be the only weapon she had. Her command, her family, spread out to either side. Maybe she had failed them, maybe her mission had been a bust and they would all die here, but they would die together. Jez would stand in front of them until the end, and that was enough.

Mokey was blathering. Jez supposed she ought to listen. "—and deign to condescend, you—"

"Falconer Commander!" a very young voice cut over the comm. "There is movement to our rear. Atop the ridge!"

Some of the Falcon 'Mechs turned, but most looked unsure. Only the Lambda machines responded with any efficiency, aiming weapons at the southwest ridge as silhouettes began appearing along it, glinting in the dawn sun. They were few, so painfully few, but before them marched an aura that made them giants. They strode with the weight of reputation earned, and the anger of spurned gods seeking vengeance upon the mortal world. Black and red were their colors, and the eyes of the hound logo emblazoned on their breasts smoldered, hungry as the yawing barrels of their guns.

Jezebel's heart soared. A *Hollander* stood with them. She had waited long enough.

A bulbous SM1 hovertank pulled to the fore, its colossal autocannon accusing the combatants below. "Please, don't let us interrupt you."

Jez knew that voice, hated that voice—and in that moment loved it. How fortunes changed. A moment ago, she'd had no hope, but now the Kell Hounds and her Crescent Hawks stood poised like the jaws of some massive beast, with Falcon flesh between its teeth.

"Took you long enough." Jez mostly succeeded in keeping the glee from her voice. "Do you want to play anvil, or shall we?"

A *tsk* came over the open comm. "Do you know who the Falcons sent to kill you, Jezebel? We've monitored them since they left Somerport. These aren't warriors. This bastard marched his *sibkos* out here. You've been shooting at children."

A shard of ice pierced Jezebel's gut. Somerset, home of Somerset *Academy.* She should have seen it sooner, would have if she hadn't been blinded by their numbers. These Falcons lacked cohesion, bungled their maneuvers, missed half their shots. Even *solahma* and test-downs were better than that. Two unseated Falcon MechWarriors limped back across the no-man's-land, the taller one virtually carrying his bloody companion, who appeared to be a limb short. They looked of an age to call her mother. Bile rose in Jezebel's throat, and in that moment, she hated the Falconer Commander more than anything in the universe.

"Children are an Inner Sphere concept," Falconer M'oko said. "My cadets are not whiny freebirths with dripping noses sucking their mother's teats. They are Jade Falcons, bred to be warriors, and warriors they will be."

Jez kicked the smoking wreckage of the *Rifleman* she had dueled. "What kind of warrior will this one be?"

"The strong prevail, the weak are culled. It is our way. Those who survive today will take their place in our *touman*."

"So, none of them, then. I may not like the place you have put me in, but if someone tries to kill me and mine, I will try to kill them right back. As you have already seen, I am better at it than you. You should have rushed me with everything you had. It's what your Khan would have done. Now you get to choose which knife to turn your back to."

Pol's voice came on their command channel. "Jez, we can't shoot kids. Not even Falcon kids."

"I'm open to suggestions," Jez said, but Pol had none. There was nothing left but to wait, and probably shoot.

"Death in battle is what we strive toward." M'oko's words sounded rote, as if this was merely another lecture for a hall full of bored students. "My charges are Mongol brave, Mongol strong. We have numbers enough to assure a Pyrrhic victory, and that is acceptable."

The Falcons held their ground, facing both threats in a tight set of lines. The time was near.

A new voice cut across the comm, older, more assured. "*Neg*, Falconer Commander, it is not acceptable. I cannot allow this to proceed."

"Star Captain Bennet!" M'oko barked. "Keep your place!"

"This *is* my place!"

Jezebel caught her breath. *The Lambda Galaxy machines!* They were not cadets beholden to a Falconer, and their leader seemed blessedly disinclined to ritual suicide. Jez listened as Bennet vented, new possibilities bubbling in her mind.

"This is not a Trial of Position, *Falconer*. It is a combat operation, and *you* will listen to *me!*" A ripple passed through the Falcon lines. Someone was listening. "Your Mongol ways will have no victory here, Pyrrhic or otherwise. You would succeed only in depriving the Clan of a generation of fine warriors, and such waste cannot be condoned. What will you say to Malvina Hazen when you have no graduating class for her?"

Everyone, Hawk, Falcon, and Hound, held their breath. M'oko could back down, he must if he wanted to save lives, but doing so would wreck his reputation, drop him from his cushy position at Somerset Academy into a *solahma* infantry unit, or flush him into the lowest tier of the warrior caste, policing civilians with a baton instead of a BattleMech. Falcons were nothing if not proud.

"It does not matter." M'oko sighed. "Combat is engaged, blood is shed. Honor must be satisfied."

The Falcon 'Mechs girded themselves. Jezebel's Hawks drew closer together. Atop the ridge, the Kell Hounds never wavered, guns trained on the mass of Falcons sitting exposed on the valley floor.

Staring down each branch of the metaphorical crossroads that she had marched to, Jezebel despaired at her dire choices. Only one dusty and untrodden path might lead somewhere besides annihilation. It wasn't really a choice at all. She put her foot on that uncertain path and walked forward.

"Star Captain Bennet, would you accept a *batchall* from an Inner Sphere freebirth? One your cadets could learn from rather than die in?"

A long pause. "What do you propose?"

"A Circle of Equals, according to Clan rules. One 'Mech each."

"Can I trust you to abide by our rules?"

"It's mutually assured destruction if I don't. I don't hate you that much."

"Nor I you. It is the duty of a warrior to stand between their people and destruction. I see you understand that. I accept."

"Very well. I am Jezebel Youngblood of the Crescent Hawks. What forces defend these hatchling warriors?"

"What?" M'oko sounded on the verge of apoplexy. "My cadets are not—"

"I will defend! And I will thank you to remain silent, Falconer Commander." A beige *Thunderbolt* stepped from the Falcons' ranks and raised its arms. "I am Star Captain Bennet of Clan Jade Falcon. In accordance with the ritual of *zellbrigen*, I choose this valley as our battlefield. In this solemn matter, let none interfere."

A chorus rose from the assembled Falcons that shivered Jezebel's spine. *"Seyla."*

Polonius Allard stood at the ready beside her. "Let me do it."

With Pol at the controls, his *Scourge* was probably the deadliest 'Mech in the company. Duma Grauss' *Vulture Mk IV* could surely hold its own, so could the *Mangonel* piloted by Kress, her little Wolf adoptee. But this was not their fight. She was the Crescent Hawk exemplar, the Youngblood, and all eyes were on her. Hawk eyes, Falcon eyes. Hound eyes. Youngblood eyes.

"Only one way out of this, Pol. The Clan way. I led us in, I'll lead us out." Jezebel stepped into the no-man's-land and raised her arms as Bennet had.

*Gray Lady* was not the PHX-7K *Phoenix Hawk* she had inherited from Grandpa Jerry. That old Vicore beater had died early in her career, under the guns of a Marik *Juliano* during Operation Hammerfall. *Gray Lady* came from a Wolf factory, and bore an aesthetic more fitting of a *Phoenix Hawk*. And Clan-grade weaponry, that was nice, too. *Gray Lady* had put many of Jezebel's enemies into the ground, but they were foes of a size to her. Falcon *Hellhound*s and *Cougar*s, Wolf *Lobo*s and *Wulfen*s, Marik *Griffin*s, Kurita *Dragon*s and *Ninja-to*s. This foe outclassed them all. This was a *Thunderbolt*, the perennial zombie of the Inner Sphere,

unstoppable and terrifying even before the Clans had buffed its speed, armor, and weaponry. Assault 'Mechs feared the *Thunderbolt IIC*, and *Gray Lady* was a *Phoenix Hawk*. A scout 'Mech.

"If you choose to fight with such a small 'Mech, then I will bid away my medium lasers." Bennet wasn't mocking her, but displaying an aspect of Clan warfare the Falcons had abandoned in recent years. Jez appreciated it.

"Bargained well and done. Shall we begin?"

She flipped her three pulse lasers to the same firing circuit. Aided by *Gray Lady*'s advanced targeting computer, they would land on target virtually 100 percent of the time, but their damage was minimal. Bennet's heavy lasers could tear through her armor with one or two shots. Mobility was her greatest defense. He was a Falcon and she was a Hawk, but only one of them could fly.

Bennet scored the first hit, peppering Jez with long-range-missile fire as she kicked *Gray Lady* to her incredible maximum speed. Dodging left to foil his aim, Jez took to the skies, rocketing over Bennet's head as lasers cracked through the air on either side of her. She scored the *Thunderbolt*'s left shoulder with laser pulses and landed behind it. Bennet swiveled left, tracking her movement with the laser hanging below his left arm. *Excellent!* He was left-handed, responding automatically instead of protecting the damaged arm. If the *Thunderbolt IIC* had a weakness, it was those fragile heavy lasers and their tendency to explode when tickled. Jez triggered her anti-personnel Gauss rifles while her lasers cycled, stripping away little more than paint, but every fleck counted.

Heat flooded her cockpit, but Jezebel loved it. She tended to run *Gray Lady* hot, boiling coolant like the blood in her veins. She ran, she fired, she dodged, while Bennet stoically returned fire, relying on stability and armor rather than maneuverability. His lasers missed more often than they hit, but after a few minutes, he had painted *Gray Lady*'s wireframe readout in shades of yellow and angry red. Jezebel's more accurate fire had pierced the *Thunderbolt*'s torso and melted the medium lasers he wasn't using, but overall, his armor held.

One of her shots finally breached the armor over the *Thunderbolt*'s left-arm laser housing. Bennet turned to shield the side, but Jezebel jumped in close, firing everything she had. It was one of her lowly Gauss rounds that slipped through, pinging around the laser's charging coil and unleashing what it found there in a ball of blue lightning. Most of the *Thunderbolt*'s left side collapsed, but it didn't fall.

The loss seemed to correct Bennet's balance, bringing the blocky LRM on his right shoulder into line. He fired. Missiles pushed through *Gray Lady*'s ruined armor, tearing up the myomers on her right leg.

The *Phoenix Hawk* wobbled, trying to stand on muscles that were no longer there.

Bennet followed up with a laser blast that severed the leg below the knee. Jezebel felt the unpleasant sensation of falling, and instinctively stuck out *Gray Lady*'s arm. The barrel of her large pulse laser met the ground and snapped clean off. Her 'Mech's right hand crumpled, and Jezebel slammed her head hard, saved from a collapsed skull by her neurohelmet.

Blinking through blurred vision, Jez saw the *Thunderbolt* looming overhead, the barrel of its remaining heavy laser glowing eagerly. "Are you dead, Jezebel Youngblood?"

"I'm not that lucky. I can't stand. I can't fight. You win, Star Captain." Jezebel bit her tongue and forced out the words. "I humbly request *hegira*."

All activity in the universe seemed to have paused. Nothing moved, and not even M'oko had a fool's opinion to spew into the void as all present waited to see what honor meant to Star Captain Bennet.

"Granted. Depart this world and fight another day."

Jez supervised the loading of *Gray Lady* into one of the *Trinity*'s 'Mech bays with mixed emotions. The Falcons had claimed the remaining salvage, including the Hawks' other downed 'Mechs, but Bennet chose not to seize anything else as *isorla*. The other DropShips had arrived to recover their charges, but there was one battle yet to fight before the Crescent Hawks could depart Somerset.

Sitting on a crate in the bustling hangar, Jez watched the door with her gut twisting into knots. It slid open, and there *she* was, backlit by the morning sun. Calamity Kell—older, angrier, more tempered, wearing the last fifteen years as a whole murder of crow's-feet, and streaks of gray in her once-colorful hair.

She took two steps into the room, nose wrinkled against something foul. "Bitch."

"You took the word right out of my mouth."

No observer, Hound or Hawk, interfered in the shouting match that followed. Words were said but not heard, and that was probably for the best. Jezebel burned with that need to shout, to tear someone down, to be *right*. She hated it, but she also treasured it. It was the fire that drove her to win, and there was nothing quite like sating it.

After a minute, some unspoken limit was reached and both women fell silent, angry eyes turned away, nothing forgiven, nothing forgotten.

"You want a drink?" Jezebel finally asked.

"Several."

Callandre disappeared in the direction of the mess. The Kell Hounds filed into the *Trinity*, battle-worn souls glad to seek out an old familiar face and share tales from their long years of separation. They arrived to cries of appreciation, laughter, and a sense of homecoming.

Jezebel looked them over, greeting the ones she knew and didn't know equally, for they were all beloved. Among them, there was one who mattered more than the others, standing at the rear, smiling politely as Pol regaled her with some story, hands tucked neatly into the rear pockets of her MechWarrior's shorts. Jez hadn't seen her in almost a decade, and was surprised at how old she looked. Still the same round face, still the same dirty-blond hair tied in a neat ponytail over one shoulder, but Jen was older now. They all were.

Jen saw Jez looking and slowly crossed to her. "'Surrender Jennifer'? That was your whole message?"

"Yes."

"Do you know how much it pissed her off?"

"God, I hope you'll tell me."

Then they laughed and threw their arms around each other, and Jezebel could not stop her tears. She shouldn't have to.

Jen Youngblood wiped at her own face as they came apart. "What is this about? Why me?"

"I thought you were dead. Since Arc-Royal. I thought I was the last of us. Remember what Grandpa Jerry always told us about family?"

"Something about sticking by no matter what?"

"Yeah. I kind of forgot the exact wording." Jez snorted a laugh. "Point is, we should stick together, now more than ever." She waved a hand to encompass the *Trinity* and all it held. "You belong with us."

"You mean *you* belong with *us*, right?" Callandre had returned, tapping a half empty bottle of Timbiqui Dark against a crate like a judge's gavel.

Jezebel's smile vanished. "Jen is a Youngblood. She belongs with the Crescent Hawks."

"That's fine." Callandre drained her brew, swirling the last gulp. "She can be a Hawk. But the Crescent Hawks belong with the Kell Hounds."

Jez took a step toward Callandre. "I know what you're doing. You think you're Morgan Kell, calling back his regiment. Gonna get the old gang back together and go avenge yourself on the universe."

"That's the plan."

"It's not the same, Callandre. Malvina Hazen is worse than a million Yorinaga Kuritas, and you don't have Morgan's people."

Callandre sniffed. "If I had Morgan's people, I'd already be bashing down Malvina's door. Instead, I have you."

"You don't have me." Jezebel's lip was curling, as it always did. "You don't have any of us."

"Your command wouldn't exist if not for my uncle! The Kell Hounds trained you, equipped you, and filled your ranks. You *are* Kell Hounds, and that makes you mine."

All the warmth drained out of the room. No one wanted the screaming to start again, but they seemed resigned to hearing it. The mingled Hawks and Hounds watched helplessly as the irresistible force moved inexorably toward the immovable object.

Jezebel took a deep, calming breath. Then a second and third. "Where have you been since you lost our homeworld? Not so much as a hello for a year. I've had messages from home come through the Falcon blockade telling me most of my family is dead, but nothing from you." Jez thrust a finger at Jen. "Nothing about *her*!"

"Well, there she is. You're reunited, so let's put this foolishness behind us." Callandre swirled the dregs in her bottle. "I'm not asking, Jezebel."

"You're not asking, and you're not getting. Our reliance on the Kell Hounds ended long before Arc-Royal fell. The Crescent Hawks are independent." Jezebel stepped close enough to smell the beer on Callandre's breath. "I sought you out for one reason, and that reason is standing beside me now. You may leave now."

Callandre glanced at Jen. "This your decision, or hers?"

Jen didn't respond. Callandre and Jezebel snapped their heads toward her, each silently demanding her allegiance.

Jen wouldn't meet their eyes, gazing instead at her companions. "It has to be a choice."

"Good idea," Callandre said. "Why don't we let the Crescent Hawks decide? Let's put it to a vote."

She started to step onto a crate to call for attention, but Jezebel pulled her back by the arm. "Get down! *I* will address my people, not you."

Callandre gave her a gaze to melt steel, but stepped back nonetheless. Jez called for order. Almost everyone who wore a Hawks insignia was here, MechWarriors, pilots, techs, and all the various support personnel who kept them running. Jez knew all of them, loved all of them. The question to ask was if they loved her.

"Crescent Hawks. My friends, my family. My great-grandfather, Jason Youngblood, once said that sometime in your life you'll reach a major crossroads, when you have to decide who you are. We're at it. Callandre Kell is calling back everyone with a Kell Hounds past. She wants to rebuild the Hounds and take the fight back to the Falcons. Maybe she will. Maybe she'll even take back Arc-Royal. But that's a long number of years down a hard road."

She picked up a pry bar; it felt better to have something in her hands. "The Hawks came from the Hounds, as I did, as did many of you. We were Kell Hounds before we were Crescent Hawks, and many of us still think of ourselves as Hounds." She threw down the bar. "I don't."

A muttering rose among the crowd. Many nodded agreement, some just shifted from side to side. Back in the corner, DevilJack Callahan looked to be quietly taking bets.

Jezebel raised her hands for silence. "We've been on our own five years now, ever since Timkovichi." Hearing the name of the world where the Kell Hounds nearly died made Callandre turn away from her. *Good.* "Five years we've had to provide for ourselves. Five years where the contracts were ours, not subbed out from the Hounds. Now Callandre wants us to come back to the fold like nothing's changed. From what I've seen, the Hawks will damn near double the Kell Hounds' current strength. There's no doubt we'd be stronger together. But I have my own plans for the future, and they *don't* involve running away to lick our wounds."

She took a breath that hitched slightly. "Maybe some of you disagree. That's fine. I understand. If you've got more family in the Hounds than in the Crescent Hawks, then this is your chance to join them. I won't hold it against anyone who wants to go with Callandre. It's your choice. Go ahead and make it."

Jez stepped down and waited. Her MechWarriors stood at the fore, their expressions mixed. Black Barton Deckert stood with arms crossed, dour and unreadable as always, but he did not move. Nor did Isla and Kress. The little Wolves would stay with the woman who was their pack leader, until a new one bested her. That wasn't yet. Alise, Sweetbottom, Bailey. They all stayed.

First to step forward was Romulus Halstead-Kell, his bandaged arm in a sling. He shrugged with an apologetic smile. "It's in the name." He was only a Kell by marriage, but Jez understood.

Yasmine came next, wiping her eyes. "I'm sorry, Jez," was all she said. Jez nodded, face twitching a bit, and embraced her.

That seemed to open a floodgate, as more personnel shifted to stand with Callandre. Cherie Devereaux was the only other MechWarrior she lost, but about a third of the Hawks' support staff deserted Jezebel.

Then Divebomb Engelson came to stand before her. She'd expected some of her pilots to go, but all of them? The entire Crimson Hawks flight went to Callandre's side.

After a few moments, the shifting subsided. The Kell Hounds and Crescent Hawks stood apart.

Callandre nodded, formal, emotionless. "I guess that's settled, then."

"I guess so," Jez said.

"Well..."

"Well."

Callandre nodded curtly, then turned away.

One person had not participated in the separation, hanging back by the door. Polonius Allard leaned casually against the wall as Callandre approached, his usual smirk absent.

"You coming, Pol?" Callandre asked. "You're a Kell, too."

Pol heaved a sigh appropriate for the crossroads and shook his head. "It's just a name. I'll make my own destiny."

It took several more hours to transfer equipment. At the end, the *Trinity* felt like a house devoid of furnishings, colder, yet wide open. Captain Bloom declared the ship fit to fly, and her engines rumbled to life. Jez stood outside, binoculars on the Falcons still camped at the far end of the valley, ensuring that the Crescent Hawks did, in fact, leave.

Footsteps brought her around. Jen stood beside her.

"You on board?" Jez asked.

Jen smiled in a sad, resigned way. "'Mechs are loaded. Let's get out before *she* notices."

A short, wiry man accompanied Jen. Jez squinted at him, feeling a stab of irritation at how close he stood. "Who's that?"

"Jason Jackowski. Friend of mine. We call him Vulture, for some reason. He's coming with."

"Like hell." Jezebel sneered. Yeah, she didn't like him. "We don't take stragglers."

"He has a *Galahad*."

Jez ran her tongue across her front teeth. "Pulse-laser variant?"

"You know it," said the short, ugly little guy.

"Okay, you're in." She poked Jen's chest. "He's your responsibility. You walk him and keep him fed. And give him the test. I want his results before we reach the JumpShip."

"What test is that?" Vulture asked.

Jen took his arm. "Citadel Challenge. All potential Crescent Hawks have to take it."

"What if I fail?"

"Then we keep your 'Mech," Jez said as she walked away. "And space you."

Jez didn't see Vulture turn green or ask Jen for advice.

"Don't fail," Jen said as the new Crescent Hawks lifted off.

**MILITARY ACADEMY OF SOMERSET**
**SOMERPORT**
**SOMERSET**
**JADE FALCON OCCUPATION ZONE**
**9 JANUARY 3148**

Dawn came, and Bennet found himself again in Falconer Commander M'oko's office, waiting as M'oko leaned over his holotank, his uniform wrinkled and stained. They had not spoken since Bennet's victory, maintaining a respectful distance from each other. The warriors of Bennet's Binary discussed the incident, as M'oko's cadets surely did, but Bennet kept out of it. He knew he had done right. If he had to collect another enemy over it, then so be it.

"Falconer Commander, you should know that I do not regret my actions."

"Neither do I, Star Captain." M'oko lifted his head from the valley of icons. Bennet recognized North Gormley. "It turns out that you were right. Simulations—many simulations—show that had we engaged the mercenaries in Mongol fashion, we would have died. Only about twelve percent of scenarios yield victory, but even then, all of my cadets are lost." He rubbed at the black bags under his eyes. "Yours was the correct action."

"It does not fill me with joy to be right, Falconer Commander."

"It should. Battlefield victory is hard to come by, moral victory even more so. I do not often admit that I am wrong. My report to Galaxy Commander Tamara Faulk will reflect your exemplary judgment."

Bennet relaxed a bit. "It seems the old ways are not without merit."

"Indeed. But Khan Malvina demands Mongols, and Mongols she will receive. This batch, though, may be more tempered." M'oko offered a rare, pensive smile. "A moment will come when warriors such as you ascend again. When it does, I hope you seize it."

**CRESCENT HAWKS BARRACKS**
**PRIMETREE**
**HOOD IV**
**LYRAN COMMONWEALTH**
**16 FEBRUARY 3148**

Jez went looking for Jen, because she wanted to. Because for the first time in long weeks of apathy, she felt good.

She found Jen in the hangar, admiring her *Hollander* in its new blue and gray. She'd see the yellow stripe Jez had painted down the 'Mech's back some other time.

Jez held out a bottle. "Here. A little taste of home."

"Is that one of Grandpa Jerry's reds?"

"3113. Best year he ever had, or so he said. I can't tell the difference."

Jen took the bottle and popped out the cork. "It's all in the balance. How did you get Cliff to part with it?"

Jez smirked. Their cousin, Cliff the Stiff, parted with nothing easily. "Assuming I told him."

"Aw, Jez, you'd steal from family?" A hint of playfulness, a hint of reproach, just like old times.

Jez snatched it and took a pull like it was cheap whiskey. "Cliff is a James, not a Youngblood. We make war, they make wine."

"Damn good wine, though." They ambled slowly down the line of 'Mechs, trading the bottle between them. Jen inspected each towering war machine in turn, until they came to the end, where *Gray Lady* loomed in its cradle, a tiger at rest. "So...where is it, Jez?"

Jez kicked at an imaginary rock. "Where is what?"

"You know what."

As an excuse not to answer, Jez took a long pull on Grandpa Jerry's best. When she came up, Jen was still staring. "Where Grandpa parked it, I imagine."

Jen's eyes grew three sizes. "On Arc-Royal? Still on Arc-Royal?"

"Unless the Falcons found it and tore it up."

Jen seethed for a moment, unable to speak, then grabbed back the bottle for her own long guzzle.

"Cliff will keep it safe on the vineyard," Jez said while Jen had her mouth full. "Unless Mad Malvina's lost her taste for those damn fusionnaires, they'll never come calling."

"Why don't you have it? Cliff's got no use for it, other than—" Jen displayed the bottle's label. "A damn mascot."

"I'm a passable MechWarrior, but a piss-poor pilot. I can't use it."

Jen found the same imaginary rock Jez had just kicked. "I can," she said softly.

They locked eyes, and it was like they were girls again, running around Grandpa Jerry's estate in the Arc-Royal summer sun, plotting another escapade that would gain them little beyond a good thrashing if they were caught.

Jez took the half-empty bottle and considered it. "Well, I do need a restock. Time for the Crescent Hawks to go home."

# BATTLETECH ERAS

The *BattleTech* universe is a living, vibrant entity that grows each year as more sourcebooks and fiction are published. A dynamic universe, its setting and characters evolve over time within a highly detailed continuity framework, bringing everything to life in a way a static game universe cannot match.

To help quickly and easily convey the timeline of the universe—and to allow a player to easily "plug in" a given novel or sourcebook—we've divided *BattleTech* into eight major eras.

### STAR LEAGUE
### (Present—2780)

Ian Cameron, ruler of the Terran Hegemony, concludes decades of tireless effort with the creation of the Star League, a political and military alliance between all Great Houses and the Hegemony. Star League armed forces immediately launch the Reunification War, forcing the Periphery realms to join. For the next two centuries, humanity experiences a golden age across the thousand light-years of human-occupied space known as the Inner Sphere. It also sees the creation of the most powerful military in human history.

(This era also covers the centuries before the founding of the Star League in 2571, most notably the Age of War.)

### SUCCESSION WARS
### (2781—3049)

Every last member of First Lord Richard Cameron's family is killed during a coup launched by Stefan Amaris. Following the thirteen-year war to unseat him, the rulers of each of the five Great Houses disband the Star League. General Aleksandr Kerensky departs with eighty percent of the Star League Defense Force beyond known space and the Inner Sphere collapses into centuries of warfare known as the Succession Wars that will eventually result in a massive loss of technology across most worlds.

### CLAN INVASION
### (3050—3061)

A mysterious invading force strikes the coreward region of the Inner Sphere. The invaders, called the Clans, are descendants of Kerensky's SLDF troops, forged into a society dedicated to becoming the greatest fighting force in history. With vastly superior technology and warriors, the Clans conquer world after world. Eventually this outside threat will forge a new Star League, something hundreds of years of warfare failed to accomplish. In addition, the Clans will act as a catalyst for a technological renaissance.

### CIVIL WAR
### (3062—3067)

The Clan threat is eventually lessened with the complete destruction of a Clan. With that massive external threat apparently neutralized, internal conflicts explode around the Inner Sphere. House Liao conquers its former Commonality, the St. Ives Compact; a rebellion of military units belonging to House Kurita sparks a war with their powerful border enemy, Clan Ghost Bear; the fabulously powerful Federated Commonwealth of House Steiner and House Davion collapses into five long years of bitter civil war.

### JIHAD
### (3067–3080)

Following the Federated Commonwealth Civil War, the leaders of the Great Houses meet and disband the new Star League, declaring it a sham. The pseudo-religious Word of Blake—a splinter group of ComStar, the protectors and controllers of interstellar communication—launch the Jihad: an interstellar war that pits every faction against each other and even against themselves, as weapons of mass destruction are used for the first time in centuries while new and frightening technologies are also unleashed.

### DARK AGE
### (3081-3150)

Under the guidance of Devlin Stone, the Republic of the Sphere is born at the heart of the Inner Sphere following the Jihad. One of the more extensive periods of peace begins to break out as the 32nd century dawns. The factions, to one degree or another, embrace disarmament, and the massive armies of the Succession Wars begin to fade. However, in 3132 eighty percent of interstellar communications collapses, throwing the universe into chaos. Wars erupt almost immediately, and the factions begin rebuilding their armies.

### ILCLAN
### (3151-present)

The once-invulnerable Republic of the Sphere lies in ruins, torn apart by the Great Houses and the Clans as they wage war against each other on a scale not seen in nearly a century. Mercenaries flourish once more, selling their might to the highest bidder. As Fortress Republic collapses, the Clans race toward Terra to claim their long-denied birthright and create a supreme authority that will fulfill the dream of Aleksandr Kerensky and rule the Inner Sphere by any means necessary: The ilClan.

### CLAN HOMEWORLDS
### (2786-present)

In 2784, General Aleksandr Kerensky launched Operation Exodus, and led most of the Star League Defense Force out of the Inner Sphere in a search for a new world, far away from the strife of the Great Houses. After more than two years and thousands of light years, they arrived at the Pentagon Worlds. Over the next two-and-a-half centuries, internal dissent and civil war led to the creation of a brutal new society—the Clans. And in 3049, they returned to the Inner Sphere with one goal—the complete conquest of the Great Houses.

# SUBMISSION GUIDELINES

*Shrapnel* is the market for official short fiction set in the *BattleTech* universe.

**WHAT WE WANT**

We are looking for stories of **3,000–5,000 words** that are character-oriented, meaning the characters, rather than the technology, provide the main focus of the action. Stories can be set in any established *BattleTech* era, and although we prefer stories where BattleMechs are featured, this is by no means a mandatory element.

**WHAT WE DON'T WANT**

The following items are generally grounds for immediate disqualification:

- Stories not set in the *BattleTech* universe. There are other markets for these stories.

- Stories centering solely on romance, supernatural, fantasy, or horror elements. If your story isn't primarily military sci-fi, then it's probably not for us.

- Stories containing gratuitous sex, gore, or profanity. Keep it PG-13, and you should be fine.

- Stories under 3,000 words or over 5,000 words. We don't publish flash fiction, and although we do publish works longer than 5,000 words, these are reserved for established *BattleTech* authors.

- Vanity stories, which include personal units, author-as-character inserts, or tabletop game sessions retold in narrative form.

- Publicly available *BattleTech* fan-fiction. If your story has been posted in a forum or other public venue, then we will not accept it.

**MANUSCRIPT FORMAT**

- .rtf, .doc, .docx formats ONLY
- 12-point Times New Roman, Cambria, or Palatino fonts ONLY
- 1" (2.54 cm) margins all around
- Double-spaced lines
- DO NOT put an extra space between each paragraph
- Filename: "Submission Title by Jane Q. Writer"

**PAYMENT & RIGHTS**

We pay $0.06 per word after publication. By submitting to *Shrapnel*, you acknowledge that your work is set in an owned universe and that you retain no rights to any of the characters, settings, or "ideas" detailed in your story. We purchase **all rights** to every published story; those rights are automatically transferred to The Topps Company, Inc.

**SUBMISSIONS PORTAL**

To send us a submission, visit our submissions portal here: **https://pulsepublishingsubmissions.moksha.io/publication/shrapnel-the-battletech-magazine-fiction**

17773018R00239